DAUGHTERS DREAR

THOMAS EDWARDS

Black Rose Wri-ing | Texas

The author grants the final approval for this literary material.

First printing

This is a work of fiction. Names, characters, businesses, places, events, and incidents are either the products of the author's imagination or used in a fictitious manner. Any resemblance to actual persons, living or dead, or actual events is purely coincidental.

ISBN: 978-1-68513-246-0
PUBLISHED BY BLACK ROSE WRITING
www.blackrosewriting.com

Printed in the United States of America
Suggested Retail Price (SRP) $23.95

Daughters Drear is printed in Calluna

*As a planet-friendly publisher, Black Rose Writing does its best to eliminate unnecessary waste to reduce paper usage and energy costs, while never compromising the reading experience. As a result, the final word count vs. page count may not meet common expectations.

PRAISE FOR

DAUGHTERS DREAR

"San Antonio's Old World charms serve as a major backdrop in this dark, fictional battle to save the New World. It's the tale of a seasoned crime reporter versus vampires, wrapped up in apocalyptic fear and Southern charm. You'll want to bite into it, too, as a reader."

—Brian Kirkpatrick, Texas Public Radio

"Thomas Edwards has written a real page-turner in his first novel, *Daughters Drear*. Edwards weaves the tight tale of an old-fashioned, pipe-smoking, trench-coat wearing San Antonio Tribune reporter covering a story about bloodthirsty assailants. Reporter John Blackwood is investigating a series of unexplained events after trying to meet a source at a graveyard and is always one step ahead of well-meaning police. Edwards' novel captures the reader by the throat as they can't wait to see what happens next."

—Eraldo "Dino" Chiecchi, author of "*Josue — A Young Man's Life Lost to Suicide*"

"Entertaining and intricately written, *Daughters Drear* will satisfy horror fans of all dispositions whether they're new to the genre or well-traveled in it."

—Daniel Tucker, writer/director/editor of "*Nothing But the Blood*"

For those who helped me hold back the darkness —
Camille, Caitlin, Matthew and, of course, Florence.

DAUGHTERS DREAR

PROLOGUE

San Antonio

December 18, 1994

Every town harbors its share of old, vacant houses where the past slumbers uneasily, where shadows clump thick as tar, stirring even when there's no breeze; where voices whisper between creaking floorboards and groaning rafters. These are forlorn dwellings where age and dust have settled upon stone and timber as heavily as a funeral shroud.

The Birkenstadt Haus is such a place. A poor relation to its richer, more modern cousins spaced along the tree-covered lots of Argyle Lane (where, if you have to ask how much a home costs, you can't afford it), the weathered pile broods in the manner of an old man exiled by his family. Alone at the top of the road, the abandoned mansion clings to the edge of the Olmos Bluffs, an ancient limestone escarpment north of downtown. Spread below the bluffs is Olmos Basin Park, a wooded natural bowl threaded by Olmos Creek and thickened by an abundance of pecan trees, gnarled oaks and Ashe junipers, which the locals call mountain cedars. The basin remains a wooded oasis surrounded by urban sprawl.

Above the trees, anyone standing on the top deck of the Birkenstadt Haus commands an unobstructed view of the city skyline to the south.

Yet despite the spectacular panorama, the dwelling's reputation grows more unsavory each year. For generations, tragedy has dogged the fates of those associated with the manse, beginning with Gustave Birkenstadt, the German brewer who erected the home in 1846. He spent a fortune raising the mansion with native limestone.

From his balcony, Birkenstadt kept a watchful eye on his brewery a few miles away, where the waters of the San Antonio River powered his mill. He could judge how hard his crews worked by the smoke belching from the stacks.

Prosperity did not last long.

Three years after arriving from Germany, the brewer lost his son and only child during a border skirmish with Mexican forces. Mere weeks later, his wife — never well after the arduous sea voyage from Holstein — succumbed to a wasting disease. Alone and wracked by grief, the old burgher retreated into the shadowed confines of his mirthless home, once the site of grand balls and sumptuous feasts. The townsfolk saw less of him. He paid fewer visits to his brewery until one day he vanished.

•   •   •

Some claimed he trafficked in dark rites from the Old Country, hoping to return his son and wife to existence; others whispered he went crazy and became forever lost among the bottomless caves honeycombing the basin. In the end, his fate remained unknown. Eventually, the family solicitor shuttered the place.

Over time, others came, finding the grand mansion a gem too tempting. Invariably they left, or died, often under tragic circumstances. Other times the new occupants disappeared, adding another layer of mystery to the lore of the Birkenstadt House, and further cementing its reputation as cursed.

On this winter's eve, an hour before a sullen sun slips below the horizon, the headlights of a Ford Explorer wash over a For Sale sign staked in the front garden. The SUV's magnetized door placards proclaim, "Alamo Metro Home Sales: Texas Independence at an Affordable Price."

The Explorer pulls into the circular drive, tires jarred by fissures in the pavement. Four faces inside the vehicle stare up as the Explorer crunches to a stop. As the home looms over the vehicle, the SUV's lights reveal weathered walls, streaked by ochre runnels from years of rainwater. The front doors, once polished mahogany, are dull and padlocked.

Three stories above is a sloping tin roof, partially eaten by rust. A series of narrow chimneys thrust into the sky like mummified fingers. Rows of cracked or missing windows watch the desiccated garden below, resembling eyes gouged from a skull.

Ben Wade, the pride and joy of Alamo Metro Home Sales, exits the driver's side and stands on the bricked path winding to the front door, stomping his spit-shined boots to warm his feet. A hearty plume of air blows from his open mouth, scented by mint gum. A big grin splits his beefy face as the other doors of the Explorer open.

"Now aren't y'all glad you came along for the ride?" he booms, throwing arms wide. "Your castle in the sky."

The front-seat passenger emerges first and surveys the grand vista of manse, cliff, forest and a sky just starting to glimmer with stars. He's a tall, well-built man with laughter in his eyes.

"It's beautiful. Just what we're looking for," Dr. Vincent Malory says. Wade notes how the man stands with legs slightly apart, hands planted on hips, his mannerisms announcing to the world the good doctor does not fear a challenge — especially from an old fixer-upper.

Wade, salesman extraordinaire ($2.5 million in sales so far this year, and if he can unload this place, a cool $3 mil by Christmas), keeps his glance fixed on Malory and allows his grin to stretch even wider. He is much older than the physician, with a crest of white hair that wouldn't have looked out of place on a television evangelist. He clutches a cowboy hat, the blunt fingers curling and uncurling around the brim.

A trim blonde who's far too young for the worry lines already creasing her forehead joins them. She studies the house with undisguised aversion, then turns and regards her husband quizzically.

Wade recognizes that look, an expression that says "slow down, honey." Wade knows he needs to get the missus on his side pronto if he wants to make the sale. Shouldn't be too hard, he thinks. Mrs. Malory seems nice enough, maybe a little brittle after a long day, but not one of those snooty gals he deals with so often, the kind with plastic boobs and lips so plumped a bee might have stung them.

And, even if the doc didn't bite and the deal fell through, there was that other caller who wanted to look the place over. Wade couldn't quite recall the name, which was scrawled on a Post-it Note back on his desk. Some big-time lawyer fellow or personal assistant who'd just rolled into town, that's what he remembered. He could follow up on that lead tomorrow, if he needed to.

Never let an opportunity go by, that was his motto.

"Vince," the woman scolds, her small mouth turned down, "you can't be serious. We just got here. We haven't even been inside yet."

She clucks her tongue. "Besides, I wanted to see the Queen Anne over on Harrigan, but now the light's gone."

The laughter in Dr. Malory's eyes dims just a bit, as though his wife's lament is just the latest in a long line of complaints he's learned to endure.

"I know, honey," he says, waving his hands. "But I couldn't help it if I had to work late at the hospital."

With a theatrical flourish, he indicates the lab coat he still wears.

"I'm the new guy, remember?"

Though he protests, it's not with any real rancor. Then he snaps his fingers and mock-slaps his forehead.

"Oh yeah, it's payday. I was rushing so much I forgot to grab my check. When we're done, I'll go back, pick it up and I'll treat you to a nice dinner. Promise."

He gives her an affectionate peck on the cheek.

Not placated, Kristin Malory's frown deepens.

"Your idea of a 'nice dinner' is Tex-Mex," she scolds, though she stops short of stamping her feet. "I'm cold, too, and it's too dark here to see anything."

Wade's canny eyes drift from wife to husband, giving no hint this is a marital drama he's seen played out in one form or another many times. He knows sometimes it's best to let the clients talk things out first. He'll step in when needed. That's always been the secret to his success—listening and timing. Being pushy never much got him anywhere.

Vincent Malory chuckles, taking a deep breath of the chilly air. He exhales and reaches for his wife's shoulders, gives her a gentle squeeze.

"Oh, come on, Kristin! Can't you just feel the energy here? The vibes?" His perfect doctor smile dazzles, rivaling the city lights on the horizon, a carpet of diamonds under a sky filling with thick, gray clouds. "And look at the view! I'll bet it's the best in the city."

Her frown stays frozen. She seems to shrink deeper into her faux fur coat. From where he stands, Wade can tell the husband's arguments haven't swayed the missus just yet. He may need to jump in after all.

"'Feel the energy'? 'Vibes'?" she snorts.

Malory gently releases her shoulders.

"The history, Kristin! The history—you can feel it in the air. This place comes with a pedigree. How can you not love it?"

The pinched look on her face shows Kristin Malory is far from being won over. But Wade sees the ice melting. The doctor's enthusiasm is infectious.

"How long have we wanted a place like this?" Vincent Malory presses. "How long? A place with atmosphere, a place to build family traditions? A home that's unique, not a cookie-cutter box like that place we're renting? Think of the parties we can throw. We'll be the talk of the Medical Society. Besides, the price is right. Soooo right."

"Maybe that's because the place is falling apart?" she suggests dryly, but without the scolding tone.

He ignores the gibe, his smile growing even bigger.

"Maybe this is the place to have that second baby we've been talking about? It's pretty big ... hmmmm? The kind of place a kid could rattle around in."

That did the trick. Now, Wade can practically hear the ice breaking.

"And wouldn't it be nice to spend Christmas in our own home instead of the rental?" Malory throws in.

Kristin, warming to the idea, starts grinning. Wade wasn't sure they could close on the house before Christmas, seeing as how the holiday was only a week away, but the doctor was on a roll. No sense interrupting him.

"Okay," she relents, waving her hands. "But I didn't say anything about buying it. Let's just go inside and look around, then we'll talk."

The husband squeezes her hand. Wade can see the battle is half-won. From the look on her face, Kristin Malory knows it, too.

"Is this place haunted, dad?"

The three adults turn at the sound of a child's voice. Wade's enthusiasm slips a notch. Now comes real trouble — the kid.

Sam Malory, seven years old and normally filled with boundless energy, is not budging from the Explorer's back seat, where he peers uneasily at the house. He seems to vanish into his baggy sweater, the human equivalent of a turtle hiding in its shell.

His dad reaches over, unfastens the child-restraint belt and lifts the boy from the car, hugging him.

"Don't you worry about any ghosts, Sam my man," his dad says, using the nickname that never fails to elicit a grin from his son. "If we see any, we'll just say 'boo' first and scare them away."

This time Sammy doesn't smile. Instead, he scrunches his mouth the way only boys can, a look half-clown, half-sage that makes a parent's heart ache.

"The kids at my new school say this place is haunted," he murmurs, not letting go of his father.

"Awww, come on, Sammy," his dad says. "That's nonsense."

Wade watches as the boy's wide eyes rove over the dark walls covered in withered trails of ivy, the shattered windows, the gaps in the upstairs railing.

"It scares me," the boy whispers into the scratchy stubble of his father's cheek. "My friends say bad things happened here."

Sammy's thin arms tighten around his father's neck. His dad carefully disengages the boy, sets him down, drops to a knee and stares into Sammy's stricken face with a very thoughtful look.

"C'mon, Sammy. Who're you going to believe? Your dad or a bunch of second-graders?"

Sammy drops his chin and kicks at the frozen dirt with a sneaker.

"You, I guess," he says after some reflection.

"That's my boy," his dad says, tousling his hair.

Wade studies the child, who doesn't look the least bit reassured. Time to earn his commission. He addresses the boy, knowing full well the parents are listening to every word.

"Oh, folks do tell some colorful tales regarding this place—I won't lie to you," Wade says, his tone sweet as a grandmother's cupcakes. "But you know what, Sammy? That's all they are—just stories. Hogwash. Not an ounce of truth to them. Heck, no one's even lived here for fifteen or twenty years."

Sam nods but keeps his silence, examining the scuff marks made by his sneakers.

Personally, Wade has never believed the stories anyway. Local claptrap, what his old man would've called pure bull spit (on account he didn't cuss).

"Wow," breathes Kristin Malory. "An honest Realtor. This place really has people talking about it?"

Wade gives her his best "aw shucks" look, dons his 10-gallon hat and cups his ham-sized hands over his heart with a flourish.

"Yes indeed. Can't deny that. Called the Birkenstadt Haus in these parts, on account of the German brewer that done built it in the 1840s. But you gotta remember these stories are oooold. Stories from before I was born—waaaay before. And I ain't no spring chicken. You just can't put any stock in something that musty."

She giggles — a little too hesitant, a little too forced. But it's good enough for him.

Wade purses his lips and sizes up the family. Dad was sold— Wade recognizes that stargazer look right away. Momma was close; he had her figured right enough — a perky little social climber. An old house with a little history, a little harmless scandal, something setting her apart from the other doctors' wives — that was the prefect recipe for the missus. But the boy definitely needed a little more convincing.

"It just needs some fixin' up, that's all," Wade continues, fixing his gaze on Sammy. "With a little shine and polish, it'll look good as new. Why, you won't even think of those stories no more."

Wade's "trust-me" eyes bore a path straight to the boy. The mother and father lean in, listening; judging, Wade knew.

The boy still gazes at Wade with uncertainty, but Wade can hear the gears turning with mom and dad. He presses on, not wishing to lose momentum.

"So what do you say we go inside, have a quick look-see? No harm in that, right Sammy?"

Before any dissent is voiced, Wade walks to the bed of the SUV. Vincent Malory trails him. Wade opens the back hatch and rummages through an assortment of items—a tarp, a stack of For Sale signs, flares, a toolbox—and picks up a flashlight.

The Realtor starts up the stone steps to the front porch.

Malory calls after him, "Shouldn't we lock your car?"

Wade grins, never breaking stride. He's pawing the keys to the padlock in his pocket.

"Nawww," he twangs. "Ain't nobody gonna bother it. This is the safest neighborhood in the whole dang town."

The screaming started not much later.

CHAPTER ONE

Few places are as intriguing as the newsroom of a metropolitan newspaper. Not just another office, a newsroom is a communications hub where up-to-the-second information is the only commodity of any value and anything five minutes old is already depreciating.

A modern newsroom hums with quiet energy, a far cry from the cacophony of the old days. Gone are the clacking weather wires, the ringing bells of the news-service teletypes, the rapid-fire tapping of manual typewriters. The only similarity between past and present are the crackling police and fire scanners and the reporters who monitor them.

Some things never change.

On this night, however, the San Antonio Tribune's scanners remained unusually silent, a state that left a lone police reporter bored to tears. He sat hunched over his desk, waiting for something — anything — to happen.

John Gwydion Blackwood chewed on an unlit briar pipe and swirled the coffee grounds in his empty mug. He wondered—not for the first time—whether a career as a newspaper reporter promised much of a future. Long hours, low pay and readers who only called to complain made the job unappealing far too often.

Yet he had to admit there remained a certain attraction to his vocation. Blackwood firmly believed journalism is a profession where the starry-eyed man or woman can still save the world, righting wrongs one sentence at a time.

Just the same as any other calling, journalism had its exciting days and ones less so, and unfortunately, this day counted among the latter.

He glanced at the clock over the Metro Desk. Almost 7 p.m., which meant five hours left on his shift. His spirits rose — plenty of time for a decent story to develop. So far tonight, the pickings remained slim. Two hours ago he covered a house fire with no injuries—well, no human injuries, though a cat named "Sandy Claws" checked into that big litter box in the sky. The owner, an elderly spinster named Eugenia Finster, related to Blackwood between heaving sobs how the unfortunate tabby had been a Christmas gift two years earlier, hence the name. He wrote it up as a metro brief for tomorrow's edition.

With a sigh, Blackwood settled his cup into a hole in the chipped varnish of the desk. He regarded the gold inkwell inscribed on the mug. The cup had been a little something extra he received during last year's ceremony at the Investigative Reporters and Editors convention in Houston to accept the Reporter of the Year award. His groundbreaking series on the twisted life and very twisted times of the so-called Bookstore Butcher had solidified his reputation as the "dean of South Texas police reporters."

Two years gone since the Butcher's demise, thoughts of the brutal psychopath hiding behind the cherubic face and horn-rimmed glasses still haunted Blackwood. That story nearly became his epitaph, principally because the Butcher came close to adding Blackwood to his victims.

With a shiver, Blackwood pushed those memories aside and tried to recall if he had any "evergreen" stories he could harvest for tomorrow's paper. Maybe dust off an old Crime Stoppers cold case?

But after more thought, he instead decided to pay a visit to San Antonio Police

Department headquarters over on West Nueva and throw himself on the mercy of the night detectives. As long as he brought doughnuts, they might toss him a proverbial bone ... At least a story worth a byline.

The phone on his desk rang, as insistent as a needy child.

He glanced down, feeling a spark of hope. The words "Pay Phone" and a downtown exchange glowed on the Caller ID screen. Would this answer his prayers for a good story? He reached for the receiver.

"Blackwood," he said.

With my luck, it's probably someone who didn't get their paper, he thought.

A man's low voice responded. There was a strange quality to his tone, a sound that reminded him of sandpaper rubbing against silk.

"Hello," the caller politely said. "Is this Mr. Blackwood, the crime-beat reporter?"

"Speaking," Blackwood said, automatically pulling his notebook from his back pocket. A pen—his favored Mont Blanc—appeared between his fingers.

A dozen feet away, one of the televisions mounted above the clustered work stations comprising the Metro Desk showed black clouds crawling across a satellite picture of San Antonio. The accompanying graphics predicted a sixty percent chance of light snow. Blackwood's head rose to regard the screen, brow furrowing. Snow in South Texas? Really?

Snow fell in San Antonio with the same frequency as cactus sprouting in the arctic.

"Mr. Blackwood? Hello?"

The reporter returned to the present.

"Right.—Sorry. How can I help?" Blackwood's attention lingered a moment longer on the TV.

The caller softly chuckled.

"Actually, I might be able to help you," he said.

Blackwood shifted in his seat, the weather report dismissed for now.

"How so?" Blackwood asked, now mildly interested.

The caller quickly answered.

"I frequently read your stories. You have a singular voice, Mr. Blackwood. Your articles on that monster, the Bookstore Butcher, especially riveted me. Very frightening."

Blackwood gave a rueful smile despite the favorable mention.

"You read those?" Blackwood said.

The caller chuckled again.

"The public library has copies," the man said. "I read a lot. My job involves—local research."

A long pause ensued. Blackwood heard the speaker take a deep breath, as if determining a way to broach the reason for his call.

"Very riveting," the voice repeated.

Blackwood tried picturing the man. Probably in his late 30s. Given his precise speech, his careful enunciation, he likely belonged to a professional class. Very well-mannered—almost old-fashioned. But an edge lurked in his voice, a palpable sense of apprehension Blackwood had no trouble detecting.

"You write about the dark side, Mr. Blackwood. You seem to have a—how should I put it?—an understanding of such things," the caller said.

"It comes with the territory," Blackwood said. "I've been covering the crime beat a few years now."

Get to the point, mate, he said to himself. *I've no time for a chinwag.*

"Hell's bells, yes, I imagine it does," the caller softly said, giving no sign he sensed

Blackwood's urgency. "But handling the unusual ... the tragic ... appears to be something you do well. The strange. Or all of the above, such as that Bookstore Butcher maniac."

He placed extra emphasis on "the strange."

Blackwood moved the pipe from one side of his mouth to the other. Until tonight, thoughts of the Butcher hadn't crossed his mind in months, and now twice in just a few minutes?

If only he could forget.

The Bookstore Butcher, alias Matt Linkin, stalked through life a proverbial wolf in sheep's clothing. Linkin was the manager of a greeting-card store; his affable manner and meek appearance disguised the blackened soul of a serial killer. His terrible exploits paralyzed the city for weeks. After tracking down his victims by address labels left on magazines sold in a second-hand bookstore, he broke into their homes, bound his targets and suffocated them with plastic bags. Then he nicked a treasured memento as a way of keeping his prey "alive."

The Butcher taunted the police by sending cryptic letters to the newspaper—to Blackwood—even as the body count mounted. Clues left in the missives allowed Blackwood to piece together a pattern and, eventually, an identity. Though most of SAPD's finest had viewed Blackwood as nothing more than a boyish amateur playing sleuth, an open-minded homicide detective named Frank Gruene came to trust the reporter enough to ask for his help. The pair ultimately ended the murderer's reign of terror during a deadly confrontation.

The caller's voice pried Blackwood from his memories.

"I have a very unique story to tell, Mr. Blackwood. Something that makes the Butcher look like a child. Interested?"

His voice rose slightly, as though afraid Blackwood wouldn't take the bait.

He needn't have worried. Blackwood remained nothing if not eternally curious.

"I'm listening," the reporter said. The tip of his Mont Blanc pen settled on a page in the notebook. Blackwood decided he could spare five minutes. The night detectives could wait.

"Good," the man said. "I think you're just the person to write the story. You understand death and evil, it seems."

True, Blackwood agreed mentally. There are advantages to writing about the violently departed. A card taped to his computer summed up his views on the subject: "Mortuos non petendam." Roughly translated, "The dead can't sue."

The caller cleared his throat.

"So tell me," the reporter prodded.

The man's tone shifted, becoming sharp and insistent.

"Oh no, not over the phone. Hell's bells, Mr. Blackwood, I'm smarter than that. We need to meet. In person. I want to look into your eyes. Make sure you can be trusted."

Blackwood imagined the caller standing on a dim street corner, coat pulled up against the cold, his shoulders squeezed into the call box and his head down, covered by shadow.

"Besides, they're watching me," the caller whispered.

"They?" Blackwood said, straining to hear.

"Indeed, 'they,' Mr. Blackwood. A very nasty bunch of people. You could say they're close to each other—very close indeed. And let's avoid any mention of their fearsome agents."

In spite of the ironic tone, Blackwood had no trouble discerning the fear in the man's voice.

"If they find out—if they even suspect—that I've talked to a reporter, you will never hear from me again."

Another long break followed.

"There must be ground rules first. But to do that, we must visit—face to face, Mr. Blackwood. Face to face. There is no other way. Then, and only then, will all be made clear."

"Very well," Blackwood said. The caller's paranoia did not surprise him. In fact, experience had taught him this kind of parlay was typical during these types of conversations. "Where do we meet?"

"Someplace quiet. A place where we won't be disturbed," the man suggested.

His voice dropped another octave, this time so low Blackwood almost couldn't hear him.

"I harbor a secret so terrible not even the dead will speak of it," the man said in a breathless voice. "Taking that into consideration, I suggest we meet at Oddfellows' Cemetery. Do you know it?"

Blackwood combed his memory for a minute, then nodded while jotting down the location. He raised his eyebrows. What a strange phrase, even melodramatic — "not even the dead will speak of it." He'd interviewed many tipsters during his career, but no one had ever quite put it like that before. Points for originality.

Blackwood wondered about the caller's sanity.

"Yes—it's over on the East Side," the reporter said. "Near Chandler and North Dogwood; not exactly a splendid neighborhood." He'd covered enough gang shootings and crack-whore deaths over there to know.

The caller didn't seem too perturbed.

"But nice and quiet, Mr. Blackwood. No one will disturb us. The locals think the place is haunted."

"Then it shouldn't be too hard recognizing you — you'll be the only one standing," the reporter said. He lobbed another question. "I don't suppose you can say who you are?"

The caller answered with an inquiry of his own.

"Can you guarantee my anonymity?"

He spoke in a hushed voice.

"Make no mistake. It's not me I care about. There is another person who could be affected, and I don't wish to see her come to harm."

Blackwood hesitated before responding. His editors took a dim view of anonymous sources. The trust of readers is earned based on disclosing information, not withholding it, they always argued.

However, the Bookstore Butcher case taught him to trust his instincts, and every mental alarm he possessed told Blackwood that while the caller might sound crazy, he had a story to tell. If this turned into an exclusive, the editors would be the first to forgive him for agreeing to protect the source's identity.

The way he saw the situation, he had nothing to lose.

"Yes," Blackwood finally answered. "You can remain anonymous."

A heavy sense of responsibility settled on Blackwood's shoulders the minute the words left his lips. He did not make such promises lightly. Reporters went to jail for less.

In for a penny, in for a pound, he thought.

The caller sucked down a deep breath.

"Oddly enough, Mr. Blackwood, hiding my identity now does me little good. I am already a dead man. Hell's bells, a dead man indeed. I just want to protect her — my ... friend."

Blackwood sensed the man relaxing.

"For your record-keeping purposes only, my name is James Grant. I am employed by the Akel-Dama Corporation as personal counsel to the CEO, Tobias Revnant."

"Could you spell that, please?" Blackwood said. Grant obliged him, sounding out the letters. Blackwood read the characters back to him, then stared hard at his notes. What kind of name was Akel-Dama? An acronym? And why did this Tobias chap sound familiar?

He opened his mouth to ask, but Grant started speaking again.

"Though trained as a lawyer, these days I am what you might call an 'acquisitions specialist.' A rare-acquisitions specialist, to be precise. I've only been in town a few weeks."

Blackwood heard Grant shift his position. Was he glancing over his shoulder?

Grant sighed heavily.

"I've made a very fascinating discovery, Mr. Blackwood. A very dangerous discovery."

Grant spoke slowly, precisely, as though he wanted to make sure Blackwood heard every word. The reporter turned down the volume knob on the police scanner above his desk.

"I'm all ears," Blackwood said.

"And I will tell you everything when we meet — say, midnight?"

Blackwood nodded.

"Agreed," he said.

There was a long silence from Grant.

"One other thing, Mr. Blackwood."

"Yes?"

"I detect an accent. Slight, but there. Please forgive my curiosity, but are you English?"

Blackwood frowned. He heard this question too often.

"It's complicated," he said, feeling uneasy sharing his life story with a stranger.

"Tsk-tsk," Grant said, decrying his reticence. "I'm opening the book of my life to you — and at great peril to myself. The least you could do is enlighten me a little bit."

Blackwood sighed. After a moment's consideration, he concluded there really wasn't any harm in answering. Like most reporters, he preferred asking questions, not answering them.

"Long story short: I'm an American, but I also hold a British passport. My father is a retired Air Force general. He grew up on a ranch in West Texas. My mum is from a seaside town called Aberystwyth. A beautiful little place in Wales, not England. Dad's a fighter pilot. They met during his tour at RAF Lakenheath, got married, had me and then divorced. I spent part of my life in Wales. So what you hear is a kind of hybrid Welsh accent. Not English."

Grant clicked his teeth.

"I see. Good Celtic stock."

Blackwood glanced at the clock a third time, mindful he still wanted to head over to SAPD. Time to wrap this up.

Grant seemed to sense the session was over.

"Very well. Then I'll see you at midnight — the witching hour. How appropriate." He tittered mirthlessly. "Don't forget—Oddfellows' Cemetery. Come to the south gate. The lock is broken. Just yank on it. I'll wait by the big mausoleum. You can't miss it."

"Until then," Blackwood said.

"Good, very good," Grant said. He whispered his next sentence, as though talking to himself: "We must keep them from breaking the circle."

The reporter's eyebrows rose.

"Breaking the circle?" he repeated. "What is –."

Grant clicked off without uttering another word.

CHAPTER TWO

Blackwood rose and grabbed his tweed jacket off the back of the chair, a hundred questions racing through his brain. The contemplation, however, was short-lived. A breathless man with a beard the color of a wildfire rushed into the newsroom, his boots screeching to a stop in front of Blackwood. A bulging camera bag heavy enough to leave a dent in the floor hung over a broad shoulder. A Nikon with a huge lens dangled from his neck.

"Are you a news-lovin' sonofabitch?" the man thundered.

Blackwood thrust one arm into the jacket, then the other, not missing a beat. He barely looked up as he draped a long trench coat over the jacket and straightened his tie.

"I am," he said in a deadpan voice.

Smiles flitted across the faces of the other reporters hunched over their terminals. The routine, though familiar, never lost its hammy charm.

"Then have I got a story for you, you uptight limey," the newcomer promised, voice booming like a fire-and-brimstone preacher in the pulpit.

The crime writer fought to suppress a smile.

"Hullo, McGowan," Blackwood said.

Robert McGowan's lower lip, at least the discernible part under his mustache, twitched in mild irritation. Cousins the pair might be, though even a studious observer would have found it difficult to note a family resemblance. McGowan—flame-haired, beefy, disheveled, often chomping on an unlit cigar. Blackwood—thin, blond, neat, never far from his straight-stem briar, with gray eyes like steel points. Trading jabs had become routine for the trans-Atlantic relations.

"Ha. Ha. Ha," the photographer said, each syllable delivered with an attitude. "And while you're busy ticklin' my ribs, tell me you heard the hostage incident on the scanner?"

Blackwood's blank expression answered McGowan. He cast a guilty look at the volume knob on the black box, which he'd turned down when Grant called.

"Bexar Regional Hospital? A crazy-ass gunman? People in the ER held at gunpoint? FUBAR?" McGowan pressed.

Blackwood pointed to his phone.

"Sorry, haven't a clue. A source — well, a potential source," he corrected himself, " — rang me up with a tip. I'm meeting him later in the cemetery."

"Well, luckily I *was* listening to the scanner," McGowan sighed. A hand the size of a bear's paw clapped Blackwood's shoulder. "Let's go, cuz. This time you drive — you need the practice. And remember, stay on the right side of the road, okay?"

As they turned to go, McGowan noticed a candy jar on the desk next to Blackwood's. Curious, he extracted a strand of black licorice.

He popped the treat into his mouth, chewed and then made a face.

"That tastes like ass!" he said.

"And you would know this how?" Blackwood said.

McGowan spat sticky gobs into a trashcan.

"C'mon. We're wasting time," he said, not bothering to hide his irritation.

The photographer headed to the elevator and Blackwood fell in step. The crime writer yelled something to the night metro editor about his destination. She didn't even look up from her keyboard, just waved a hand.

"Yeah, I heard McGowan," the editor said. "Everybody did."

Someone over on the State Desk snickered.

As the cousins waited on the elevator, Blackwood cast a thoughtful glance at the photographer.

"Hang on. Something you said back there—what was it?" He tapped his head, remembering. "Oh, right. FUBAR?"

McGowan guffawed.

"Gotcha, didn't I? Add that to your dictionary of American slang. 'Fucked Up Beyond All Recognition.' A favorite expression from my glory days in the Marines. And from the scanner traffic I heard, this deal at the hospital qualifies."

The elevator doors whooshed open. They entered the carriage.

Blackwood walked out of the Trib a minute later and felt something cool and liquid touch his cheek. He gazed up at the night. Dozens of small, shiny dots flickered in the downtown streetlamps. More followed, until thousands of tiny flakes fell to earth, turning slow, silent cartwheels before coating the streets and sidewalks.

"Look at that!" McGowan breathed, as excited as a child on Christmas morning. "Snow! Actual snow. I can't believe it."

Blackwood had the opposite reaction.

"Odd," he said, frowning. "Very odd indeed."

CHAPTER THREE

The first thing Dr. Sabrina Hagen noticed when she glanced up from her desk was the snow dusting her office windows. More flakes spiraled down in the distance, caught in the glare of the parking-lot lights across from the museum her family had owned for nearly a century. Beyond the lights, darkness gathered among the trees of Brackenridge Park, nestled in the city's heart, and through those, one could just glimpse the wandering ribbon of the San Antonio River winding past the massive building.

Sabrina sighed and leaned back. The slightly crisp air when she left home this morning didn't seem unusual for "winter" in South Texas. But snow? Unusual. No, not just unusual. Extremely rare. Quite often in the Panhandle, sometimes Dallas, but not here, not this far south.

Raised in sun-drenched San Antonio, Sabrina felt oddly drained by the unaccustomed sight. Most would have been ecstatic, but for her snow foreshadowed road closures, accidents, blackouts, frozen pipes and headaches. During her post-graduate studies in Massachusetts, she dreaded the winters. But at least people in Cambridge knew how to deal with snow. It would paralyze folks in San Antonio. Hardly anyone in this part of the world even knew how to put on tire chains.

Though Sabrina's new position as interim director of the Anderson Museum kept her too busy to peruse the latest scientific journals (*thanks grandmother*, she thought, and then instantly felt ashamed), she couldn't help but wonder whether the environmentalists' fears regarding a potential connection between greenhouse-gas emissions and global warming would prove true.

She pushed a strand of blond hair from her face.

I need a vacation, she thought. *Someplace with plenty of sun, palms, margaritas and everybody in shorts and sandals.* Then she chuckled, realizing she'd just described San Antonio most of the year.

She glanced at her watch with a yawn. Oh my. Where had the time gone? Still so much to do! Her ice-blue eyes swept the paperwork piled on her desk, eliciting a frown. At this rate, she wouldn't finish until midnight.

A knock on the partially open door startled her. Ben Murray, the Anderson's development officer, hovered at the entrance to her grandmother's office—*no, my office now*, she corrected herself; *I've got to get used to saying that*—wearing a congratulatory grin.

Sabrina waved him in. He didn't need a second invitation and entered the room faster than she could blink. His smile grew wider, like a hopeful schoolboy seeing his favorite cheerleader.

"Congratulations on getting the final funding, Dr. Hagen," he said, raising a coffee mug in her honor. "Great job at the meeting today with the suits from Alamo Bancshares. So much for those creeps from Akel-Dama."

She returned the grin, though hers wavered.

"Thank you, Dr. Murray," she responded, lifting her own mug with coffee gone cold hours ago.

Ben crossed the room, clinked cups and took a sip from his. Sabrina waited, sensing he wanted to say more.

"Well, you actually did it," he said. "You got those tightwads from the bank to underwrite the new exhibit. It won't cost us a dime. And, we get to keep the relic. No selling to Akel-Dama, despite their truly generous offer."

She brushed aside the compliment. She had no intention of selling the relic — right, grandmother? Your will made that abundantly clear.

"*We* did it, Ben," she said, emphasizing the plural. "You, me, the staff. It didn't happen overnight, but we got Alamo Bancshares onboard. Thanks to them, we have the last bit of funding in place. The real challenge is getting the exhibit ready in three days."

She groaned and put palms to her temples. "Three days!"

Ben rubbed his salt-and-pepper goatee with a faraway look.

"'Myths & Magicks of Spanish Tejas,'" he broadcast, waving his hand like an impresario. "I love the title."

His tone became thoughtful.

"Don't worry. We'll make the deadline," he said with an earnest face. "We're going to pack them in – Sabrina."

She pretended not to notice he dropped the "Dr. Hagen." Instead, she stretched, cat-like, working out the kinks in her back that came from sitting too long. She ignored the way his eyebrows rose appreciatively.

"Making deadline won't be easy," she said. "The centerpiece still has to be mounted. And while I admit the old book looks sturdy, it is 800 years old. We need to be careful."

Ben threw back his head and gave a throaty laugh.

"If anyone can make the deadline, it's you," he said with a burst of confidence Sabrina didn't share.

Still, she appreciated his faith in her. Sabrina respected Ben as a colleague, but she sensed he wanted their professional relationship to blossom into something more.

Not going to happen. That's all she needed right now — another complication in her life. Having laid Mimi Anderson in the ground only two months ago left an ache that wouldn't go away. No one could fill that void, and she preferred to face her grief alone. Besides, Sabrina was still learning her way around the museum. She didn't need an entanglement with someone whose check she signed, no matter how pleasant he seemed.

Ben studied Sabrina's features as though attempting to read her mind.

"It's too bad your grandmother—and your parents—aren't here to see this. They would be proud of you. Real proud. You've done a great job as the new director, and now this—getting your first major exhibit off the ground."

Interim director, she wanted to correct him; she was only here to get things back on track, shore up the financials, square the books, and then she'd be returning to her old life as an archaeologist. Her father had been an archaeologist and her mother worked as his assistant. The cooperative relationship proved fulfilling for both (*despite the cave-in at the excavation; don't forget that little tragedy — it only left you an orphan*), and Sabrina knew she could do worse than follow in their footsteps.

Yet she had to admit Ben's optimism raised her spirits; Sabrina had shed too many tears lately, and kind words remained a salve for invisible wounds.

So instead of correcting him, she softly offered, "I hope so."

She had not asked to be named interim director of the Anderson. But her grandmother's fatal heart attack changed everything, and Sabrina had little choice but to take over at the board's insistence. Nor did she have any idea what her parents would have thought — both had died so long ago without her ever knowing them.

Her parents' last discovery in the caves beneath Mission San Jose, in fact, had spurred this exhibit, so many years in the making. If it hadn't been for their dogged efforts, and Sabrina's own research into a forgotten crate locked in the museum's vault, "Myths & Magicks of Spanish Tejas" would never have gotten off the ground. The projections from the Marketing Department — which had spent months playing up the exhibit's so-called "book of mystery" — indicated record attendance, promising to make the venture the museum's most lucrative in years.

Lord knows they needed a blockbuster to draw the crowds again. Attendance over the last two years had gradually tapered off, biting into the bottom line. Something as old-fashioned as wax statues and stuffed animals didn't impress kids enraptured with computer games and cinematic special effects.

But the new exhibit couldn't miss, marketing said. Old legends, Spanish explorers and an enigmatic book that raised more questions than answers — blended with interactive displays and state-of-the-art animatronics — virtually guaranteed a sold-out crowd. Hence the need for extra funding; the museum had never mounted anything this elaborate. Not even "Texas Jurassic," and that had been pretty awesome.

"It'll be great," Ben predicted.

Walking over, he gave her shoulder a gentle squeeze. Not hard and not long, just a gesture that said, "I could be more than a friend."

Sabrina started shuffling papers. It gave her a reason to move away without seeming rude. Ben got the hint, cleared his throat and began inching to the door. Yet he seemed reluctant to leave.

"So where is 'Mr. Sign the Dotted Line'?" he asked. Though innocent in tone, the question spiked the air with the thrust of a dagger.

Sabrina wouldn't take the bait, just kept her eyes glued to an invoice. She clicked and un-clicked a ballpoint pen, pretending to read.

Ben patiently waited by the door and repeated himself.

"So, have you heard from James Grant?"

She glanced up, keeping her gaze neutral. Did she detect just a wee hint of green flickering behind Ben's round spectacles? If she had to guess, she would have said he seemed just a tad jealous of the acquisitions specialist from the Akel-Dama Corporation.

This did not surprise her—the two men were nothing alike. James was everything Ben wasn't; an expensive dresser, well groomed, outgoing, worldly, quick on his feet, his words precise and to the point. Definitely charming, but with a hint of the rogue. There always seemed to be a secretive air about him, something unspoken. Unlike Ben, who always carried a whiff of needy under the scent of his Aramis.

Why are the scoundrels always more appealing, she wondered.

Sabrina put down her pen before answering.

"I haven't heard from Mr. Grant today," she said, her tone cool. "But I don't think he's too happy with us."

Ben appeared to suppress a smile.

"Let me guess: Your refusal to sell the relic didn't sit well with our corporate friend?"

"No," she said, pursing her lips. "No, it didn't."

She took a breath. "Not so much him, was the sense I got. He was more worried about his boss' reaction, I think."

Ben snorted. "Well, duh. It's only the centerpiece of the Anderson's biggest exhibit in years." He shook his head in disbelief. "Grant never even said what they wanted it for."

She raised the pen and met Ben's gaze with what she hoped was a sisterly look. Something that broadcast the word platonic.

"I'm sure he's fine," Sabrina said, though she didn't sound entirely convinced. When she let James know by phone yesterday that Alamo Bancshares planned to underwrite the exhibit, he became quite upset, but it was more from concern about his employer's temper than anything else. That was easy to understand, considering his employer was Tobias Revnant, the billionaire software developer unaccustomed to taking no for an answer.

Sabrina had never met Revnant, not even during the negotiations (she'd seen his mug plastered on the cover of TIME last year, that was about it), but Grant in his more candid moments painted a picture of a brilliant but aggressive entrepreneur fueled by ambition, ego and even rage.

Ben shrugged, appearing unfazed by her apprehension.

"I wouldn't worry," he assured her, crossing arms and leaning against the doorway. "Grant's a big boy."

She gave him a pointed look that said, "Stop prying." Ben changed gears quickly. He fixed his gaze on the large window behind her cluttered desk.

"Hey, what's the deal with the snow? Totally weird, huh? The radio mentioned some power failures and school closures."

In the fading light, his eyes seemed big and moist, reminding her of a puppy.

Sabrina mumbled something about being too busy to listen to the news, then returned to her paperwork. He turned to go, now looking a little wounded as she busied herself reading a proposal for a geology exhibit.

"OK. See ya," he said over his shoulder.

He disappeared. Sabrina started drumming on her desk.

"— Three, two, one," she whispered.

Ben's head popped back into her office.

"And Sabrina — Dr. Hagen," he corrected himself, "you did fantastic today."

Always the last word, she thought, but not too unkindly.

"Thanks," she said. "Now let's keep our fingers crossed and pray we can get this behemoth completed."

Three days – my God, are we insane or what, she wondered.

Ben Murray flashed a thumbs up.

"Who's worried?"

"Right," she said under her breath. But she knew there was plenty to worry her. There always was.

CHAPTER FOUR

Twenty minutes after Ben departed, Sabrina Hagen finished signing invoices, exhaled loudly and counted her blessings. What a whirlwind these last days had been.

Securing the needed funding for "Myths & Magicks of Spanish Tejas" from Alamo Bancshares only seventy-two hours before the unveiling may have struck her staff as totally insane, but it gave Sabrina a legitimate excuse to turn down Akel-Dama's repeated overtures to purchase her parents' discovery, the indecipherable book reputedly outlawed by the Vatican centuries ago. Her father in his journals cited ancient records at the Holy See as attributing authorship of the tome to the so-called "mad monk" Pierre DeGulliot in 13th century France.

But authorship might be too strong a word, based on information her dad unearthed in other church records. DeGulliot merely copied symbols to the vellum pages from cuneiform fragments discovered even earlier in the Holy Land. If the book had a real name, it remained a mystery; the glyphs on the cover defied translation. The symbols and diagrams scrawled on the inside pages, painstakingly copied from the fragments by DeGulliot, remained as incomprehensible as the title on the front.

Church fathers, for reasons her father could never discover, called the book *Pactum est Maledictus*. In English, "The Covenant of the Cursed." They sent it to the New World more than two centuries ago to be buried and forgotten.

But incomprehensible or not, and as much as the enigmatic James Grant intrigued her, Sabrina wasn't ready to part with the relic. She would not betray her grandmother's final wish: The book must stay on the museum grounds. Mimi's last will and testament remained clear on that point.

Why Mimi kept the relic locked in the basement vault for three decades, not even the will revealed the reason.

If Sabrina had to be honest, another consideration made her reluctant to do business with Akel-Dama. Grant never made clear why Tobias Revnant so desperately wanted the antiquity. No matter how often she pressed James, he would not disclose the reason, only shove more money at her.

His reticence to discuss his employer's interest in the artifact set off alarms for Sabrina. She learned long ago to trust her instincts regarding such things. It never failed her, allowing Sabrina to survive everything from drug cartels to malaria while on excavations in Central America. Just because she was back in Texas running the family business didn't change that.

Unfortunately, the museum's board didn't share her caution. They only saw dollar signs with every offer Akel-Dama waved under their noses. The directors ignored the relic's potential archaeological significance. The board only thought of balance sheets and bottom lines. And though Sabrina inherited her grandmother's seat at the table, the other members could still outvote her.

Though everyone in town admired Mimi's charitable nature, Sabrina quickly learned her dear grandmother lacked any real business acumen. Sabrina's grandfather — Mimi's husband — built the museum's success on his own father's booming oil business, which he inherited, but his death when Sabrina was just a little girl living in their household left a financial void at the

Anderson that tested Mimi and found her wanting. An internal audit after Mimi's demise only confirmed she may have excelled at mounting Old West displays and reattaching dinosaur bones, but she was no bookkeeper. In fact, the Anderson teetered on the brink of financial collapse. "Myths & Magicks of Spanish Tejas" was a do-or-die gamble. But would it be enough?

• • •

The long hallway seemed unusually cold to Sabrina. Rubbing hands against her arms, she drew her black leather jacket tighter around her frame. A quick glance at her watch showed a little past eight. She hurried her steps—the workmen wouldn't stay much longer. Above her, the skeletal arm of a tree scratched against a gallery window like a hungry child begging to come in. She turned a corner, surrounded by paintings of raspa vendors, ice houses, chili queens in El Mercado, mom-and-pop taquerias on Guadalupe Street and flamenco dancers in front of the Alamo. This was the "Tejas Moderno" wing, which she'd helped design during a break from grad school a few years ago.

Her destination, the Spanish Colonial wing, waited at the end of the corridor.

The sounds of sawing, hammering and drilling grew louder as she approached the massive arched doors. The tread of her Doc Martens echoed on the marble floor, a counter-beat to the work crew's din. Mimi Anderson may have arrived at the museum each day in pearls and heels, but not her granddaughter. Sabrina believed in dressing comfortably — scarves, leggings, sweaters, leather jackets and jean skirts.

"*Que pasa, senorita?*" one of the crew politely said as Sabrina entered the cavernous Great Hall housing the Spanish Colonial wing. He rose from the case he disassembled, wiping dusty hands on an apron.

"Not much, Pascual," Sabrina answered, her heart warming at the sight of Pascual Gonzales. Solid as a rock, the handyman had worked at the museum for more years than she could count, repairing everything from broken doors to torn eagle feathers. Her grandmother had doted on Pascual, treating him like family. Sabrina saw no reason not to continue the practice.

"We are making good progress, see?" Pascual said, waving an arm to take in the hall. His grin beamed through a bushy black mustache.

Two other laborers rose from where they drilled a panel and gave her a short, courtly bow. Sabrina returned the acknowledgment with a smile and a nod, her eyes sweeping the room.

What she saw pleased her. Drop cloths, paint cans, buckets of nails and scattered tools littered the parquet floor, but in spite of the mess, the displays appeared almost ready. At the hall's south end stood lifelike conquistadors in curved helmets and cuirasses, leading a hooded Franciscan priest to some unknown destination. When the time came, the animatronic figures would spring to life with the flick of a switch. Not far away rose a life-size replica of a corner of the courtyard from Mission San Jose, which she knew would be filled with 3-D projections of Indians and mendicant friars, some of them equipped with soundtracks to explain the challenges of frontier life in the Spanish Empire. An interactive map of 18th century San Antonio showing the Alamo and the other original missions strung along the San Antonio River, with a toggle that provided an overlay of the modern city, covered an entire wall.

In the center of the hall, of course, on a black granite dais inside a stainless-steel glass case, the very centerpiece of the exhibit, the magnet she hoped would draw a curious — and paying — public, sat the famous mystery tome of Mission San Jose.

Except the case stood empty.

"Pascual," she began, voicing a trill of worry. "Why isn't the book mounted?"

Her vision didn't lie. Both the book and the black-oak chest that cradled it for so many centuries—unearthed by her own parents on that ill-fated dig—were nowhere in sight. Then, she noticed the large wooden crate containing the items squatting next to the display, the boards still nailed shut.

She saw something else, too. Someone had splashed a cross on the box, the red paint still wet. Her mouth dropped open.

Pascual did not respond at once. Instead, he sighed and glanced sideways at the two laborers, then swiveled in her direction looking sheepish.

"I am sorry, Dr. Hagen," he began, his voice stammering. "These men won't touch it. I will have to mount it later."

"Later?" she asked. "But the unveiling is in three days. The exhibit absolutely must be ready by then, Pascual."

She fought to keep the irritation out of her voice.

"*Si, si,*" he said in a rush. "I know." He cast his eyes to the floor, then looked back up at her, wringing weathered hands. "I will have it ready. I promise."

He shot an angry look over his shoulder at the two men, both of whom muttered and directed fearful glances at the crate. Sabrina had no illusions as to who painted the rough cross.

Shaking her head, she walked over to the crate, her eyes riveted on the runny cross. Her annoyance rose the longer she stared. Turning right, she spotted a can of red paint shoved into a corner, just behind a life-size Coahuiltecan statue. She drew up her shoulders.

"Any idea why they did this?"

Pascual shook his head, almost wincing.

"Ignorance, *senorita*, pure ignorance. They didn't even want their pictures taken for the museum newsletter. They said something along the lines of keeping their souls tied to their bodies."

Sabrina rested her chin in her hand. Superstitious nonsense ... But she'd encountered the same thing during excavations in the Yucatan. She'd been just as annoyed then.

Everything—absolutely everything—depended on the display being ready. The relic represented the heart and soul of "Myths & Magicks of Spanish Tejas." The entire advertising campaign centered on the legend of the *Pactum est Maledictus*, which marketing had played up as a book of dark lore banned by the Catholic Church.

But that was just a public-relations tool, for pity's sake. Half truths and a little embellishment. A way to whet the public's appetite and boost attendance.

No one in their right mind actually believed that garbage.

Obviously someone does, a little voice said inside her head. Sabrina glanced once more at the laborers, trying to control her temper.

The men continued murmuring, the words coming so fast she couldn't keep up even if she understood their dialect. Not Spanish; some native tongue from Mexico's interior.

They began backing away.

"Can you understand them, Pascual?" she asked.

He shrugged. "Not really, *senorita*. I think it's a kind of Nahuatl. We get by talking Spanish, but their Spanish is not so good."

They were not part of the regular work crew; Sabrina saw that in an instant. Black hair cropped short in a bowl cut, blunt noses, features as hard as stone, and glittering obsidian for eyes. She shook her head in frustration.

Pascual hastily added, "They come from that day-labor point over on West Commerce. The subcontractor doing the track lighting brought them. He left; they stayed. But they are good workers, ma'm. Hard workers."

"If they were good, Pascual, they would have helped you assemble the display," she said, her words sharper than intended.

But then she caught the glum look on his face and her anger cooled. Sabrina knew she couldn't afford to be too harsh. Pascual was doing his best with what he had.

She vented a frustrated sigh, her stern expression softening.

"I'll tell you what, Pascual," she said. "Why not dismiss these men for the night, and then you and I will mount the book ourselves?"

Looking ashamed at the prospect of the boss dirtying her hands, the handyman nodded, then turned to bark at the laborers; a little too roughly perhaps, but they appeared more relieved than anything. They dropped their heads in that little bow again, breathing "*gracias, gracias*" several times, then beat a hasty retreat across the wide hall. On their way out, they grabbed a pair of tattered ball caps and rough woolen coats from a table by the door.

As soon as they left, Sabrina put her hands on her hips, looked at Pascual and said, with a determined air, "Shall we?"

Getting her hands dirty didn't bother Sabrina, so long as the job got done.

CHAPTER FIVE

The Jeep Cherokee Sport's tires squealed to a stop inches from the police barricade. The sawhorse that stretched across the blacktop lane blocked any ingress or egress to the ambulance bay in the rear of Bexar Regional Hospital. A San Antonio Tribune logo in Old English script could barely be seen under the dirt-streaked doors of the company vehicle, affectionately dubbed the Crime Jeep by the paper's five police reporters.

Officer Peter Clemons zipped up his black leather jacket, flexed gloved hands and marched forward. His job meant keeping the media away from the emergency room during the unfolding hostage situation.

Except for the Trib, he reminded himself. Captain Gruene's orders. Unusual, but to be followed. Behind the patrolman's silhouette, the monolithic hospital dominated the dark skyline, a slab of high-rise glass, lights and stainless steel soaring above low hills once home to cactus and mesquite but now covered by labs, clinics, hotels and fast-food joints.

Clemons swiveled the sawhorse aside. The Jeep pulled next to him and the driver's window rolled down.

A man with sharp cheekbones smoking a pipe held the wheel; a flame-haired bear sat next to him, pawing through a camera bag.

"Thank you," the driver said. A hundred yards west in the hospital's main parking lot, a forest of satellite dishes and antennas rose from an assembly of TV and radio news vans.

"You're supposed to be over there," Clemons said, nodding in that direction, "but the captain must like you. Drive slow and report to the command post. Don't go anywhere else."

The patrolman's mouth tightened in a grim line.

"There's a real psycho down there," Clemons warned.

•   •   •

In the cramped parking lot outside the emergency room, a tense Capt. Frank Gruene hovered behind a squad car, silently praying the hostage situation unfolding just yards away wouldn't go from worse to absolute meltdown. Members of the command staff clustering around him consulted blueprints of the hospital, then spoke quietly into radios. Gruene had eyes only for the partially opened automatic doors of the darkened emergency room, which remained ominously quiet. During his twenty-year career, the commander of the violent-crimes unit could recall few episodes that approached this one in terms of volatility.

A lunatic appearing out of nowhere now held a dozen people at gunpoint inside the emergency-room waiting area. Hospital security identified the assailant as a new doctor named Vincent Malory. The situation started innocently enough forty minutes earlier when

Malory showed up, asked a clerk for his paycheck, then inexplicably turned and wrestled a pistol from an unsuspecting security guard. Malory shot the guard point-blank in the face, then pumped another round into the chest of a nurse who ran to the fallen man's aid. Both died on the spot.

All this Gruene witnessed on footage recovered from a security camera. Unfortunately, the good doctor had since disabled every surveillance device in the ER. After forcing other medical staff and waiting patients to barricade all inside doors with furniture and vending machines, Malory methodically blasted the cameras and the lights. He also fired into a breaker box near the nurses' station, disrupting all power including the heat. That left the automatic rear plate-glass doors to the ambulance bay partially frozen open — just wide enough to admit one person at a time, no more.

Whatever else he might have been, Dr. Malory was not stupid. In minutes, he'd eliminated any chance of escape for his hostages or a rapid rescue from outside. Gruene vowed not to underestimate him.

So far Malory refused to answer the phone, nor had he issued any demands. A vaguely glimpsed shadow pacing back and forth suggested the hostages remained constantly in Malory's sight. He maintained a prudent distance from the doors, too. Occasionally a stab of light glinted off a gun barrel.

For now, the officers ringing the parking lot kept their distance, alert and watchful behind a semicircle of patrol cars, but the captain knew they didn't have the luxury of time.

A police helicopter buzzed overhead, the dancing ovals of its searchlights sweeping the asphalt.

Normally, Gruene would make time his ally. In standoffs, negotiations and patience usually resulted in a peaceful resolution.

But not tonight. Thanks to the unusual weather, the temperature continued dropping; worse, many of the hostages suffered from ailments requiring immediate medical attention. They'd come to an ER, after all. The situation also presented a logistics nightmare. The methodical evacuation of the remainder of the hospital through exits on the other side of the building promised to last hours. Moving patients out of the ICU and surgical suites was taking longer than expected.

Gruene ground his teeth in frustration and turned to the dour lieutenant at his side. From the corner of his eye, he spotted two figures emerging from a San Antonio Tribune Jeep. One wore a trench coat, tie flapping in the wind. Seconds later, he detected a familiar whiff of pipe smoke tinged with molasses.

He addressed the lieutenant.

"George, what's the ETA on SWAT?"

"Another fifteen minutes, captain," George Poe said. "They had to retrieve the secondary command van."

"Why the delay?" Gruene said, his frown mirroring Poe's.

"It was in the shop for maintenance. The primary is at a Neighborhood Watch meeting where some councilman is speaking. They call that good community policing, sir."

Poe's sarcasm was not lost on the captain.

Gruene grunted, then forced himself to take a deep, calming breath. "Fine. Keep me posted."

The lieutenant nodded and left. Gruene now had time for Blackwood. The two newsmen patiently waited a few feet away behind a pickup with a bumper sticker that read, "Welcome to Texas. Now Git."

The captain approached the pair and took turns pumping their hands. He tried to smile, but what emerged was a crooked line, the kind cartoonists draw to show stress.

"Blackwood," he said, forcing some cheerfulness into his voice. "And McGowan. Glad you yellow rat bastards could join the party."

That was Gruene's nickname for the press, of which he held a dim view, but around Blackwood and McGowan the appellation amounted to a private joke.

"Likewise, Captain Gruene," Blackwood returned, correctly pronouncing the name as "Green." Though he'd saved the man's life, out of respect, he used Gruene's rank when in public.

The captain hailed from a long line of Hill Country Germans, born and bred in New Braunfels where folks still brewed their own beer, fermented sauerkraut in earthenware pots stashed in the garage, played polkas and celebrated Oktoberfest in lederhosen.

Somehow, Blackwood couldn't picture Gruene prancing in green suspenders.

"Fancy telling us what this is all about?" Blackwood asked.

Gruene grimaced and jabbed a hand at the ER.

"You want the short version? It's FUBAR."

The reporter couldn't help but glance at his cousin, who only shrugged with an "I-told-you-so" expression.

•   •   •

Blackwood absorbed the scene in a single, laser-focused glance. His keen gaze registered enough detail to fill a book.

An abandoned ambulance partially blocked the ER's automatic glass doors. Blackwood noted at least twenty other cars and a commercial vehicle crowding the lot, not counting the squad cars. A placard on the commercial vehicle — a Ford Explorer — read "Alamo Metro Home Sales."

Intermittently revealed by the police helicopter's searchlights, a few people inside the darkened waiting room squatted on the floor with their backs to a wall. Their expressions ranged from fear to resignation.

A man in a lab coat waving a handgun flitted briefly into view, then disappeared.

Lt. Poe returned and wordlessly handed a clipboard to Gruene. He also carried a Thermos and some cups.

A minute later, over scalding mud disguised as coffee, Gruene briefed the newsmen. He kept a cautious eye on the ER, but so far Malory continued to ignore their calls. Though mystified by the good doctor's lack of demands, Gruene reminded himself that at least no one else had died. Yet.

"Ready to take some notes?" he asked Blackwood.

Blackwood flipped open his notepad. His favored Mont Blanc pen appeared in his hand. Gruene didn't waste time and started talking.

"Our friend down there is Dr. Vincent Malory, 34, a cardiac specialist who moved here a few months ago from Alexandria, Louisiana. That's M-A-L-O-R-Y, one 'l.'"

Blackwood narrowed his eyes. "Any family?"

"Neighbors said a wife and a young son, but we haven't been able to locate them yet. The hospital gave us a home address for a leased residence off East Mulberry. I sent a uniform to check. No one was inside the home, but there's a Volvo sedan in the driveway registered to Malory. We're looking."

Growing silent, Gruene regarded the dark eddies in his cup. Then he looked up and offered additional details.

As he spoke, an icy wind ruffled Blackwood's straw-blond hair. His pen scratched across the paper. Gruene wondered why the reporter didn't use a tape recorder, then remembered Blackwood saying something once about the risk of batteries dying and losing an entire interview. Gruene didn't believe that was the real reason. Blackwood was just old-fashioned. Anybody else would just pack extra batteries.

Gruene sucked air between his teeth, then took another sip of coffee, wincing at the taste.

"Malory's a partner in a local cardiac clinic over on Datapoint Drive, but he also worked extra shifts at the ER."

"Extra shifts?" Blackwood repeated, his steel-gray eyes glittering.

Gruene shrugged. "Probably to pay off some medical-school bills. Don't let the flashy Mercedes and ski trips to Jackson Hole fool you — most doctors are in debt up to their asses. The new ones, anyway. Apparently, the ER gig started a month ago, from what the hospital administrator told us."

"Any prior problems with this chap?" Blackwood said, his pen hovering over the notebook the way a spear-fisher waits to impale a catch.

The captain shook his head and said, "Not a one. Spotless record. Not even a traffic citation."

Gruene consulted a notecard a detective handed him earlier. He could barely read the handwriting. He ended up putting on his glasses, which he rarely wore. The pair slid to the end of his nose.

Sighing, Gruene pushed them back up.

"One of these days I will get a new set," he promised.

The wind blew harder. Snowflakes laced in the breeze struck flesh with the force of bitter nettles. Pulling up the collar of his coat, Blackwood gazed at the sky. Gruene followed his stare.

The captain finally noticed the full moon, and for some strange reason that only made the wind's bite more bitter. Old-timers around the department claimed a full moon always brought out the crazies. Until tonight, Gruene always considered such talk just a myth.

Blackwood gave the captain a level gaze and asked the obvious question.

"Motive?"

Gruene crumpled his Styrofoam cup and pushed it into a plastic bag hanging from a squad car's door handle. The lines of his face sagged with weariness. Blackwood imagined all he really wanted to do was head home, curl up before a fire and read a good book, preferably one detailing the American Civil War or the Tudors. The captain remained a committed history buff.

"I have no fucking idea. Nobody else does, either." Shaking his head in bafflement, he added: "And if you quote me, don't use the word 'fucking,' okay? I don't think that will please the chief."

A thin smile played across Blackwood's features. Gruene's wife just happened to be the chief's sister.

"Not to worry. You realize, don't you, that I've heard your brother-in-law use the same word a time or two?"

Of course, he wouldn't use the expletive. The Trib was a family newspaper, after all. But more to the point, there was no need to get Gruene in any more trouble. He already would have a hard time explaining to the chief why he allowed a reporter — even Blackwood — into a hostage scene to begin with. The chief tolerated their friendship, but that didn't make things any easier when other media complained about "favoritism," which invariably happened. Still, nothing in the General Manual barred an incident commander from deciding who could be at the command post.

"Should he change it to 'gee whiz'?" McGowan asked, patting his vest pockets for a film roll.

Gruene chuckled but didn't reply, only shifted his feet. His eyes scanned the ER's half-opened doors. Frosty breath twirled curlicues in front of his hollow cheeks. Although short for a police officer, not quite 5-foot-7, Gruene made up for the smallish stature with a robust build, honed by daily workouts in the Police Headquarters gym. A regulation haircut and a neat mustache added to his air of vitality.

Blackwood asked, "Why the ER?"

Gruene couldn't help but laugh, although what emerged was a strangled chuckle.

"Today's payday. Believe it or not, that crazy son of a bitch came to collect his paycheck."

Anticipating Blackwood's next question, he added: "Payroll is next door to the ER."

The police reporter shook his head in disbelief, scribbling faster.

"Demands?" Blackwood asked.

"None," Gruene answered. "He won't pick up the phone. Night CID tried calling several times."

The captain glanced into the trash bag and regarded the crumpled cup. Then his gaze tipped to Blackwood.

"Frankly, the good doctor has us by the short hairs. We can't storm the ER without risking lives. But we have to do something — it's getting colder and there's a lot of sick people to consider."

Blackwood grew thoughtful, then spoke. "What about SWAT?"

Gruene released a long breath.

"They're on the way. I hope it doesn't come to that."

Blackwood's head rose from his notes. The squad cars' bar lights painted his face red and blue in a dance of masques.

The crime writer tapped the notepad with his pen. McGowan lowered his camera, the strap around his neck pulling taut.

"Two dead and a bunch of shivering, sick, frightened people," the photographer breathed.

Blackwood replied without hesitation, the enthusiasm in his voice unmistakable.

"Talk about a great story."

Gruene and McGowan exchanged resigned glances.

CHAPTER SIX

From Sabrina Hagen's vantage point next to the sleek display case, the old book didn't look like much, just a ragged collection of vellum pages sandwiched between two stiff leather boards. A few sheets smattered with indecipherable script protruded from the closed volume.

Nestled a foot below, a small chest carved from black oak as shiny as a patch of fresh oil squatted on a second shelf. For centuries, the chest served as the repository for the ancient book. Both artifacts were recovered during the cave-in that claimed her parents' lives during the dig at Mission San Jose all those years ago.

Across from the case, the packing crate's lid stood propped against the wall. Straw padding spilled out of the box like the innards of a toppled scarecrow. Sabrina tried to ignore the cross on the side, the paint still glistening.

With Pascual's help, they had assembled the display in only a few minutes. Now, while the handyman busied himself connecting an armature, Sabrina reached inside the open cabinet and traced a gloved finger along the edge of the book. Even through the latex the cover felt strangely cold.

Lost in her perusal, Sabrina drifted back to a moment three months ago and a lifetime away, recalling the somber reading of her grandmother's will in the family attorney's office. Sabrina was the only person present; Mimi's aged sister, estranged from the Andersons for years, was incommunicado somewhere in Europe. Not that it mattered. Mimi had designated Sabrina the sole heir and executor when she turned 18, adding to the rift between the siblings.

The fall day outside felt warm and vibrant, but inside those carpeted halls of burnished wood and quietly whirring air conditioning, time stood still. Until then, life had been nothing but a rushed, numbed blur for Sabrina, starting with the phone call informing her about Mimi's fatal heart attack.

Yet that morning in the lawyer's office may have been her oddest experience yet since returning home, especially learning about the unexpected codicil in Mimi's will mentioning the relics. Even stranger was the warning never to allow the artifacts to leave the museum.

"There is no leeway on this," Aloysius Hobbes informed her, his lined face as stony as a granite sculpture. In all his years as the family attorney, Sabrina couldn't remember him ever smiling. "Your grandmother was quite adamant on this point, Sabrina. These items must remain at the museum in perpetuity. Any deviation will result in the immediate termination of your access to the family trust."

Sabrina opened her mouth, but Hobbes cut her off with a wave.

"I don't know why your grandmother insisted on this—ahem—unusual request." He steepled fingers as long and withered as old twigs. "Whatever the reason, she took it to her grave."

Finished, Hobbes began arranging the documents in a folder. A silence as heavy as the law volumes lining the bookshelves settled over the office. Still stunned, Sabrina began to collect herself, grabbing her purse and rising to take her leave. That's when Hobbes' rheumy eyes bore straight into hers and he announced, "Wait, my dear, there's one other matter before you go."

Clearing his throat, he opened the top drawer of his desk and produced a crisp manila envelope.

"What's this?" Sabrina asked.

"A key," the solicitor remarked in a voice as thin and dry as onionskin. Pulling on a long metal chain, he withdrew the aforementioned key from the envelope and let it dangle.

Sabrina recognized the item the instant Hobbes extracted it from the folder. Hadn't she seen the very same key nearly every day of her young life around Mimi's neck; as inseparable from her grandmother as body and soul? Mimi never went anywhere without it, even to bed, the long chain always plunging down the necklines of her quilted nightgowns.

"Your grandmother wanted you to have this," Hobbes said, his gaze never wavering. "I'm sure you've seen it before. This key unlocks the vault in the basement of the Anderson where the artifacts are kept."

Sabrina hesitated, then accepted the proffered key. The chain looped in her palm, cool to the touch.

"Thank you, Mr. Hobbes," she said, perhaps a little too formally.

A day after the probate, she prowled the museum's sprawling basement, driven by the curiosity natural to all scientists, the innate need to know. What was so special about these—artifacts? And why keep them under lock and key?

Divided into various chambers, the climate-controlled basement—a constant 70 degrees Fahrenheit, 55 percent relative humidity—seemed to go on forever. Despite the labyrinth, Sabrina assumed locating the vault would be easy, based on hazy childhood memories of trips into the basement with Mimi. She was wrong. After an hour navigating shipping crates, Mesoamerican sculptures, suits of armor, a Mayan sarcophagus and hundreds of other retired displays piling up in the Anderson's innards, she finally located the vault in a remote compartment. She probably walked past the door at least three times before, but no small wonder. A floor-to-ceiling oil canvas of Mexican revolutionary Emiliano Zapata hid the heavy iron door, cunningly recessed into a wall.

Other than Sabrina, it appeared no one else had trod that corridor in a blue moon; undisturbed dust as thick as a shag carpet layered the concrete floor.

Sabrina grunted as she moved the painting. Blinding clouds of dust rose to coat her face, arms and jacket. After gulping great draughts of air to clear her throat, she began a careful examination of the door. That's when she spied the archaic lock set into the winter-gray metal.

Sabrina inserted her grandmother's key and swiveled her wrist. She heard a satisfying click as a heavy metal bolt retracted on the other side of the massive door.

She turned the handle, waiting pensively as the portal swung inward on hinges that needed oiling.

Stepping just inside the threshold, her fingers fumbled for a light switch and found one. The illumination cast by a single, unadorned bulb revealed a small room. Wearing a puzzled expression, she ventured inside.

The coldness of the chamber, a drop of several degrees from the rest of the basement, snatched her breath away. Every exposed inch of skin prickled with gooseflesh. Dust thickened the air. A single crate holding the relics rested in the center. But even that didn't grab her attention as much as the white, sparkling powder sprinkled in a circle around the box. She dropped to a knee, delicately poked a finger into the crystals, sniffed and took an exploratory lick. She instantly recognized the taste. Salt. Her brows scrunched. Why would anyone pour salt around a packing crate?

As Sabrina rose to her feet, her mouth dropped open. Though Mimi never impressed her as particularly religious, Sabrina stared at several crosses, Stars of David and other ecumenical icons adorning the walls. Careful not to disturb the salt circle, Sabrina paced the chamber, scrutinizing the holy symbols. During the inspection, her eyes alighted upon perhaps the strangest sight so far: three words chalked on the back wall, none of which she recognized.

Sanvi, Sansavi, Semangelaf

Like the vault itself, the scrawls raised more questions than answers.

A polite cough returned her focus to the here and now, in the echoing expanse of the Spanish Colonial Wing.

"I must brace the shelves, *senorita*," Pascual said, studying her with mild concern.

"Of course, Pascual," Sabrina murmured, shaking her head to clear the memories.

He shuffled to a toolbox and removed a hammer.

The handyman dropped to a knee and began assembling the supports. Sabrina's thoughts returned to the book, which brooded on the shelf as though contemplating her in return.

• • •

According to her father's painstaking research, legends compiled by one Virgil Elizondo, an 18th century bishop at Mission San Jose, shed more light on the *Pactum est Maledictus* than the scant records in the Vatican library.

Though Elizondo acknowledged no translation existed for The Covenant of the Cursed, he nonetheless declared the book anathema to holy mother church and called it a "doorway to annihilation." The very few and very ancient stories documented by her father, Professor Toren Hagen, claimed the book to be a grimoire of alchemy and heretical lore written in a lost language.

Examining Mimi's private papers painted a picture for Sabrina of the time and effort her grandmother spent trying to fathom the artifact's mysteries, which ultimately proved fruitless. Failing as the church fathers before her had failed, Mimi could not discover the book's secrets.

Eventually Mimi gave up. Still grief-stricken over losing her only child and bitter over her inability to plumb the mysteries of the instrument of Marta Hagen's death, Mimi sealed the relics in the vault and let them slip from her mind.

Old, dusty and forgotten.

But on that fateful day when Sabrina ventured into the basement, an idea began taking root as she stood contemplating the crate and the mysteries within. Though at first the notion seemed crazy, she admitted within her "madness" lurked the motivation to accomplish some real good for the museum. While fully cognizant of her grandmother's final prohibition, Sabrina remained acutely aware Mimi also had left the Anderson in financial shambles.

And that's when the notion of a new exhibit grew. Could this puzzling and utterly unfathomable artifact hidden by the Holy See on the edge of the Spanish Empire two hundred years ago be the answer to the museum's woes? Was it so preposterous a notion the old book might see the light of day as a bona fide money-making exhibit? Add some animatronic models, interactive displays and plenty of publicity, and what would she have? Why, a blockbuster attraction that could push the museum back into the black.

Or so she hoped. And who would object? Certainly not Mimi (a pang of guilt struck her at such a thought), nor the old attorney, so long as she stuck to the letter of the law.

After all, she wouldn't be violating her grandmother's instructions ... the book would remain on the museum's grounds and would never, ever leave, exactly as Mimi ordered.

The only real difficulty, especially since the Anderson itself lacked deep coffers, would be enticing financial backers. But the investors were out there — Sabrina felt certain. Mimi had plenty of friends who owed the museum favors.

A win-win situation, Sabrina reasoned as she lingered that morning in the vault.

• • •

Faintly, Pascual's hammering reached her ears. Pulled once more from a web of memories into the present, Sabrina leaned into the cabinet again and reopened the book. She studied the words (symbols? hieroglyphs?) to pass the time while the handyman finished up. This wasn't her first attempt at deciphering the illegible scrawls, which Mimi once described as "scratch from a rooster on peyote." As usual, Sabrina's fruitless inspection left her mildly irritated.

But as she started to shut the cover, a cold blue light flashed from inside the book, catching her by surprise. The glow faded the second it registered on her retinas.

Had one of the overheads flared out, she wondered. A quick scan showed nothing amiss with the fluorescents. The lights shone so brightly, it wasn't a trick of the shadows.

Though somewhat startled, but still more curious than afraid, Sabrina gently peeled back the book's cover, peering inside. What she spied wrenched a gasp from her. Before her widening eyes, the marks on the pages moved. Shifted. Just a hairsbreadth, so slight as to be barely noticeable. But enough to jolt her.

"What?" she whispered in a choked voice.

Questioning her eyesight, Sabrina tore her gaze away, then looked again. Now, of course, everything appeared normal — the same old chicken scratch. Slashes and strokes, deep crimson on every page, making about as much sense as splotches from a madman's paintbrush. But this time nothing moved.

Nerves, she told herself. *I'm just anxious about the unveiling. That's all.*

She blinked several times to clear her field of vision.

There? See, nothing strange—she told herself.

The characters stirred again, inkblot scorpions sluggishly shrugging off the sleep of eons.

She rubbed tired eyes, hoping that would help. But when she removed the balled fists from her sockets, the shimmying of the symbols had only grown worse. They twirled and tumbled on the parchment. For a moment, she wondered if the hall's powerful lights created an optical illusion tricking her mind. The sounds of Pascual's labored breathing seemed as distant as the echoes down a tunnel. She wanted to call out, but couldn't lift a tongue grown heavy as a brick. Her pulse pounded in her temples, and she shook from head to toe.

The letters, scrawls, runes or whatever they represented picked up speed, spinning like bottomless whirlpools. She felt them pulling on her mind, an insistent tugging at the shores of consciousness, drawing her thoughts like a rudderless boat out to sea. There was worse to come. Within seconds, Sabrina became aware of a presence. Something brooded in the deep black beyond.

With growing dread, she realized the thing could sense her, too. It possessed sentience ... arrogant, superior — malevolent. Not human. Or, more aptly, more than human. Magnificent, immense and utterly vile, all simultaneously.

Sabrina decided enough was enough. Time to put the book away.

But when she tried to close the pitted leather cover, her fingers felt glued to the pages. Try as she might, she couldn't let go. She wanted to slam the thing shut, but it felt as though invisible hands gripped hers, holding them in place. Utter cold seized her, cementing her to the spot. Even worse, the symbols on the pages now pulsated as though alive, creating the appearance of angry creatures ready to crawl — or worse, leap — off the page.

And there was something else, too.

Whispers ... frozen, haunted whispers. They wrapped around her consciousness, holding tight with the force of frost-encrusted tentacles. A single voice arose above the cacophony, commanding, imperious, as sharp as a glass shard buried in ice. She couldn't make out the words, but she didn't need to. Menace hung in every utterance. If only she could shut her ears. Whatever lurked in the darkness beyond made her flesh want to crawl off her bones.

She could bear no more. Summoning every ounce of will she possessed, Sabrina slammed the book shut with enough force to rattle the display case. Taking a halting step backwards, she dropped quivering hands to her sides.

Her head shook in denial.

What just happened? she wondered, aghast.

Against her better judgment, she held a lungful of air, waited a moment, then cautiously inserted her fingers between the pages and cracked the cover once more. Steeling herself, Sabrina took a long, hard look, heart pounding against her ribs.

Nothing appeared amiss. Just weird little lines on treated animal hide. She deflated with a grateful sigh.

A goofy smile lifted the corners of her mouth. She felt very relieved and a little foolish.

I need to get some sleep, that's all.

She nodded vigorously, agreeing with herself. Just a fatigue-induced hallucination, nothing more. Had to be.

Sure, keep telling yourself that, her little common-sense voice said, the one that reminded her to feed the parking meter and to look both ways before crossing a street.

"*Senorita*, I am done," Pascual announced. He knelt on the floor, inspecting the now-secured brackets. He showed no awareness of what had just happened, and Sabrina — who felt silly enough already — decided it was best not to say anything.

"Time to return the objects to the basement?" Pascual said.

The vast hall seemed to absorb any noise; there were no other sounds except the slight hiss of wind chasing its tail around the eaves outside.

"The ... basement?" she stammered.

"*Si*," he answered, nodding. "You said the insurance company requires the book to stay in the vault when it's not on display."

"Yes ..." she answered, struggling not to feel guilty about her little white lie. Her voice came out small and drained. "Yes, Pascual, of course."

The truth was, insurance had nothing to do with returning the relic to its cozy little circle of salt in the vault. Sabrina couldn't explain why, but the decision just felt right. As much as she scoffed at the hint of menace in her grandmother's last testament, she knew Mimi probably had her reasons for keeping the artifact under lock and key.

And after what she'd just witnessed (not real, not real, she chanted to herself), Sabrina wondered if Mimi had known more than she let on.

Glancing at Pascual, then shifting to the case, Sabrina summoned her most resolute voice and said, "Let's do that, shall we?"

Twenty minutes later, the book rested securely in its crate downstairs. As she swung shut the vault's heavy iron door, Sabrina couldn't shake the familiar feeling there lurked a sly awareness to the tome, as though it still watched her.

Don't be absurd, she told herself.

Sabrina and Pascual trudged back upstairs.

On his way to the exit, Pascual stopped to remove his dusty apron and snatch a wool jacket hanging from a wall peg. As he fed his arms into the sleeves, he called out.

"*Senorita?*"

"Yes, Pascual?"

"I know the Anderson is not the place you want to be right now," he said, his earnest expression mirroring how carefully he chose each word. "This museum was your grandmother's calling—God rest her soul. All of us loved her like our own *abuelita*. But you should know—and I speak for everyone—you are doing a good job. *Muy bueno.*"

Warmth flushed Sabrina's cheeks.

"Why thank you, Pascual," she said. "But I can never fill my grandmother's shoes."

His face offered a slight grin.

"No, that is true. But you are making tracks of your own." He turned to go. "*Feliz Navidad, senorita.*"

"Merry Christmas to you, too, Pascual."

She watched his back recede as he walked away, marking the tread of his work boots down the long hallway. Eventually, his footsteps faded. She turned and confronted the empty display case, pleasant feelings evaporating.

The words ... twisting and turning ... A voice inside my head...

She swept the disconcerting memories from her mind, but the sense of disorientation, of being thrust into some dark, hidden world she never imagined existed, refused to go away.

CHAPTER SEVEN

Lt. Poe returned with his hand wrapped around a megaphone. Gruene reached for it.

"SWAT is here, captain," Poe said. Apple-red spots on each cheek rubbed raw by the wind stood out from a face as pale as ashes. Gruene seemed to relax. But only slightly.

"Get 'em over here," he ordered. "Let's end this."

• • •

No matter how many times Blackwood watched the elite Special Weapons and Tactics team, he still had to convince himself flesh-and-blood humans breathed under the all-black uniforms, body armor, helmets, tactical goggles and balaclavas.

The driver of the armored SWAT van, a sergeant protected behind a bullet-resistant windshield, barked an order into a dash-mounted microphone as the vehicle rolled to a stop. The fortified doors at the rear of the shield-plated vehicle swung open to disgorge the occupants. Despite their heavy combat boots, the troopers dropped to the ground in quick succession. They gripped AR-15 assault rifles with MagLites attached just below the dull metal of the barrels. Each officer also carried a .40-caliber Glock strapped to a thigh holster, and smoke grenades dangled from their web gear.

They assembled in a single line without a sound. McGowan moved in and snapped a few shots.

Over to the side, Blackwood puffed on his battered briar but remained silent. Gruene stood next to him, face hard as alabaster. The SWAT sergeant approached at a brisk walk.

"Captain," said the commander. Blackwood noted a trim, thirtyish Hispanic man with thin lips, deep hollows in his cheeks and somber eyes. He wore a black, featureless ball cap instead of a helmet.

"Welcome to the party, sergeant," Gruene returned.

"Wouldn't miss it, sir," said the sergeant, whose name tag spelled RODRIGUEZ. He stood well over six feet with wide shoulders and a jaw jutting like a basalt cliff. "Has the situation changed since dispatch notified us?"

"No, nothing. Lt. Poe faxed you the building schematics and suspect profile; did you get them?" Gruene asked.

"Yes sir."

Giving the ER doors a quick but comprehensive glance, the sergeant asked, "How many hostages?"

"Eight to ten, as best as we can tell. Our suspect — Dr. Vincent Malory — is armed with a Colt Detective Special. He took it off a security guard and killed him with it. Carries six rounds, witnesses report hearing two shots fired so far. No other weapons or extra ammo that we can determine. There's a second DOA, a nurse. Unknown how many others dead or injured. Malory disabled all cameras and barricaded the exits. No demands so far."

The sergeant considered this information, raising eyebrows as dark as charcoal slashes. He looked down, saw the megaphone clutched by Gruene. Awareness dawned on his face.

"You're a trained negotiator, right sir?"

This fellow doesn't miss much, Blackwood thought.

Gruene sucked a tense breath between clenched teeth.

"Yes I am, sergeant. I did two years with SWAT."

Rodriguez absorbed the information, then asked, "What do you advise?"

The captain paused a moment before answering.

"Normally, I'd let this guy sit on his thumbs, but the temperature is dropping and we've got some very sick people in there. He won't pick up the phone, so we need to establish verbal contact."

He looked resigned. "I guess I'll handle the honors."

"Understood," Rodriguez said. His expression said he didn't envy Gruene.

• • •

The wind died down, as though weighted by the gravity of the situation unfolding at the hospital's back doors. But the cold only became worse, draining life, movement and resolve.

Blackwood shrugged off the icy fingers caressing the exposed square of his neck, his gray eyes fixed on the clinging darkness of the ambulance bay. Only the rumbling engine of the SWAT transport and the muffled thuds of the troopers' boots reached his ears. The officers marched in two lines behind the heavy-duty vehicle. Blackwood noticed the van approached the bay at an angle, protecting the tactical team with its metal bulk. He knew nothing less than a rocket could punch through the reinforced hull of the military-surplus carrier.

The van came to a stop about sixty feet from the ER doors. With a loud clang, a row of roof-mounted spotlights switched on, twin suns transforming darkness into day. The beams illuminated eight hostages huddled on the floor just inside the sliding doors. A few gasped and threw hands over their eyes to block the harsh glare. The vehicle's public-address system crackled to life. Gruene, sitting in the passenger's seat, spoke into the dash-mounted microphone as his unwavering gaze locked on the doors. No need for a megaphone now.

"Doctor Malory," Gruene's voice hissed tinnily. "This is Capt. Gruene of the San Antonio Police Department. Please put down your weapon and come into the light with your hands on your head. You will not be injured if you cooperate."

Something stirred in the shadows just out of the lights' reach.

"Eat shit!" bellowed a man's strained voice.

Gruene tried another tactic.

"Doctor, we are here to resolve this matter peacefully. Why not release some hostages? Surely you must be hungry or thirsty. We could trade. Maybe a sandwich and some hot coffee in return for letting a few of those people go? Or at least some warm blankets for them?"

A scornful laugh echoed from the section of the ER the lights couldn't reach.

Next to Gruene, Sgt. Rodriguez waved a hand outside the driver's side window, a gesture directed at the lead man in each column and passed down the line. The SWAT officers quietly flowed around the van while a sharpshooter climbed on top. He shouldered a high-powered rifle mounted with an infrared scope.

When Gruene spoke again, his voice carried an unmistakable air of controlled patience.

"Doctor Malory, please do not make this any more difficult. I repeat: Put down your weapon and come out. We can end this peacefully. No one has to get hurt."

Gruene paused, seemed to consider something on the floorboard, then raised his head and leaned closer to the microphone.

"If nothing else, how about releasing just those folks who require immediate medical attention? Please."

But instead of a profane retort or even something worse, Malory surprised everyone by stepping through the gap between the doors and onto the loading dock, a lopsided grin spreading like a stain across his face. A revolver dangled in his right hand. In the stunned silence that followed, he just stood there blinking at the bright circles of the spotlights.

Then he turned and waved the gun inside the partially open doors, barking at the hostages.

"Y'all come out and say hello," Malory invited.

A desultory, downtrodden line of eight people walking single-file, including a very pregnant woman, shuffled from the ER, heads lowered. Malory waved the gun, grunting; the captives assembled in front of him, forming a protective shield. Tears on some of the captives' cheeks glistened in the light.

Blackwood gazed over their heads and studied Malory. Under ordinary circumstances the doctor might have been handsome, but tonight his knotted brown hair hung in unkempt strands. The wind parted the folds of his lab coat, revealing a bloody streak coating the untucked designer shirt underneath.

Malory's eyes glowed with manic intensity as he surveyed the phalanx of officers. The silly grin on his face stretched wider.

After a second, he took an exaggerated step forward and planted himself next to the pregnant woman, casually placing the revolver against her temple. A young, pretty Hispanic girl, she barely looked twenty. Even from where he crouched behind a patrol car, Blackwood could hear her whimpers intensify.

The SWAT officers, who formed a half-ring around the bay, raised their rifles.

"Do not fire," Sgt. Rodriguez ordered, speaking into a radio transmitting a signal to the troopers' headsets. "Repeat: Do not fire."

"You have no idea what's going on," Malory said, keeping the revolver pointed at the girl. She wore a thin cotton T-shirt, an unzipped jacket and shorts. Dragon tattoos crawled up and down her bare legs, which shivered. Whether from fear or the cold, Blackwood couldn't say.

No one moved. Malory giggled.

"No idea," he repeated, but this time in a falsetto voice. "Try to take me, boys.—Just make sure you're faster on the trigger."

He pushed the barrel against the woman's temple. Her eyes snapped shut, and she began muttering a prayer in Spanish. Malory's hand shook. The gun barrel bobbed up and down, reminding Blackwood of a cork on the water.

Malory swept his surroundings with a single glance and leveled a sickly smile at the watchers. For the merest second, his eyes alighted on Blackwood and rested there. Their gazes locked. A dark, unreadable expression clouded Malory's features as his face swallowed that Tilt-a-Whirl smile. Then, in what seemed a deliberate and calculated move, he winked at the crime reporter before returning his attention to the SWAT van.

"Come and get me!" the doctor taunted.

Blackwood's heart leapt into his throat.

Did he just wink at me...?

What the hell was that all about? The wink — no random act, for sure — became indelibly imprinted on his mind.

He glanced at McGowan. If the photographer noticed, he didn't give any indication.

Malory stood his ground, coughed deep in the back of his throat and spat something viscous on the loading dock. A few of the SWAT officers shifted uneasily.

Malory cried out, an ululation fueled by fear and madness.

"I'm breaking the circle!" he said, voice cracking. "I'm breaking the circle!"

Every hair on Blackwood's head stiffened. Where had he heard that expression before?

It took a moment, and then a violent breath escaped him with the force of a punch to the gut. His blood went cold.

James Grant had said the same thing an hour ago.

"I'm breaking the circle," Malory repeated with a titter.

Icy claws skittered along the ridges of Blackwood's spine.

That same damn expression. Did Grant and Malory know each other? It seemed unlikely, but worth asking Grant. And what did the phrase mean, anyway?

The questions kept chasing each other around Blackwood's stunned mind.

A strangled cry rose from the ER entrance. The air crackled with enough tension to split a tree.

"I have no choice!" Malory yelled. "I am commanded to break the circle!"

He bit off the words like a dog snapping a bone, ending with a screeching laugh.

"Commanded," Blackwood thought. As in taking orders? Another strange word choice. Another mystery.

Squatting behind the squad car, Blackwood rotated on his heels and gazed into the SWAT transport's open passenger door. Sitting on the edge of his seat, Gruene sucked down several long breaths as though to calm himself, but Blackwood recognized that look — the captain was losing patience.

"Dr. Malory, put the gun down. Do it now," Gruene barked.

The physician ignored the instruction. He spat once more and began trembling. The revolver shook in his hand. A second later, he pointed the barrel downward.

Blackwood stopped taking notes and stared, astonished, as Malory's movements became more agitated. A score of primal emotions flashed across his tormented features, but primarily abject terror. Malory began twisting and turning, squirming like a fish caught in a net. The contortions reminded Blackwood of someone trying to wake from a nightmare.

Then, as suddenly as the fit began, the seizure stopped. Malory squinted and blinked. Blackwood could see his grip on the handgun tightening. The barrel rose again, touching the bridge of the woman's nose. A little cry escaped her pale lips.

Ignoring the pregnant woman, Malory faced the assembled officers. A river of sweat dripped from his crinkled brow.

"Something's coming!" he shouted hoarsely. "You've never seen anything like it. Big, bad and mad. Really mad."

He shoved the girl to the ground, where she crumpled in a startled heap. The other hostages stood petrified; some cried, others murmured prayers. Ignoring them, Malory spoke next in a low, considered tone, almost sad.

"To be honest, I'm not sticking around. It's not gonna be pretty and I don't like the cold."

Before anyone could make a move, the doctor thrust the revolver barrel between his parted teeth.

A renewed fit of trembling shook his frame, an attack far more pronounced than before, and the weapon just as quickly leapt out of his mouth. Then, like a pendulum, the barrel began to swing back and forth, with one of the doctor's white-knuckled hands trying to force it between clenched teeth and the other trying to push the gun away. To the horrified observers, it looked as if Malory warred with himself. Some of the hostages began inching away.

Blackwood unconsciously rose from his crouch and stared straight into Malory's eyes, called there by an impulse he didn't understand. Malory's frantic perturbations ceased as he returned the journalist's searching gaze, his agonized eyes searing a path directly to Blackwood's brain.

Two words, uttered so low as to be almost unheard by anyone else, escaped the doctor's lips. To Blackwood, they were as loud as cannon shots.

"Help me," Malory pleaded.

For the merest second, the unearthly glare dominating Malory's expression dropped away. Blackwood saw only desperation and regret—regret so profound a chill passed through his soul. Then just as swiftly, the look vanished, snuffed out like a candle.

The man who stood there now laughed thunderously. His eyes blazed with the fires of a dying sun.

In the next second, Malory swung the revolver around, shoved the barrel into his gaping mouth with a bone-jarring thud, and then softly — as if he had all the time in the world — squeezed the trigger.

CHAPTER EIGHT

With the hour growing late, Blackwood and McGowan wasted no time returning to the newspaper. Juan Cantu, the night city editor, stepped from the break room holding a cup of coffee just as Blackwood burst out of the elevator. McGowan remained in the lift, headed for the Photo Department one floor above. Cantu wagged a finger at the crime writer. Steaming coffee sloshed across his red sweater, but the editor didn't notice.

"I hear you've got a news brief," he deadpanned.

Blackwood faked a frown.

"Right," he said. "It's a brief that belongs on Page One, above the fold, with a headline in 60-point type."

Cantu shook his head with a knowing grin.

"Follow me, grasshopper," he said. "Give me the gory details."

Blackwood trailed him into the newsroom. As they walked, he flipped through his notebook, providing Cantu a synopsis. Yet ... he didn't share everything.

"Help me."

It seemed only Blackwood heard the desperate plea, for when he questioned his cousin and Gruene, both regarded him strangely and said his ears must have played tricks on him. When the reporter insisted Malory had indeed spoken those words, Gruene politely suggested his friend might need a vacation.

But Blackwood, who listened to others for a living, never doubted what he'd heard.

"Help me."

Not wanting to appear rattled at a crime scene, Blackwood decided he could ponder the mystery later. He was on deadline, after all.

Cantu reached his desk and dropped into his chair, which sighed as air rushed from the cushions.

"That's one helluva story, vato," Cantu said. "I've talked to the copy desk and we're holding page one. Unless something else breaks, we'll get you above the fold. Graphics started a locator map."

"If it bleeds, it leads," Blackwood said, reciting the news media's age-old mantra.

Cantu nodded. "What about the art? Any good?"

Blackwood shut the notebook. "McGowan shot it."

Cantu clapped. "Then it's Page One for sure."

The editor chewed thoughtfully on the cap of his Bic pen. Cantu was older than Blackwood, but only by a year. The two went back a ways, having spent their early careers together as police reporters. In those days, their roles were reversed and Blackwood played the mentor. Not one to lack ambition, Cantu set his sights on climbing the newsroom ladder and eventually left the streets Blackwood still adored. Today he filled the unglamorous role of night city editor, but Blackwood harbored no doubt that someday Cantu would sit behind a mahogany desk as editor in chief in one of the executive suites overlooking the Alamo.

The police reporter shoved the dog-eared notebook into his back pocket.

"Now bang that puppy out—you don't have much time," Cantu said.

•   •   •

Blackwood flung himself into his work. He was nothing if not a fast writer. He'd composed most of the story in his head even before leaving the hospital. Words and sentences flowed through his fingers to the keyboard and emerged on the computer screen, the story practically writing itself.

Occasionally he glanced up at the newsroom's soaring windows. Limned with frost, the panes revealed Christmas decorations strung along the streets. Blinking multicolored lights offered a reassuring touch of holiday cheer. Around him, phones rang, keyboards clicked, conversations hummed. The world moved on.

On the screen of a television overlooking the City Desk, a Latina TV reporter did a "breaking news" segment from the hospital. The wash of the camera lights caught snow flurries pirouetting behind her. Judging from her grimace, the cashmere coat buttoned to the throat didn't seem to be keeping her very warm.

Blackwood returned to his article. Filtered through the lens of memory, he saw again the demented physician surrounded by SWAT troopers, the revolver clutched by an unsteady hand, the light from the tactical vehicle's lamps flowing like quicksilver along the barrel. He could hear Malory's lab coat whipping in the wind, could still see the gunman's inexplicable twitching and turning, a crazy marionette performing a macabre dance.

And what did Malory mean about someone big, bad and angry arriving soon? That one stumped even Gruene.

Something menacing and cold lurked in Malory's glare. Something inhuman. And then, just moments before pulling the trigger, Malory's eyes shifted, became normal ... or as close to normal as possible given the circumstances.

"Help me..."

Despite the newsroom's warmth, Blackwood shivered.

"Help me ..."

Blackwood shoved the memory aside, fingers playing on the computer keyboard like a concert pianist as he finished his story. Like all reporters, deadlines dictated the rhythm of his life. Every assignment had the potential to be a command performance.

On the TV, a radar image depicting the gray mass of an approaching ice storm replaced the correspondent.

Five minutes later, Blackwood "fixed" the final draft, pushed back from the computer and plopped his penny-loafers on the desk.

His trench coat, which he'd forgotten to remove, got rucked up around his shoulders.

"Finished," he called out.

Looking greatly relieved, Cantu flashed a thumbs up and glanced at the wall clock. Just shy of 11 p.m. Blackwood had made the Metro edition deadline, but barely.

"Cutting it close, buddy," Cantu said.

Blackwood barely heard. The editor's typing and the rest of the newsroom chatter receded as fatigue crept through his limbs and deadened his senses. His eyelids lowered.

A few minutes later, Cantu got up and patted Blackwood's shoulder in passing.

"That'll be the best-read story in the paper tomorrow, *vato*."

He disappeared around the corner, presumably to grab more coffee — the fuel powering all newsrooms.

Blackwood sighed, keeping his eyes tightly shut but his ears tuned to the fire and police scanners.

Rousing himself a little later, a glance at his Mickey Mouse watch showed the famous rodent's white mittens at half-past eleven. Stiff-Arm Bob, the overnight or "dogwatch" police reporter, wouldn't relieve him until midnight. And Danny Rocha's shift started in the morning; he'd handle any follow-up story.

This is how the paper's 24-hour criminal justice team worked: Each incoming reporter updated stories from the last shift — arrests, bonds, victim's conditions, their names after notification of next of kin — plus covered any breaking news. Some days it could feel like trying to catch Niagara Falls in a thimble.

The police-beat reporters also kept a running log of their stories and background notes in the computer accessible only to them called the "Polog." Very little fell through the cracks.

Blackwood stuffed tobacco into his pipe. He fully intended to fire up the bowl the second he walked out of the building. But there was something else, wasn't there? Something nagging him ...

Blackwood shot forward in his chair, the soles of his shoes smacking the floor with the force of a book dropped from a great height.

Grant! In all the excitement, he'd completely forgotten about his agreement to meet the mysterious caller at midnight.

Blackwood dialed the photo department. His cousin picked up.

"Remember the bloke who rang me?" Blackwood asked. "Wanted to meet in Oddfellows' Cemetery?"

He sensed McGowan nod.

"Yeah," McGowan said, sounding underwhelmed, "you did. Remember me telling you we missed dinner? Me hungry."

He made pig sounds for extra emphasis.

Blackwood propped his elbows on the desk. Dinner could wait.

"I'm sure it won't take long," Blackwood pressed. "He's likely just some nutter."

Cradling the phone between shoulder and ear, Blackwood rubbed his temples, easing away the weariness. The night had been long and difficult, and it wasn't over yet.

When his cousin responded, Blackwood could hear an equal measure of weariness and resolve.

"Sure, let's freeze our asses off in a creepy cemetery while we starve," McGowan said. Then he sighed. "Okay. I guess we can stop at The Pig Stand afterwards."

Blackwood's spirits brightened.

"Meet you in the lobby, then."

The receiver clicked off, as good an answer as any for Blackwood.

CHAPTER NINE

True to his meticulous nature, James Grant arrived early at Oddfellow's Cemetery. Sliding his black Mercedes-Benz E320 behind a dumpster just outside the gates, the attorney grabbed a fresh pack of Gitanes and climbed out. A keen gaze from under eyebrows trimmed straighter than a ruler's edge swept the alleys and abandoned buildings, seeing nothing amiss. Although a long Burberry coat draped his thin frame, he still shivered. The wind nipped at his cheeks like an angry dog. Rings flashed on moisturized hands as he lifted his collar. While he tarried in the sedan's open door, the invisible claws of the breeze snatched a postcard forgotten under the driver's seat, overlooked somehow during one of Grant's innumerable trips to an exclusive detailing service.

Engrossed in a survey of his surroundings, he never noticed the four-by-six-inch square fluttering away. Instead, Grant turned and faced the high walls enclosing the cemetery. His pencil-thin mustache twitched in distaste.

Frowning, the self-styled acquisitions specialist closed the door and sliced open the Gitanes with a spotless nail. He gently shook the box, tumbling out a cigarette. Cupping one hand, he fired the end with a Zippo brush chrome windproof lighter (a collector's item, he assured Dr. Sabrina Hagen during their introductory meeting, pausing to light the Virginia Slims dangling from her lips; she'd given him a cool but studied look; he'd known then he had her attention). Puffing nervously, he stood on pavement as cracked as a desert riverbed, keeping a careful watch. The minutes ticked by, each one as long as a century. When the heat from the ash warmed his cheeks, he threw the cigarette away and lit another.

Brushing back hair so stylishly coiffed the locks could have been a plastic mold, Grant narrowed his eyes and glanced at his Rolex. Still too early for the reporter. Though the surroundings appeared deserted, Grant couldn't shake the feeling someone watched him.

Probably wouldn't hurt to get out of sight, he thought, and began moving. He carried no illumination, assuming a flashlight would only attract unwanted attention in this disreputable neighborhood. Stopping in front of the wrought-iron gate (how typically Victorian, he noted with casual aplomb), Grant turned and gave the lifeless street one last sweep, then shook the broken lock. The latch tumbled open and he wandered through, quietly closing the panel behind him. With a practiced move, he flicked away the second cigarette, confident the new snowfall would extinguish the embers.

The cemetery swallowed him.

Heading for the grand mausoleum — the rendezvous point — Grant glanced again at his watch. Just shy of midnight. He had no idea if Blackwood was a punctual man. Maybe he wouldn't show up at all. Nevertheless, Grant planned to wait as long as he could. The reporter was his last hope. There was nowhere else he could turn.

A few days ago, he'd gone to a priest. The cleric proved less than helpful, even hostile. So here he was, now, in a freezing cemetery, pinning his hopes on a man he'd never met and wasn't even sure he could trust. What if Blackwood didn't believe him?

Around Grant, the graveyard shifted as though in a dream, a rising breeze scattering thin blankets of snow like powdered sugar. Numbed fingers drew his coat tighter. Shadows cast by memorial candles ensconced in several tombstones — an old Mexican burial custom — grew and shrank with his passage, their tiny flames flickering in prisons of colored glass.

Intrigued by the candles, Grant at first didn't notice the tendrils of mist creeping across the grounds. Eventually glancing down, he regarded with a puzzled expression the pale river of fog lapping at his polished Italian loafers.

It was then Grant experienced the first faint stirrings of disorientation, a mental whisper telling him things didn't feel quite right. In seconds, the drifting fog became a gauzy shroud clinging to every surface. He noticed he could no longer see the gate. And the mausoleum had disappeared from view.

He stopped to get his bearings, seeking a familiar landmark. But buried by snow and cloaked in darkness, everything looked the same. Even the little grave candles offered no help. Each pinprick of light became indistinguishable from its neighbor, identical flickering nimbuses shining wetly in the fog. Pressing his lips so tight they looked like an old scab, he started to retrace his steps.

Minutes later, after recognizing a stone cherub he'd passed three times, Grant's heart sank with the realization he walked in circles. Even the moonlight betrayed him. Swollen gray clouds like belching smoke slid across the pale orb, dimming whatever illumination could have helped him find his way. Cursing himself for a fool, Grant wished for the flashlight he'd left tucked snugly in the Mercedes' glove box.

After a moment's reflection, he decided his best bet was finding the wall and following it to the gate. There, he would wait for the reporter on the street, even if it meant exposure. He preferred taking his chances with the crack whores and gang members, rather than staying in this cursed cemetery another second. Nothing about the place felt right.

The world around Grant remained utterly silent, his own breathing the sole refrain in his ears, now coming a little faster and more ragged. The only other noise was crunching snow underfoot. Fighting to keep calm, his eyes darted in all directions.

The wall couldn't be far away. But he only spied more headstones. As crazy as it sounded, they seemed to have multiplied during his wandering. Grave markers of varying sizes, some so old only a stitch of moss held the crumbling masonry together, closed around him and marched out to the limits of his vision. The shifting snow didn't help, smoothing and flattening the ground beneath the undulating fog, turning the boneyard into one unbroken carpet of white that hid his footprints. Grant doubled his pace.

After a few minutes, his footfalls gradually slowed and then halted altogether. Hell, who was he kidding? Time to accept the inescapable. He remained irrevocably lost, and Grant began to suspect nothing that existed in the natural world had any bearing on his predicament. His growing suspicions pointed to forces beyond his control.

The cold air didn't stop beads of sweat from prickling his brow. Grant stared hard into the shadows and swallowed. He could feel the balance between light and dark shifting. Somehow *the others* suspected his betrayal. The Forgotten One, or its fanatical Adherents, sensed he had broken the code of silence.

Grant had known it was only a matter of time before he faced discovery by those who commissioned him to gain the release of the relic. They had eyes and ears everywhere. The Synod of the Noose and their dark allies would stop at nothing to silence him.

No matter. Grant didn't regret forsaking his agreements, binding or not. Not one bit. What they planned was monstrous beyond words.

Yet his defiant thoughts couldn't stop fingers of dread from curling around his guts and squeezing. All the bravado in the world wouldn't chase away the knowledge forces he couldn't begin to comprehend marshaled against him. The question now was how much time remained.

Grant urged his feet to move faster.

Must find that gate...

But after several minutes of fruitless searching, the accelerated pace proved too brutal for the two-pack-a-day smoker. The thin figure in the long coat slowed to catch his breath, features pinched as he leaned against an old grave marker. Grant knew he should keep moving, but the stitch burning in his side said different.

"Not used... to running so ... much," he wheezed.

The cold air seared his throat, but after a minute also revived him. Sucking down one last deep breath, Grant was about to start walking again when he heard a noise that stiffened every hair on his body.

Laughter. A soft, sibilant hiss drifting from the shadows that pierced his ears with the sharpness of a blade. He gasped, knowing in his bones no trick of the wind, no settling of the ground, produced such an evil sound. Something inhuman had come calling. Something wicked. As the laughter grew louder, more mocking, ice formed in the pit of his stomach. Grant peered at the empty space between the gravestones where the sound originated, his sleek leather shoes rooted to the spot by terror. The shadows appeared to be massing in a dark, smoky ball.

The vapors seemed alive.

Grant violently rubbed his eyes, hoping the sight was just a crazy illusion brought on by lightheadedness. No such luck. Nothing changed when the sparks and pinwheels in his vision cleared.

His heart beat behind his ribs with the force of a bird slamming against its cage.

The gathering darkness coalesced into three rippling shadows, as though a knife carved a trio of jagged silhouettes from the cloth of night. From these holes in space the cackles issued.

As Grant stared slack jawed at the shifting outlines, the shapes grew more solid, more defined. A stench bored into his nostrils, so foul he felt the hairs curl up and die. Unless his olfactory senses could hallucinate, these things — whatever they might be — possessed corporeality. Ice water filled his bowels.

The figures started gliding in his direction. It didn't escape Grant's notice they left no footprints in the snow.

Drawing closer, the shapes resolved into torsos, arms, hips, breasts and raven tresses billowing around pale ovals slashed by thin, cruel mouths. Bottomless black holes passed for eyes. To Grant's fear-struck gaze, the arrivals appeared vaguely feminine. But similarities to anything human ended there. Protruding from below their shoulder blades, great leathery squares resembling folded sails swam into focus. These unfurled and flapped with hesitant movements, as though testing an unfamiliar environment. Gasping, Grant recognized the spreading appendages as wings, bat-like and immense, crisscrossed by a network of veins thick as a man's finger.

His throat constricted even as a scream struggled to explode. Panic overtook him. He began running, ignoring the rip burning in his side.

Against his better judgment, Grant couldn't resist the temptation to cast a look back. What he beheld withered his soul.

The memorial candles decorating the tombstones started winking out. One second a flame guttered in its stained-glass jar, only to disappear in a puff of smoke, and the one after that and the one after that. Ebon wings smothered the wicks as they flowed over them.

He doubled his pace, gibbering. The very ground conspired against him. Roots appeared from nowhere, tripping his uncertain feet. Sent sprawling, Grant knocked over a lit candle. The flames caught easily in the brittle weeds, whipped by the rising wind. Grant didn't care. He had other worries. Grunting and straining, he rose and scurried away on unsteady legs.

The wind became fierce, striking up a symphony of creaking wood among the trees. Sticks and leaves flew into his face. Arms and hands flailed to prevent being blinded.

Peering between splayed fingers as he ran, Grant at last could make out the mausoleum just ahead. A rusty iron gate clanged like a ship's bell rung by a lost mariner. Faint hope stirred in his aching breast. If only he could reach the mausoleum, he might have a chance. Close and bar the door, wait until daylight.

He shot forward with renewed speed.

Grant reached the enclosure, sensing the pursuers close upon his heels. He wasn't about to look behind him again, though. The gate beckoned, and beyond that, just across a little square decorated with cheap plastic flowers, a stout door that opened to the long, windowless building.

Grant's shuffling feet carried him through the gate, which he slammed shut. He stumbled across granite flagstones to the mausoleum, then yelped in surprise when the heavy door swung inward. In the gloom within, only bronze nameplates, some green with rust, greeted his frenzied stare. He entered the chamber, the air heavy with faded memories pressing upon him. Whirling to shut the door, he spied a dead-bolt lock above the handle. Forged from reliable, solid steel, the mechanism wouldn't bend or break. His heart swelled with relief — yes!

All he needed to do was sit tight inside this abode of the dead and wait out his unholy pursuers. Didn't the legends say these things couldn't stand the rising sun?

But just as he started shutting the door, claw-like hands shot through the gap separating wood and stone, curled around the frame and yanked with such ferocity the heavy oak tore from its hinges. The door went flying, splintering yards away among the headstones.

With a cry of despair, Grant sank to his knees and cradled his head. Any reserves of will evaporated. The figures oozed inside, circled him and coldly regarded the cowering man. Resigned to his fate, the hunted could only raise his face and gaze blankly at the hunters.

That's when Grant screamed. Their eyes! Those empty sockets burned with undying malice, freezing his soul. The blank orbs held him motionless as though binding his limbs with steel. Paralyzed, he could only shake as fangs sharper than any knife flashed in the gloom.

As the abominations slaked their ancient thirst, Grant's cries became truly inhuman.

CHAPTER TEN

McGowan stomped on the Crime Jeep's accelerator like a brick was tied to his foot. The downtown lights speckled the dusty interior of the vehicle, which raced along empty urban canyons framed by skyscrapers. The speedometer needle climbed ... forty-five ... fifty ... The Jeep drifted on the icy surface. McGowan glanced off a curb over correcting.

He didn't even blink.

"Bloody hell," Blackwood yelped.

"Quit worrying," McGowan shot back. "It's company property. It's paid for."

Noticing his cousin's grimace, he added, "You're the one who got his panties in a twist about meeting this guy. I'm just trying to get you there."

As Blackwood's fingernails dug into the armrest, the Jeep angled up a ramp onto the elevated span of U.S. 281.

The massive base of the 750-foot Tower of the Americas soared into view, looming over the expressway like a titanic sentinel. Christmas lights crowned the rotating restaurant at the top. Built for the 1968 World's Fair, the iconic needle rose into the clouds above the twinkling cityscape, a testament to pan-American engineering and as fancy as a holiday postcard.

The picturesque view had little effect on Blackwood, who only stared ahead, his gray eyes like points of frozen metal.

An emergency tone blared from the police scanner. Twisting the volume knob, Blackwood leaned closer to the dash-mounted speaker.

A dispatcher asked for a night utility detective to respond to a body found at the scene of a grass fire. The detective asked her to repeat the address, which she did. The reporter's heart thudded into his stomach. He recognized the location as Oddfellow's Cemetery.

Twirling snowflakes clotted on the window; the wipers shushed-shushed them into sticky little slurries while Blackwood considered this decidedly alarming turn of events.

McGowan's goofy grin vanished. He must have recognized the address, too. The darkness outside seemed to jump at them.

"Ain't that where your source is meeting us?" McGowan said.

Blackwood nodded.

"Yes," Blackwood said, drawing out the word.

He chewed on his pipe stem. McGowan leveled a worried look at him.

"Are you thinking what I'm thinking?"

"I'm afraid so," Blackwood said.

•   •   •

When Detective Rutherford Stewart from the Night Criminal Investigation Division arrived at the cemetery, Patrolman Enrique Espinoza — the first officer on the scene — heaved a sigh of relief. About time, the patrolman thought. Let the "defectives" handle this mess. Another night-utility detective accompanied the lean Stewart. The second guy was a hard-looking Hispanic in a faux leather Members Only jacket and cowboy boots. Espinoza did not remember his name.

A small crew of firefighters worked in the distance to extinguish the burning grass. The flames' glow painted the detectives' faces in shades of red and orange.

"Who's handling this?" Stewart asked.

"I am, sir," Espinoza said. "I was on routine patrol when I spotted the fire, and then I found the ..." he seemed to struggle for the appropriate word "... remains over by the mausoleum."

Their heads swiveled to regard a pulpy mass humped up in the shadows, just out of reach of the firelight. For that, Espinoza was thankful.

Stewart nodded grimly.

"Step into my office," he said, waving in the general direction of the cemetery, "and tell me all."

•   •   •

While Espinoza and Stewart talked, the San Antonio Tribune Jeep pulled up. Two figures emerged and walked purposefully toward the crime scene, their shapes — one lanky, one broad — outlined against the dying flames.

"Aw crap," a policeman on perimeter duty groaned. "News media."

The officer moved to intercept the pair. Over by the mausoleum, Stewart caught sight of Blackwood and McGowan. The detective abruptly held up his hand, signaling Espinoza should wait, then his long legs began scissoring at a rapid clip toward the two newsmen.

"Don't worry about these guys," Stewart called out to all the officers within earshot. "They can stay, as long as they spell my name right."

He made the gibe warmly, and Blackwood extended his hand when they met up. The scarecrow of a detective returned the shake with a firm grip.

"Hullo, Rutherford," Blackwood said with a faint smile. The other night detective in the Members Only jacket joined them. Blackwood pivoted and pumped his proffered hand next.

"Good old Blackwood. Checking up on us colonials?" Rudolfo Aguirre greeted him, chuckling. When he finally let go of Blackwood's hand, the crime reporter could barely feel his fingers. Aguirre spent a lot of off-duty time lifting weights in the SAPD gym.

"Rudy. Always a pleasure," said Blackwood, trying hard to ignore his tingling digits.

Aguirre's mahogany skin, neatly combed hair with squares of gray at the temples, and a broad, flat nose gave him a certain regal appearance — likely from some fierce Aztec forebear.

The police reporter had known the pair for years, and over time they had become not only a wellspring of news stories, but friends, too.

By now uniformed-detective investigators started swarming over the grounds in their black coveralls and jackets marked "evidence team." One of the DIs unspooled a roll of yellow crime-scene tape, encircling the bloody remains.

Another DI hefted a video camera from the trunk of his cruiser and began shooting footage. Blackwood nodded at the two night detectives, then moved to the edge of the tape and studied the dark mass piled on the frozen ground.

He had seen much death in his time, and heard the screams of the dying more times than he cared to remember, but what he stared at now sent a shiver through his frame that had nothing to do with the dropping mercury. From the glistening lumps embedded in the snow, Blackwood's inspection traced spatters of blood winding to the mausoleum's little courtyard, only to disappear inside the building. That's when he noticed the missing door. The darkness at the entrance yawned like a skull's gap-toothed grin.

He turned to McGowan and told him bleakly, "There's nothing here to shoot. We could never run this."

"Huh. The 'Cheerios factor,'" McGowan said, putting the camera back into its bag.

Blackwood could tell by the look on his face his cousin didn't seem all that upset. Of the pair, McGowan was the more squeamish, which always struck Blackwood as rather odd, considering his cousin's deployment to the Middle East when he'd been a Marine. Or maybe that explained it.

"'Cheerios factor'?" Aguirre said, appearing at their side.

"It's an old journalism expression," Blackwood said. "The Trib is a morning paper. A lot of our readers read it over breakfast. Hence, the 'Cheerios factor.' We avoid running graphic photographs to avoid giving our audience an adverse reaction."

McGowan groaned and looked at Aguirre apologetically.

"What the 'perfessor' here is trying to say is that you don't want mommy, daddy and junior puking in their cornflakes because of nasty pictures in the paper."

"Makes sense," Aguirre said after a moment's thought.

Stewart pulled a pack from his coat and shook out a cigarette.

"You know," he said, touching a lighter to the tobacco, "someday you won't even have newspapers. They'll be as outdated as cave paintings. I've been reading how people will get all their news on these home computers whenever they want. And then they'll shrink those screens until you can carry them around with you, like the video wristwatch from 'Dick Tracy.' It'll be news all the time, twenty-four hours a day, seven days a week. I don't know how you guys will keep up."

He took a thoughtful drag, grinning at the somewhat apprehensive looks on the newsmen's faces.

"Relax, guys," he said. "That's probably decades away."

Blackwood appeared doubtful. If that was the future of newspapers, it had already arrived. Only a few weeks ago, and with little fanfare, the Tribune launched a rudimentary website.

Of course, nothing got posted until after the stories appeared in print first. An ongoing debate between the bean counters and his editors revolved around whether to charge for the online content. A paywall, the paper's chief financial officer called it. So far, viewers could read articles on the site for free; Juan Cantu thought that set a bad precedent. After all, why pay good money for a print subscription when you could read articles on the computer for no charge, even if they appeared a day later? And what happened if the publisher or the suits at corporate decided reporters' stories should go on the website first — free or otherwise? What would happen to print then? Advertisers understandably might flock to the new medium, just as they had to radio and television. And zeroes and ones on a screen cost a lot less than newsprint, ink, a press crew, diesel, a fleet of delivery trucks and drivers.

Reaching inside his back pocket, Blackwood withdrew his notebook. The future will take care of itself, he figured. Right now, he had a story to cover.

He forced himself to look down once more at the pulpy mass coated by shimmering ice crystals, wondering if the remains spread at his feet really belonged to James Grant. But who else could it be?

That conclusion left him feeling unsettled. Here was a first. He'd never had a source die on him, at least not like this. It seemed like he'd spoken to Grant not hours but a lifetime ago—a much saner lifetime. Before the hospital and before Malory.

With a jolt, Blackwood realized Grant had all but predicted his own demise.

They're watching me, Grant warned him. And how to explain "breaking the circle"? An expression both men — now dead—had uttered.

Swallowing hard, Blackwood regarded the heavens. Clouds threatening more snow drifted on, but only for the moment. Behind them, the horizon filled with an unbroken layer resembling stacked blankets of black fleece. The crisp air kissed his sharp cheekbones with icy lips, clearing his head.

McGowan tugged at his elbow, letting his breath out.

"You need to tell them about this dude," the photographer whispered.

Blackwood nodded, the weight on his shoulders getting heavier.

A dozen conflicting emotions warred on his face as he sought Stewart. The detective glanced up from inspecting the ground.

"We need to talk," Blackwood said.

Stewart registered the unusually serious look on Blackwood's features. He waved his hand in a direction away from the firefighters, patrol officers and evidence technicians.

"Step into my office," he said for the second time that night. The expression was one of his favorites.

When Blackwood finished his story, Stewart made no response at first, just puffed on a cigarette. By now, Aguirre and McGowan had joined them. In the distance, firefighters wrestled the blaze into sullen embers. Smoke drifted around them.

"And that's all you have?" Stewart prodded gently. "His name is James Grant, he's a lawyer —."

"An acquisitions specialist, rare items," Blackwood interjected.

"And he works for some outfit called the Akel-Dama Corporation?" This from Aguirre.

"And he wanted to give you a big scoop, but didn't say what it was?" Stewart added.

"Don't forget — he told you, 'They're after me,'" McGowan offered.

Their barrage of questions finished, the trio regarded Blackwood intently. He nodded.

"I wish there was more," Blackwood said regretfully. "Quite frankly, I thought he was just daft."

Aguirre put a finger to his chin. "Akel-Dama," he murmured. "Why do I know that name?"

Stewart scratched the thinning hair of his crew cut. He was an avid reader; Popular Mechanics and Gun Digest numbered among his favorites. His lean features registered dawning remembrance.

"It's a big computer firm in Dallas, I think. They're a major defense contractor. And they're in San Antonio setting up a new operation."

Aguirre shot his partner a doubtful glance. "And just how do you know all of this?"

Stewart tapped his forehead.

"Elementary, my dear Watson. I read the business pages," he said, then winked at Blackwood.

As they bantered, Blackwood rubbed hard at his temples, struggling to remember more.

Stewart gave him a consoling pat on the arm.

"Don't blow a fuse," he said. "If there's anything else, you'll think of it. You gave us a name. That's something to go on."

"I suppose you're right," Blackwood said. All the air seemed to have left him.

Aguirre stamped his feet to stay warm.

"Well, a name is a good start," he said. "None of the DIs has found a wallet or anything else to give us an ID."

Bending down, Stewart examined shards of what appeared to be a partial jaw smashed into the snow. His knees creaked as he rose, a shadow crossing his face.

"Making a positive ID from dental records is not going to be easy, considering most of his teeth are missing," he said. "And some of his fingers are gone. There's a couple left. They can test for prints at the medical examiner's office."

"Man, who would do this?" McGowan whispered.

Who—or what, Blackwood silently wondered.

Aguirre looked up at Rutherford, who stood a head taller.

"We'll run the name though NCIC, TCIC and the PiPs file. We're bound to come up with something. We'll also check utility and phone records."

The senior detective nodded.

"Good idea. I just hope he didn't give our friend here a fake name. Then we're back to square one."

The two investigators lapsed into silence, then shared a knowing glance.

"It doesn't have to be right now," Stewart said, turning to face Blackwood, "but at some point you'll have to give us a sworn statement."

Blackwood didn't argue. After years of covering the police beat, he knew the drill.

"Right. Just let me file my story first. I'll come to your office before your shift ends."

"Sure. Otherwise you'll have to deal with the 'daylight darlings'"— he used Night CID's nickname for the dayside homicide unit — "and they're not as fun as us."

Stewart gave him a thoughtful look.

"Will your story mention this guy called you?"

Blackwood pursed his lips, mulling over the question.

"I think it's wiser if I wait until you lot confirm the ID. No need to jump to conclusions. Right now I'm just planning on a bare-bones piece about a mutilated body found in the cemetery."

Stewart clasped hands and rocked back on his heels.

"Good pun," he said. Blackwood shot him a quizzical glance.

"Bare bones?" Stewart supplied.

Blackwood brought a hand to his forehead with a pained expression.

"Oh, that's not what I meant."

An evidence technician waving a clipboard appeared at the detective's elbow, needing Stewart to sign something.

Blackwood flashed a wan smile at the detective, but already his thoughts raced ahead with the speed of a locomotive. Grant was dead, or somebody he thought was Grant, and that meant more questions than answers. Loads more.

Breaking the circle ...

In the end, he still had a job to do. He strongly felt Grant's death was only the tip of the iceberg, and the story promised to be much bigger than he originally suspected. Follow the threads, see where they lead. First and foremost, he needed to figure out the secret Grant planned to divulge.

That's where to begin.

The evidence technician walked off and the detective regarded the crime reporter. Blackwood's glance locked with Stewart's. In the darkness, Blackwood touched pen to paper, ready to scribble furiously. His words would pin history to the page. Working on the story kept him busy, kept him focused. He needed that anchor right now.

"Always dedicated," Stewart remarked.

Blackwood inclined his head.

"Or deranged," he said. "Now, let's get down to business, shall we? What happened here?"

Stewart didn't immediately answer. Instead, the detective inched the pack of Camels out of the breast pocket of his leather coat, turned his skinny back to the breeze and lit a new smoke. After replacing the lighter and the crumpled pack, he took a long, reflective puff.

"Don't use my name, okay? Just do that thing where you say, 'police said.'" The reporter nodded in agreement. Easy enough.

"I've been a policeman for almost twenty years, and fourteen of those as a detective. I've seen a lot of DOAs in my time, but never one like this."

A trace of bewilderment tinged the veteran investigator's voice, and something else, too. If Blackwood hadn't known better, he would have thought Rutherford seemed horrified.

"Well, since I'm not quoting you, care to speculate?" Blackwood said, probing Stewart's lined face. "Is this a freak accident or an actual homicide?"

In reply, Stewart turned to Officer Espinoza, who patiently waited just outside their little circle.

"Espinoza, what did that paramedic tell you while you were waiting for us to arrive?"

Espinoza gave a calm and controlled reply, but the look in his eyes hinted at something much darker.

"The EMT said, 'Check the zoo for escaped animals.'"

"Really?" Blackwood said, cocking his head in astonishment.

"No shit," Espinoza said matter-of-factly.

Blackwood's pen flashed across his notepad. "Is that on the record?

Espinoza offered a strained smile.

"The 'no shit' part or the zoo?" the patrolman asked.

"The zoo," Blackwood said, amused.

"It's going into my report, so yeah, I guess it's on the record."

The patrolman shot a questioning look at Stewart. The senior officer nodded, then swiveled his head to study Blackwood. A filament of smoke from the detective's cigarette traced a question mark in the air.

"There's your headline," Stewart said, taking another drag. "I'll update you when we know more. And yes, Rudy's checking on the zoo."

The reporter's eyebrows lifted. Granted, the zoo was only a couple of miles away in Brackenridge Park, but the idea of a grown man being mauled to death by an escaped beast in the country's seventh-largest city seemed preposterous.

"You don't actually think an animal did this?"

He saw doubt register in Stewart's eyes.

"No, but we have to check all leads," the investigator said. "There are no witnesses, no prints to lift. And you heard Rudy — no ID. Three strikes."

Blackwood ran a hand through straw-colored hair.

"So maybe it's a robbery that went south? That qualifies as capital murder," he said, referring to a homicide during the commission of another felony.

Stewart vented a long sigh, a clear signal he thought this was just as unlikely as an animal attack.

"Your guess is as good as mine."

The night-utility detective turned to Espinoza.

"Officer?"

"Sir?"

"Give Blackwood the particulars: Date and time of call, what you found, all the jazz that goes into the public offense report."

With a final tip of his head in the reporter's direction, Stewart moved off to consult the evidence team. In the distance, a dog howled. Its lone, mournful cry carried over the cemetery's high walls. By now the clouds had returned, pierced by scattered shafts of frozen moonlight.

After giving Blackwood the "particulars," Espinoza asked, "Notice the door?"

Blackwood cast a glance at the mausoleum.

"It's missing."

Espinoza's forehead wrinkled. "Not anymore. We found it about twenty yards away. In pieces."

Blackwood made a face.

"Somebody dragged the door over there?"

That didn't make any sense. But what about this did?

Espinoza raised and lowered his hands in puzzlement.

"More like threw it, based on the way the debris is spread around. Shattered like kindling. At least that's how it looks to the evidence guys."

Blackwood sucked in a breath. Questions swirled in his gray eyes.

"But that thing must weigh, what, two or three hundred pounds?"

"Yeah," Espinoza said, folding the cover over his report.

"Impossible," Blackwood said. "Nobody can throw a door that heavy that far."

Espinoza shrugged. "Mister, I just work here."

Gooseflesh prickled along Blackwood's back.

What happened to the door ruled out an animal attack, as far as he was concerned. An enraged beast — a bear? A lion? — might knock down a door, but not consciously hurl the object. Perhaps an elephant had the strength, but as far as he knew, the pachyderm exhibit closed two years ago and the animals lived on a nature preserve near New Braunfels. So if not an animal, then what? What could toss a heavy door halfway across a cemetery and have strength left over to tear a man to pieces?

Aguirre walked up, flashlight in hand, just as Espinoza took his leave.

"No tracks. Not man, not critter," he announced. "And the zoo reports all cages are secure."

Aguirre paused a beat. "Based on the evidence we found inside the mausoleum, we think the attack occurred there. Then your mystery caller's remains were dragged outside. Not sure if he was still alive by then." He glanced over his shoulder and made a sour face. "I hope not."

He gave Blackwood a searching look, seeing the multiple questions stamped on the reporter's face.

"The medical investigator's on his way," Aguirre said. "Maybe he can shed a little more light on this cluster."

Blackwood tapped his pen against his notepad.

"You look beat," Aguirre offered kindly.

"I am," Blackwood admitted. "But there's never any rest for the wicked, eh?"

CHAPTER ELEVEN

December 19
1:07 a.m.
The medical investigator from the Bexar County Medical
Examiner's Office and Crime Lab arrived in due course, grumbling
the second he opened the squeaking door of his dented red pickup
and climbed out.

"What a shitty night," he breathed, more in weariness than
annoyance. His gaze swept the rest of them.

"I just finished the Malory case. I didn't think anything could be
worse." He rose on tiptoes and craned his neck for a look over their
shoulders at the crime scene. "I guess I was wrong."

He walked toward the mausoleum, everyone parting to let him
pass.

Blackwood inclined his head; the investigator offered a breezy
wave in return. Blackwood and David "Paco" Martinez went back a
few moons. The amicable medical investigator had never been one
to pass up an extra breakfast taco or cinnamon roll. He often
chuckled, "My mirth matches my girth." Paco knew how to throw a
good party, too, and always invited the Trib's police reporters to his
family's annual Tejano dance at a bingo hall on West Avenue. No
one made better tamales than his wife.

Donning thin rubber gloves and slinging a camera over an ample
shoulder, Martinez went to work, gingerly probing the scattered
body parts with a metal pointer that extended like a car antenna.

After a moment, he placed the camera on the ground and dropped to a knee with a heavy release of breath.

"Are you sure he's dead, Paco?" a DI asked. A few nervous chuckles rose from the gathered officers. Even the most grizzled among their ranks had never seen anything like this before.

Rising to his feet with a grunt, Martinez thrust the pointer at the remains, pivoting first to the right and then left.

"I pronounce this part dead, and that part over there, and that part, too," he said, never breaking a smile.

"What about this one, Paco?" the same DI asked, pointing with the toe of his boot at a misshapen mass that could have been a kidney, the frosted blood iridescent in the moonlight.

"Yeah, all right, that one, too," the investigator responded. Falling to his knees again with all the grace of a feed sack, Martinez continued his up-close-and-personal inspection of the late James Grant. The investigator's flashlight beam traced a corkscrew pattern over the remains.

Several minutes passed, punctuated only by grunts issuing in short bursts from the heavyset medical investigator. He rose and then bent down again, repeating the motion several times during his examination. At one point, he fished a pen from a pocket, clicked the end and jotted notes on a small yellow legal pad; afterwards, he produced a tape measure and recorded distances between the clumps. The detectives, the DIs, the patrolmen, the journalists and even some firefighters watched in both disgust and fascination as Martinez performed his grisly job with quiet efficiency.

"I can tell you one thing," Martinez said. "This guy's definitely looking at a closed-casket funeral."

The investigator straddled what appeared to be the chest, his face just a few inches above a smashed ribcage. Not for the last time, Blackwood marveled at Martinez's strong stomach.

After another minute or two, Martinez rose to his feet on creaking knees, put a gloved hand to his double chin and made a puzzled sound.

Stewart leaned in his direction. "What is it, Paco?"

Martinez shook his head. The frown on his face deepened.

"Call me loco," he said, "but given the amount of trauma, there should be more blood. A lot more."

He whistled. "Where did it go?"

Blackwood politely coughed.

"Well, he is torn to pieces," the reporter said.

Martinez shot him an annoyed look.

"The average human has one and a half gallons of blood," he said, his pointer hovering over what might have been the head. "In spite of what you see, there's only enough here to fill a thimble."

Stewart rotated his bony shoulders as though warding off a chill, then thrust hands into his coat pockets.

"Are we talking exsanguination?" he said, clearly disturbed by the implications.

McGowan, rummaging in his camera bag, suddenly halted.

"Exsang—uh, what?"

"It means purposefully drained of blood," Blackwood answered, then shifted his attention to Martinez. "How about it, Paco? Did someone actually remove the victim's blood? Or did it just seep into the soil?"

But how, he asked himself. The ground is frozen solid.

Martinez raised his hands defensively, apprehensive about the line of questioning.

"That's for the medical examiner to say after the postmortem, *vato*. I just bag 'em and tag 'em." His lozenge-shaped body bent back down, but the look on his face remained troubled.

No one said anything after that. In the silence that followed, Martinez picked up his camera, pressed his eye against the viewfinder and adjusted the lens with fingers the size of small sausages. A series of bright flashes momentarily blinded the onlookers.

"This guy didn't die a very pleasant death," he said, putting the camera back on the ground. Probably comes out of his paycheck if he breaks it, Blackwood thought. Which, if he recalled, Paco always said wasn't enough.

"The autopsy should give us a cause of death, but I'd say this guy was — well — chewed apart," Martinez said. "There are bite marks all over him. Or what's left of him."

He gave the others a pained look. "Really weird," he added.

Without saying a word, Stewart and Blackwood exchanged worried glances. They both knew the zoo reported all cages secure.

"If the zoo reports no escaped animals, then what did this?" Blackwood asked in an uncertain tone.

A few mental tumblers began falling into place. A cemetery ... dismemberment ... remains drained of blood ... Hints by the victim of shadowy, threatening people watching him ... A ritual killing was starting to look more possible, though that scenario still raised several questions. Yet to Blackwood, that prospect seemed just as unlikely as being mauled by a renegade zoo animal. He'd covered two ritual killings that he knew about during his career, and read accounts of many more, and in none of those cases had anyone been "chewed apart."

"Wild dogs?" Stewart ventured, sounding incredulous at his own words.

Now he's grasping at straws, Blackwood said to himself.

"Possible, but unlikely," Martinez said, seeming to dismiss the prospect outright. "They'd have to be starving. And big. And there's plenty of garbage to eat on the streets. A lot less trouble than a grown man."

He shrugged. "Why attack something that fights back?"

After clucking his tongue and consulting his legal pad, Martinez glanced over at the detectives.

"How old do we think this guy is?" he asked.

All heads swiveled to regard Blackwood, who returned their stares with a pained expression.

"I've never laid eyes on the chap, remember? He rang me up. We talked briefly on the phone, that's all."

The expectant gazes lingered.

"Fine," Blackwood said. "If I had to a guess, I'd say mid-thirties. Most likely. Why?"

Martinez scrunched his brow.

"Just wondering," he said, but Blackwood knew better and kept staring. Unable to ignore that withering gaze, Martinez sighed. "It might have something to do with the extreme trauma, the cold or even some pre-existing condition, but the skin — or the fragments of skin — appear abnormal."

Aguirre stepped forward. "Define abnormal. We see a lot of abnormal in this job."

Martinez took a deep breath, weighing his answer.

"The fragments are very brittle. Or aged. Think of cracked leather or beef jerky. Devoid of moisture."

Martinez gave Blackwood a stern look.

"That's off the record, buddy."

Stewart, who had been speaking quietly into his police radio, lowered the black box and regarded the others.

"Just for grins, I had dispatch run the name James Grant minus a date of birth through local utility records. Four hits came back. The most recent entry is for a guy who's thirty-five."

Blackwood's gaze traveled from Martinez to Stewart.

"Grant said he'd only been here a few weeks," the reporter said.

As the medical investigator resumed his probe, Blackwood pushed aside his growing bewilderment and focused on taking notes, his spidery shorthand punctuated by slashes and dashes only he could read. He did this for two reasons, both practical: The shorthand saved time when he recorded quotes from fast talkers; and if some lawyer ever subpoenaed his notes, they offered little value by being indecipherable.

Inside the crime scene tape trembling in a bitter wind, the medical investigator began preserving the remnants of the victim's hands, slipping small paper bags over the rigid fists and sealing them shut with a rubber band. The covering protected the nails and skin from any further contamination. During the autopsy, a forensic pathologist would scrape under the fingernails. Whatever Dr. Bucks recovered—blood, hair, saliva, paint, dirt, food—often revealed a very interesting tale, one that started at the microscopic level and often finished in a courtroom.

As the cataloging process dragged on, Blackwood grew restless. The wind leeched the warmth from his skin. A sudden vibration in his pocket reminded Blackwood he carried one of the new mobile phones issued by the Tribune — what McGowan called an "electronic leash." The glowing Caller ID displayed a familiar number: SAPD homicide.

Gruene must be trying to reach me, Blackwood surmised.

Time for a stroll, maybe restore some feeling to his bones.

"This is all terribly interesting, but I need to stretch my legs," he told McGowan.

McGowan absently nodded, now busy shooting pictures of the medical investigator from angles that didn't reveal the deceased. These photos the Trib could run without worrying about the Cheerios factor.

With a quick wave to Stewart and Aguirre, Blackwood ambled off, skirting the crime scene but otherwise not watching where his footsteps led.

Once out of sight, he dialed homicide. Normally the dayside detectives wouldn't be there so late, but he guessed — correctly — the Malory case kept everyone burning the midnight oil.

"Homicide," a gruff voice answered.

"This is John Blackwood, returning a call to Capt. Gruene," he said.

"Hold on."

Gruene picked up a second later.

"Capt. Gruene."

"Frank. You rang?"

He could hear Gruene take a deep breath.

"Yeah. We ran across something at the hospital that might interest you."

Blackwood's chin rose.

"Do tell," he prompted.

Gruene cleared his throat. "This is off the record for now, okay? Save it for one of your follow-up stories."

Blackwood nodded; Gruene somehow sensed his assent.

The reporter thought of Paco's comment from a moment ago. *The off-the-records are really piling up tonight.*

"We reviewed security-camera footage of the parking lot," Gruene said. "It showed Malory arriving in a Ford Explorer."

Blackwood exhaled, watching his breath collect in a frosty cloud.

"You're telling me this because the vehicle wasn't his, right?"

He could sense Gruene knitting his brows.

"Good guess. We ran the plates. They're registered to a Ben Wade, a real estate agent for Alamo Metro Home Sales."

Drifting snowflakes dusted Blackwood's London Fog. He regarded the shiny diamonds for just a moment before replying.

"I remember seeing the vehicle outside the ER." He shifted the tiny phone to the other ear. He wasn't sure he'd ever get used to the device. "How did Malory get his hands on this chap's car?"

Gruene answered the question with a question, but it sounded like more of a statement.

"He's new in town and looking for a home? They could've met at Wade's office or somewhere else, drove together to visit a property and, for whatever reason, the good doctor 'borrowed' the SUV."

Blackwood considered this for a moment, then decided Gruene's explanation made sense. He said as much.

"Well, that's our working theory," the captain said.

Blackwood could hear oiled rollers squeaking. He imagined Gruene leaning back in his chair, the old-fashioned kind that twirled and scooted across the office.

"We tracked down the manager of the realty office," Gruene said. "Had to wake him up. He said Wade hadn't been seen since this morning. Er, yesterday morning."

Blackwood pursed his lips. "Odd."

"And there's still nobody home at the place Malory rented with his wife and kid," the captain added. "I've had a blue-and-white go by three times now."

Blackwood sensed the direction the conversation was taking.

"Did the owner know where Wade was going?" he asked.

"There were three properties, according to the log book. They always have the agents sign out so they can track appointments. Two commercial, but the last one was a private residence in Alamo Heights. Big place. Old place."

Blackwood's gaze drifted past the headstones to regard the drifting snow coating the ground, settling in layers neat as stacked blankets. The occasional moonbeam turned the crystals into glittering silver.

"What property, Frank?"

Gruene sighed.

"Ever heard of the Birkenstadt Haus?"

•   •   •

After the call, Blackwood wandered through a city built for the dead, deep in thought. Gruene had given him much to ponder.

Absorbed in his ruminations, Blackwood barely stopped before his bowed head bumped into the graveyard's high stone wall. Adjusting his footsteps, he turned right to follow the enclosure, his glove idly trailing the mortared limestone. He soon faced a wooden door fashioned from knotty slats. Curious, he tugged on the horseshoe-shaped handle. The weathered portal swung open, revealing a gloomy street beyond. Blackwood's protruding head turned right, then left.

There wasn't much to see, just a wide, empty lane bordering the cemetery. Sagging buildings of crumbling brick and splintered wood stretched for several blocks. A frigid breeze rattled loose boards and pushed discarded wrappers, foam cups and other rubbish along the street like flakes of dried skin.

The drifting debris reminded him of what Martinez said about the victim's flesh. Cracked. Devoid of all moisture. And no blood.

The medical examiner's report should shed more light on the strange circumstances — unless they had to wait on a toxicology screen. Those could take six weeks. Gruene or the district attorney, however, could request expedited results.

Blackwood pushed those concerns away for the moment. The deserted lane beckoned. Stepping through the door, his roving gaze focused on shadows clinging to a decaying property straight across the road. The gloom there seemed thick and suffocating.

Blackwood started turning around when a patch of darkness detached itself from the shadows and moved forward into the light cast by a lone street lamp.

A hiss rose from the reporter's throat.

"What the hell?" he said, feeling very exposed.

The illumination revealed little, but what it hinted sent ice water coursing through his veins. A man, or something shaped like a man, stood across the street staring in his direction. Veils of shadow concealed the newcomer's face, but not so his attire. He wore a long cloak, a rough tunic and woolen trousers that brushed the tops of worn leather boots tied with laces. A floppy, wide-brimmed hat covered his head. To Blackwood, it looked like a medieval woodcut had come to life.

They stared at each other — well, Blackwood gaped at the black hole where a face should be — neither speaking, separated by a ribbon of frosted asphalt gleaming like a frozen river. Try as he might, Blackwood couldn't discern a single feature. Then, whether by design or other motivation, the figure shifted, and the sickly yellow glow grudgingly provided by the street light added definition to the face under the hat. Now the reporter could trace the outline of a broad, flat nose; a thick, coarse beard hanging down like Spanish moss; and the crease of a slight, judgmental frown. The stranger's eyes remained hidden.

For a long time, the quiet lingered. The figure offered no greeting, no introduction, no explanation. His right arm rose with purpose, straight up from his side as though cranked by a lever. A long forefinger as crooked as a bent stick pointed at the journalist.

Blackwood couldn't tear away his gaze. Apprehension seized him. Could this be Grant's killer? If so, did he know Grant phoned the newspaper? Had this improbable figure returned to the scene of the crime to catch Blackwood defenseless and unprepared, a loose end to be tidied up?

Somehow that didn't seem likely, and yet Blackwood sensed the strange figure's appearance was no accident.

Blackwood tensed, readying for a fight or flight. He cast around for a weapon. Plenty of broken bottles littered the pavement, just none within reach. By now, his mouth had gone dry; his tongue felt heavy as a log. But it soon became apparent a confrontation was not the visitor's intent. Instead, the finger swung away like a well-oiled gun turret, pointing down the street. At first, Blackwood didn't understand, so he just kept staring straight ahead at the empty space under the stranger's enormous hat, fists clenching and unclenching at his side.

With an air of impatience, the man wagged the long finger, then poked the air twice for emphasis.

Finally, the message registered with Blackwood. Swallowing hard, he tore his eyes away and followed the direction indicated by the extended digit.

To his surprise, he spotted a dark sedan parked only a few yards away, concealed behind a dumpster. A spotless Mercedes. Newer model, he noticed. Empty and dark, the car sat close to what Blackwood now realized was the front gate to Oddfellows' Cemetery. Though he and McGowan had driven past the exact spot an hour ago, it was no wonder they hadn't seen the vehicle. The huge bin was turned at such an angle that it completely obscured the car.

Blackwood's head rose knowingly. Suddenly, everything clicked. *Grant's car. It must be*, he thought. *Who else?*

He turned and gave the hooded figure a curious look. The cloaked man in the wide-brimmed hat lowered the finger, then dipped his chin slightly in wordless acknowledgement. The rest of the face remained shrouded. Nodding to show he understood, Blackwood returned his attention to the sedan.

Willing himself into motion, Blackwood walked to the car for a better look. Sidling up to the vehicle, his keen eyes noticed a spent cigarette on the ground just under the driver's door, probably left in the exact spot where the preoccupied motorist — *Grant*, his mind filled in — absently flicked it before venturing into the cemetery.

Blackwood tugged on the door handle. Locked, of course. No surprise there.

Cupping his hands and pressing his face to the driver's window, the reporter peered inside. It occurred to him that he might be disturbing a potential crime scene. But he knew as long as he remained careful, no evidence would be tainted. Nor did he worry about leaving fingerprints because of the lamb's wool gloves he wore.

His eyes strained to pierce the gloom of the sedan's interior. From what little he could tell, the inside looked neat as a pin, nothing out of place.

Somewhat disappointed, Blackwood straightened up. He'd been hoping to discover a clue—a briefcase, papers, pictures, crucial or damning documents, secret diagrams, blueprints—anything that might tip him off to what Grant planned to reveal during their conversation. Blackwood wanted to know what was so important that it cost a man his life.

He remembered his nameless benefactor lurking across the street. Curiosity trumped caution. Perhaps the man — in his mind he'd already nicknamed him Big Hat — could reveal more.

Blackwood rotated on his heel, his hand half-raised in a grateful salute and a query on his lips. Getting answers had become more important than being afraid.

"Thanks –," he began, but his voice tapered off.

The dim pool of light cast by the streetlamp shone on an empty spot. Bewildered, Blackwood's eyes swept the lane. Nothing stirred, and even the breeze had subsided. The moon sailed higher, the silver disk cresting the angled roofs of the abandoned warehouses, but its cold light revealed no one and nothing in either direction.

"So much for an interview," he muttered.

Not willing to go chasing down blind alleys, Blackwood put aside thoughts of the mysterious benefactor and resumed his inspection of the car. Maybe he'd overlooked something. But the sedan yielded nothing. Not even a bumper sticker.

Taking out his notepad, he began sketching the luxury auto just in case the Art Department wanted a design element to accompany a future article. Though Blackwood wore gloves, his hands quickly grew cold. As he flexed numb fingers to force some warmth back into them, the Mont Blanc pen slipped and clattered to the street.

Blackwood bent down to pick up the writing instrument. That's when he noticed a small piece of paper or cardboard lodged under the left front wheel. Grasping the fragment, he stood up and beheld a postcard.

Only then did the notion occur to him the card might belong to Grant.

The postcard appeared to be one of those gag varieties found in gift shops, hotels, restaurants and roadside stops from Beaumont to El Paso. This particular specimen depicted a beaming cowboy astride an armadillo the size of a pickup. Waving a 10-gallon Stetson, the cowboy kicked up his boots, framed by a broiling desert landscape of cactus and mesas.

The caption read: "Howdy Buckaroo! Everything in Texas is BIGGER!" Blackwood had seen other tourist mementos just like this one, only substitute giant jackrabbits for the armadillo.

Turning the card over, Blackwood discovered what seemed to be hastily scrawled notes and a strange symbol.

A minute passed as he attempted to read the cramped, thin handwriting. Accustomed to deciphering his own poor penmanship, the characters gradually coalesced into legible script. What Blackwood saw gave him a jolt. Three names stood out:

Father Louis Dragoti/UIW

Dr. Sabrina Hagen/Anderson Museum

John Blackwood/SA Tribune

His heart started racing as he considered the script. He recognized his name only, not the others. Who were they? More contacts?

Curious. A line crossed through Dragoti's name.

Blackwood tried not to trip over his own thoughts, which chased each other like wheeling birds. Why strike the name? Did this Dragoti — whoever he was — prove a dead end?

The entry showed the priest worked at the University of the Incarnate Word, a respected Catholic institution in the city's silk-stocking district.

That wasn't all. Blackwood next scrutinized the jumble of other characters scratched on the card's surface. They sharpened into identifiable but very curious figures before his narrowed eyes: A circle and, inside, three identical symbols — XXX.

Finally, he regarded a single, uneven line of copy, sandwiched near the left corner, and wondered at the meaning: Covenant of the Cursed. The words drew a blank.

He had no clue what any of this meant. Did the design and words have a bearing on Grant's grand conspiracy?

Blackwood groaned. Why couldn't Grant have made things more simple? Leaving behind a journal or a tape recording would have suited the reporter just fine.

He stared at the card, willing the words and symbol to impart their mysteries through mental osmosis. When that didn't happen, he sighed. There was not much else he could do, and he'd been gone from McGowan for some time now.

He copied the names, the phrase and made a crude drawing of the symbol, then replaced the scrap under the tire. He felt a twinge of guilt about disturbing potential evidence. But then again, he hadn't known it was evidence when he'd first spotted the postcard, had he? Just more street flotsam.

Rationalization—what a safety net, he scolded himself.

Feeling immensely tired, he trudged back to the others. In just a few words, he revealed his discovery to McGowan. He didn't mention the man with the face swallowed by shadows — Big Hat. He'd already gotten enough grief for mentioning Malory's "Help me." No need to travel that road again.

McGowan swore.

"Is this night never going to end?" his cousin asked.

Blackwood didn't answer as he went to find Stewart.

CHAPTER TWELVE

By the time the sun rose — a wan, ghostly dot dimmed by winter's haze — the freakish weather's grip on the city had only tightened. News-radio stations reported dozens of neighborhoods and thousands of homes paralyzed by rolling blackouts and loss of water pressure, as well as major road closures. Things could have been worse, though. Being the week of Christmas, schools were shuttered for the break, which at least cut down on traffic and kept rush-hour roadway mishaps to a minimum.

Downtown, thin sheets of black ice coated the parking lot reserved for Tribune employees, making footing treacherous. Blackwood almost fell clambering out of his car — a classic black 1969 Ford Mustang Fastback, once the pride and joy of a local drug kingpin. Seized as an asset forfeiture during a narcotics raid, Blackwood bought the car — "for a steal," he liked to quip — at a police auction. He felt lucky to score the ride on his normal reporter's salary, which was more tailored to a Yugo (and a used one at that).

Though Blackwood had the day off, he couldn't sit on the sidelines while someone else wrote the next Grant story. That meant banging out a solid follow-up himself, something more substantial than the brief filed at 2 a.m. and flown in by the press crew for a few hundred afternoon editions only. It never bothered him to work on a story on his day off. Blackwood didn't have a wife or kids, didn't have many outside interests and didn't like sitting around the house watching the telly, so coming to the newsroom was an easy choice. The newspaper was more of a home to him anyway than the bungalow he rented.

Knowing Cantu, the editor would assign a team of reporters to the Malory episode, probably for the Sunday lead — most likely Danny Rocha, the morning police reporter; Finlay Goddard from the medical beat; and maybe a general assignment writer to do the grunt work. A suicidal doctor triggering a SWAT standoff at the city's biggest hospital tended to be a rare occurrence. Tongues would be wagging across town. Though Sunday papers tallied the highest circulation, Blackwood didn't mind if someone else worked on the Malory follow. He'd broken the story—that was good enough for him.

More to the point, Dr. Malory did not scribble Blackwood's name on a postcard, nor phoned him to drop hints about a sinister conspiracy before being ripped apart in a graveyard.

Which made the saga of the acquisitions specialist more pressing. And personal.

The wind ruffled Blackwood's thin blond hair and whipped his tie over his shoulder as he walked to the paper a block away. His freezing lobes made him wish for a cap or earmuffs, and he huddled deeper into his trench coat.

Just a straight shot down the street rose the faded limestone walls of the Alamo, arguably Texas' most famous attraction. The old Spanish mission looked oddly dwarfed by the downtown high-rises. Over the last 300 years, the city sprouted up around the venerable outpost, the source of so much lore ever since the vastly outnumbered Texian rebels made their ill-fated stand there in March 1836 against the soldiers of the Republic of Mexico and their despotic leader, Antonio Lopez de Santa Anna, during the Texas war for independence. Not one Alamo defender survived.

Just a month later, rebel forces rallying under the cry "Remember the Alamo!" routed the Mexican army at San Jacinto, creating a new nation and putting Texas on a path to eventual U.S. statehood in 1845.

In modern times, reality and legend collided daily at the site. Tourists fed on a diet of cinematic Westerns often voiced disappointment encountering the mission's small size and the absence of sweeping desert vistas crowded with tumbleweeds and cactus. They instead found an urban landscape of cultivated palm trees, heritage oaks, hotels, offices, curio shops, fast-food chains, big-name stores, the iconic River Walk and streets bustling with traffic.

Reaching the corner, Blackwood shifted his attention from the Alamo to consider the gray old lady of the Trib looming several stories above him. He crossed the street and entered a door marked EMPLOYEES ONLY (the "servants' entrance," McGowan liked to say). Blackwood headed to the newsroom first. The place remained quiet for a change, almost docile. The television sets ringing the City Desk chattered at low volume with stories about the rare snowfall.

Blackwood left a note taped to Cantu's computer terminal, informing the editor he planned to do a "folo" on the cemetery case.

Skipping the stairs for the elevator, Blackwood punched the button for the fourth floor, home of the news-research department. He intended to comb through the archives to see what he could discover about Grant, the Akel-Dama Corporation, Sabrina Hagen and Father Louis Dragoti.

•   •   •

Blackwood pushed his way through the double swinging doors of the newspaper's morgue — a euphemism for the repository where all the old stories went to be buried. The room resembled a cramped library. Before him stretched metal bookshelves sagging under alphabetically arranged manila envelopes containing articles clipped from the newspaper and filed away — but never quite forgotten. The smell of faded newsprint and ink filled the air. Computers mounted on desks in the rear provided links to the nascent World Wide Web through Netscape Navigator, as well as reams of data from other sources thanks to the paper's recent LexisNexis subscription. A row of cubicles with microfiche viewers lined the wall.

One shouldn't think it unusual Blackwood remained ignorant of the Akel-Dama Corporation. Other than crime and courts stories, as far as he was concerned, the rest of the articles printed in the Trib — including business stories — constituted mere filler crammed between the ads. Death always sold more newspapers anyway. (Well, that and sports; San Antonians idolized their Spurs). Morbid interest is the circulation department's best friend, he liked to say. Put a 60-point headline on page one above the fold screaming "Orphans Killed in Bus Crash" and copies fly off the racks. Add a deck headline announcing "Driver swerved to avoid puppy" and a second press run is guaranteed.

With assistance from Mandy Bennett, the on-duty news researcher, Blackwood collected a handful of files, sat down at a rickety corner desk and began pawing through the contents. Pulling tidbits from the various stories, his notebook rapidly filled with crucial background details.

Researching a story using scattered clips is like painting by the numbers. Sometimes it takes awhile before a picture emerges, Blackwood told himself.

During his reading, he learned Tobias Revnant, a billionaire regarded as a technological visionary, founded the Akel-Dama Corporation in the mid-1970s and continued running things to this day. The entrepreneur made his fortune in microprocessors and something called software, building on that revenue stream by landing several Department of Defense contracts. Also considered very elusive, Revnant apparently never granted interviews, so not much was known about him personally. Two months ago, a company spokesman announced the firm planned to vacate its

Dallas headquarters and relocate to San Antonio, home of several military bases.

City leaders wined and dined Revnant to secure the deal, including offering a very favorable tax abatement worth sixty-million dollars over ten years. The charismatic Mayor Raul Solis orchestrated the courtship, of course. In return, Revnant guaranteed to provide seventy local, high-paying, white-collar jobs.

Blackwood scratched the stubble of his cheek. He'd left the house in such a rush he'd forgotten to shave. Fatigue clung to him like a second skin. He'd found his slumber fitful and short, filled with vague, troubling dreams that vanished like smoke the second his lids opened.

He stifled a yawn and scanned more articles. While the stuff about Revnant proved mildly interesting, none of the stories mentioned Grant. That didn't surprise Blackwood. He'd already formed the distinct impression his mysterious caller was not one to seek the limelight, proving more elusive than his boss.

Time to change tactics. He wasn't writing about Grant's employer, after all. Blackwood got up, stretched and ambled over to the H row.

After locating a manila envelope marked "Hagen," he returned to his seat, turned the packet upside-down and shook out the bundle. A handful of yellowed news stories fluttered to the table.

During the next half hour, an examination of the wrinkled cuttings yielded biographical details about a Marta Hagen (nee Anderson) and her husband, a Norwegian-born archaeology professor named Toren Hagen. Blackwood also discovered related briefs mentioning Mimi Anderson — an oil heiress, Marta Hagen's mother and the director of the Anderson Museum, which the family founded in the 1920s. The first mention of a Sabrina Hagen took a little more digging, but eventually he found an obituary from the late 1960s listing her as an infant, the surviving daughter of Marta and Toren Hagen.

The next story raised Blackwood's eyebrows.

The article recounted how a freak accident claimed the lives of Professor Hagen and his wife during an archaeological excavation. While they collected historical artifacts discovered in a cave near Mission San Jose, a gas main exploded, causing a partial collapse. The professor and four graduate students died instantly, while his wife — nine months pregnant—suffered extensive third-degree burns. A priest at the scene braved the flames and carried her from the tunnel. In spite of his heroism, she only survived long enough to deliver her daughter, Sabrina, in an arriving ambulance.

A paragraph later, the story identified the rescuer: a young cleric assigned to Mission San Jose named Father Louis Dragoti.

Blackwood's head snapped back.

"So that's how it fits together," he breathed. "Dragoti saved the Hagen baby."

He read further, but the account didn't elaborate on the nature of the artifacts, nor what happened to them; those details remained frustratingly scarce. The story did relate the University of Texas at Austin sponsored the excavation, over the objections of the Archdiocese of San Antonio. Apparently the church even went to court to block the endeavor, but as the cave existed on private property just outside the mission grounds, the state district judge ruled the church had no jurisdiction. The diocesan attorneys also failed to sway the jurist with their arguments about potential acts of religious desecration. Blackwood wondered if a copy of the lawsuit still existed at the District Clerk's Office. Checking for that would be a priority on Monday.

As is customary, the bottom of the story included routine funeral arrangements and survivors, listing Marta Hagen's mum, Mimi Anderson; the daughter, Sabrina; Marta Hagen's maternal aunt; and the professor's relatives in Narvik, Norway.

Blackwood leaned forward. Now things had gotten interesting. Linking his fingers, he cracked the knuckles. Two other reporters sitting nearby winced at the sound.

He couldn't find much more on the cave-in, but other stories confirmed Mimi Anderson carried on as director of the Anderson even after her daughter's death. Blackwood nodded thoughtfully. He knew the place, just north of downtown in Brackenridge Park. He'd driven past the granite edifice a thousand times — a big, neoclassical building nestled amongst the oak trees, overlooking a bend in the San Antonio River.

He rose, rubbed a leg that had fallen asleep, returned the envelope to its empty spot on the shelf, and wished for a cup of tea. Then he moved to another aisle and found the As, which led him to a packet labeled "Anderson Museum."

Taking the file with him, Blackwood sat down and began digging through the brittle clippings.

A recent obituary for Mimi Anderson caught his attention first. The paid write-up, which ran in the classifieds, listed a granddaughter named Sabrina Hagen as a survivor. The obit didn't say what Anderson died from, other than a "short illness."

Next, he located a press release from two months ago announcing Dr. Sabrina Hagen's appointment as the museum's interim director in the wake of her grandmother's unexpected demise. The write-up related Hagen held a doctorate in archaeology, just like her late father.

"I suppose the apple doesn't fall far from the tree," Blackwood remarked, his curiosity growing. What would Grant, a lawyer for a high-tech firm, want with the curator of a museum?

An acquisition, of course. Museums deal in rare items, said the voice inside his head that always spoke when he turned on his reporter radar. *Indeed. But, what kind of acquisition?*

Only one way to find out, and that meant paying a visit to Dr. Sabrina Hagen.

That left one other name on the list: Dragoti.

Blackwood's lips pressed in frustration, but a glimpse at his Mickey Mouse watch showed the hour had grown late. He had an appointment at SAPD.

He returned to Mandy's desk, but the news researcher was nowhere to be found. Probably getting a Big Red and a barbacoa taco, which happened to be her go-to Saturday morning treat.

He scribbled a note requesting any information she could find on Dragoti and the words "covenant of the cursed."

•   •   •

Blackwood carefully navigated the ice-packed roads to McGowan's apartment and picked him up. Thirty minutes later, a uniformed officer ushered the pair into Gruene's office in the Violent Crimes Division on the second floor of SAPD headquarters, a gray, white and aquamarine building stamped in the mold of the "mod" architecture of the 1970s.

Wearing a haggard expression, the captain sat hunched over his desk. A large map of the city hung on the wall behind him. Civic awards, commendations, a photograph of Gruene sharing a handshake with Gov. Ann Richards, a large oil painting depicting bluebonnets and a Persian throw rug added a little color to the drab government office. Classical music drifted from a radio perched on a bookshelf, the volume turned low.

The captain barely looked up when they entered.

Blackwood's eyes shifted to the folders and crime-scene diagrams spread across Gruene's desk. He drew closer, confirming his suspicions the reports dealt with the Malory and Grant cases. Like most reporters worth their salt, he could read upside-down.

"John, isn't this your day off?" Gruene grumbled by way of greeting. Underneath the captain's gruff demeanor, Blackwood caught a faint smile flickering on his drawn lips.

Without waiting for an invitation, the newsmen sat down in leather chairs across from the captain.

Blackwood feigned bruised feelings.

"Frank, I could ask the same of you. Did you even go home?"

Gruene gave a rough chuckle, then sat back in his seat.

Normally an immaculate dresser, this morning the captain looked as if he'd waltzed with a tornado. A relief map of the Rockies had less wrinkles than his silk shirt. Spilled coffee added a splash of color to a sleeve. The Windsor knot of his tie was yanked down level with his breastbone.

"Got me there," Gruene said, twisting his neck to get the kinks out. "I stayed to oversee the Malory case, and then night CID brought in that other cluster, the 'Hamburger Helper' from the cemetery."

Gruene began to usher the papers back into their folders.

"You here about Malory?" he asked.

"No," Blackwood said. "The 'Hamburger Helper.'"

McGowan snickered.

Gruene pondered this, but didn't seem surprised.

"Worried because your name is on that postcard?" he asked.

Gruene's question didn't surprise Blackwood. The reporter hadn't dared reveal to the night detectives he'd handled the evidence under Grant's car, including copying down the names and cryptic scribbles. When Stewart took his statement, Blackwood was fine letting the detective "reveal" the reporter's name was emblazoned across a giant armadillo's backside on a postcard "found" by the evidence technicians. Stewart did this out of sheer decency, but he never mentioned Hagen nor Dragoti. A true professional, Stewart was doing his duty to maintain the chain of evidence; Blackwood didn't begrudge his reticence.

Gruene fixed Blackwood with a probing stare, waiting for an answer.

"Worried? Perhaps a tad," Blackwood said, though not absolutely sure "worried" constituted the appropriate word. More intrigued, to be honest. He'd faced worse threats from prison gangs. "My real concern is that Grant wanted to tell me something obviously very important, and died for his troubles. I wish I'd asked him more questions when he rang."

"You and me both," Gruene said, then softened his tone. "But I looked at your statement to Night CID. How could you know the guy would be dead in a few hours?"

The captain drummed his fingers on the desk, then stirred in his seat.

"By the way, the medical examiner says fingerprints confirm it's him. Not that Dr. Bucks had a lot of fingers to work with," Gruene said, cocking his head in Blackwood's direction. "But other than that, you probably know as much as we do. You always do your research, John."

"I stopped by the Trib this morning and skimmed the clips," Blackwood acknowledged. "Trying to fill in the gaps. But we didn't have anything on Grant. Not a scrap. Got anything you can share?"

The captain flipped open the folder and donned his reading glasses. Blackwood took out his notepad.

"So I guess you know Mr. Grant worked for –," Gruene consulted one of the reports, "the Akel-Dama Corporation. He's a lawyer."

Blackwood acknowledged the fact with a nod.

"And a rare-acquisitions specialist," Blackwood said.

The captain jotted a note in the margin of the report.

"His boss is — was — a man named Tobias Revnant," Blackwood continued. "You may have heard of him."

Gruene nodded, then responded.

"Well, I can't say I know much about Mr. Revnant, other than what I've read or seen on TV," Gruene said. "He's filthy rich, from what I understand. Some kind of high-tech guru. If he sneezes, he makes money. I'm sending Detective Galvan to take a statement from him. You've met Galvan. A damn good investigator, high clearance rate. The company's set up headquarters in the Tower Life building, over on South Saint Mary's. Penthouse suite, very pricey. Maybe Mr. Revnant will have a few answers for us."

Blackwood crossed one leg over the other, resting his notepad on a bony knee. "So what else did the ME say?"

Gruene turned a weary expression to the window, his tone mystified. Then he contemplated the reporter.

"The medical examiner said he's never seen a case like this. Very little blood and skin the consistency of an old boot. Dr. Bucks uses a lot of highfalutin terms in the initial report he faxed over — skin turgor, hypovolemia, exsanguination — but I think it can be summed up in one word — 'weird.'"

"'Exsanguination. I know that one," McGowan said, looking pleased with himself.

Gruene rolled his eyes, then continued.

"The lab is running toxicology tests now. Maybe the guy had some kind of medical condition, like psoriasis. Or was taking something."

"It is damned peculiar," Blackwood said.

"Peculiar?" Gruene huffed. "For a reporter, you have a wonderful gift for understatement. That's like calling the sinking of the Titanic a 'setback.' And we still don't know what killed our complainant. Best guess? Bucks thinks it might have been feral animals, like dogs. At the scene, you heard about the bite marks on the bones, right? Animal Control has extra patrols in the area, but so far no one has reported anything unusual."

Blackwood tapped his pen against the notepad, failing miserably to look surprised. He'd heard the same theory last night. Then as now, he found the explanation ludicrous. No ravenous pack of pooches killed Grant, of that he felt sure. If such an assessment represented Dr. Bucks' best idea about what occurred, then the case had the medical examiner just as stumped as the rest of them.

"Do we know anything more about James Grant, other than what he said to me?" Blackwood said.

Gruene downed a swallow of coffee from a mug that said "Living Legend" above an etching of his badge number, making a face. He leaned across the desk and consulted a second file, not very thick.

"I can give you some basic bio details, based on what Akel-Dama's HR department sent us. He was 35, never married, resided in

Houston before joining Revnant in Dallas, and apparently lived alone. Galvan went by his apartment early this a.m. and the landlord gave him entry. Funston Place, just off Broadway. Know the street?"

Blackwood nodded. "Mahncke Park, right? Nice area, old Craftsman bungalows, streets with trees."

Gruene inclined his head and continued. "Galvan said the place looked spotless; pretty much like the car. This guy was either Mr. Neat or Mr. Obsessive-Compulsive."

"Or Mr. Cover-My-Tracks," Blackwood offered, thoughtfully chewing on the stem of the unlit pipe that popped into his mouth. The reporter fought an urge to light the tobacco. San Antonio had only recently adopted an ordinance prohibiting smoking in municipal buildings. If he lit up, Gruene would have to arrest him.

"There was something, though. Something a little unusual," the captain said, turning a page of the report. "Galvan said there were two large wooden crates in the living room. One filled with crosses and Stars of David, and the other packed with wooden sticks."

"Crosses and Stars of David?" McGowan echoed.

"Sticks?" Blackwood joined in.

"Dozens and dozens," Gruene said. He flipped another page, examining some color photographs attached to the file by a large paperclip. Then he held them up for the visitors to inspect.

Blackwood furrowed his brow. "Those aren't 'sticks,' Frank. They look more like fat dowel rods or short posts."

McGowan fished in a vest pocket, extracted a magnifier loupe and wagged a blunt finger at Gruene. The captain handed over the photos. McGowan tipped them and pressed the monocle-like device against the images. Squinting, he gave the shots a photographer's thorough appraisal in quick succession.

"Hmmm," he breathed. "Those 'sticks' are sharpened at one end, like the stakes to hold up a tent." He grunted. "Not really great photos, Frank."

Gruene, who was busy scanning another file, stared stonily over his glasses and cleared his throat.

"Sorry, Robert … Not all of us have fancy news cameras," he said, his tone anything but apologetic. "Besides, I haven't had a chance to read the whole file yet. I was still on Malory when you girls strolled in, remember?"

Another question sprang to Blackwood's mind.

"Were the crates open?"

Gruene steepled his fingers. "No, the evidence boys pried the boards off. In fact, the landlord said the crates arrived yesterday afternoon, but only after Grant had left the apartment — left in a big damn hurry, in fact, the landlord said. 'Skedaddled' is the word he used, honest to God. Since Grant was gone, the landlord unlocked the apartment for the deliverymen and signed for the crates."

He laid hands flat on the desk, palms down.

"Grant never came back," the captain said.

"'Skedaddled,' huh?" McGowan echoed. "Now how's that for speaking Texan?"

"'Departed in a hurry,'" Blackwood supplied, scribbling in his notebook and then lowering his face to take a better look at the bundle of pictures, including interior shots of the apartment.

The pictures revealed a wood floor, a sensible couch, a roll-top desk in the corner … He and McGowan exchanged a puzzled glance.

"What are those scraps of paper covering the walls, Frank?" the reporter asked. "They're everywhere."

The captain stared at the indicated photos from his side of the desk.

"Bible verses," he said flatly. "Galvan said the place is plastered with them. Every room, even the shitter."

"Holy crap," McGowan stage whispered. If he was trying to be funny, no one laughed.

Blackwood parted his lips to ask another question. Gruene ran a finger down a few lines of type in the report and cut him off.

"Hold your horses, Goldilocks. The inventory is still being catalogued. And before you ask, there wasn't anything special about the crosses or the Stars of David. They were just religious objects.

Unremarkable, nothing of any value. Not gold, not silver, not even chocolate with sprinkles. Just wood and plaster. And don't ask me what he intended to do with any of that stuff. I'm not about to speculate. Maybe we'll find out after we follow up on a few leads."

By "leads," Gruene meant the other people whose names graced the postcard, Hagen and Dragoti, but Blackwood said nothing about those. Instead, he took a minute to absorb what the captain mentioned about the crates, his mind churning. If this wasn't strange, then he didn't know what counted as such. Grant hadn't impressed him as particularly religious, though he knew practically nothing about the man. What would Grant want with religious objects? Was he superstitious? Were they part of an art collection? Or a component of the negotiations with the museum? And what about the Bible passages on the walls? What purpose did those serve?

He directed his gaze back at Gruene, who looked simply beat. The officer's face, already wreathed by a healthy five o'clock shadow, darkened with frustration.

"What did the neighbors say?" Blackwood asked, putting the crates and Bible verses aside for the moment.

Gruene shook his head.

"There aren't any. It's an old house that's been subdivided. The other apartments are vacant. But the landlord said Grant was never any trouble; quiet, paid the rent on time, no loud music—a model citizen. Just went about his business. If he had enemies, the landlord didn't know about them. Of course, the guy had only been there two or three months."

The captain's gaze drifted to the window again, his attention diverted by the battleship-gray clouds scudding across the sky. Then his focus sharpened and he returned his attention to the two newsmen.

Blackwood turned a page in his notebook and spoke again.

"So there's no note, no letter, no diary, no files, no records of any kind, nothing left behind by Grant to explain why somebody wanted to kill him?"

The captain hesitated for just a second before replying.

"Like I said, we hope to get some answers soon. Galvan got an evidentiary search warrant from Judge Quintanilla and recovered a computer and a bunch of floppy disks from Grant's place. Who knows? Maybe that'll tell us something. It'll take a while. We have to ship them to the Department of Public Safety lab in Austin, let their tech boys play with it."

Blackwood twirled his pen between thumb and forefinger.

"My guess is, you won't find anything. Seems like Grant really wanted to cover his tracks."

"I won't argue that," Gruene said, rubbing at the stubble peppering his jaw.

Blackwood fired off another question.

"Have you reached next of kin?"

Gruene consulted the paperwork.

"Still looking," he said. "When Grant rented the apartment, he filled out a form designating emergency contacts. There's a cousin in New Orleans and an aunt who lives way the hell up in Salem, Massachusetts. So far we haven't been able to reach either one. Law enforcement in both states is checking."

"Fine. Then I'll still hold off using his name in a story for now," Blackwood said, pressing on. "What about here in the city? Any friends?" He had a particular reason for asking.

After all, Grant mentioned he was trying to protect someone ... a "her."

Blackwood wanted to know if he'd meant Sabrina Hagen.

Using his index finger, Gruene turned a page in the folder.

"The landlord mentioned a female acquaintance. The guy recalled seeing a woman drive up once or twice to fetch Grant. She had a Land Rover, he remembered that. Seem's the landlord's a nosey old fart. When he asked Grant about the lady, our complainant just said she was a friend showing him around town."

"Girlfriend?" Blackwood interjected.

Gruene stretched his neck again, then pursed his lips as he considered the question.

"Honestly, we don't know. Oddly enough, Grant left a new mobile phone behind in his apartment. A pretty pricey Nokia. Not sure why he didn't take it with him last night. Might've come in handy. Anyway, we found a woman's number in the address book. We still need to speak with her, but I think they're one and the same."

Blackwood's scalp tingled.

"Who's the woman, Frank?" Blackwood asked, though he already knew the answer.

"I figured you'd ask," the captain sighed, giving Blackwood a shrewd glance.

Gruene wordlessly pushed the folder across the desk with the tips of his fingers. He watched Blackwood's reaction as the reporter scanned the file.

"Sabrina Hagen," Blackwood whispered, nodding. He'd already worked it out, but this was the confirmation he needed.

So this was Grant's "acquaintance" — the name on the card, who also just happened to be the director of the Anderson Museum.

What's the connection? he thought. *Was Grant in negotiations with Hagen about a museum piece?*

The notation carried an address and a phone number. Blackwood recorded both in his notebook. When he finished, he gently closed the folder and pushed the file back across the desk to Gruene, who licked dry lips.

They regarded each other for a beat and Gruene sipped his coffee.

Blackwood tried to figure out why a man as methodical as Grant would decide not to take his mobile phone with him when he went to the cemetery, a potentially dangerous place given its proximity to crack dens, prostitutes and gang hideouts.

Then an idea struck him.

"He called me last night from a pay phone," Blackwood said. "I suppose he was afraid 'they' could track him through a mobile phone. I've read somewhere that's possible."

His eyes moved from Gruene to McGowan.

"He seriously wanted to stay off the radar," McGowan said.

Gruene parted another manila folder.

"We're checking the records with the phone company for all the calls made from the two pay phones just blocks from your paper. We don't think he was very far away."

"Two? There must be a dozen," Blackwood said.

Gruene gave him a questioning look and pointed to a boxy mobile phone charging on his desk.

"Where have you been?" he said, pointing to the device. "These things are taking over. They're going to make payphones obsolete. The city issued this one to me. I'm under orders from the chief to carry it, day and night."

Gruene's expression soured. "Too much like an electronic leash, if you ask me."

Blackwood, suddenly conscious of the metallic lump of the phone in his own pocket, nodded, conceding the point. The radio on Gruene's shelf switched from Beethoven to news, an announcer's muted voice mentioning President Clinton and yet another allegation in the Whitewater probe. Meanwhile, the captain studied the file's contents one last time, then closed the cover.

"Thanks," Blackwood acknowledged gratefully.

"Don't mention it," Gruene said. "Just remember to spell 'anonymous' correctly."

CHAPTER THIRTEEN

By the time Blackwood and McGowan reached the Mustang, heavy clouds had formed into bloated fingers grasping the sky, ready to squeeze the warmth from the city. Heralding the advent of a coming snowstorm, a fierce wind pushed by the front rattled Christmas lights strung along Nueva Street outside the police station. Whipped by the gale, the lines sang a mournful dirge.

Inside the scant warmth of the car, Blackwood fumbled with matches and lit his pipe. Soon, blue-tobacco fog curled out of a window cranked open just a hair. Without a word, he pushed "Synchronicity" by The Police into the cassette player. "King of Pain" began playing. A second later, the engine gunned to life.

He pulled out of the media parking lot. The Mustang's wheels churned through slippery gray slush.

"What's next?" McGowan asked. "Go talk to this Hagen chick?"

Blackwood turned down the volume.

"That's the idea," he said.

Shimmering in the wan winter light like an iridescent black beetle, Blackwood's classic Mustang rounded the downtown ramp that herded traffic from Interstate 10 West to U.S. 281 North. His mind turned as circuitously as the multiple lanes of the elevated expressway, his gaze absently roving across skyscrapers, a sea of gray rooftops, frosted skylights and hooded vents belching smoke.

Lost in thought, he never noticed when his mobile phone, which he'd tossed into the alcove between the driver's and passenger's seats, began vibrating. McGowan's bushy eyebrows rose.

"Gonna answer that?" the photographer asked after a minute spent watching the phone jump around.

"It's ringing?" Blackwood said, glancing down. The photographer gave his cousin a pitying look, then picked up the device.

"What a techno dumbass," McGowan announced, examining the phone. "You somehow put the ringer on vibrate." With a disparaging sigh, he flipped open the screen and answered for the reporter, whose two hands remained firmly locked around the steering wheel. Negotiating the icy lanes, Blackwood didn't look like he would let go for anything.

"Not John Blackwood here," McGowan answered, the corners of his mouth turning down in a smirk. After a beat, "You want to speak to the perfessor? OK."

He offered the phone to his cousin.

"Mandy Bennett, from news research," he said.

Blackwood hesitantly released one hand from wheel and pressed the phone's cool surface to his ear.

"Blackwood."

Mandy's distinctive East Texas drawl ricocheted off the side of his head like a firecracker in a tin can.

"Howdy, John. I got yer note," she said, sounding almost giddy. "At first I couldn't find anythin' in the clip files about this Father Dragoti guy. Then, I had the bright idea," (which came across as "ideer"), "to head on down to the stacks in the basement, where the files being shipped off to be digitized are stored. Fer the online directory we're buildin'.'"

Blackwood tilted his head.

"We're digitizing our clip files?" he asked.

Mandy snorted. McGowan shook his head and rolled his eyes.

"Duh," his cousin said with disdain.

"'A course," Mandy added. "Dontcha read my newsletters? Right now we're getting ready to send everything about the missions and the Archdiocese over to the archive company. You're lucky ... By Monday, all of that stuff would've been gone for a couple of weeks."

The news researcher held a deep breath, then released it.

"Any hey, I found some stories from the early 1970s 'bout a lawsuit connected to an explosion and cave-in next door to Mission San Jose. Tragic. A whole lotta finger pointin' at a dead archaeologist and the university. A real blame game."

Blackwood felt his pulse quicken. "Great work, Mandy. The clips — where are they?"

She chuckled hearing the eagerness brimming in his voice.

"I 'rescued' 'em and left the whole bundle at the Crime Desk. Merry Christmas, Johnny boy."

•　　•　　•

An hour later, after an extended layover at the newspaper so Blackwood could review the clipped articles, he and McGowan returned to the highway. Fresh snow falling on top of black ice made the drive treacherous. With no snowplows in the city's motor pool, regular dump trucks loaded with salt and chat lumbered along doing the best they could to keep the roads open.

The locals joked only two seasons existed in South Texas: summer and more summer. Which explained why the bizarre wintry conditions now smothering the city took such a toll. San Antonians easily endured blistering heat and punishing drought, but scatter a few snowflakes across the ground and everything grinds to a standstill. Though the landlocked region experiences the occasional hard freeze during an average winter, deep snowfalls occur with the frequency of a tidal wave, and paralyze the city just as effectively.

The Mustang fell in line with other traffic, though the road wasn't crowded. As the flurries increased, cars slowed to timid crawls, taillights flashing like semaphore signals as drivers stomped on their brakes.

McGowan gave his cousin an expectant stare.

"So what's the scoop?" he asked. "Anything enlightening in those clips?"

"Very enlightening," Blackwood said. Dropping into a lower gear, the Mustang lurched forward to edge around a stalled Toyota pickup.

The clips Mandy dug up proved to be pure gold. The stack detailed a class-action lawsuit filed in state district court by the parents of the four graduate students killed in the accident at the dig site outside the walls of Mission San Joe. The University of Texas was named as a defendant in the legal action, which alleged gross negligence on the part of the school and Professor Hagen.

Evidence presented during the trial included testimony from survivors, some of whom shed light on a certain young priest named Dragoti.

McGowan gave the morose pickup driver a sympathetic nod before asking his next question.

"And what did you discover?"

Blackwood didn't answer at first. Instead, his attention remained focused on the slippery road, watchful eyes tallying the vehicles pulling over to the shoulder. Old Man Winter hammered the city on an anvil of ice.

Satisfied he wasn't going to skid off the blacktop, he broke his silence.

"Did you know, Robert," he said, "that during the vice-regal period in New Spain, churches performed some of the same functions that museums do today, serving as storehouses or repositories for relics, sculptures, paintings, books and sacred objects?"

"History ain't my bag," McGowan said.

"Well, apparently history was rather important to a certain Professor Toren Hagen and his wife Marta, according to those old articles. Back in 1969, they were part of a University of Texas archaeological team conducting an excavation at Mission San Jose. They located a hidden cave just outside the church property."

"You mean that old mission by the abandoned drive-in? On the South Side"

"The very same."

McGowan appeared to consider this.

"What were they looking for? Buried treasure?" He grinned, but Blackwood's expression remained grim.

"I don't think so, but the stories are rather vague on the specifics," Blackwood said. "Based on the testimony, it was a relic of some kind, sent from Rome to be hidden on the frontier of the New World in the 1700s. I gather it was religious in nature. The Hagens learned about this artifact from an old diary penned by Bishop Virgil Elizondo, the curate at the mission in its early years. Professor Hagen translated excerpts and published them in a scholarly journal, which was introduced as an exhibit during the trial."

"I'll bet that was a runaway bestseller," McGowan said dryly. "When's the movie coming out?"

"Anyway," said the reporter, ignoring his cousin's stab at humor, "there was a terrible accident, an explosion, during the excavation. It caused a fire and a cave-in. Professor Hagen was killed, as were several members of his party. Grad students."

McGowan's light-hearted expression switched to astonishment.

"Damn.—What caused the explosion?"

"Good question. The utility company conducted a very thorough investigation and determined a natural-gas pipeline ran from the mission through the dig site. During the proceedings, an inspector testified the archaeology crew must have ruptured the pipe, causing a spark to ignite the gas. The parents who filed the suit claimed UT — or really, Professor Hagen — should have known about the gas line."

McGowan's facial muscles stretched into a tight mask.

"Explains the lawsuit. Somebody smelled money."

"Yes. This turned into a very long and very expensive proceeding," Blackwood said. "The university spent years tied up in court. Eventually, there was a settlement, which was sealed."

Ahead of him, an elderly woman in a silver Mercedes-Benz slammed on her brakes. Cursing under his breath, Blackwood quickly veered the Mustang around the sedan. The Ford's wheels spun for just a second or two, then managed to grab the road, no harm done.

"How does Sabrina Hagen fit into all of this?" McGowan asked, his iron grip relaxing on the door handle. A drive on an ice-choked highway with his cousin behind the wheel felt about as calming as riding in a barrel over Niagara Falls.

"Marta Hagen was assisting her husband during the excavation. She was pregnant with a daughter," Blackwood told him.

"Preggers and working at a dig site? Tough gal," McGowan said, visibly impressed.

"Nine months," Blackwood said, sliding gloved hands along the steering wheel. "The child was delivered in an ambulance just after the paramedics arrived. A healthy baby girl, no worse for wear. With her dying breath, the mother named her Sabrina."

Keeping his eyes glued to a roadway dotted by idled or sliding vehicles, Blackwood carefully removed one hand from the steering wheel, fished in a coat pocket and pulled out a Bic butane lighter. He cracked open the window an inch, lit his pipe and took a few deep, reflective puffs.

The wind whistling through the gap brushed his left cheek like a frost maiden's kiss. Blackwood resumed his account.

"A Roman Catholic priest at the mission named Louis Dragoti heard the explosion and rushed to the site. Two survivors testified this was not his first appearance that day. He'd come earlier and quarreled with Toren Hagen, trying to convince him to shut down the operation."

"Isn't Dragoti the other name on that mystery list?" McGowan said, his mouth opening with an "ah-ha" expression.

Blackwood started to nod when suddenly both hands tightened around the wheel. A Cadillac in front abruptly dropped down to 20 mph; Blackwood flashed his lights and the Caddy moved over, allowing the Mustang to pass.

"What was the padre's beef?" McGowan asked, his bugged-out eyes shrinking back into his skull.

"Witnesses told the court Dragoti was assigned by the Vatican to San Jose to monitor the excavation, which took place just outside the mission's walls on private land. That meant, of course, it was also outside of the church's jurisdiction. From what I gathered, the Vatican felt Hagen was on the verge of committing sacrilege. Apparently that led to a row between Dragoti and the professor."

McGowan scrunched his brow in puzzlement.

"What did he have to say for himself at the trial?"

Blackwood shook his head.

"Dragoti was a no-show. The Vatican conveniently recalled him immediately after the accident. When the subpoenas started flying, Dragoti was nowhere to be found. The church probably sent him to some country that isn't even on a map."

"Sounds like the Vatican helped him disappear," McGowan said.

"Too right," Blackwood said. "Anyway, when Dragoti returned to the site after the blast, he found Marta Hagen and carried her to the ambulance. She'd been at the mouth of the cave and was thrown several yards by the explosion. The blast left her barely alive, but she lived long enough to deliver the baby."

McGowan shifted to face Blackwood.

"That priest probably saved the kid's life," he said, now uncharacteristically solemn.

Blackwood's chin rose and fell in acknowledgement.

"Dragoti also administered Last Rites to the others," Blackwood said.

The photographer studied the road.

"What do we know about Sabrina Hagen?" he asked.

"A little," Blackwood responded after another puff. "She became an archaeologist, just like her father. Her family runs the Anderson Museum. She took over the museum a few weeks ago after the death of her maternal grandmother, Mimi Anderson."

Blackwood spotted the exit for East Hildebrand Avenue, the turnoff for Sabrina Hagen's neighborhood, and dropped into silence. He angled the Mustang off the highway, wondering what additional light she might shed on this conundrum which, by his reckoning, had snowballed from her connection to a slain acquisitions specialist to include her ill-fated family and her father's dispute with a missing Vatican envoy.

He needed answers and he needed them fast. A deadline loomed.

CHAPTER FOURTEEN

The Mustang threaded an icy street framed by a canopy of frozen oaks, their limbs stripped bare by winter's loveless embrace. The sprawling homes of the upscale neighborhood rose like citadels from yards as big as football fields. In good weather, those lawns would be trimmed as smartly as a military recruit's haircut, but for now only undulating snow blanketed dead carpets of brittle grass.

A minute later, Blackwood located the Anderson homestead — an imposing, two-story Spanish hacienda with a red stucco roof, jutting beams and whitewashed walls. The Mustang turned into the circular driveway and rolled to a stop. The two newspapermen emerged from the auto and stood on the blacktop for a moment, rubbing their hands and getting their bearings.

"Well, shall we?" Blackwood suggested. McGowan waved him ahead with a theatrical flourish. Brushing shoulders, the pair started up a path of slate paving stones winding through a garden dotted by dormant cactus and hardy agave plants.

Soon they stood before a door the size of a banquet table, inset with a small, octagonal window protected by cross-hatched bars of wrought iron. Blackwood grabbed the matching knocker and pounded the thick wood.

Seconds ticked by. Their breath misted as they waited for someone to answer.

"Perhaps no one's home," Blackwood said at last, wondering whether he should knock again. McGowan stepped forward.

"Allow me," the photographer said, pointedly polite. He jammed his finger into the doorbell for several seconds, pressing so hard the skin around the nail bled white. The chimes inside buzzed urgently, as if catching their mood.

"Really, Robert," Blackwood said as the ding-dong refrain faded. McGowan's lips tightened.

"I'll never understand how you can be so bloodthirsty and so fussy at the same time," he shot back.

As Blackwood's mouth opened to issue a retort, the door swung inward. The pair glanced up like naughty schoolboys caught bickering. A tanned woman sporting a blond bob stood there; she wore a slight smile as she regarded them.

"You must be Mr. McGowan and Mr. Blackwood, from the San Antonio Tribune," she announced.

Struck speechless, the cousins remained rooted to the spot. The woman's hint of a smile became a wide, impish grin.

Noting their confusion, she laughed softly. That's when Blackwood noticed her eyes. Blue. The deepest, purest blue he had ever seen, glittering like flecks of fjord ice.

She weighed the puzzled looks on their faces.

"I'll bet you're wondering how I know your names," she said, anticipating Blackwood's question. "Easy. A police captain called thirty minutes ago to say a detective would be coming by to take my statement. He warned me two newsmen might show up first."

After pausing to let that sink in, she spoke again, her tone charged with an undercurrent of humor.

"He also said I didn't have to talk to you if I didn't want to."

The woman seemed to be trying to make up her mind about whether to let them in.

Blackwood and McGowan shared a knowing glance, one name flashing wordlessly between them: Gruene.

"He did, did he?" Blackwood said, returning his attention to the woman on the doorstep.

Again, that smile, fresh, honest and as big as a cloudless sky in June. She nodded, her long, natural eyelashes brushing the chilly air.

"I'm Dr. Sabrina Hagen, by the way," she said.

She extended a hand to shake theirs; small, but not delicate, the skin a little dry, a little rough, and the grip as firm as a vise. It reminded Blackwood the woman was a scientist, an archaeologist, someone who worked outdoors, who dug in the ground, who probably knew how to "rough it" better than he did.

She noticed the biting air as a slight shiver caressed her frame. Stamping feet anxiously, she looked both men up and down.

Sighing, she beckoned to them, evidently arriving at a decision.

"Well, neither of you looks very dangerous. Come in. You're going to catch your cold out there. And if you're not, then I am," she insisted.

She turned, steps carrying her into the cavernous house. Blackwood and McGowan shared relieved glances at the invitation and followed her inside, shutting the door behind them.

Sabrina glided across the hallway's red Saltillo tile, her steps soft, graceful and quietly self-assured, like a cat.

Moving deeper into the house, the tile yielded to polished wood floors. Thick ornamental rugs swallowed their footfalls as they traversed several large rooms, the chambers cluttered with antique furniture. White sheets covered many of the pieces; others stood exposed, surfaces coated with a fine layer of dust. The carved mahogany wainscot and wood moldings created a reverential air, while the pervasive silence added to an impression of time frozen in place. None of the rooms looked lived in.

"I was in the study when I heard the chimes. I thought you might have been the mailman, just a little early," she said. "Good thing you didn't knock. I never would have heard you."

"Right, just us ink-stained wretches," Blackwood said, ignoring the smug "I told you so" look on his cousin's face.

Sabrina shot Blackwood another fey grin, flashing a perfect row of white teeth. Revealed against the amber light of the wood-paneled rooms, she reminded Blackwood of a fairy — breezy, curious and a twee mischievous, perhaps.

"Want some coffee? Newspeople live on coffee, right?" she asked, tossing the question over a shoulder. Ahead of them, the entrance to the kitchen beckoned.

Blackwood studied Sabrina as she strolled into the large, airy space. Her swept-back hair only accentuated the delicate tips of each ear, curved like little question marks. Her sartorial tastes ran to what Blackwood would call "biker chic" — a tasteful black leather jacket, a fleece pullover the color of sun-kissed pollen and a black leather vest. Thick, rolled-over skier's socks topped off black stirrup pants tucked into a pair of leather boots. The form-fitting hug of the fabric stenciled the firm muscles of her calves and thighs.

Sabrina pointed to a long wooden table in the middle of the kitchen. Ristras — strands of red and green chiles and garlic bulbs — dangled from blunted hooks sunk in the wall. Several copper-bottomed pots orbited just above a pitted butcher block. A heavy, old-fashioned gas range glowered against the far wall like Vulcan's forgotten forge.

"I'm not a bad cook, but I hardly ever come in here," Sabrina admitted as her guests settled themselves into a pair of stiff-backed chairs as timeworn as the table. A leg on Blackwood's measured a hair short, so it rocked a little every time he shifted his weight.

"This is the undisputed realm of Consuelo, our — my — housekeeper."

Blackwood couldn't help but notice the quick shift of pronouns.

"She makes the best *enchiladas verdes* in the city, bar none," Sabrina continued. "She's been here as long as I can remember. Her pork tamales every Christmas can't be beat. Remind me to give you some before you leave."

Sabrina hovered over a gleaming chrome-and-glass coffee press, futuristic enough to belong on a space station.

"What's your poison? We've got Irish mocha, cafe amaretto, French roast—."

"French roast is fine," Blackwood said.

"Anything black and hot," McGowan seconded.

"French roast it is," she said.

With precise, economical movements, Sabrina flowed around the kitchen, preparing the coffee.

"It'll be ready in a minute," she told them, twisting a dial on the stove. A burner under the kettle whooshed to life.

She sat down at the head of the table, slipping a pack of Virginia Slims from her jacket.

"My first this morning," she proudly said, tapping a slender cigarette against the tabletop. "Actually, I'm trying to cut down, but with everything that's happened lately, well, you know. Old habits die hard."

She shrugged, as if neither expecting nor seeking approval. A second later, she nodded in Blackwood's direction.

"Is that a pipe, Mr. Blackwood?" She pointed to the stem sticking out of his coat. "Feel free to light up."

"If you insist," he said.

She watched him retrieve the battered briar and tamp a wad of tobacco into the bowl. Fishing in his pocket, he extracted a yellow box of Swan Vestas and lit a match, touching the flame to the springy plug of cavendish. The soft glow in Sabrina's eyes reflected the glare of the burning phosphorous, like sunshine glinting off an iceberg. Those same cool, appraising orbs rose as she watched gray smoke rings float past his sharp cheekbones to the high ceiling.

"Quite a little ritual," she said.

Blackwood shrugged, not sure why her scrutiny left him feeling self-conscious. Without a word, she reached over, plucked the still-burning match from his fingers and touched her cigarette. As the fibers crackled to glowing life, she blew a smoke ring that passed through his.

"Thanks," Sabrina said nonchalantly, as though she did this sort of thing every day.

Visibly impressed, Blackwood's thin eyebrows lifted.

The kettle began to sing. Sabrina rose from the table, lithe as a puma. She poured the boiling water into the coffee press, waited a minute for the mixture to steep and then pushed down the plunger. The aroma of perfectly brewed coffee flooded the kitchen. Opening a cabinet door, she located three mugs and tipped the press over each. Being careful not to burn herself, she picked up the cups and delivered them to her visitors.

"Powdered cream, sugar and sweetener are on the table," she said after depositing the mugs in front of her guests. "If you want, milk and half-and-half are in the fridge."

She tentatively sniffed the air.

"Mmm... that tobacco smells wonderful. Reminds me of pancakes and Sunday mornings."

Blackwood nodded, but didn't add anything to the conversation. Sabrina resumed her seat and caught him scrutinizing the design on his cup, which represented some ancient Mayan or Aztec deity.

"I got that at the gift shop where I work," she said.

"You're employed at a gift shop?" Blackwood said, befuddled. "I thought you —."

She drummed balled fists on either side of her head.

"Sorry, sorry," she said. "Not making myself very clear, am I? The gift shop in the museum where I work, that's what I meant."

"Ah, I see," Blackwood said, then added sympathetically: "The Anderson Museum, which you now direct after the death of your grandmother, Mimi Anderson."

He took a breath.

"Our condolences."

She bowed her head, a shadow darkening her features. When she looked at him again, flecks of moisture clung to her lashes. Sabrina wiped them with the back of a hand.

"Thank you," she said, then paused a beat. "I see you do your research."

Producing a tissue from a pocket, she dabbed at her eyes one more time. Straightening her back, Sabrina took a cautious sip from her cup and pursed her lips.

"So, what do you want to know?" she asked.

She gazed directly into his eyes, taking his measure.

Out came his notebook. He decided to be just as direct.

"What can you tell me about James Grant? I'm writing a story about his death. I understand you knew him."

Sabrina put down her mug and peered at the wood grain running the length of the table, as though she could read a message there no one else could decipher.

"James? Yes, I figured you weren't here to do a feature on our new exhibit, which we're unveiling in two days," Sabrina said, her leather jacket rustling as she moved in the chair. "It's called 'Myths and Magicks of Spanish Tejas,' by the way."

She added hastily, "That's 'magicks' with a k."

McGowan rumbled with a sound of appreciation.

"Catchy name," he acknowledged. "I like it."

"Thank you," she said. Then she regarded Blackwood again.

"So you want to know about James? All I can tell you is that he was negotiating on behalf of his employer, Tobias Revnant, to buy a relic from the museum, a very rare, 800-year-old artifact, which is in fact the centerpiece of this exhibit," she said. "Our discussions ended—abruptly—a couple of days ago, after I repeatedly told him I wouldn't sell to his company. I haven't heard from him since."

Listening to her, Blackwood detected just the hint of a Texas accent, very urbanized, with the r's rolled soft or even missing, and vowels often dropped from the small connective words, like "th'" for "the." Still, years of travel to all those dig sites had beaten the twang out of her vocal chords, unlike his cousin, whose boisterous speech — born of open skies and windblown plains so flat you could watch a dog run away for a week — tended to be peppered with phrases such as "y'all" and "I guaran-damn-tee it."

Sabrina's expression turned sad and tired in the same second, as if that's how she'd really felt all along, and the little tour through the house, brewing coffee and the confident attitude had all just been part of an elaborate performance to hide some deeper pain.

Blackwood gave her a searching look.

"What else can you reveal about these negotiations?" he said.

Her chin rose and she took a long drag on the cigarette. Before she could answer, McGowan wondered aloud if he could shoot her picture. She shrugged.

"I'll probably break your camera," Sabrina said.

"Not likely," McGowan said with a bearish grin, getting to his feet and snapping off a few frames.

"Before I say anything else, is this going to be in the newspaper?" she asked her other guest. Sabrina seemed unconcerned about the photographer hovering just inches away.

"Yes," Blackwood said, purposely avoiding any questions about whether she wanted to be quoted.

She slipped into thought for a moment.

"OK, but the museum board will be mortified. They don't like anything that hints of scandal. The directors are a stuffy crowd. And, like I mentioned, we have a big event coming up, this new exhibit. We've been advertising ... radio, television, even your newspaper."

Sabrina placed her chin in her hands, sliding a delicate pinky nail between those even white teeth, and narrowed her eyes. She gave him another long stare.

"But, they say bad publicity is better than no publicity at all, isn't that right, Mr. Blackwood?"

"That is what they say," Blackwood answered.

McGowan finished clicking away and reclaimed his seat.

Crossing her legs, Sabrina cupped a knee in her hands.

"Let me give you some background. It may be helpful. When Mimi — my gram — passed, the board asked me to take over. I was in the Yucatan on a dig. I caught the first flight back and the board named me interim director an hour after I landed. Reluctantly, I accepted. Just doing my family duty, I guess. Frankly, I'm hoping when my great-aunt returns from abroad, she'll take the job. I'm not really the sit-behind-a-desk type."

Sabrina gave a final puff and finished the cigarette by crushing it in an ashtray shaped like Texas.

"I had barely moved into Mimi's office when James Grant showed up, three weeks ahead of an Akel-Dama corporate advance team. He said the company was relocating to San Antonio and wanted to create a good first impression. 'Become a better corporate citizen,' that's how he phrased it. They wanted to buy the artifact I mentioned in exchange for underwriting the entire exhibit. Revnant planned to transfer the relic to his private collection and have an exact replica created for the museum."

She cast a sidelong glance at the wall.

"I didn't like James at first," she admitted. "There was something, well, kinda creepy about him. And he wore the most expensive suits; kind of a showoff."

A wistful smile creased her face.

"But he grows on you, I guess. He could be very sweet. James knew quite a bit about the Spanish colonial or missionary period. His knowledge rivaled my gram's. We went to dinner a couple of times, had some drinks, but nothing serious. He was new in town, you know? And I hadn't been home in a long time, so I guess I was new, too."

Blackwood carefully formulated his next inquiry.

"I must ask: Did Grant have any enemies? Ever mention anything about being in trouble with someone?"

Her eyes closed and hands fluttered to her face.

"No, no. Never. Not to me, anyway," she whispered. A choked sob escaped her. "I can't believe he's dead."

Sabrina pressed her lips so tight the reporter worried they might bleed. Eventually she vented a deep breath and ran a hand through her hair. Visibly struggling to calm herself, she picked up the Virginia Slims lying on the table and eyed the pack.

The reporter shifted his line of questioning to her negotiations with Grant.

"What led him to your museum?" Blackwood asked.

Regaining her composure, Sabrina won the battle against temptation and lowered the pack. Taking a breath, she started to fill in the blanks for Blackwood.

"At some point, Tobias Revnant — for whatever reason — developed a keen interest in 17th and 18th century vice-regal Spanish artifacts; the type of pieces produced in the New World or brought here by the Spanish Empire. Because of James' specialized knowledge, as well as his legal training, Mr. Revnant sent him on 'fishing expeditions.' James traveled extensively visiting collectors, museums, universities, dig sites; anyone who might have what Mr. Revnant searched for."

As she spoke, Blackwood made a connection.

So that explains why Grant described himself as an acquisitions specialist.

"James told me Akel-Dama owned land in New Mexico where they conducted laser-guidance tests for a military targeting system, a remote place that came with the ruins of a very old and forgotten church. Catacombs under the sanctuary contained mummified remains preserved by the desert air. A group of Akel-Dama technicians stumbled across a sealed letter in one of those crypts that pointed to the existence of an extremely important artifact buried right here in San Antonio, near Mission San Jose."

A cloud slid across her features.

"As it turns out, that document contained information on the very relic Tobias Revnant had spent years looking for. There was only one problem."

She paused, and Blackwood took a shot in the dark with his next question.

"Your father already discovered the relic Revnant wanted at Mission San Jose, hadn't he? That's what cost your parents their lives."

He removed his pipe and took a tentative sip of the coffee, then replaced the mug on the table, awaiting her answer.

Her gaze drifted to the frosted window above the tiled sink, but her eyes seemed to be looking at something more distant.

"Yes, my dad discovered the artifact years earlier and it was already in possession of the Anderson. To complicate matters, my grandmother left precise instructions in her will the museum was not to part with this — relic — for any reason whatsoever."

There was a slight pause. "She never explained why. For twenty-five years the relic remained in the basement vault under lock and key, where I found it only after the reading of Mimi's will. I knew about it, of course, but the first time I ever laid eyes on the object was just after her death."

As she spoke, Sabrina's fingers hesitantly grasped a metal chain looped around her throat. She withdrew a key and stared at it for a few seconds, then met Blackwood's gaze.

She didn't need to say anything. He already sensed what the key unlocked.

"How did your grandmother gain possession?" he asked.

She glanced at her nails, holding them at arm's length as her head dipped down. Though the rest of her looked like she'd just stepped away from a fashion shoot, Blackwood wondered about the unadorned nails with the blunt ends. But then again, he reasoned, a manicure wouldn't last long at an excavation prying pottery shards and old bones from stubborn soil.

She lifted features chiseled by mourning.

"My grandmother owned the land outside the mission, where my dad and his team conducted their excavations," she said in a low voice. "My dad talked her into buying the parcel. He didn't want the church having any claim to his discovery. Mimi regretted that decision the rest of her life."

"This thing made you an orphan, and you're putting it on display?" McGowan interjected, incredulous.

She didn't seem surprised by his reaction.

"The museum is in dire need of a financial shot in the arm, gentlemen. For legal reasons, I can't dip into my family's personal oil fortune to prop it up, so I had to find another source of revenue."

When she spoke next, the whiff of desperation in her tone gave way to unmistakable pride.

"You need to understand: My grandmother dedicated her life to locating artifacts that reflect the 500 years of European exploration in the Southwest. She wanted to make history accessible to the general public, make it alive and real and not just boring words in some textbook. More than 600 works of art recovered or donated from architectural sites, other museums, churches and private collections here in the States, Mexico, South America and Europe are curated at the Anderson."

She allowed her voice to float off, a faraway expression on her face. Then she took up the thread of her narrative again.

"As I've mentioned, the relic is the heart of the new exhibit, the centerpiece of 'Myths & Magicks of Spanish Tejas.' For now, we're not revealing the exact nature of the artifact until the grand opening. We've only been offering broad hints in the marketing campaign," she said.

McGowan nodded with approval.

"Kinda building the suspense, the mystery," he said, slurping his coffee. "Smart of y'all."

"Exactly," Sabrina said. "Creating a sense of anticipation."

"Again, I like it," the photographer said in solidarity.

Blackwood waited with an impassive expression for the mutual-admiration session to conclude. Sabrina turned to face him.

"Akel-Dama wanted the artifact. Wanted it badly. James — well, his company — kept throwing more and more money at me— ungodly amounts—but I kept saying no," Sabrina said.

She brought her hands together around the coffee mug and stared over the rim.

"Lately, things have been a little rough for the Anderson. Mimi's death didn't help, but on top of that, attendance is down. People today, especially kids, aren't as interested in traditional museums as they used to be. Stuffed animals and suits of armor just can't compete with video games and Hollywood blockbusters with special effects."

The point of her chin rose.

"But this new exhibit might just turn things around."

"If the museum is in such dire straits, why not just sell the artifact to Revnant?" Blackwood asked.

Sabrina made a little noise in her throat.

"You're forgetting the provision in my grandmother's will. Pawning off the relic is not legally possible. There would be recriminations both for myself personally and for the museum."

"Still, aren't you defying your grandmother's final wishes by putting this relic on display?" Blackwood pressed.

Sabrina glanced up, appearing a little taken aback by the query.

"Not in the least," she said, a prim tone surfacing, almost defensive.

She picked up a small silver spoon, contemplated her reflection for a moment in the metal, then stirred her coffee.

"Mimi's will stipulates the relic can't leave the museum grounds," she said. "And it won't. I just took it from the vault and moved it upstairs for the exhibit, where it can do some good. I've got a lot of employees who depend on the museum to feed their families and pay their bills. The Anderson is a cornerstone of San Antonio culture; it needs to stay afloat. I'm banking on this new exhibit to do just that."

Her answer sounded rehearsed, a little too pat, as though she had turned this very thought over in her mind for quite some time to justify her actions.

After considering her reply, Blackwood moved on with a follow-up question.

"So you must have found some local sponsors with no strings attached?"

"Oh, we did — Mimi left this mortal coil with a few people still owing her some big favors," she answered. "Alamo Bancshares eventually coughed up some funding. My great-grandfather, the oil baron Holden Bergheim Anderson, was one of the founders."

Picking up the pack of cigarettes resting on the table, Sabrina gave it a penetrating look. With a frown, she put the box back down.

Her eyes shifted from Blackwood to McGowan and back to Blackwood.

"But if your grandmother kept the relic a secret all these years, how did Revnant learn it was housed in your museum? Or Grant?" the reporter asked.

"Revnant has deep pockets, Mr. Blackwood," Sabrina said. "Given his connections in government and business, I doubt very much escapes his notice. Or maybe James learned the details first and reported back to him. Maybe he heard about the relic from the old court case, which I assume you looked up. James was a lawyer, after all. He would have been able to dig up the files after the lawsuit was settled all those years ago."

Blackwood put down his pen, rubbed the bridge of his knuckles and then looked at her head on.

"The newspaper stories never mentioned the true nature of this 'relic.' And the court documents were sealed after the undisclosed settlement was reached. Revnant must have made some educated guesses — or paid somebody off," Blackwood said, flipping a page in the notebook. "So what exactly is this artifact?"

A look of caution rose on her expression and he quickly added, "You have my word I won't mention it—for now—in my story, but I must know, if only for my own records."

Sabrina's shoulders relaxed a smidgen; his reply seemed to offer the reassurance she needed to hear. One of his talents was getting people to trust him in short order, which explained why Blackwood had become the newspaper's best interviewer.

Evidently he'd won her over. For now, at least.

"A book," she said, her reply unequivocal and direct. "An indecipherable, timeless book written in gibberish that has no discernible literary value. One that has resisted all efforts at translation. Yet it was considered so heretical the Catholic Church hid the book on the far-flung Spanish frontier under guard by an army of priests and soldiers."

Her last statement drew a curious stare from Blackwood.

"Why showcase a book with no value?" he wondered aloud.

She challenged his gaze with a direct look of her own.

"I said no apparent literary worth, Mr. Blackwood," she answered. "But it has plenty of historical value, not to mention its potential benefit as an object of pure curiosity. Perhaps even legendary. And that's what the museum is counting on. We want to draw people to the exhibit like moths to a flame."

Blackwood leaned forward.

"And how are you going to do that?"

"We're selling this as the discovery of a reputedly heretical work banned by the church. A book that so terrified Rome the pope ordered the king of Spain to get rid of it in the New World."

She stared at both visitors, steel flashing in her blue eyes.

"I'm hoping the exhibit puts the Anderson solidly back in the black," she said.

McGowan drained his coffee.

"Must be one hell of a book," he said.

"You don't know the half of it," Sabrina responded. "I don't suppose you've ever heard of 'The Covenant of the Cursed'?"

McGowan answered with a blank stare. Blackwood took a slow sip of coffee.

"I have," he said.

CHAPTER FIFTEEN

The air seemed to rush out of the room. Sabrina kept her silence for several seconds, then tilted her head back and rubbed her temples.

"You've actually heard the name?" she asked, not bothering to hide her surprise. Her demeanor became deadly serious.

Her next query sounded more like a demand: "Where?"

The single word hit like a jab to the chest. Blackwood paused, thinking carefully before answering. He couldn't reveal he'd violated a crime scene, but he needed to come clean on a few details to maintain her trust.

The woman had been through a lot lately; he didn't want to add to her troubles—or create any for himself.

"I don't know how much Capt. Gruene told you about the scene where Grant died, but a postcard found at his car listed three names — mine, yours and the priest who pulled your mother from the cave-in: Father Louis Dragoti."

She regarded him with a cool stare.

"Interesting. I recognize Father Dragoti's name, of course. When I was a little girl, Mimi told me he saved my life. We can discuss that later. Right now, I want to know how you learned the title of the relic. That's a closely guarded museum secret."

Her tone remained insistent.

"Go on," she urged.

"Also written on the card was the phrase 'Covenant of the Cursed.' Nothing more," Blackwood continued. "I had no inkling as to the meaning until now."

He tried to keep his face expressionless. "You just confirmed it for me."

Sabrina lit another Virginia Slims, trying to hide both her irritation and admiration at the effortless way he'd just coaxed the equivalent of a confession from her.

Her eyes rose and she gazed at him expectantly.

"What else?" she prompted.

"That's all I know," Blackwood said, throwing up his palms in a show of innocence. "You needn't worry about any leaks regarding your exhibit. That card is evidence and I doubt the police will be releasing its contents."

He tried smiling, but Sabrina countered with a stony gaze.

"And you? Will your story reveal the title before the exhibit opens?" she asked.

She tamped ashes from the cigarette, eyebrows raised.

"No. I'm writing about Grant's death, not here to violate trade secrets," he said. "I'm a police-beat reporter, not a features writer."

She studied him wordlessly for a few more seconds, but Blackwood's answer seemed to mollify her. The red apples flaring in her cheeks lost some of their luster. After a second, her brow loosened and the corners of her mouth smoothed out.

He pushed on.

"I say, that's a rather strange name — 'The Covenant of the Cursed,'" he said.

"Agreed — and that's only one of the titles," she said.

The conversation led Sabrina to mentally review her perusal of the book last night and the strange effect it had upon her. She grew unnaturally quiet. Blackwood saw the shiver that softly rattled her frame.

She moved her chair back a few inches, scraping the floor. Despite her best efforts, a low gasp escaped her throat as visions of those strange, incoherent characters on the pages danced and twisted once more before her mind's eye. Taking a deep gulp, she pushed away the memory, hallucination, whatever it was, then began rubbing both hands vigorously. Not to warm them but almost as though performing an unconscious act of cleansing. Finally, after several seconds, she glanced apologetically at her visitors, whistled a low breath between clenched teeth and put hands in her lap to still them.

Sabrina opened her mouth slowly, working to get her voice under control.

"In the vulgate, it is called 'The Covenant of the Cursed,'" she said, taking another breath. "My father's research confirmed the pages were illuminated — copied — by the mad French monk Pierre DeGulliot in the 13th century from fragments brought back decades earlier by crusaders returning from the Holy Land."

The wind outside picked up speed, nosing around the house like a hungry wolf. Blackwood moved closer to the table and regarded Sabrina over hands clasped around his mug.

"What about Bishop Virgil Elizondo? That was his diary they discovered in New Mexico, wasn't it?" he said.

The question produced another raised eyebrow.

"My, my ... Bishop Elizondo. You know about him, too? You really do your research, Mr. Blackwood."

"John," he said, weighing whether her assessment praised or denigrated him. "John is fine. And yes, I do my research. The stories in the Tribune's clips about the lawsuit mentioned the bishop. No surprise there."

Sabrina gave him a searching stare.

"Yes, it was Bishop Elizondo's journal the technicians found in the crypts of the abandoned church. My father possessed a copy, 'liberated' somehow from the Vatican Apostolic Archive."

She tapped more ashes into the ceramic Texas tray and gave him an appreciative nod.

"'*Pactum est Maledictus*,'" she announced in a matter-of-fact voice. She noted the way Blackwood's forehead knit in studious concentration as he attempted to decipher the title.

She made things easier.

"'The Covenant of the Cursed' in Latin. That's the official, sanctioned named the church gave this unsanctioned text — '*Pactum est Maledictus*.'"

She curled a strand of hair behind an ear. Around the kitchen, shadows lengthened as morning stretched into afternoon, though the snow-choked skies made it difficult to tell where one started and the other ended.

"Bishop Elizondo wrote that the *Pactum est Maledictus* contained 'a curse to freeze the soul of the world,'" she explained.

"A curse?" McGowan murmured.

Weaving a smoke trail in the air with her cigarette, Sabrina provided an explanation.

"To our ears, it probably sounds like superstitious nonsense, but trust me, the matter was deathly serious to the bishop," she said. "The more he learned over time, the more frightened he became. He had a vision once, or a nightmare, connected to that book. All he could remember was the phrase, 'Break the circle.' It's unfortunate, but he never explained the meaning."

An electric jolt arced through Blackwood upon hearing "break the circle."

"Break the circle?" he repeated, unable to keep his voice from quivering. Sabrina nodded, scrutinizing his worried expression and the way his jaw hardened.

"Break the circle," she echoed.

He jotted down the words and circled them several times, pushing so hard his pen punched through the paper.

"Bizarre," he said, trying to keep his voice level. "Grant used a similar phrase when he rang me."

The words were burned into his brain.

"We must keep them from breaking the circle."

And not just Grant. Remember what Malory blurted out?

How could he forget?

Ice coursed through Blackwood's veins. Beneath his feet, he felt a cosmic wheel turn, another tumbler falling into place. The room grew very quiet and he repressed a shudder. From across the table, Sabrina met his slate-gray eyes and tipped her forehead.

"It's not surprising James mentioned that phrase," she said. "He did his research, too."

Blackwood's pipe had gone out, but he didn't notice.

"Grant specifically said someone had to be stopped before they broke this circle," he said.

McGowan clinked a spoon against his cup.

"Ain't that what 'el loco' doctor said at the hospital last night? Somethin' about being commanded to break a circle?"

He regarded Blackwood.

"What's that?" Sabrina asked, also staring at the reporter.

Blackwood frowned. He'd assumed Sabrina knew about the siege, but he had to remember not everybody read the paper first thing or turned on the news the minute they woke up. In a few words, he filled her in on the hostage situation.

"That's weird," she remarked when he finished. "Could James have known this guy?"

Blackwood's gaze circled the kitchen before answering.

"I rather hoped you'd know."

Sabrina's head moved back and forth, a puzzled look stamped on her face.

"If James knew Dr. Malory, he never mentioned it."

Looking frustrated, Blackwood peeked at his Mickey Mouse timepiece, the seconds ticking away. If he planned to make the afternoon deadline for the Sunday editions, he would have to put aside the matter of a possible Malory-Grant acquaintanceship and move on to his next question.

There would be time for more inquiries — more stories — later.

"How did your grandmother gain possession of the book?"

Sabrina shot him a blank stare.

"I thought Texas had laws about the recovery of historical objects. Why didn't the book end up in a state museum or archive?" he added.

"Didn't I mention Mimi bought the land?" Sabrina said in a low tone. "In Texas, believe it or not, there are no laws safeguarding archaeological sites on private property. Except for human remains, relics discovered on private land belong to the owner, who then determines the disposition of the object or objects. Thus, my grandmother had first dibs."

Blackwood considered her statement.

"But didn't the university fund the excavation?"

The corners of Sabrina's eyes tightened.

"After the lawsuit was filed, the university wanted nothing to do with the artifact. They probably wouldn't have cared if Mimi tossed it back in that hole and blew up the entrance."

Blackwood gazed at her.

"Did your grandmother recover anything else?"

"Just a 300-year-old chest carved from black oak," Sabrina said. "Somewhat well-preserved even after the explosion, but otherwise unremarkable. We think it held the book."

She caught his curious stare.

"It's not the box I care about — John. Since returning home, I've spent hours studying the book," she said. "I was looking for a clue as to why Revnant was so keen to get his hands on it. James played those cards close to his chest, though. I never did learn the reason."

Blackwood said nothing, but he harbored no doubts that whatever had alarmed Grant — and perhaps got him killed — revolved around this mysterious book.

Sabrina considered something he'd mentioned earlier.

"You brought up Father Dragoti. Like I said, my gram mentioned him sometimes."

He studied her hair, which glowed in defiance of the reluctant light admitted by the window.

"I suppose I should be grateful to him for saving my life, but I've never formally met Father Dragoti. Is he even alive?"

Blackwood caught himself still staring at the gauzy, golden nimbus around her head and snapped back to the interview.

"I'm trying to sort that out myself," he said, perhaps too quickly. "I know the Archdiocese sent him out of country before the trial started. Did Grant ever mention him?"

Sabrina wrinkled her brow, once again racking her brains.

"Honestly, not that I recall. But it can't be a coincidence his name was on that card. James was very methodical, if nothing else."

She smiled ruefully. Blackwood tapped his chin with a thumb.

"Hazard a guess?" he asked.

After pondering his question, she shrugged.

"James must have contacted Father Dragoti about the relic. The priest undoubtedly knows something. I mean, why would he warn my father to shut down the excavation? Mimi also talked about that."

She cast a long glance out the window again, allowing the conversation to hit a lull. Then she resumed speaking.

"If James met with Father Dragoti, or learned anything from him, it's a mystery to me."

Her blue eyes glowed as she scanned him up and down.

His mind leapt ahead. Blackwood turned the pad over and started writing on the blank backs of the pages.

"Is there anything else you can tell us?"

The lines of her mouth narrowed.

"Well, after going through Mimi's papers, I learned she conducted extensive research on the book. She kept the relic's existence a secret, but made a few discreet inquiries with some linguists and etymologists, anthropologists and a couple of other 'ologists.' She mailed facsimiles of pages to them, but not one of the specialists could make heads or tails of the words, if that's what they are. There's no Rosetta Stone for this thing."

She idly traced a finger around the whorls of the old table.

"I'm guessing that one day, after years of banging her head against the proverbial wall, my grandmother convinced herself the whole thing was just an elaborate hoax. Maybe that's why she locked the artifact away and forgot about it."

She raised and waved the finger, a hint of bewilderment in her voice.

"Yet there's something about the relic that must have made her … well, apprehensive."

"How so?" said Blackwood, his face alight with curiosity. Sabrina hesitated before replying.

"When I first entered the vault, I found religious symbols — crosses and the like — hanging on the walls, and the book and the chest were circled by a ring of salt. There were also some words drawn on the wall I didn't recognize. Three of them; Hebrew, perhaps."

Both Blackwood and McGowan exchanged startled expressions. Toying with the key around her neck, Sabrina shrugged and shared a troubled glance with them.

Her statement brought to Blackwood's mind the crosses and Stars of David the police found in Grant's apartment. What connection, if any, existed between the two, he couldn't begin to fathom. He drew a big question mark in his notebook.

McGowan posed the next inquiry.

"Why salt?"

"Ancient beliefs say a circle of salt keeps evil spirits away," she said.

Her voice, tinged with regret, became husky.

"The whole thing's a pity, really; Mimi was so certain she had a major discovery on her hands. She absolutely wanted to break new scientific ground. She wanted her daughter's death—my mother's — not to be in vain."

Sabrina rested folded hands on the table.

"Mimi studied other ancillary works, manifests drafted by the imperial Spanish government and liturgical documents left by the church. A few contained scattered, tantalizing references to a book of forbidden knowledge, hinting at alchemies and heresies," she said.

Her voice trailed off.

"So that's where the idea for the exhibit came from," Blackwood said, filling his pipe again. A match flared to life and caught the tobacco.

Sabrina watched the dancing smoke rise to the ceiling before replying.

"It suggested a theme of a cursed or haunted book, yes," Sabrina answered. "I agreed to the promotion after consulting with our marketing department, but I'm a scientist. I don't believe in that kind of stuff."

"But it sells tickets," McGowan offered.

Sabrina didn't dispute the point, just gave a tacit nod of her head.

Blackwood shifted in his chair, which creaked as he leaned back and stared at the ceiling.

"Still, you said something about the book made your grandmother apprehensive," he said, leveling his gaze. "Why else would there be the religious icons and the salt?"

Silence filled the room again, except for the wind outside, before Sabrina answered.

"In his journal, Bishop Elizondo kept insisting the book harbored something impure and vile, even though he couldn't translate a single sentence."

Catching Blackwood's questioning look, she added, "Elizondo and the relic had a long, dark association. When the soldiers and priests transporting the tome arrived back in, oh, 1736, he was the one who demanded it be sealed in the cave, outside the mission, beyond sanctified ground."

Planting elbows on the table, she offered a bitter smile.

"Later, the bishop went into seclusion at the monastery in New Mexico, taking a vow of silence. He died there."

She stood up, glided to the sink and rinsed her empty cup.

A second later, she returned to the table, her boots clicking on the tiles.

"You're British, I can tell," she said to Blackwood. She faced McGowan. "What's your story, cowboy? You sound local."

The photographer chuckled. "We're cousins, but I'm not as fancy as the perfessor here. I'm from West Texas, salt-of-the-earth folk. Ranchers. Our dads are brothers."

Turning and jabbing a finger in Blackwood's direction, she asked, "Then why does he speak with an accent?"

Blackwood tried not to bristle at the mention of an "accent." McGowan took a sip of coffee before answering.

"His dad was an Air Force pilot. Uncle Hampton met his mom –."

"Mum," Blackwood quietly corrected.

"—Mom," McGowan said with extra emphasis, "when he was stationed in the UK. M'boy Spanky here was born there."

Sabrina did a double-take and peered closely at the pair, clearly trying to detect a family resemblance.

"Hmmm ... Well, yes, I can tell you both have the same nose. Cousins? Imagine that," she said.

Sabrina gave them both another inspection.

"Well, cousins, don't forget the big event. The exhibit opens in two days in the Spanish Colonial wing, curated as part of the San Jose collection."

She offered Blackwood a sideways glance.

"You two should come to the preview party. It's at seven tomorrow night. Be warned—it's black tie. I'll put you on the VIP list."

Blackwood shot her a look of mock panic.

"Can't say with any certainty that I own a dinner jacket." He glanced at McGowan, who caught his drift.

"Well, y'all, I got a clean pair of jeans and shiny new boots," McGowan drawled. "Don't that count as dressin' fancy?"

Sabrina giggled.

"Believe me, I know how you feel," she agreed, pointing both forefingers at herself. "I'm not much on dressing up myself, as you can see. Just do your best."

The lighthearted moment passed. Her hands began to tremble and she covered her face, locking fingers.

"Poor James. Who would do this?" she said, lowering her hands to reveal a lost expression.

She gave Blackwood an imploring look.

"That's what I hope to find out," he answered.

Sabrina brushed at the corners of her eyes and smiled weakly.

"I know he was upset after I found another underwriter for the exhibit, but I still wanted to be friends. I even promised to go with him to look at a house he was sizing up for Mr. Revnant."

Busy inspecting his notes, Blackwood barely heard her, but McGowan, being polite, asked: "Oh? Whereabouts is that?"

The window over the kitchen sink darkened as clouds bloated with snow lumbered across the sky. Their muted light rolled along the crinkled surface of Sabrina's jacket like moonlight skimming a wavy sea.

"Oh, it's just an old place here in the neighborhood," she answered. "Just a few blocks away, actually. Creepy old mansion some say is haunted. It's called the Birkenstadt Haus."

Blackwood's jaw fell to the floor. He almost dropped the coffee cup half-raised to his lips.

"Pardon?" he spluttered.

CHAPTER SIXTEEN

Somehow, Sabrina talked the newsmen into letting her drive them to the Birkenstadt Haus. She presented a convincing argument: She'd grown up in the neighborhood, she knew a shortcut, she'd been inside once on a dare years ago and she'd planned to go there anyway with Grant.

"I'm the perfect tour guide," she informed them. "And I won't charge you."

After a few halfhearted attempts to dissuade her, Blackwood relented and McGowan actually seemed to enjoy the prospect. They headed out in Sabrina's Land Rover, one of the old-fashioned, sturdy models Blackwood recalled from innumerable jaunts during shearing time at a cousin's sheep farm in mid-Wales.

On the way, Blackwood related what Gruene revealed last night: Ben Wade, the real estate agent from Alamo Metro Home Sales, had more than likely taken Dr. Malory and his family to preview the Birkenstadt Haus. He explained to Sabrina that in the wake of the hospital incident, both Wade and Malory's family remained unaccounted for. From what Gruene told him, no one from the homicide unit had gotten over to the Birkenstadt Haus yet to confirm they'd been there. The case was only a few hours old, after all, and any officer who could have conducted a patrol-by was probably tied up on calls related to the freakish weather.

The detective assigned to the case — Galvan — also was probably still taking a statement from Grant's boss, Revnant. But, patience was not one of Blackwood's virtues when a story deadline loomed, so he resolved in Sabrina's kitchen there was no time like the present to visit the old place. The police could get to it when they had time; he didn't.

As they drove, day became night under massed clouds dark as smoke, even though the dashboard clock read early afternoon. The trees along the way assumed odd, feverish shapes, as though stripped, bent and twisted by the hands of a doomed sculptor.

Blackwood sat up front. McGowan, perched in the back, thrust his shaggy head between the seats.

"So what's the yarn behind this place?" he asked Sabrina.

Their driver, who clearly relished her role as a tale-spinner captivating the professional storytellers in her presence, softened her voice to a theatrical whisper.

"Well, I can't say I know the full story, but I'll tell you what I remember. I heard the tale a long time ago from Mimi."

Both men gave Sabrina their full attention.

"The story begins with a German brewer, Gustave Birkenstadt, who immigrated with the Prince Karl group in the 1840s to establish the Adelsverein — a German colony in Texas. He's the one who built the brewery that's still downtown on the river."

McGowan grimaced.

"You mean Texas Gold Star? That stuff's horse piss," he said.

Sabrina snorted. "That's what the beer company is called today, after multiple mergers and acquisitions. I forget the original name. Anyway, he also built a mansion on a cliff overlooking Olmos Basin. That's the Birkenstadt Haus. If you squint hard enough, you can see it from U.S. 281, just above the Olmos Dam."

She took a breath.

"Back then, the Birkenstadt Haus sat way out in the country. Today, it's virtually in the middle of the city. Everything grew up around it."

Blackwood spoke up.

"No surprise there. The basin is the geographic heart of San Antonio. The headwaters of the river originate there. The Spaniards built their missions along its banks."

Sabrina murmured a confirmation.

"Things were going great for old Gustave, at least at first. Then his wife became ill. Sadly, she didn't last long. She died from some wasting-away disease. Consumption, they called such things back then. Today, we'd say cancer. But Gustave's misfortunes had only just started. About three years later, his son was killed during a skirmish with Mexican soldiers. It's said the old German's grief drove him insane."

She shifted to a lower gear so the Land Rover could handle an icy incline. Then she turned into an alley running behind a row of ornate Queen Anne homes, their gables dusted with snow to resemble decorations on a cake. Strings of blinking Christmas lights draped each home.

"The legends say Herr Birkenstadt began consulting with shamans and brujas, seeking a path to the dark arts," Sabrina said, her head turning to admire the decorations as they drove past.

"To what end?" interjected Blackwood, scrunching his forehead.

"Why, he wanted to bring his son back from the dead. His wife too, maybe, though the stories never really say," Sabrina said. "Over time, folks saw less and less of the brewer, until eventually he disappeared altogether. It's as though he vanished into thin air."

McGowan released a long breath.

"Good story, but what really happened?"

Sabrina glanced at him, her brows contracting.

"There are limestone caves running the length and breadth of the Olmos Basin," she said, "that are quite deep and mostly unknown. They're under the mansion, too. Take it from an archaeologist, the few tunnels that have been explored have yielded a treasure trove of artifacts offering ample evidence that humans have inhabited this area for at least ten thousand years. Millennia before the Spanish set foot in the New World, Native American tribes camped around the basin's springs and practiced their rituals in those caves. It always amuses me when people say the Europeans 'discovered' Texas. People lived here for thousands of years before the first Spanish expedition crossed the Rio Grande."

A faraway look came into her eyes.

"Into those same caverns, folks say, descended the brewer, where he attempted to summon unclean spirits to return his loved ones to the land of the living. No one knows what happened to Gustave, but it's been said his tortured soul still wanders those dark places snatching the unwary."

She vented a little chuckle. A hand left the steering wheel and waved dismissively.

"Of course, this is just an old wive's tale, something parents told their kids to make sure they didn't stay out too late."

A trace of scorn in her voice mocked those childhood fears. Still, Blackwood wondered just how much of the story she considered mere doggerel and how much fact? Experience had shown him there usually is a kernel of truth to most legends, no matter how outlandish.

"What about the Birkenstadt Haus now?" Blackwood said.

She shrugged. "Coming apart at the seams, last time I saw it. Abandoned for years. Anyone who moves in moves out soon after."

Blackwood reflected on this.

"What did Grant want with the place?" he said.

Sabrina spun the wheel to maneuver around an abandoned Volvo with a faded Clinton-Gore sticker plastered on the back bumper.

"I don't know. He just told me he had a couple of places Revnant wanted him to check out. I guess his boss is getting tired of living in penthouses."

Those lapis lazuli eyes darted to Blackwood.

"James loved local history, and this place oozes with it."

Soon they reached Argyle Lane, a long, narrow street running along the rim of the Olmos Bluffs like a scar down the back of a sleeping dragon. A few stately homes spaced far apart on large lots lined the road, the eaves girded by gleaming icicles.

Sabrina drew alongside the curb and braked. The trio's bundled forms clambered out as soon as the vehicle came to a complete stop. The breeze tugging at their exhaled breaths turned the plumes into white cats chasing their tails.

Above them, neglected and nearly forgotten, the brooding hulk men called the Birkenstadt Haus stood silhouetted against the swirls of a charcoal sky, looking like something out of an Edward Gorey print. Blackwood could sense decades of memories lurking behind those jagged windows, gathered in the shadows the way beetles cluster under a toppled headstone.

His stomach tightened in anxiety.

Sabrina bent down to adjust a leather strap on her motorcycle boot. Tugging hard, she closed a snap and bobbed her head.

"Let's get started," she said, getting to her feet. "I'm already freezing my you know what off."

A rusted iron gate stood open to the grounds. The men from the newspaper fell in step behind their guide, who strode through with a determined air. The knot forming in Blackwood's midsection hardened into a brick.

The reporter automatically cataloged their surroundings. The house appeared not so much an abandoned dwelling as a weather-stained accretion of blackened stone, shattered windows and rot-riddled boards rising three stories above the weed-choked grounds. Watery stains trailing down the walls created an impression the old pile constantly wept. Looming over the street like some beached, decaying sea beast, the mansion's antiquated rows of chimneys and rusted vents thrust into the frosty air in the manner of exposed ribs.

The three visitors trod a bricked path winding past an empty fountain, and then climbed steps to the front porch. The door appeared to be hewn from a solid block of aged walnut.

Blackwood's curious but guarded gaze roved up and down the house, which he supposed could best be described as gothic. Everything about the place felt wrong to him. Human hands may have built the house, fitted stone to stone, pounded nails and slotted boards, but over the years the dwelling transformed into something else, something that no longer belonged in this world. Not truly.

Had the Malorys really been interested in buying this old wreck, he wondered. Or this mystery man, Revnant? How could anyone want to live in such a place? The very air of the grounds smelled stale and rotten, as though piped from a tomb.

Around them all remained still. Not a single creature stirred nor uttered a sound; no birdsong, no barking of a neighbor's dog, not even the drone of traffic crawling along the expressway a half mile away, across the forested bowl formed by the Olmos Basin.

Sabrina tried the door. It wouldn't budge.

"Hmm... locked. Of course. Go to the back," she instructed. "That's how we'll get in."

Since she'd explored here as a child, Sabrina by silent agreement continued leading the way. The ground not covered with snow became wet and slippery. A light mist sprang up. The footing became precarious. Why some of the garden remained frozen and other parts boggy, Blackwood couldn't fathom. Then he recalled Sabrina mentioning caves under the cliff. Could heat vents or thermal springs deep beneath the house be the cause? That might explain both the thickening mist and the soft ground, which now squelched obscenely under his shoes.

"Heads up, everybody," Sabrina said, interrupting his thoughts. She pointed to the right, but nothing could be seen through the fog sliding like sheets of wet gossamer over the ground.

"Be careful," she warned. "There's a steep drop over there."

The mist parted, and Blackwood saw what she meant. Fifteen yards away, the property ended in a sheer cliff plummeting to the basin below. He craned his neck for a better look over the edge, but all he could see were the snow-dusted tops of heritage oaks, cedar elms and pecan trees.

"When I was a kid, there was a safety rail along the edge," Sabrina said, frowning. "I guess it rusted away."

A few steps later, she led them to a back porch converted into a long wraparound deck. Tattered screens vibrated in the wind, and the termite-burrowed wood reeked of damp and mold.

The fog rolled away long enough to reveal a sight out near the cliff that jolted Blackwood.

"What the hell?" he said with a gasp. He abruptly stopped just short of the porch, the mud gurgling as the icy morass clutched at his heels. McGowan rammed into his back.

"What's that?" the photographer asked, also catching a glimpse of the object in the haze. Peering intently into the gloom, Sabrina slipped wordlessly between the two men.

Wearing aghast expressions, the trio struggled to absorb the sight of a stone cross planted upside-down in the yielding earth. A light coating of snow dusted the craggy base and outstretched crosspiece.

McGowan sucked in his breath.

"Now that ain't right," he spat.

"That's not all," Blackwood quietly said. "Something's painted on it."

He jerked his gloved hand upwards.

In dripping red letters that couldn't be older than an hour or two, someone had scrawled "Sarvaelo est suelto."

Sabrina, her voice restrained, translated: 'Sarvael is loose.'"

Blackwood sensed her hovering behind his shoulder. Her breath tickled the back of his neck in warm, agitated bursts.

McGowan dropped his camera bag to the squishy ground with a plop. He began snapping off a series of shots.

Sabrina hunched up her shoulders, wearing a deeply troubled expression.

"Who would do such a thing? Vandals?" she asked. Apprehension dug furrows into her forehead. "And what's Sarvael? A gang? There are no gangs in this neighborhood."

Both turned expectant, questioning gazes to Blackwood. The reporter didn't have much to offer, but he knew one thing for certain — this was not the work of any gangbangers. In his extensive encounters with local street and prison elements, as well as an exhaustive mental reference of territorial graffiti or "tagging," he'd never heard of an outfit called "Sarvaelo," nor encountered any common gang committing such a desecration.

This reeked of something more malicious, more intentional. More — directed. Perhaps even at them, which left him feeling both perplexed and anxious.

"I haven't a clue," he finally answered. "This is a new one. Frankly, I don't think a gang did this."

He stole a glance at his Mickey Mouse watch, painfully aware of the approaching deadline for his article.

"I suggest we file this under 'to be investigated later' and move on," he said. "I'll do some digging after I turn in my story."

McGowan grunted his assent, bending down to slip his camera back in the bag. He closed and zippered the flap with a grim expression.

"Fine by me," Sabrina said, her voice remaining troubled.

Giving the upside-down cross one last distasteful glance, they trekked up wooden steps to the covered porch.

With a firm grip, Sabrina pulled open a rickety screen door and walked through, footfalls tattooing an unsettling creak. The wind pushed dead leaves that skittered like frightened mice across the warped floorboards. The structure appeared to be an add-on, Blackwood decided; the architecture appeared more 1940s than 1840s. Probably the corroded ceiling fans above their heads gave it away. No furniture existed, although someone at some point had paid a visit, as revealed by a cluster of empty Big Red cans next to a crumpled paper bag with a Taco Cabana logo.

Sabrina steered them to a closed door at the end of the enclosure. Sheafs of peeling paint turned the pitted surface into a sickened beast sloughing off decaying skin.

Her fleece-lined glove closed around the doorknob and rattled the tarnished brass fixture.

"Locked," she said. "No surprise there."

She shared a conspiratorial wink with the men.

"No problem," she said.

Sabrina's forefinger angled downward, pointing to a hinged wooden flap about three feet wide and knee high.

"That's how we get in?" Blackwood asked, eyeballing the diminutive aperture. "A bloody dog door?"

"Are you shittin' me?" McGowan chimed in.

The gloomy surroundings did't prevent Sabrina from grinning.

"I got in just fine when I was eleven," she informed the pair. McGowan gave her figure an up-and-down appraisal.

"No offense, ma'am, but you ain't a little girl now," he said.

If his offhand compliment made her uncomfortable, Sabrina betrayed no indication. She slipped out of her motorcycle jacket and unwound her bumblebee-striped scarf, which seemed to go on for a mile.

"Here, hold these," she ordered Blackwood, who took the proffered items with a bemused expression. Sabrina then dropped to her hands and knees, leaned forward and cautiously thrust her head through the flap.

"Smells a little musty," her muffled voice drifted back to the waiting men. "Going in," she announced with a plucky grin, and wiggled effortlessly through the small door.

A second later, Blackwood and McGowan could hear her fumbling with the lock from the inside.

"Got it," she yelled triumphantly.

The door swung open on hinges so creaky the neighbors three blocks away must have heard.

The Anderson's interim director greeted the pair with an almost smug grin.

"Please, come in, won't you?" She curtsied. Blackwood handed back her jacket and scarf, then walked inside, gray eyes absorbing every detail.

He found himself standing in a large, dim chamber that must have been a den or a family room. Cobwebs drifted lazily among the nooks and crannies, and thick dust smothered every surface. The tongue-and-groove flooring had long ago lost any luster, the wooden boards crisscrossed by a century-and-a-half's worth of scratches, slashes and scuff marks.

Blackwood made a face.

"I supposed you'd call this a real fixer-upper," he said.

"I'd have to agree," Sabrina quietly said. She shifted her gaze from Blackwood to roam the room, which was dominated by a large fireplace and rows of empty bookshelves. A few old pool cues rose like spears from an iron stand, but any billiard table appeared long gone.

Blackwood found a light panel and toggled the switch.

Nothing. He sighed.

"Thought as much," he informed the others.

McGowan patted him on the shoulder, pulled a flashlight from his camera bag and turned it on.

"Like a Boy Scout, I always come prepared," he said.

The beam danced along the wall, exposing gaping holes in the wallpaper.

"Do you have another torch?" Blackwood asked.

Nodding, McGowan handed a second, smaller flashlight to Blackwood, who accepted the metal cylinder with a grateful nod.

The last in line, the photographer shut the porch door.

Blackwood edged across the room, his penny loafers scuffing a trail in the dust.

With his longer legs, he scissored past Sabrina and made his way to a hallway outside the den; the others followed, their images reflected as elongated blobs in a fractured mirror stubbornly clinging to the wall. Every step reverberated through the long corridor with a kind of prolonged echo, as though they traversed a deep tunnel.

They located a sizable kitchen next. Blackwood paused on the threshold, his gaze performing a careful examination of the space. Sucking in a deep breath, he moved a few paces inside to make room for his companions. The beam from his flashlight roamed across old cabinets and fissured granite counters. Entering behind him, Sabrina and McGowan stopped and hovered just inside the door. They peered over his shoulder with faces as big as harvest moons. The kitchen contained an old gas range, the burners removed. Oily water pimpled by viscous bubbles fat as toadstools filled the sink.

The cone of light from McGowan's flashlight traced a circuit around the kitchen. To their left, a pair of swinging metal doors streaked with rust led to parts unknown.

Foregoing the double doors for now, they turned to the right and entered another lengthy hallway, walking as cautiously as cats tiptoeing through a room of dozing Rottweilers.

The corridor grew gloomier the farther they went. A tangle of shadows on the wall became a net that tightened around them, as dark and suffocating as the inside of a coal sack. Blackwood groped along the chipped wainscoting. The flashlight beams didn't illuminate the passage so much as punch a hole through the clinging blackness. He could feel Sabrina's searching fingers grasp his coat.

She pulled alongside him as they continued down the hall.

"Are you all right?" Blackwood asked.

She nodded and inhaled a deep breath.

"Yes, I'm fine," she said, but the quiver in her voice told another story.

Moving on, they came to the front foyer, which had seen better days.

A sweeping staircase curving into the blackness above dominated the chamber. On the ground floor where they stood, a grime-covered statue of a nymph missing a nose glared from between a couple of cracked vases on a marble table, relics abandoned by some nameless inhabitant decades ago. The foyer felt weighted down by an air of sad gravity. Blackwood cast a glance at the large front door, which he knew to be locked.

He then looked down at the scattered gaps his flashlight revealed between the wooden floorboards, victims of time and decay. The mournful gloom filling those empty spaces appeared bottomless. No telling what existed down there; likely a basement, but certainly a precipitous drop that could snap a leg or break a neck.

For some reason, an image of the basin's endless limestone caves flashed in his brain, the engines of water and erosion over the ages transforming the porous rock into a labyrinthine honeycomb. Forget a basement. Did the darkness beneath their feet plunge into those sunless depths? Ignoring the chill that seeped into his bones at such musings, Blackwood returned his attention to their surroundings, not that they offered any more comfort.

"Watch your step here," Blackwood warned.

In the foyer, all sound seemed smothered under the high ceiling. Blackwood allowed his flashlight to flow up the stairs. Doorways looming like open graves punctuated the second-story landing. Darkness as thick as ink-soaked cotton choked the third floor.

Tracing the beam with a wary gaze, Sabrina hugged herself.

"This place gives me the creeps," she said. "It looks much, much worse than when I was a kid."

They crossed the room without incident, the floor groaning like the deck of a listing ship, and presently faced a pair of impossibly tall, sliding doors pulled from pockets in the walls.

Shards of glass from shattered panes in the doors littered the floor, glinting with the dim luster of faded diamonds. Beyond the aperture, the trio observed a large, empty room lined in the same aged walnut as the front door. A gargantuan fireplace anchored the far end.

Must have been a formal parlor, Blackwood thought.

Blackwood turned sideways and slid between the partially open doors. He continued to hold the lead, Sabrina and Robert following in his footsteps. The police reporter walked a few more paces and stopped. He cast the flashlight beam around the yawning interior, dust motes pirouetting in the murky air the way the muck of an undersea grotto is disturbed by passing divers. The funnel of light hopped from spot to spot, pausing briefly on furniture outlined under drop cloths and cold ash heaped in the fireplace. Fitted wood panels high over their heads spanned the ceiling.

A chandelier suspended fifteen feet above them tinkled quietly. Blackwood hoped a breeze was at work, though he couldn't see any open windows.

McGowan whistled.

"Home sweet home," he said.

"Nothing sweet about this place," Sabrina retorted. "There's only decay and loss—deep, deep loss."

She rubbed her arms. "Can't you feel it? You would go mad if you stayed in this house for very long."

Blackwood stroked his chin, realizing more truth lurked in her words than she might realize. How long had Dr. Malory been here?

"Then let's keep this visit as short as possible," the reporter said.

He turned right, staring down a new corridor.

"Where does that lead?" he said, staring at the passage ahead.

"A small ballroom, if I remember correctly," Sabrina said.

Blackwood entered the corridor. McGowan and Sabrina dropped in behind him, their features churning with uncertainty.

Shadows swimming in the hallway seemed to take on a life of their own. Sabrina's fingers felt for and grasped Blackwood's free hand; she moved forward with him. Too intent on not stumbling in the darkness, he didn't read too much into the gesture.

A door appeared on their left and Blackwood stopped, gingerly pushing the panel open and shining his flashlight inside. From the look of the place, this had been a study at one time.

He paused under the lintel. The others once more clustered behind him, peering around the back of Blackwood's head. The light being more pronounced here thanks to a row of large windows, Sabrina appeared less ill at ease and gently disengaged her hand. McGowan's beam joined Blackwood's, the twin shafts of light skipping over vacant shelves, a battered roll-top desk and an overturned swivel chair mounted on bent rollers. Empty squares on the oak-paneled walls spoke of missing picture frames. Blackwood wondered what portraits they held, what stories they once told now lost to time and neglect.

His reverie evaporated as Sabrina let out an explosive gasp, her mouth opening as wide as a fish landed on a bank. Startled by the outburst, Blackwood followed her bugged-out gaze and pinned the flashlight beam to the wall. In lettering crusted over with a dull copper sheen, someone had scrawled "Break the Circle" in uneven, dripping script.

He swallowed audibly. Sabrina spoke first.

"Is that dried –?" she began tremulously.

"Blood? Perhaps. I don't see any discarded paint cans," Blackwood said, stepping closer for an inspection. Although struggling to remain clinical, his grip on the flashlight tightened.

"The fact it's here only convinces me even more that Dr. Malory was not in possession of his faculties," he said, his tone barely above a whisper.

"You think he left that?" McGowan croaked. "But whose blood is it? I mean, if it is blood?"

Blackwood pushed his answer through gritted teeth.

"I don't know who left it, Robert. And I hope it's just paint."

He sighed in frustration. First the desecrated cross, now this. What the hell was going on? Was the same person or persons responsible for both? The mysteries just kept piling up in this place, and their intent in venturing here had been to seek answers, not find more questions.

"I suppose we'll just have to keep searching," Blackwood said.

He focused on making the hand holding the torch remain steady. The thought occurred to him that if the substance smeared on the wall proved to be blood and not the result of some macabre prank, their brazen entry into the house potentially contaminated a crime scene.

That could prove legally problematic if the house became tied to Malory's lethal rampage at Bexar Regional last night.

"Don't touch anything, don't leave any fingerprints," he said, a rueful expression branded on his face. He could just imagine what Gruene might say regarding their unauthorized presence. Blackwood reluctantly made a mental promise to call him, though he knew the captain wouldn't be thrilled.

By unspoken consent, the trio started moving again. McGowan's broad shoulders twitched as he walked past the disquieting message on the wall.

Their journey resumed down the long hallway, which ended at a pair of swinging metal doors, each with a fractured port window. Cracked glass ringed the circular frames like crystal fangs.

Must be the grand ballroom, Blackwood thought.

Pushing on one of the doors. he stepped into an enormous chamber vaulted by a soaring roof. He held the door ajar for his companions. Sabrina and McGowan filed past. Once inside, he let the door swing back on protesting hinges and joined them.

Blackwood took a moment to take stock of their new surroundings.

Like the rest of the property, the ballroom had seen better days. Much better. Broken folding chairs littered the dance floor, which didn't appear very stable. As in the foyer, large gaps had eaten through some of the boards. At one end of the long chamber, tattered curtains, maybe velour but so moth-eaten one couldn't really tell, enclosed a small stage. Another pair of doors off to the side presumably connected with the kitchen; they'd seen those same doors a little while ago from the opposite side. Large floor-to-ceiling picture windows lining the west wall had long ago lost most of their glass. The filmy plywood nailed over the empty spaces bucked and heaved in a frigid, whistling wind. Pushed through ragged gaps in the wood, bits of fluttering snow chased each other on the current. A rank, wet odor rose from puddles pooled across the slatted floor.

Sabrina, meanwhile, began to circle the ballroom with a measured pace, being careful to dodge the gaps between the broken floorboards. Her pert nose wrinkled in disgust.

"God, this place smells worse than the kitchen," she said.

The longer the companions studied their surroundings, the deeper their collective spirits sank. Out of all the chambers visited so far, the ballroom by far seemed the most depressing. Blackwood tried hard to imagine what the grand chamber must have been like on some long-ago night with the tinkling of champagne glasses and an orchestra playing a waltz.

The thought had barely left his mind when an ominous crash, a groan so loud it seemed the house itself gasped in pain, caused the trio to whirl on their heels. The sound of splintering wood pushed their nerves to the breaking point.

One of the thick curtains over the stage, either by design or simply from old age, had tumbled down into a moldy heap. McGowan and Blackwood automatically swung their flashlight beams into the darkness revealed behind the little stage.

Gradually three dim objects began taking shape.

At first glance Blackwood took them to be nothing more than weighted burlap sacks hanging by ropes from the upper scaffolding, perhaps counterbalances stuffed with sand or sawdust to hold the heavy stage drapes in place. Fine particles drifted down from the weathered fabric to sprinkle the stage, which probably hadn't felt an actor's tread in ages.

Blackwood approached the proscenium, being careful to avoid the missing slats in the ballroom floor. But as he drew nearer to the trio of dry, lumpy sacks, his inspection revealed new and unsettling details.

The shape on his left registered larger than the others, the one in the middle was small and child-size, and the object on the right slim and petite. Each figure tapered to a blob about the size of a melon, pointed downwards.

A 10-gallon Stetson cowboy hat rested on the stage under the larger shape, ice crystalizing on a brim as wide as a pond. The frigid breeze roaming the dancehall gently twirled the flaking sacks in a counter-clockwise motion. But as the bundles slowly rotated into his light, Blackwood realized with a start that what he'd mistaken for just whorls of burlap amounted to something much worse.

A chill ran down his spine as the deep indentations in the misshapen balls resolved into mouths. Irregular knobs that could only be teeth studded the ragged holes, ringed by papery lips peeled back in a rictus of pain. The dark blemishes he at first mistook for black stitching or little buttons revealed themselves as shriveled eyes frozen in silent anguish. For a mere second, the last second in which the world he knew still made sense, Blackwood hoped—no, prayed—that he merely gazed upon simple stage props, perhaps scarecrows or grossly misshapen puppets left over from some long-forgotten play. But, as his steps inexorably pulled him toward the objects the way a cork is sucked into a whirlpool, all doubts vanished as to what — or whom — had been found.

When the realization fully hit him, a cold hand squeezed his heart and he stumbled backwards. If it hadn't been for Sabrina appearing beside him and catching him under the arms, he would have lost a leg in one of the floor's yawning holes.

Then she almost dropped him as awareness dawned on her own features.

"Oh my god," she breathed. "Oh my god." Her voice came out pained and thin, a cross between a hiss and a low shriek.

As he and Sabrina continued to stare, unable to tear their eyes away, other horrific details emerged, making even the hardened police reporter reluctant to continue his examination.

These weren't props. They were human remains. These people — these poor, poor souls — had somehow been rendered into lifeless husks and strung up like strips of dried jerky.

Blackwood wondered if he'd ever sleep peacefully again.

"No, no, no," Sabrina muttered through fingers splayed across her gaping mouth.

McGowan stumbled against Blackwood. His big hands shook clumsily as he attempted to extract his camera from the bag. The effort took three attempts.

"Mummies?" he whispered in stark disbelief. "What're mummies doing here?"

Finally Blackwood discovered his voice. He struggled to pull his thoughts together, and when he spoke, his words came out as a tortured whisper.

"Not mummies. Not mummies at all. I think we've found Malory's family and Ben Wade."

CHAPTER SEVENTEEN

Blackwood made a call to SAPD on his new mobile phone. His prediction that Capt. Frank Gruene would be less than pleased after learning their well-intentioned excursion violated a crime scene proved accurate, though the reporter figured he did the Police Department a favor. After all, he'd stumbled across a triple homicide that might otherwise have gone undiscovered, at least for a few more days. Time and decay are both critical factors in a murder probe.

Still, when Gruene pulled up to the Birkenstadt Haus with a fleet of wailing patrol cars in his wake, the homicide commander's greeting registered colder than the winter air that left Blackwood and his companions shivering while they waited by the curb for the police to arrive.

After exiting his unmarked Ford Crown Victoria, Gruene curtly nodded at McGowan, muttered a gruff hello to Blackwood and offered a brief handshake by way of introduction to Sabrina. He then wasted no time ordering the three of them sequestered in separate patrol units. Blackwood stifled a wave of irritation at the captain's decision. The clock was ticking. He absolutely needed to return to the newsroom and write his story while the details remained fresh in his mind.

However, in fairness to Gruene, the captain only followed standard procedure for all material witnesses at a homicide scene, a fact Blackwood knew but nonetheless resented.

And no small wonder. This was shaping up to be the story of his career. The blanched expressions on the officers' faces as they rotated in and out of the crumbling 19th-century relic left no doubt the Birkenstadt Haus had just entered the record books as the setting for one of the most macabre and inexplicable slayings in Alamo City history. Certainly no one there, not even Gruene with nearly 30 years on the force, had ever encountered such atrocities. And that was saying something for the man who'd cornered the infamous Bookstore Butcher — with a little help from a certain reporter now working himself up to a slow boil inside a prowl car.

• • •

"Hope none of y'all has a hot date. We need to take your statements, but we can do the prelims while we're here," Gruene drawled a few minutes later after having the three interlopers transferred to his city car. His Texas twang hung in the air like sour notes from an old guitar.

He shot a sideways glance at Blackwood.

"This is getting to be a habit with you, John," he added, not hiding his annoyance. "If you keep showing up at crime scenes ahead of my officers, you're going to make the department look bad."

Blackwood's gray eyes bored through the floorboard, hard as twin shards of flint, but he said nothing.

Gruene settled into a contemplative hush and sipped coffee delivered minutes earlier by an evidence technician, who'd also brought java to the three "guests" in the unmarked car. The reporter's brooding silence didn't seem to faze Gruene. He was no stranger to Blackwood's moods.

"We'll keep these interviews short, I promise," Gruene said. "And Dr. Hagen, I would appreciate it if you would go ahead and speak with Detective Galvan. He's here—and very keen to talk to you about Mr. Grant."

Sabrina, sitting with a vacant expression in the back seat next to McGowan, nodded imperceptibly. Blackwood's head rose when he didn't hear a verbal response. Though he'd only known the woman a few hours — very revelatory hours, to be sure — her brooding silence seemed uncharacteristic. Twisting around to study her, his expression switched from frustration to worry upon seeing the lost look in her eyes. He resisted the urge to offer some pithy assurance that everything would be just fine, to tell her this wasn't the worst thing he'd ever seen. But he held his tongue for fear of lying. This absolutely was the worst thing he'd ever seen.

On top of Mimi Anderson's untimely demise, Grant's death had also taken a toll on Sabrina, that much was apparent, and Blackwood worried the horrors in the ballroom may have pushed her over the edge. She'd barely uttered a word since their stumbling, mad scramble from the nightmarish house.

As Gruene's car idled and the heater pumped welcome warmth into the cabin, the captain for his part stared straight ahead through a windshield coated by glittering ice, lost in his own thoughts. Then he spoke again, his attitude softening somewhat.

He swiveled to regard Blackwood.

"I do realize you could've just driven away, taken your sweet time to write your story and then called us," he said. "I guess we owe you."

"No good deed goes unpunished," Blackwood murmured, glancing for the umpteenth time at his Mickey Mouse watch. The gesture was not lost on Gruene, but he had his own priorities.

An early dusk started to fall. The sinking sun broke through the dark clouds to trace fiery reds and golds in a razor-thin line shimmering across the horizon. As Blackwood's untouched coffee cooled, he watched porch lights snap on at the well-appointed houses of the neighborhood. Homeowners wearing faces stamped with curiosity, worry or even annoyance kept emerging, braving the arctic temperatures to see the cause of all the fuss. Officers crunched across yards covered in fresh powder, fanning out to talk to some of the onlookers.

Gruene pressed stubby thumbs to his temples and rotated them, clucked his tongue and then faced Blackwood again.

"John, old buddy, I'm going to throw you a bone, but this bone you have to bury until I tell you it's OK to dig it up."

He gave Blackwood a penetrating look. "You can use it in a story, just not yet. *Bueno?*"

A long pause followed while Blackwood considered the offer, and then he reluctantly nodded. He hated agreeing to these terms, but experience had taught him such *quid pro quo* deals with the cops usually paid off in the long run for the newspaper. A string of page-one exclusives under his byline testified to the benefits of sometimes holding back on one or two juicy items for the moment.

The crinkles around Gruene's brown eyes flattened as he stared hard at the reporter, carefully formulating his next words.

"The medical investigator's in there now, finishing his preliminary examination, but from what he told us, it looks like our victims expired the same way as the complainant found in the cemetery. We can't blame this one on a wild animal."

Blackwood straightened up, all irritation evaporating.

"Drained of blood? Tissue aged prematurely?" he asked. Under his feet, the world tilted a few more degrees toward darkness.

Gruene nodded. "Yeah. Crazy, isn't it? These three—we're pretty sure it's Wade, Malory's wife and the missing kid — are nothing more than human tissue paper. Literally no fluids in their bodies. No blood, no water, no fats, no mucus, nothing."

McGowan stirred from his silence.

"How is that even possible?"

The captain shrugged, being careful not to slosh his cooling coffee after removing the lid.

"I don't know, Robert. Dr. Bucks at the ME's Office is still conducting tests on the first victim from last night."

Gruene scrunched his brow and leveled eyes with Blackwood.

"Toxicology results are pending, and we've asked Dr. Bucks to put a rush on the cases. It's obvious the same person or persons are at work here. Maybe the killer's using some kind of acid, or the victims are injected with a fast-acting corrosive agent."

Gruene's jowls darkened with frustration. "We'll know more when the tests are finalized. That's still a few days off."

McGowan brought his coffee cup to his lips, took a cautious sip and then spoke in a doubtful voice.

"I can see one guy in a cemetery getting overpowered and—injected, then hacked apart for good measure," he said, taking a deep breath. "But how do you take down three people at once and turn them into—um, Kleenex?"

He made a face. "Could that nut job at the hospital have killed them all? He's a doctor. Was ... a doctor. Maybe he got his hands on some chemicals or poisons in a lab?"

Blackwood dropped his chin into his hands, mind churning like a river in a downpour.

"No, it couldn't be Malory," he said after some thought. "That's just not possible. Even if he did have something to do with this –," he pointed to the house, "he couldn't be connected to Grant's death. Dr. Malory took his own life at least two hours before Grant showed up at the cemetery. In fact, Grant and I were on the phone when the siege began at Bexar Regional."

He knit his brows. "What's the connection? Is it this damned house?"

Gruene gripped the steering wheel, knuckles tightening in resignation. He shook his head.

"Like I keep saying, we don't know." He bit his lower lip. "But if you have any ideas, John, feel free to share. You seem pretty good at finding your way into my crime scenes."

• • •

Not much later, Blackwood and Sabrina sat inside her Land Rover. The archaeologist had spoken to Galvan, as requested, and seemed to be regaining her composure. Blackwood wasn't surprised; this was someone who organized major excavations in faraway climes, probably dealing with everything from malaria to drug runners. He was good at reading people and, unless he was mistaken, Sabrina seemed the type to quickly bounce back from adversity.

"Captain Gruene seemed to know you pretty well," she finally said.

Blackwood smiled ruefully.

"Oh, we're old chums," he responded. "Remind me to tell you the story sometime."

By now a caravan of TV news crews had arrived. McGowan lingered outside Gruene's car, finishing his coffee. Blackwood wondered why his cousin tarried.

The newspaper reporter switched his attention back to the new arrivals, eyeing them with some annoyance because they reminded him of his own deadline.

Sabrina glanced at him, noticing the peeved expression coloring his face.

"Worried about making your print time?" she asked.

"Eh?" Blackwood absently said, then realized her meaning. "Oh, you mean my deadline?"

Her brows knit together.

"John, you have a mobile phone. Can't you call your editors, just like you did Capt. Gruene? When I watch those old movies on TV, I always see the reporter rushing to a phone booth to call the newspaper with a hot scoop."

A look of surprise crossed his face. He briefly wondered why he hadn't thought of the idea himself.

"You're rather clever, I'll give you that," he said.

Sabrina folded arms across her chest and smiled.

"I try," she said, and he knew then she'd toppled whatever walls had briefly closed her off to everything else. She seemed almost back to normal.

Patting himself down, Blackwood located his mobile phone in a coat pocket, extracted the device, flipped the cover open and dialed the City Desk's straight line. He connected with Juan Cantu on the first ring. After a brief conversation, the metro editor located a seasoned rewrite man on the copy desk.

Though not the same as coming in and banging out the story himself, it was better than nothing. Time had grown too short for a return to the newsroom. Blackwood fed his notes to the rewrite man, composing sentences in his head as he went along, answering questions, correcting spellings and genuinely feeling pleased with himself.

The process went faster than expected, and Blackwood finished in a few minutes. Rewrite switched him back to Cantu.

"I think we're all good here, John," the city editor said.

Blackwood sighed, feeling a weight lift from his shoulders. No busted deadline. Reputation saved. That also meant the story would run Sunday, in the edition with the highest circulation of the week.

"Great story, excellent hustle," the editor added. "Hands down, this beats anything else we've got for Sunday, even the weather package — although it's close. The whole city is shutting down. Massive power failures, trees down, streets iced over, the whole works. Road and utility crews can't keep up."

Blackwood watched a mob of video photographers and their reporters, microphones and boom mics thrust forward like daggers and spears, surround Gruene under the Argyle Lane street sign. The captain's pained expression showed he'd rather submit to a root canal than hold a press conference.

Over the phone, Cantu heaved an expansive breath.

"We'll post a short version of your story online as breaking news, tease the longer article in the Sunday print edition. It's part of corporate's new strategy to attract more readers to the free website, then get them to subscribe to the print."

Blackwood's voice sounded doubtful.

"Is that wise? Giving away stories for free on computers before they run in the paper?" he asked.

He couldn't help but recall Rutherford Stewart's prediction that web content would someday replace the printed newspaper.

Blackwood could hear Cantu chewing noisily on the plastic cap of a Bic felt-tip pen, just like he always did.

"This is too big a story to wait until tomorrow's editions, especially since it involves that doctor's family. We need to beat TV and radio," the metro editor said. "Besides, it's not the whole story, just a taste of what's to come in the Sunday paper."

"I suppose so," Blackwood said, not bothering to hide his misgivings. He was getting ready to add another thought when a new sight distracted him.

Over by Gruene's unit, McGowan downed his coffee and started walking towards the Land Rover. One of the TV reporters broke off from the others and made a beeline across the street to head him off.

Only McGowan didn't seem surprised. He slowed to a halt and smiled warmly at the woman; she grinned back. They appeared to be acquainted with each other, bending their heads in conversation for a few moments. Trading more grins, they parted ways a second later, but not before the woman tentatively touched McGowan's elbow.

Dimly registering Sheryl Crow's "All I Wanna Do" drift at low volume from the Land Rover's speakers, Blackwood pondered this rather interesting development. He thought he recognized the reporter ... Wasn't she the one on the television yesterday in the newsroom delivering the weather update, talking about the snowstorm's impact on the city? Carla Rodriguez, that was her name, right? Worked at KLIK, channel seven. A recent addition, he recalled. Moving up-market from some station down in the Valley.

How did Robert know her? Had he been waiting for her?

Cantu started speaking again.

"Get some rest," the editor suggested. "This is your day off, *vato.*"

Blackwood snapped back to the conversation.

"Can't. Not yet. I'm dropping Robert off at the paper to process his photos. Fair warning — you won't be able to use most of them. Cheerios factor."

Scarecrows ... rotating above the stage ... Man, woman, child. Correction. Things that had once been a man, a woman and a child...

"Understood," Cantu answered thickly. "Okay. Gotta go. Garza's writing the weather sidebar and I need to look at it."

The line went dead, as sudden as the wind closing a door. Blackwood tucked the phone back in his pocket, wondering where this story would take him next.

CHAPTER EIGHTEEN

Sabrina drove the newsmen back to her home, where Blackwood retrieved his Mustang. Afterwards, he dutifully transported McGowan to the Tribune to develop his photos. The cousins traveled in silence; Blackwood didn't ask about the girl from KLIK-TV.

After appearing briefly at the City Desk to see if Cantu had any other questions concerning the story, Blackwood decided to take his editor's advice and call it a day.

Riding the elevator down to the lobby, he exited the carriage and crossed the checkerboard marble floor, barely noticing a locally famous series of 1930s murals arranged around the ceiling. Though antiquated, the panels depicted the relatively unchanged process of how a newspaper is printed, from the felling of mighty trees in a forest and a trip to the pulp mill, to sheets of newsprint eventually stretched on a thrumming press. His only thought: Maybe someday they'll add another painting showing a news story on a computer screen.

He pushed his way through the heavy front doors framed in glass and brass and stepped outside. The brisk weather slapped him awake.

Filling his lungs with a cold rush of air, he fished in his pocket for his keys. Across the street, engines revved to life as the weekend advertising staff started heading home.

The snow swirled around Blackwood on his way to the car park reserved for newsroom personnel, located on the far side of the building. Leave it to advertising to get the choice slots closest to the front door, he grumbled.

(A steely eyed corporate man in the finance department once informed him, "Sales reps make money. Reporters cost money. To the victors go the spoils.")

Overhead, the night sky looked as thick as a tar pit. No stars glimmered.

Taking a shortcut through an alley, head dipped low against the biting wind, Blackwood's mind kept returning to the strange events of the past forty-eight hours. The reporter shivered, one hand pinching the collar of his coat to keep the warmth in.

He emerged from the alley, spotting his Mustang dead ahead.

Drawing alongside the car seconds later, keys clutched in a gloved hand, Blackwood heard someone faintly speak his name. His head shot up. He noticed the dim silhouettes of three figures standing by a dumpster at the lip of the alley. Mildly surprised, Blackwood wondered how he'd missed spotting them.

He blinked and stared again.

Empty. Nobody loitered next to the dumpster. One of the plastic lids flapped in the breeze with all the gusto of an angry elephant's ear, but nothing more.

Rubbing tired eyes, Blackwood decided, with some justification, the recent, unrelenting exposure to suicide, murder and mummified corpses had combined to make him just a tad jumpy. He unlocked the car door.

"Johnny ... Johnny Blackwood," a voice cooed. Louder this time, riding on the wind.

The three figures now reappeared in the alley. The amorphous shapes all shared the same height and same build, their shoulders touching in the outline of cutout paper dolls. For just a second he considered the possibility they might be gang members planning a carjacking or transients wanting a handout. But the weather was too cold for crime and too harsh for charity, and he dismissed both notions.

That didn't explain how one knew his name, though.

"Johnny, me fine bard," the voice teased. Purring a little.

Blackwood made an exasperated sound.

"Hullo?" he said.

No response. The three shadows stood rooted to the spot, directly facing him. The silence lengthened.

Perhaps these were coworkers waiting on a ride, or a press crew taking a smoke break. All right — that would explain how they knew his name. In truth, Blackwood didn't really care. He just wanted to head home. He gave the trio a dismissive wave.

"I'm knackered. Good night," he said, gathering up the coattails of his London Fog so the door didn't tear the fabric. He scooted in.

Blackwood didn't recognize the next sound that reached his ears, at least not at first. But it made the hair on his arms and back bristle. He dipped his head, listening, curiosity as always replacing alarm, the hem of his coat still gathered in a clenched fist. Then he realized what he heard.

A low, thin growl rose from the alleyway. Other growls joined the first.

What happened next occurred so rapidly Blackwood didn't have time to register the chain of events, only accept them. Almost faster than the eye could follow, the trio stood next to his car, their outlines more sharply defined under the parking lot's lights. Three women, he noticed with a shock, wondering whether his mind played tricks on him as he tried to reconcile their seemingly instantaneous appearance. He harbored a vague notion they had literally flown over the asphalt.

Deep inside his head, a little voice reminded him that people couldn't fly. The dim lights and the snowfall must have fooled his bleary eyes.

Then he glanced down at the powder carpeting the car park and that's when his guts really started churning. The only footprints leading to the Mustang belonged to him. The rest of the lot remained undisturbed.

Jolted by fear, he started closing the door.

"Not so fast, Johnny me lad," one said in a voice like a snake's hiss choked with dust.

A spidery hand shot out, grasping the door frame in a steel grip. Blackwood yanked on the handle, but the door wouldn't budge.

"Let go," he demanded, his voice small.

"We want to play, Johnny," the one holding the door announced mirthfully, her mouth peeling back in a leer that said play was the last thing on her mind. Casually reaching inside the car, she grabbed him by the arm of his coat and yanked. His head jerked forward, reluctantly followed by his neck. Pain exploded in his skull as his head banged against the frame.

With reflexes that surprised even him, his right hand shot out and grabbed the steering wheel to keep anchored inside the car. The woman refused to release his left arm and started pulling, trying to dislodge him.

"Dammit," he squeaked. She was much stronger than she looked.

Low laughter whistled from the lips the shade of roses dipped in blood, followed by a blast of sulfurous breath washing over him like the riptide from a cesspool. Enveloped by the miasma, Blackwood nearly vomited. Tears brimmed in his burning eyes.

"Ugh," he spat.

His grip tightened even more on the steering wheel. The same hand also clutched his keys, but he didn't dare let go to insert them in the ignition.

The other women joined their companion and ringed the door, all three plainly toying with him. Grand halitosis or not, their beauty left him stunned. Simultaneously fascinated and repulsed, Blackwood couldn't tear his gaze away; the fabled sirens of legend who lured hapless sailors to their deaths on storm-tossed rocks couldn't have been any more alluring. Long, pitch-black hair fell past shapely shoulders and swept over the pale ovals of their bare breasts; their smooth-as-satin skin, though corpse white, rippled with muscles. Somehow not a goose pimple showed on those colorless limbs despite the arctic temperature. Their ears ended in delicate lupine tips. Their only nod to fashion were dark loincloths girded by jeweled belts fitted with jagged obsidian daggers.

But above all else, their eyes held him prisoner, drawing him in and threatening to suck him down into twin whirlpools of churning darkness. He'd never seen anything like those orbs before. No pupils, no irises, just black marbles as cold and lightless as the ocean's deepest trench, and filled with a malevolence just as crushing.

No mercy existed there.

A lull stole over Blackwood. He felt himself captivated, starting to go limp. Under their relentless, eternal stares, his will ebbed away.

With a crack like thunder, a rusted sign hanging on the car park's chain-link fence—UNAUTHORIZED VEHICLES WILL BE TOWED AT OWNER'S EXPENSE — rose and fell, lifted by a gust of wind. The clatter set off a Ford Escort's car alarm.

As one, the three women whirled with unbelievable speed to glare in that direction, breaking contact with Blackwood's mesmerized eyes. Shaking a groggy head, he averted his gaze, some primal part of him realizing the hypnotic pull of those soulless sockets could drain him of all sense of self-preservation, leaving him as vulnerable as a sleeping baby.

Every square inch of his body shook from what amounted to a full-on psychic attack. When the women swiveled around to pin him once more with those bottomless pits, he refused to look directly at them. He could feel their eyes fruitlessly clutching at his mind, trying to bend his will.

It wouldn't work this time. He wouldn't let them.

"Johnny," whispered the one tugging on his coat, "come out and play. Don't make me come in there."

Struggling to resist the temptation to look into their eyes again, he instead regarded the trio with a peripheral sweep of his vision. They could have passed as sisters, except now he noticed the one latched onto his coat possessed a feature the others didn't — a prominent white streak running through her jet-black mane.

Another said, "We don't bite," then giggled and added, "Well, that's not true. We do bite. . . A lot."

Their mouths slowly parted, revealing malicious smiles. Any illusion of glamor disappeared the very second their lips pulled back. Blackwood swallowed a scream. Inside the impossibly large ovals of their maws, sharpened teeth punched through mottled gums like bone shards thrusting from an infected wound.

The one sporting the white streak leaned further in, adroitly plucked the keys from his numb fingers and flung them across the parking lot. They ricocheted off the dumpster and landed with a forlorn tinkle in the alley.

"This is not happening," Blackwood mumbled, straining to break her unyielding grasp. He watched in helpless fascination as a transformation came over her. The clutching fingers stretched out, becoming unnaturally elongated, while the nails grew more pointed, sharpened, thrusting from the skin like chitinous blades.

Claws.

Consumed by mounting panic, he almost released his desperate hold on the steering wheel.

The moment blossomed into a dark epiphany for Blackwood. Between one thunderous heartbeat and the next, as the woman-thing lowered her meat grinder of a mouth ever so slowly to his exposed throat, John Gwydion Blackwood arrived at the soul-numbing realization the world no longer operated according to the norms he knew. Probably never had, but like most, he'd spent his life blissfully unaware of such horrors — even as someone who chronicled the worst deeds one human could visit upon another. Those episodes paled in comparison to what he faced now.

Dread seized him. He was the most scared he'd ever been in what appeared to be his soon-to-be-cut-short life.

"Bloody hell," he muttered as the gibbering funnel of a mouth and dozens of steak-knife teeth drew dangerously near his carotid artery, the creature's fetid breath as heavy as a moldy rag soaked in offal.

His timid protestation prompted peals of laughter from the trio, a mocking ululation that made a vulture's raspy hiss sound as tender as a lullaby. Blackwood wanted to slam palms over his ears, but he couldn't let go of the steering wheel or he'd be dragged from the car. He slid low in his seat, paralyzed and waiting for the inevitable.

But the nagging, insistent little voice inside his head hadn't stopped speaking either, reminding Blackwood of something else, something vitally important ... His reason for existence. The justification for his survival.

He needed to finish his story. There was a job to do.

He'd been in tight situations before, the diminutive voice reminded him ... Maybe not this bad, but bad enough ... Worst of all, of course, was the final encounter with the Bookstore Butcher. Truly a demon in human form.

Like a deck of cards reshuffled, the memories flipped through his frenzied mind with one image standing out: Matt Linkin, aka the Bookstore Butcher, his maniacal features looming over a barely conscious, bloodied Lt. Frank Gruene. Linkin's hands rising, his fists molded around a hunting knife gleaming in the shafts of moonlight pouring through a long picture window. Blackwood saw himself bursting into the chamber, doing the only thing he could do. He lowered his head and charged like a battering ram before the blade could thrust downwards. He could still feel the thud of his skull slamming into Linkin's midsection with a gut-wrenching crunch. Even now, the ear-splitting shriek rang in his ears as the psychopath lost his balance, arms pinwheeling, and toppled backwards, plunging through the plate-glass window on a 22-story fall that brought a fitting end to the serial killer's reign of terror.

Yes, he'd been in tough situations before — and came through each and every one relatively intact.

So why should this one be any different, the voice asked.

These things before me are clearly monsters ... but so was Matt Linkin, and I survived him.

As the memories unspooled in the flickering cinema of his brain, a metamorphoses began to occur. A sense of calm settled over Blackwood. Not the motionless stupefaction of a sheep resigned to the wolf's fangs. No, this was the serenity of self-preservation. Of calculation.

Certainly, he would die someday... but not today.

Blackwood's head shot up, chin thrust forward in defiance.

"Piss off," he growled.

Blackwood released the steering wheel, bunched his knuckles and slammed a fist into the monster's face.

Unprepared for the impact, the thing wearing the guise of a woman emitted a bloodcurdling screech and fell backwards. Blackwood couldn't tell whether he'd caused any real damage; the screaming seemed borne more of astonishment or rage. He didn't wait to find out. Forcing frozen muscles to move, he slid across the passenger seat (smashing his crotch into the gear shift, which elicited a howl almost as loud as the creature's), fumbled with the door handle and scrambled out of the car.

Looking none the worse, only annoyed perhaps, his would-be assailant rose in a single fluid motion, a shadow brought to life. She and the other weird sisters (the only name he could come up with on such short notice) lingered on the other side of the Mustang, hissing and spitting with the vehemence of a kicked-over basket of vipers.

Blackwood assumed they were not accustomed to dinner skipping out on them.

For his next act, he practiced the better part of valor and ran away.

CHAPTER NINETEEN

He wasn't exactly sure where to run, but the most logical destination seemed the south gate. From there, Blackwood could make his way to the Alamo two blocks away, then lose himself among late-night shoppers and tourists thronging the River Walk. He resisted the urge to turn around for one last look at his assailants, concentrating instead on just getting away. Had he done so, he would have seen the trio regain their otherworldly composure and beam huge, predatory grins. They lowered their heads and started after him.

With his back turned, Blackwood also didn't witness the rapid change coming over the women. The creamy alabaster skin he'd admired minutes ago disappeared under a carpet of coarse hair sprouting like blackened moss; eyebrows became thick as the bristles of a wire brush; and their faces seemed to melt and reform, assuming a bat-like aspect marked by sunken cheekbones and flattened slits for noses. Twin, curved horns began growing from their heads.

Low growls boiled from their throats. Half-moons glowing like pools of neon blood flickered in the oil-dark sockets of their narrowed eyes. Forked tongues darted at the chilly air.

He only managed another several paces when — inexplicably — he found himself surrounded again. The sisters clearly enjoyed their hunt.

He couldn't fathom how they moved so fast. Again, the only tracks in the snow belonged to him.

"You're going to taste so good, Johnny," leered the one who'd been on the receiving end of his fist. Languidly tossing the solitary white bang from a forehead now rippling with crab-like ridges, she added, "Succulent and delicious."

The other two joined their companion's chorus of cackles.

"Indeed, bard, we shall drain the life from you. No mortal can resist our tender kisses," teased another, smacking oozing gums. Blackwood couldn't even begin to imagine how agonizing one of those "tender" kisses might be.

As he struggled to chase the image from his mind, her next statement nearly caught him off guard.

"Aye, you'll prove better fodder than that squirming whelp and his bleating mother," she said.

Blackwood's head shot backwards.

"What?" he choked.

The first swiveled to contemplate the second, the pair forgetting him for a moment.

"Shame about that healer, though," white streak said, funneling a rancid sigh between the shards that passed for teeth. "Much good marrow in that one's bones, aye. What a waste to see him scuttle off."

Laughter gurgled from her companion.

"Ye needn't worry, dearie. Forgot the glam I threw over him, did you? Ensorcelled his eyes, indeed. He thought the hounds of hell themselves pursued him!"

The first nodded philosophically, considering her companion's point.

"Aye, he wouldna ken his own mother," she agreed with gusto. "Nothing but rage and doom for that one!"

Blackwood gulped down a startled breath. Their words bit deep into his ears with the sharpness of a serpent's fangs.

"What?" he exclaimed again and started forward, clearly forgetting the danger the women represented.

"Don't dismiss the traitor in the boneyard!" the third one hissed with the energy of a kettle venting steam. Like the others, she ignored Blackwood.

White lock snarled. "Aye, to reveal our secrets, to make the unholy relic known to the sons of Adam, that was his betrayal!"

The third giggled, a sound eerily akin to mud boiling from a fissure.

"Naughty, naughty man. We simply can't abide such a transgression," she said. "The secrets of the Azad'dhul are ours alone."

"Azad'dhul," they intoned in a macabre chorus, bowing their heads in reverence.

Frigid and hard, their words jammed into Blackwood's brain with the unerring aim of a falling icicle. Those bold if disjointed statements set his mind reeling. There could be no doubt they just admitted their culpability in the demise of Dr. Malory, Kristen Malory, their son, James Grant and Ben Wade. Their confession — delivered so conversationally, so light-hearted, almost like gossipy women at a tea — helped fit more pieces into the jigsaw puzzle he'd been trying to solve the last forty-eight hours.

Blackwood offered a silent prayer he would live long enough to print the revelations in his next story.

So Dr. Malory had been—what?—hypnotized? He tried remembering the term the hag used. The phrase sounded vaguely medieval, he thought — a glam, right? That explained much, including why a young doctor with a such promising career would embark on a suicidal rampage.

Sickened and angered by what he'd learned, Blackwood gritted his teeth, keeping his eyes averted while the hags continued training their soulless skull sockets on him. He entertained no doubts those holes in their crafty, angular faces would do to him what they'd done to Dr. Malory.

And "traitor in the boneyard"? Interesting way to describe Grant. Who else? During their phone conversation, which now seemed eons ago, Grant mentioned something about betraying "them." What kind of connection existed between these women and Grant? Had Grant broken trust with the trio now cornering him?

But then another thought occurred to Blackwood. What if these women were not the ones Grant feared so much? When he rang Blackwood, Grant used the phrase "a nasty bunch of people" and "their fearsome agents," or something along those lines, to describe the ones orchestrating whatever coming calamity he feared. These things in the car park certainly didn't qualify as people. Fearsome, yes, but not people. They seemed to fall under the category of "agents." Did that mean someone else held authority over these loathsome creatures, controlling them? Did they merely play the part of hellish foot soldiers, doing the bidding of an unseen master or masters? His reporter's instincts told him the concept seemed not only possible, but probable.

And what did they mean when they said Grant wanted to expose — he knew this wasn't the right word—something that sounded like "acid hole"?

Acid hole? Their "unholy relic"?

Which begged the next question: Why did these creatures pursue him? The obvious connection had to be Grant's phone call, perhaps because "the traitor" wished to reveal something regarding this "acid hole."

Seized by both desperation and curiosity, Blackwood shouted a question.

"Whom do you serve?" he demanded, not really expecting a response.

White lock's dark expression didn't soften, yet those sharp, curved ears registered every word. She surprised him by answering, though with a scowl.

"Were you to live, you would know the master by a sign — the circle and the token thrice ten," she said.

Blackwood shook his head, not understanding. A riddle? He was seconds from being killed and she told bloody riddles?

"A circle ..." he began, his confusion deepening. His ears no longer seemed to work; did he mishear? Because the woman's answer made absolutely no sense.

"... and token thrice ten?" he repeated hesitantly.

She glared hot coals at him.

"Fool," she spat. "You're wasting time. I've said more than enough."

Concentrate on the here and now, the nagging voice from his mind scolded. *Solve your little puzzle later.*

Venting an anguished cry, Blackwood dropped his ruminations for the moment to simply focus on surviving his current predicament.

In that moment he saw a chance to make a break. Timing would be everything. During their taunting and jabbering among themselves, two of the weird sisters unconsciously shifted their positions, just ever so slightly, but enough to create a small opening that led to the car park beyond.

Blackwood seized the opportunity. Acting on pure impulse, he straightened up, abruptly dashed two steps left, stopped short, feinted right, threw an arm over his face, scrunched his eyes and shrieked like a goat on fire.

For just a split second, the women — or whatever they were — froze in confusion.

Dropping to all fours, he crawled like a baby with a rocket strapped to its back through the gap between the first and second creatures. The move lacked elegance and certainly fell short of anything even remotely heroic, but he cleared their desperately grasping claws and slid into the open, the ice and grit of the broken asphalt digging into his gloved hands and knees.

Choking back a cry of surprise at the ease of his escape, he jerked unsteadily to his feet. Though free and clear, he didn't bother stopping to contemplate his good fortune. His maneuver might have bought a little time, but the trio still stood between Blackwood and the Mustang, blocking him. And even if he could return to the car, the motor wouldn't start. The keys were lost, thrown somewhere in the alley after one of those bitches ripped them from his fingers.

That didn't mean he lacked options. Scanning the lot, he recognized another vehicle that could prove useful, and which meant not only escape but a possible solution to get these harpies to beat a retreat. Shooting the weird sisters a nervous glance, he not so gracefully slid on his bum across the hood of a Volvo and sprinted to a faded, beat-up Ford F150 pickup parked in the corner. He knew the vehicle nearly as well as his own, since the truck belonged to Robert McGowan, who by now must have been deep into the task of developing his prints from the Birkenstadt Haus.

It was a foregone conclusion the cab was locked. That wouldn't be a problem. Blackwood also knew McGowan kept a spare key duct-taped to the inside of a toolbox that rattled around in the bed, right next to an old bicycle tire and a half-filled can of wiper fluid.

He reached the truck in seconds flat, shuddering and out of breath. The wind biting the back of his neck did nothing to cool his nervous sweat. Propping his elbows on the side of the bed, he leaned over, spotted the red toolbox with a peeling USMC Eagle, Globe and Anchor decal and flipped open the lid with a violent bang. Yes, the key was still there! Not wasting a moment, Blackwood ripped off the tape, held the key in fumbling fingers and managed to unlock the passenger door.

Blackwood knew better than to waste precious time casting a glance over his shoulder. Instead, guided by memory, his fingers slid inside the glove box and closed over a cool hunk of metal and polymers. Sucking in his breath, Blackwood withdrew the 40-caliber semiautomatic Glock Robert stashed there after being robbed last year, just months after his return from a duty station in Kuwait.

Blackwood always judged his cousin's response to that carjacking episode an overreaction, perhaps a symptom of lingering battle stress caused by the war, but not tonight. Thank God for Texas, he breathed, where everybody and their dog goes armed. The Police Department recently started issuing Glocks to uniformed officers — much to the dismay of the old-timers, who swore by their revolvers ("They never jam like these fucking semi-autos," one patrol sergeant groused to Blackwood) — but Robert claimed it was the best pistol around in spite of a reputation as the "plastic gun."

Tightening his grip on the weapon, Blackwood pivoted for a look behind, not at all surprised to discover the weird sisters standing motionless several yards away, their hungry glares fixed on him. Struggling to keep his hands steady, he pointed the barrel in their direction. Rather than betray any concern, though, the threesome just gave the pistol a contemptuous sneer. The one in front, she of the white streak, licked cracked charcoal lips and grinned. Blackwood felt his bowels turn to water under the unflinching scrutiny of her dead eyes, those orbs with the power he sensed could freeze a man's soul. To throw a "glam" on him. He tore his gaze away.

"Johnny," she whispered, a slow smile creasing her pallid features. "You can't escape."

Then, without missing a beat, the trio started forward in an oddly smooth motion that seemed anything but natural, merriment bubbling up from their throats in a cacophony that put fighting cats to shame. Blackwood blinked several times, as though unable to accept what he beheld.

The fact he trained a pistol on the figures did nothing to deter them. They kept coming. Their jack-o'-lantern grins only widened, garish carvings scratched in tortured wood. One dipped a claw the color of diseased ivory at Blackwood and beckoned him to approach, like he was some kind of a vassal.

"Make this easy on yourself, bard," she commanded.

"Yield, son of Adam. Yield to the Daughters of Lilith," the third intoned.

Flicking a tongue at him suggestively, she offered a lascivious smile.

"We can make this quick. We can make it … pleasurable," she purred.

"I'd rather not, if it's all the same to you," Blackwood said, throat dry as dust. Yet no matter how much he struggled to ignore the invitation, he felt an unmistakable stiffening in his loins. As his cheeks flushed with embarrassment, the woman arched a hairy eyebrow and shot him a knowing grin.

And Lilith ... Lilith—why did that name sound oddly familiar? Running the phrase through his mind, he searched his memory. Daughters of Lilith ... Later, provided he survived, he would do some research. At this stage he hadn't the foggiest. Besides, his hands were full. Her statement confirmed one suspicion, though: The women considered themselves siblings.

"Stay back," he said, attempting to put a little menace into his warning.

They tittered and continued to level their eyes at him, trying to burn a path straight into his brain.

"Put that toy away," the second sister demanded.

"Remain where you are ... Last warning," he said, wishing he'd wake up from this terrible nightmare at home, safe in his bed. His head throbbed from where he'd hit the door frame, his lungs ached from his exertions (and too much pipe smoking). Weariness weighed him down like a lead coat. He could sense their grasping minds collectively tugging at his, whispering, calling out, promising to satiate his desire and ease his pain, to open him up on an anvil equal parts suffering and pleasure.

He struggled ferociously to hold onto some small part of himself, fighting back with everything he had.

"Don't look into their eyes," he told himself through clenched teeth.

The foremost one wasted no more time, just bellowed and charged. Blackwood's jaw dropped at what the moment revealed. This close, he got his first good look at her feet. Only then did he realize they didn't touch the ground. She hovered ... no, floated as she propelled herself toward him ... somehow breaking the oldest law in the book, the law of gravity. Yellowed nails on distended toes pointed straight down, separated from the glistening surface of the icy parking lot by three or four inches.

Onward she came. Levitating. Gliding.

Now Blackwood understood why no footprints trailed through the snow.

"Impossible," he gasped. Her jet-black tresses flowed languidly behind her, reminding him of Shakespeare's Ophelia in a cold mere, locks fanned out upon the water.

When she drew less than five yards away, he knew what had to happen. He pulled back the slide of the pistol and a round slammed into the chamber with a satisfying click.

"I warned you," he said hoarsely.

Laughing maniacally, hot spittle flying from blood-red lips, the one calling herself a Daughter never slowed down.

Squaring his jaw and seeing no alternative, he drew a bead and gently squeezed the trigger. He'd learned valuable lessons over the years from his own stories on officer-involved shootings, the most important being to aim for the largest part of the target and not count bullets after you start firing. The frequent lessons plunking at tin cans he'd experienced as a boy whilst visiting his uncle's West Texas ranch didn't hurt, either.

Six rounds pumped into her torso before Blackwood's trigger finger relaxed. The gunfire echoed between the buildings like a rocket fired down a canyon.

Sent sprawling by the impact of the slugs, the thing lay motionless for a few seconds, then sat up, blinked and gazed curiously at the gaping holes stitched across her chest. The puckered, charred wounds remained strangely bloodless. Blackwood held his breath, waiting for the Daughter to scream, moan, crumple — to react. Instead, she merely sighed as though losing patience with a dull child, raised a chin capped by a few curly hairs and wagged a scolding finger. From deep within her chest he could hear sloshing noises, and before his shocked gaze, the skin around the holes started changing color, fading from crisped black to pale again.

Tendrils of flesh pushed across each of the quarter-size openings, the milky-white surfaces knitting themselves in seconds to cover the telltale punctures.

When Blackwood finally exhaled, nothing remained visible on the Daughter's chest to show any wounds ever existed, not even the faintest scars.

Lowering her head, the thing glowered at him.

This time, Blackwood didn't even need to think about what to do next. He scrambled into the truck and squeezed himself into the driver's seat. Grabbing the key he'd left on the passenger cushions, he frantically fitted the metal into the ignition and twisted. A second later — but after what seemed like an eternity — the engine roared to life. Grunting, Blackwood leaned across the armrest, slammed shut the passenger door and hit the auto-lock button just as one of the women reached the Ford. Thwarted, she uttered a bloodcurdling scream of frustration. He could actually feel his ears burn. With hands like hammers, she pounded against the pickup, leaving fist-shaped dents in the metal.

With a sinking heart, Blackwood knew it wouldn't take long before she started beating on the window. The glass wouldn't hold for long.

By now the other two charmers joined the first, the weird sisters circling the Ford while the once-tiny flecks of flame in their eyes flared with the intensity of a bonfire. White lock thrust a hairy face against the driver's side window and mashed her horrible mouth against the flat surface. Giving an ominous creak, the tempered glass strained but held against the onslaught. Her impossibly long tongue slapped against the grimed surface, writhing like some foul sea slug stranded in a tidal pool. A trail of gelatinous goo dripped down the window. Unless his eyes fooled him, tiny larval shapes writhed in the gruel.

Blackwood wanted to heave. Instead, his foot became a brick and rammed the accelerator. The truck lurched forwards, scattering the women like bowling pins. Hands became glued to the steering wheel, the ridges of his knuckles turning white as snowcaps. A line of parked cars loomed ahead. He slammed on the brakes with a yell and felt the tires fighting for purchase in the slush. The truck thankfully slid to a stop before hitting anything.

Low cackles drifted across the lot. Raising his head, Blackwood risked a quick look, not surprised to find the trio back on their feet and unharmed, eyeing him with a mixture of contempt and hunger. Would nothing stop them? Actual fury at their persistence replaced his feelings of trepidation, but he had already figured out fighting them using conventional means represented an exercise in futility. His cousin's useless pistol lay on the floorboard of the cab where he'd tossed it, and likely would stay there.

The women glided forward, though not in any hurry.

He started to put the pickup into reverse when one of the hags launched herself through the air, nimbly landing on the hood. Bunching a fist, she slammed once, then twice into the windshield, her first as powerful as a sledgehammer. The glass fissured and caved in. A wriggling hand shot through the jagged hole. Fingers as cold as a glacier wrapped around Blackwood's throat with all the gentleness of a noose.

Gagging, the reporter slapped at her impossibly strong arm and tried to pry her steely grip from his windpipe.

The woman tightened her grasp on his protesting flesh. Within seconds, yellow spots danced before his eyes; consciousness began ebbing away, his throat burning. Rising like some hellish ape on her haunches, his attacker began jumping up and down with glee, rocking the truck with a sickening motion. Gasping for what he feared could be his last breaths, Blackwood blindly fumbled for the gear shift, felt the knob slide into his questing hand, pulled it into the "R" slot by sheer instinct and smashed the accelerator to the floorboard. The vehicle hurtled backwards so fast the thing rolled off the hood with a surprised yelp. She skidded across the sheen of the iced-over car park, then popped back up with a slightly aggravated expression and flowed like spilled ink over to her sisters.

Struggling to fill his lungs with air, Blackwood wasn't watching where he steered. He cursed when the Ford clipped another parked car (the Toyota Forerunner with the I Heart First Amendment sticker belonged to Juan Cantu, he noticed with a twinge of regret) before slamming backwards into the chain-link fence separating the parking lot from Avenue E. The interlocked metal ringlets bent outward, but didn't give. Groaning, Blackwood saw he'd missed the gate by four feet. He threw the truck into first gear, pulled forward, executed a U-turn and angled for the opening.

Moving in a blur, the sisters rooted themselves between Blackwood and the street beyond.

Framed in the Ford's quartz-halogen headlights, they snarled and clawed the air, giving no sign of giving up or granting quarter.

"You asked for it," the reporter muttered. He wrenched the gear shift and gunned the engine. The pickup jumped forward, toppling the Daughters. There was a satisfying (he hated to admit) series of thuds as the truck's four-thousand pounds rolled over them. Blackwood saw the women lying motionless with what had to be bone-crunching injuries. Yet even as he spun the wheel to the left, all three levitated upright simultaneously, as though pulled by a puppeteer's unseen strings. The truck glanced against a pole and sheared off the driver's side mirror, then bounced out onto Avenue E. Crunching metal sent up a shower of sparks as the front bumper scraped the asphalt.

The street remained empty for now, Blackwood saw, counting his blessings. In the distance, down the narrow canyon formed by office buildings and the old post office, he could just make out Christmas lights sparkling on the 80-foot Douglas fir soaring above Alamo Plaza.

Now clear of the car park, he pumped the brakes and came to a stop, frozen grit peppering the undercarriage. He wanted to make sure he wasn't being followed. The reporter glanced in the cab's rearview mirror. An icy breeze blowing through the hole in the windshield kissed his bruised throat, cooling the raw, torn flesh.

No sign of his pursuers. Good. The car park appeared empty once again, though Blackwood couldn't figure out how the merry little band assaulting him could disappear so fast. Floated away? Drifted off like untethered balloons?

Somehow, Blackwood didn't think so. These characters didn't give up that easily, he'd learned. Besides, the hairs on his neck and forearms remained as stiff as a porcupine's quills. Something didn't feel right. Another glance in the rearview mirror, however, revealed nothing but empty lanes lit by the anemic glow from a few street lamps and a billboard for Big Red cola.

Far from convinced the ordeal had ended, the reporter stopped casting nervous glances into the rearview mirror and, triggered by some sixth sense, instead swiveled his head to look over his shoulder.

What he saw made the breath die on his lips.

The three weirds hovered just inches above the tailgate, their black locks teased out behind them, reminding him of oil slicks riding a wave. He could see them through the back window. They even smiled at him.

With a rustle like a burlap sack closing over kittens, three pairs of elongated shapes unfurled behind their backs — dark, leathery and crisscrossed with throbbing veins. With a visible start, Blackwood recognized the objects in an instant — wings.

The Daughters resembled nothing short of giant bats, or lunatic harpies.

At last he understood how they kept outpacing him.

Blackwood bolted upright in his seat, shook his head, rubbed his eyes and looked into the rearview mirror again. Nothing — no women, just the twinkling cityscape, falling snow and a sky clotted with black clouds. Nothing else stood revealed.

Unable to stop himself, Blackwood rotated his head very slowly to gaze once more through the back window, unaware his breath remained captive behind a prison of locked teeth.

The three women still bobbed in the air, suspended just above the tailgate. White lock even waved coquettishly.

"You're fun, bard," she teased. "You don't whine and beg for your paltry existence, like most mortals."

"Quite refreshing," opined the second.

"Aye, 'tis great sport," chimed the third. "But your quest ends tonight, son of Adam."

He fought hard to keep from screaming — both in fear and in frustration. Now he really knew the world had come undone.

They don't cast reflections.

Taking several deep breaths did very little to steady his nerves.

And they fly. They have wings. And fangs.

How is that even possible?

They started moving towards him again, flowing like dark water around the sides of the truck, faces painted with frozen shadows. Their wings sounded sonorous drumbeats against the air.

"What are you?" he screamed at them. An acidic titter bubbled up from the throat of the one with the white stripe parting her black mane.

"By your reckoning, son of Adam, we are as old as humankind," she said. "We are the demon spawn of our mother when she fled the garden. We soared above the corpse-strewn waters of the great flood, we burned bright during the revels of the flesh in Sodom and Gomorrah."

The brutal honesty he sensed in her answer stunned Blackwood.

Stiffening his spine, he decided the time had come to get the hell out of there. Sticking around for any more answers likely would cost him his life. Gritting his teeth, he punched the accelerator.

What are they, Blackwood asked himself as the truck sped away. He briefly considered the old Latino legend about the Donkey Lady, which enjoyed some popularity in the barrios on the West and South sides; a tale handed down over generations about a creature, half-woman and half-donkey, haunting roads and bridges.

But these women bore an uncanny resemblance to bats, not donkeys, and they didn't make braying noises. Besides, he'd never heard of the donkey lady taking six rounds to the chest and walking away without a scratch.

Then there was La Llorona, the spirit of a jilted woman who stole children at night to replace her own drowned babies ... Another grim folk tale popular in certain parts of town.

But no, these things were real, not myths. The purple and black bruises ringing his throat attested to that. Indeed, these beings reminded him of something else, something far more ancient than anything mentioned in the town's legends. The rumored existence of such horrible, nightmarish creatures could be found in tales common to nearly all cultures.

He ticked off his observations, struggling to stay objective in accordance with his training as a reporter.

Vampires. The word landed with an almost physical thud in his mind. *Or something like a vampire.*

The very idea seemed preposterous, the ravings of a fever dream. Yet he couldn't deny what he'd seen or experienced, no matter how incredible. But vampires — really?

Still locked in a debate with himself as he drove away, Blackwood kept casting apprehensive glances over his shoulder. But now the trio didn't seem inclined to follow him.

He couldn't say why, but they appeared hesitant, even uncertain. Then, while his wary eyes remained glued to their forms, the sisters began turning transparent and fading away, disappearing one by one like candles snuffed in a breeze.

"Sod me," Blackwood exhaled, deciding that was the final proof he needed to convince himself he'd just encountered — for lack of a better word — the supernatural.

Later, when he had time to think about why their dogged pursuit stopped so abruptly, he would recall crossing Alamo Plaza, guiding the truck onto the historical footprint of the old limestone mission, which actually continued for several city blocks across the very heart of downtown. The former courtyard, though covered in modern times by asphalt, restaurants, shops and skyscrapers, only stopping short at the terraced banks and gardens of the San Antonio River, had begun its existence three centuries earlier as a broad courtyard extending well past the Catholic chapel, consecrated time and again by waves of priests.

Holy ground.

For now, Blackwood fought to stay calm and sort his jumbled thoughts. He navigated a circuitous route just in case the monstrosities changed their minds and decided to follow him.

A moment later, as Blackwood considered whether to stay on Pecan or take Broadway, he noticed a lone figure standing on a corner watching him. This was not one of the sisters, though. The outside lights of a late-night taqueria captured a tall, gaunt shape. The features, though draped in shadow, seemed oddly familiar, and the shaggy head deliberately turned in his direction as he drove past. Blackwood did a double take. Did his eyes deceive him?

Long beard, wide-brimmed traveler's hat, dark cloak billowing in the wind.

There was no mistaking the figure—it was the man from the cemetery, the same person who directed him to Grant's abandoned vehicle. A long, crooked finger touched the wide brim of the hat and the figure tipped his head in Blackwood's direction. Could that be a toothy smile between the parted folds of the beard?

A blaring horn snapped his mind back to the street, where the pickup had drifted into the opposite lane. With a strangled cry, he swerved back to his side of the road, narrowly avoiding a collision with a Mercedes-Benz. The luxury sedan's taillights glowed in his eyes as the motorist — a crabby-looking woman in furs — sailed past, not even bothering to glance at him. Blackwood didn't care; he just wanted to know the identity of the cloaked stranger. But when he whipped the truck around and drove back to the corner, the enigmatic figure — like the Daughters — had vanished.

CHAPTER TWENTY

December 20
8:03 a.m.

Blackwood slept fitfully, tossing and turning with the violence of a dinghy caught in a cyclone. Winged shadows and slashing claws bedeviled his slumbers, until he finally snapped awake, the bruises around his neck throbbing, his skin cooling and the bunched sheets drenched with sweat. A wan slit of winter sun edged through the partially drawn curtains.

He spent a few intense moments staring up at the ceiling, scrunching his temples as the events of last night came flooding back. Did the attack actually happen? Did he really encounter a trio of bloodthirsty — for lack of a better word — vampires?

Or had the experience just been some feverish dream, brought on by fatigue and stress? His fingers traced the rough flesh of his neck, and he could still feel his skull throbbing where he'd banged it against the Mustang's door frame (though not as painful as before).

No, not a dream, then. Not by half. He made a sound partially between a groan and a sigh. Next to him, Graymalkin's sleepy head rose from the bed's plumpest pillow. The seal point Siamese glared at him imperiously, as if to say, "Can't you be still?"

The affectionate but thoroughly independent feline allowed Blackwood to share "her" 1920s American Craftsman bungalow in the Monte Vista Historic District just north of downtown, though Blackwood always seemed to be the one signing the rent check.

Time to rise, Blackwood ordered himself. After taking an extra moment to get his bearings, he swung his legs over the side of the bed, then waited another second before commanding his feet to move. With a grimace, he began walking unsteadily across the freezing hardwood floor, tracing a path from the bedroom to the living room to the kitchen, relishing little islands of warmth whenever his feet landed on an area rug. Along the way, he passed bookcases and a Welsh flag (a gift from his mother), the red dragon framed above a battered roll-top desk. A Revell scale model of an F-16 Fighting Falcon mounted on a plastic plinth soared above the desk. A smile flitted across Blackwood's lips as he recalled building the Air Force jet at age six with his dad. The elder Blackwood piloted the real version during much of his career.

Those pleasant memories faded, replaced by stark images of the nightmarish encounter on the parking lot. Somehow he'd survived an ordeal beyond anything he'd previously experienced; quite an achievement for a reporter accustomed to navigating the city's underbelly.

True, Blackwood now had some of the answers he'd been seeking, but in retrospect the frightening encounter merely opened the door to more questions.

Whom do you serve, he'd asked the cackling hag.

Her enigmatic response? *"You'll know him by the circle and the token thrice ten."*

"Were you to live," she'd also said. But survive he did. So, that meant a new riddle to solve. But where to begin? And what was this Azad'dhul? This "unholy relic"?

Two things kept coming back to him: the Birkenstadt House and the ancient book that formed the centerpiece of the Anderson Museum's exhibit — *Pactum est Maledictus.* Both had one connection in common: the late James Grant.

He glanced into the kitchen and gave the cold kettle on the unlit stove a longing gaze. Graymalkin, having silently transferred herself to a leather armchair in the living room, stretched in her sleep. Her blue eyes remained half-open in that curious way cats doze.

Blackwood's feet left the hardwood floor and met the kitchen's slate tiles. Doing his best to ignore the icicles shooting through his soles, he put the kettle on.

He rummaged in a cupboard for a tin of Twining's Earl Grey. A few packets rattled when he shook the box. He extracted two, peeled the wrappers and dropped the bags into a dragon-shaped teapot, another gift from his mum.

The kettle whistled angrily a minute later. He grabbed the handle. Steaming water arced into the teapot, moving as fast as his torrential thoughts. He revisited every second from the night before, retraced every step of that horrendous journey beginning with the standoff against the Daughters to his escape, eventually returning to the car lot, parking McGowan's truck and scouring the alley until he found the keys to his Mustang. Afterwards, he drove home in a bewildered fog, too beaten and bruised to do anything but tumble into bed.

Blackwood took a comforting sip of the tea. His hands no longer twitched, he'd gotten them under control. But his memories of last night remained a confusing eddy of images and sensations.

In short, he needed to talk to someone. Two people, actually — the only pair who might listen. And, more importantly, not brand him a lunatic. As he walked to the phone alcove, Graymalkin stirred and gave him a puzzled stare.

•　•　•

Blackwood managed to return his coffee cup to its saucer exactly one second before sneezing. A gum-smacking waitress in a polyester uniform straight out of the 1960s glanced up from the register, gazed blankly from under a beehive hairdo, saw that nothing important had blown over, and then looked back down at the tabloid she'd been reading. Elvis and Sasquatch apparently lived on the moon at a secret base, a front-page headline screamed. The yellow stretch material of her blouse stood in stark contrast to the red velvet walls behind her. Neither color existed in nature.

Blackwood removed a hand from his mouth, revealing an apologetic expression. Sabrina Hagen and Robert McGowan sat across the table eyeing him expectantly.

"Gesundheit," Sabrina said over the rim of her cup. "Or 'God bless you,' if you prefer."

"I'm not fussed," Blackwood said. He did his best to ignore the smooth curve of her neck and the way her cheeks dimpled when she smiled.

"Do you know why we say 'God bless you' when someone sneezes?" she asked. Light from the ceiling fixtures flowed along her earrings, an Incan design depicting a jungle bird in flight.

"Haven't the foggiest," Blackwood admitted, shooting a look at McGowan, who seemed to be studying one of the many culinarily inspired signs on the walls. The nearest opined, "It was a brave man who ate the first oyster."

Sabrina idly traced a nail around her cup.

"Sneezing was associated with illness and death in several old European cultures," she said. "In the Middle Ages, without antibiotics, even a cold could kill you."

He raised his cup and took a swallow. The coffee at Earl Abel's never failed to satisfy.

"In my case, it's just allergies, nothing serious," he assured her.

"Oh, I'm sure. But had this been 'ye days of yore,' anyone hearing you sneeze might've thought you were knocking on death's door," she continued.

Wearing a bemused look, Blackwood scanned the dozens of other patrons seeking warmth and food in the 24-hour diner on Broadway, fairly certain a sneeze wouldn't be noticed much over the din of conversation and clinking cutlery.

"Those superstitious Europeans," Sabrina said, pushing her hair back with both hands, "believed you ran the risk of expelling your soul when you sneezed. And if your soul went, so did your life. That's why when someone sneezes today, we still say, 'God bless you.'"

"Old habits die hard," Blackwood said.

He dragged a fork through the remains of his omelet. Sabrina's icy blue eyes didn't waver, not even to blink. He watched her study him.

"So," she said, letting the word out like air from a tire. "Here we are."

Awaiting a response, she dipped a spoon into a fruit cup, part of a sensible breakfast that included egg whites and wheat toast (hold the butter).

Blackwood offered a wry smile and signaled for a refill on the coffee.

As the waitress decanted the steaming black stream, Blackwood waited for the impossibly high beehive to topple from her head. Somehow the pile of hair defied gravity and remained in place. Her name tag read MADGE, and MADGE stopped chewing her Wrigley's Spearmint long enough to offer a toothy grin.

"Y'all need anything else, hon?" she asked, tipping the pot upright. They all said no and thanked her.

"I'll just leave the coffee here then," she declared, placing the carafe on the table.

MADGE walked away. Sabrina fixed her cup—a dollop of sugar, a teaspoon of milk—twirling the spoon until the mixture became muddy brown spirals.

"On the phone, you mentioned a 'dicey situation' last night—that's how you put it. So, what happened?" she asked.

Lowering her chin into cupped hands, she stared at him expectantly.

"Spill the beans," McGowan urged. The bacon-and-egg taco dripping with salsa in his hand seemed forgotten. The breezy tone in Blackwood's voice while chatting with Sabrina had not allayed McGowan's suspicions his cousin had something troubling to reveal.

The reporter squared his shoulders and breathed deeply. He wanted to answer in a way that made sense, but how could you make sense of the impossible? Anything he was about to say would sound insane.

"What I have to tell you ... will be very hard to believe," he began. "But I assure you, it's the absolute truth."

He spent the next half-hour relating his strange encounter from the night before, omitting nothing. Then, he also described seeing Big Hat at the cemetery, and how the enigmatic figure led him to Grant's car and the postcard with the cryptic scrawls and names.

When Blackwood finished, McGowan only stared at him, gave his coffee a long pull and quietly said, "Whoa, dude. That is some serious shit. Really serious."

Sabrina pierced him with eyes sharp as sword points.

Blackwood pushed aside his plate and sighed.

"Mind you, the whole business sounds rather bizarre. In fact, if you were to leg it right now, I wouldn't blame either of you," he said.

Sabrina didn't reply at first, just stared down into her cup as though divining a secret in the whorls of cream and coffee.

"Oh, you'd be surprised what I believe," she finally said, raising her features to meet his. "And let's not forget our little 'excursion' yesterday. I'll never get that sight out of my head."

"Me either," McGowan chimed in darkly. The two of them nodded in unspoken agreement.

Sabrina shifted in her chair, brows furrowing as she thought hard.

"John?" She let go of a long, tortured breath.

"Yes?"

"Do you think 'The Covenant of the Cursed' is at the root of all of this?" she said.

He bit back the exclamation rising to his lips. Could she read minds? Did she suspect the same question plagued him?

"I worry that James died because of that book," she added. "After learning about his connection to the Birkenstadt Haus and what we saw yesterday, I can't help but wonder."

Waiting a beat, Blackwood answered her question with one of his own.

"Do you think there's a connection, Sabrina?"

She started to say something, then paused. He could sense the hesitation in her voice. The silence dragged on, becoming an eternity.

"Do I think there's a connection?" she finally repeated, whispering. He detected more to her tone than just reluctance; fear, perhaps. Sabrina clasped her hands.

"You're going to think I'm crazy if I say anything more." The words came out like an accusation.

Blackwood shot her a sympathetic look. McGowan didn't say anything, only cast a sideways glance at the reporter.

"Try me," Blackwood said, as gently as possible. "You listened to my story and didn't call me daft."

Sabrina took a long breath to steel herself, as one might do before plunging into an icy pond.

"OK, you asked for it," she said, inhaling deeply once more. "The other night I was helping the work crew assemble the exhibit. We were running behind schedule. What's new, right?"

McGowan shot her a puzzled look.

"You assembled the exhibit? Aren't you the boss?" he asked.

Sabrina smiled. "I don't mind rolling up my sleeves and getting dirty when a job needs to get done, Robert."

No, I'm sure you don't, Blackwood silently agreed from across the table. *Whatever it takes. You're just the type.*

He found himself warming even more to her.

She resumed her narrative.

"Finally, the time came to mount *Pactum est Maledictus* in the display case. The laborers, for whatever reason, didn't want to touch it, or even go near it. They even painted a cross on the storage crate.

My foreman — who understood a little of their dialect — said they kept repeating the word 'cursed' or something like that. They had been so good up to that point. And then they went all weird on me."

Her voice sounded more mystified than angry.

"Time is money. So together, the foreman and I assembled the display. At some point I just happened to look down at the pages ..."

She paused, as though daring herself to continue.

"And then the strangest thing happened. The most insane thing ... even now, I can't accept what I saw with my own eyes."

"What did you see?" Blackwood prompted.

Sabrina's jaw tightened; Blackwood could tell she weighed whether to say more. He leaned forward, as though that would loosen her tongue.

She made a visible effort to brace herself before resuming.

"As I looked at the page, the words started to shift. To move. On their own. And I swear I could hear something ... like whispers. Or laughter. And then came the words. I couldn't really make them out."

Her face tightened with a haunted expression.

Blackwood pushed back his chair and regarded her intently, the nerves in his body tensing at her every word. Sabrina took a sip of coffee, pursed her lips and continued, fighting to keep her voice from trembling.

"Then the characters on the page began turning even more, shaking, moving like little crawling bugs, like they were alive."

She paused again, allowing enough time to let an undertone of apprehension deflate from her voice.

"I'm afraid I'm not doing a very good job of explaining things," she said, sounding frustrated.

"You're doing fine," Blackwood said, giving her an encouraging nod. Sabrina flashed him a thin smile.

"There seemed to be — I don't know — an intelligence behind the vision ... the hallucination

... the waking dream ... whatever the hell it was. A kind of ... keen — but distant — awareness. Like something malignant had woken up. I think it knew I was there; I think ... it was reaching out to me. Or for me. Trying to touch my mind."

Sabrina swallowed audibly. Blackwood could see her shiver.

"It — the awareness — felt cold. Angry. More than angry— jealous."

Sabrina uttered the next words in a voice so low Blackwood and McGowan almost didn't catch them.

"I sensed utter and absolute evil."

A nervous laugh fluttered from her.

"Sounds like nonsense, doesn't it?" she said, her tone almost apologetic. Yet something in her half-hearted denial told Blackwood she didn't want him to agree. She needed someone to believe her, to validate her observation.

In Sabrina's own mind, Blackwood sensed, she questioned her rationality as a trained scientist.

This must be so very difficult for her, he thought.

Blackwood raised his chin and attempted to reassure her.

"Believe me, after the things I've learned in the past forty-eight hours, I'm willing to accept just about anything," he said, which happened to be true. "So no, I don't think you're mad."

Blackwood studied her, concern chiseled in his features. She gave a weak chuckle that sounded forced.

"I don't know," she said, rubbing her temples. "Maybe I'm just suffering from overwork and stress. At least that's what I think. First my gram dies and I had to abandon my dig, rush back to the States, take over the museum and fight the directors. Then came the news about James. And, oh God, those bodies yesterday; and the police. ... And I *have* been burning the candle at both ends to get the exhibit ready. So much is riding on this; it has to be a success."

Using her palm, she flattened a crease in the tablecloth. Then, she began folding and unfolding her napkin, tilting her head and looking worried.

"Well, just listen to me," Sabrina said. "How foolish I must sound."

Blackwood steepled his fingers.

"Not at all," he said, scanning her worried face.

"Why do I get the feeling there's even worse to come?" she said, the words delivered swift and hard as bullets.

Blackwood narrowed his eyes but stayed quiet.

Her plaintive tone reminded him that all of Sabrina's hopes for the museum's financial recovery rested on the success of "Myths & Magicks of Spanish Tejas." The reporter knew how much was at stake. The exhibit, this book she considered potentially dangerous, ironically represented renewed life for the Anderson and prosperity for the employees who had come to trust Sabrina's family, a decades-long bond she clearly didn't wish to betray. Irrevocably tied together, a connection existed between the relic and Sabrina that literally came into being the second of her birth, whether she liked it or not.

She swiveled her head, expression hardening.

"And what I've said is not for print, gentlemen," she warned them. "I can't have this getting back to the board, especially with the preview party tonight. Everything has to be perfect."

Sabrina gave Blackwood a penetrating appraisal, which he returned with a curt nod. Preview party? He'd almost forgotten. Now, where the hell was he going to find a dinner jacket?

• • •

Their appetites satiated, Blackwood paid the tab and the trio braved the frigid world outside, crossing the parking lot with measured steps to avoid slipping on the thickening ice. Blackwood noticed the snow tumbling much faster than when they entered Earl Abel's. Soon, he realized, the city's road crews wouldn't be able to keep up. Everything would grind to a standstill.

They reached their respective vehicles parked in a little cluster. Blackwood turned to bid his goodbyes. The two newsmen and the archaeologist stood small and alone, framed against a sky the color of slate. Even the flashing neon of the restaurant's famous sign added little color to the dreary surroundings.

McGowan considered the hole in the windshield of his Ford F150 — now patched by black electrical tape and a square of cardboard — and the dented metal of the door, the shape of a fist clearly outlined.

"You know, when I came out of the office last night and saw the damage, I just assumed some asshole had broken into the truck again." He dug his hands deeper into his vest with the multiple pockets, his expression both angry and mournful as he remembered the carjacking from last year.

Blackwood's shoulders slumped.

"Sorry," he said, feeling a flash of guilt. "But it wasn't like I could leave a note that said, 'Check your policy for monster attacks.'"

Sabrina gave McGowan a comforting pat on the arm.

"It could've been worse," she said.

Shooting her a perplexed look, McGowan asked, "How so?"

"Your truck could be covered in bat guano," she said with a straight face.

The lines around McGowan's eyes crinkled and he burst out laughing. After a moment's hesitation, the other two joined in, leaving Blackwood feeling more than a little relieved.

The merriment didn't last long, though.

A pair of headlights flared in the dim morning light, capturing the three where they stood. Blackwood's head rose at the rapid approach of a black Lincoln Town Car. The long vehicle, sleek as a bullet, slowed to a stop just a few feet away.

Blackwood frowned. Now what, he wondered as the sedan sat idling. The emblem on the doors piqued his curiosity — an upraised hand with stigmata, encircled by a Latin inscription that read "Esse abiit In Oblivione."

Warned by some sixth sense the sedan's arrival wasn't an accident, Blackwood locked his eyes on the darkened windows.

Sabrina gave the official-looking vehicle a puzzled glance, then pivoted to regard him, her expression a big question mark.

Blackwood gently took her by the elbow and drew back, putting some room between them and the car.

The middle window on the passenger side lowered a crack. Someone inside cleared his throat, but the interior remained too dark to note any details other than the dim outlines of two passengers.

To their surprise, a young, athletic-looking man stepped out from behind the wheel and approached them, bestowing a kindly gaze on the trio. Underneath his unbuttoned heavy winter coat he wore a white collar, black pants, a black tunic and a glittering cross emblem stitched above the left breast.

"Please get in," the priest amicably said. His close-cropped hair was only slightly redder than the freckles sprayed across his nose and cheeks. He seemed barely older than a boy.

Blackwood, Sabrina and McGowan exchanged quizzical glances.

"What?" McGowan asked.

"Please get in," the priest repeated, still beaming and showing a wide row of perfect teeth.

Blackwood took another step back, shaking his head. None of this felt right.

"I don't think so," he said.

The cleric quietly withdrew a hand from his right pocket and trained a pistol on them. Blackwood bit back a gasp.

"I insist," the priest said, this time with a hint of steel in his voice. The shadowy figures inside the car never stirred.

McGowan sighed.

"Could things get any weirder?"

He glanced at Blackwood for confirmation, but the reporter's face remained taut as a drum. The priest waved the gun. Blackwood looked around, wondering whether to call for help, but the lot remained empty, not a soul in sight.

"Now, if you don't mind," the priest said, the demand in his tone clear.

Blackwood finally shrugged, studying the barrel of the gun.

"Doesn't look like we have much of a choice," he said.

Sabrina, whose attention seemed solely focused on the door's seal and Latin phrase, appeared to wake up.

"Yes. Okay," she said, a little more eager than Blackwood expected. The priest training a gun on them didn't seem to faze her.

Blackwood shot her an odd look. The situation had grown more surreal by the moment.

The youthful priest opened the passenger door and politely waved the three in. As they climbed inside the roomy leather interior to take their seats, they ended up facing two men.

The first passenger turned out to be another priest, but much older than the driver. Sporting a gray tonsure, his eyes burned bright as embers. His tunic also displayed the same cross insignia as the driver's, which sparkled under the cabin's dome light. But before Blackwood could utter a word, a bearded, longhaired man with a wide-brimmed hat pushed forward next to the cleric. An ironic grin Blackwood knew all too well wreathed the weathered features.

The man Blackwood nicknamed "Big Hat" swiveled his head and spoke in a slow, measured voice that was equal parts molasses and gravel.

"Mr. Blackwood. Dr. Hagen. Mr. McGowan. Good morning. Considering the circumstances, let me just say how glad I am all of you are still alive."

"You!" a thunderstruck Blackwood gasped. "Are those women back?"

Even as the man chuckled, his piercing gaze held Blackwood like glue.

"Not quite. They're not big fans of daylight. Or of me, for that matter. And they're not women. They're succubi."

He paused a moment, registering Blackwood's growing bewilderment.

"Succubi?" Blackwood said.

"Dream-haunting, child-stealing, life-draining demons in female form, born of the first vampire, Lilith, at the dawn of history," came the answer. That response only left Blackwood more perplexed.

No sooner had Big Hat spoken than the Town Car lurched forward. The Earl Abel's sign flowed past the window, then disappeared in a slanting curtain of falling snow.

"No matter," Big Hat said. "Time is short, explanations later. Just know you actually managed to outwit the three most lethal Daughters in all of creation."

Big Hat did not bother to hide his admiration.

"A remarkable feat, and one that puts you among a very select pantheon of heroes," he added. "I can't imagine the Daughters' master is very pleased right now. You've become quite a thorn in his side."

A strangled sound escaped Blackwood. All he'd done was drive away, to be honest. Well, and punch one in the face. And shoot her in the chest. His head swam with so many questions he felt dizzy.

The heretofore silent priest leveled an appraising gaze at the reporter as the big car bumped over ice clumped in the road. He spoke next.

"Frankly, I'm amazed, Mr. Blackwood. Profoundly awed is more accurate," he said.

Blackwood detected a slight Italian accent.

So far, neither man had identified himself.

"Most encounters with Lilith and her kind end badly—for humans," the priest continued. "Were this a few centuries ago, you doubtless would be anointed a king or a madman. Perhaps both."

His statement brought Blackwood forward in his seat with a dumbfounded look.

"Lilith?" Blackwood echoed. "Who is this Lilith I keep hearing about?"

The priest folded wrinkled hands in his lap.

"Many believe she was Adam's first wife—not Eve. Eve followed. And was the better wife, in spite of all that business with the Tree of Knowledge."

The priest paused.

"Lilith," he continued, his voice barely a whisper. "Hark to the words of Isaiah: 'Wildcats shall meet with hyenas, goat-demons shall call to each other. There, too, Lilith will repose.'"

Blackwood mumbled something inaudible. McGowan shot their abductors a curious look. For the moment, it seemed the newsmen and Sabrina had forgotten they'd just been kidnapped.

"Limey here said the chicks who jumped him called themselves the Daughters of Lilith," McGowan said, the strangeness of the conversation not dimming his curiosity.

A distant look came into the priest's warm brown eyes.

"Ancient, non-canonical sources say when the Creator decided to provide a mate for Adam, the first man, Lilith was brought forth upon the face of the Earth, a dark-haired woman of unsurpassed beauty. Lilith was born of clay, the same as Adam. Eve, as you recall, came from the rib of Adam."

The priest lowered his chin and stared at his intertwined fingers before speaking again. The snowy street swam in the window behind him.

"But Lilith proved to be a creature of tremendous pride. To make matters worse, she spurned Adam's embraces. She considered herself an equal and, of all things, objected to her perceived 'inferior' status. She fled the Garden."

A long sigh escaped the priest's lips.

"Adam bewailed his misfortune to God. Three angels went into the wilderness seeking Lilith. The ancient texts tell us their names are Sanvi, Sansavi and Semangelaf."

His head rose, wide eyes searching the lengthening shadows of the car's interior as the day grew darker. At the mention of the names, a shadow crossed Sabrina's face; she struggled to recall where she'd heard them before.

"The angels searched far and long, finally locating Lilith on the shores of the Red Sea," the priest continued. "They found evil incarnate. She had allowed herself to be mounted by demons, and thus gave birth to a spiteful race of incubi and succubi. Male and female vampires."

His expression turned grim. "They were terrible, mewling, hungry things," he said, eyes flashing. "The angels were in no danger, of course, and demanded that Lilith return to the Garden. She refused, pushing deeper into the wasteland with her foul brood."

His voice died away as he dusted a pants leg.

"However, Lilith knew the angels possessed power far greater than hers, so she struck a bargain in return for her freedom," the old man rumbled.

Sabrina broke her silence.

"And what was that bargain?" she asked, still working to remember how she knew the angels' names.

The priest regarded a splendid gold cross hanging from his neck before responding.

"While Lilith wouldn't disavow her threats to bedevil Adam and his descendants, she promised no human household would be harmed provided she saw an image of the names of the three angels God sent to find her."

A quick breath escaped Sabrina. The vault—she'd seen those names in the museum vault. On the wall. Of course, that's how she knew them. But for now, she kept her silence, merely hoping to learn more. Yet she couldn't ignore the penetrating gaze the priest shot at her.

She met his searching eyes with an intensity of her own. Why did he seem so familiar? Why did she feel like she knew him?

"So these things that attacked me—they were the offspring of Lilith? Her daughters?" Blackwood broke in with an ashen face.

The priest nodded solemnly. Blackwood was both fascinated and horrified, but the explanation also shed more light on the encounter. A day earlier and he wouldn't have believed a word the priest said.

Now, his brain buzzed with a thousand questions; he had no choice but to accept the validity of the man's strange tale.

"Enough about the Daughters. We have a bigger problem," Big Hat interjected, his expression turning deeply troubled.

He folded his arms and settled back into the padded upholstery, letting the shadows swallow his features. Saying nothing more, he only turned to the priest and waited.

Following his cue, the priest took up the thread of conversation, leveling his gaze not at the newsmen but at Sabrina, as though he knew her. A spark of animation glowing in her features hinted she knew more than she let on.

"But first, permit me to introduce myself," the priest said. "I am –."

"Father Louis Dragoti," Sabrina finished for him breathlessly. He tipped his balding pate in her direction, an old-fashioned gesture of respect.

"At your service."

His nut-brown eyes twinkled.

"Or, Dr. Hagen, should I say, 'At your service again'? After all, I assisted in your delivery."

Sabrina's mouth dropped open.

Without waiting for her reply, he switched his focus to Blackwood, a grin broadening at the reporter's quizzical expression.

"You have questions, Mr. Blackwood," Dragoti said. "And I have answers. But please, you must remain patient a little longer.—All of you."

Dragoti scanned the faces of the trio, then lapsed into silence.

Tired, plagued by aches from last night's encounter and burning with curiosity, Blackwood dropped his face to within inches of Dragoti's, so close he could count the veins in the priest's eyes.

"I have seen horrors, Father. A family butchered, a good man turned into a suicidal maniac, another man ripped to shreds and those ... Daughters chasing me. Can't you tell us something? It's been nothing short of hellish."

Dragoti's expression flooded with sympathy.

"I'm truly sorry for what's happened. But hellish? Quite the contrary, Mr. Blackwood," the priest softly said. "You have it all wrong."

"Then what?" Blackwood snapped, failing to keep his tone reasonable. He'd reached the limits of his patience.

The answer chilled the reporter to the marrow. Even Sabrina and McGowan appeared shocked when the priest broke his silence.

"The foe is an angel, Mr. Blackwood. But not of heaven nor of hell, for he and his ilk chose neutrality when Lucifer rebelled. As punishment for refusing to aid the heavenly host, God banished these renegades to a frozen void outside of time and space. Over countless eons, their leader — the Forgotten One — has grown vengeful and utterly insane, seeking nothing less than humanity's annihilation."

Dragoti regarded Blackwood's shocked features.

"Sarvael is his name. And he is trying to break free of his prison — an eternal circle of ice."

CHAPTER TWENTY-ONE

Despite Dragoti's plea for patience, a thousand questions rose to burn Blackwood's lips. Before he could utter a single one, the priest waved a placatory hand that doused his inquiries as effectively as a bucket of water.

"As I mentioned, explanations will come later," he promised, ignoring Blackwood's exasperated stare. "Time grows short."

Realizing he would get nowhere by pressing the issue, Blackwood reluctantly closed his mouth and bided his time. Trading a glum look with McGowan, he wedged himself deeper into his seat and watched the wintry landscape sail past.

Except there was nothing remotely prosaic about what he saw.

At different moments, abandoned cars, fallen branches or dangling power lines blocked the Lincoln's path, testing their driver's reflexes. A Broadway Bank's rapidly flashing LED sign listed the temperature as ten below zero.

Blackwood drew back in alarm. It had never been that cold here before, at least not since the last ice age.

"Where are we going?" Sabrina asked.

"To my residence — The Vicarage," Dragoti answered pleasantly, seemingly unconcerned about the treacherous weather. "The Archdiocese kindly provides my order with an humble abode near the University of the Incarnate Word."

"Are you a parish priest?" she said.

Dragoti continued to smile.

"No, no, child. I'm a professor at UIW, lecturing in comparative religions."

His glittering brown eyes shifted away from her to stare off into the distance. When he spoke again, his tone became almost reverent.

"But I'm not the scholar your father was. I worked with your parents and admired them immensely. And, I understand you've become quite an expert in the field as well. They would be quite proud of you — Dr. Hagen."

Blackwood's head tilted to one side. He recalled from the clips in the morgue the Vatican assigned Dragoti as an observer at the Hagens' dig, but the fact the priest may have been an adviser or a consultant was news to him.

Then why, he wondered, if everyone had been so cozy, did the priest take issue with Professor Hagen on that final day? Testimony at the civil trial said the disagreement arose over unearthing the relic, which Dragoti argued against. Something about committing a sacrilege ...

Either Sabrina didn't know that detail or had forgotten whatever her grandmother might have revealed to her. Flattered by the cleric's praise, her cheeks flushed a rosy red. Here was a man who had known her parents, worked with them. That meant something to her.

"Sabrina," she said shyly, gazing at her folded hands. "Please call me Sabrina, Father Dragoti."

Dragoti's kindly stare dissolved into a sorrowful expression.

"I also heard about your grandmother's passing. My condolences. We didn't always agree, she and I, but Mimi Anderson had a good heart."

Another revelation for Blackwood. The fabled Mimi Anderson had known the mysterious priest. Something else to file away.

"Thank you," Sabrina quietly said.

The big car slalomed, making everyone slide across the leather seats. The driver hissed, struggling with the steering wheel.

"Damn road," he muttered.

Dragoti frowned. "Haste, Father MacKenzie, yes, but not waste," he cautioned.

During the next five minutes, the sedan trundled over rock-hard ridges of ice and dodged the expanding snowdrifts, negotiated a series of blinking "Road Closed" signs and finally reached a wooded drive just off East Hildebrand Avenue that wound up a bluff. Located adjacent to the University of the Incarnate Word, but partially hidden by the outstretched branches of mountain cedars and hoary oaks, Blackwood realized he must have driven past the entryway a hundred times without noticing the shadowed lane. Hugging the narrow ribbon of a road, the limo climbed to Dragoti's home on the ridge, a windswept aerie of gray stone that offered a bird's eye view of half the city and the university's snow-dusted rooftops just below. Groves of oak trees blanketing the campus that just days ago glittered with strings of Christmas lights now resembled big cotton balls thanks to the unrelenting snowfall.

The sedan rolled to a stop. Dragoti pointed to their doors.

The blustery kiss of the wind scratched Blackwood's cheeks as soon as he clambered out. Standing on a blacktop drive that formed an oval below the sprawling house, the crime reporter gradually let out his breath, teeth clicking like dice in a cup. The cold couldn't be believed. He shut the car door after Sabrina and McGowan took up positions on either side, both of them shivering uncontrollably.

As his eyes swept across the building, McGowan sounded a low whistle.

"If this is what the padre considers 'humble,' I wonder what constitutes palatial," the photographer said.

Dragoti, overhearing the photographer, inclined his head.

"Welcome to my home," he said. "May our works glorify the Lord our God."

Blackwood and his companions stared up at the massive pile looming before them, their shapes dwarfed by the rambling structure. They tilted their heads back to take it all in.

The house — The Vicarage — was a four-story granite mansion situated on a couple of acres, majestically rising from the rounded outlines of a terraced lawn and garden smothered under the snow. Leaded windows shining like pearls dotted the front.

Two priests clad in matching pea coats, balaclavas and mirrored ski goggles met them on the drive to escort them up to the house. Blackwood noticed rifles — AR-15s — slung over their shoulders.

He shook his head. *This can't be right. Why would Catholic priests carry rifles?*

As if sensing Blackwood's thoughts, Dragoti coughed politely and pointed toward the slate steps leading from the drive to the sweeping front porch above.

"Shall we?" he said.

They walked single-file, Dragoti and the armed clerics leading the way, Blackwood, Sabrina and McGowan in the middle, with Big Hat and Father MacKenzie, his eyes darting in various directions, bringing up the rear.

They made their way in silence through the frozen garden, the chill wrapping icy fingers around their vocal chords. Blackwood mounted a low series of steps and stopped in front of a wooden front door as big as an upended dining table.

Dragoti pushed past him and grasped a brass knocker fashioned in the likeness of a cherub, rapping three times.

Within seconds, the door swung inward soundlessly on well-oiled hinges. A blast of warm, comforting air rushed past, filled with the Christmas scents of wood smoke, incense and cardamon.

Another priest dressed the same as Dragoti and their driver greeted them, although he didn't wear a coat. Blackwood couldn't help but notice the sidearm holstered on his hip, which he recognized as a Beretta M9 — the same pistol used by the military. He could tell from McGowan's expression his cousin also identified the weapon. The former Marine — if there is such a thing, Blackwood wondered — probably carried the same model during his Mideast deployment.

"Please come in," Dragoti said, stepping across the threshold. Blackwood swept the drive and the hillside with one last glance, then followed the others into the house.

Blackwood, Sabrina and McGowan stood for a moment in a lofty foyer lit by the soft, flickering glow of old-fashioned gas lamps, dusting the snow off their jackets and coats. A polished, wide staircase — big enough to let a bus pass — led to unknown chambers upstairs.

With the wind and cold shut behind them, Blackwood's grey eyes swept their surroundings, missing nothing.

"If you don't mind, let's keep moving," Dragoti said. "Time is of the essence."

Following Dragoti's example, the two priests who'd met them on the drive doffed their heavy coats, revealing underneath the familiar black tunics, white collars, black pants and the ubiquitous cross emblem. Even in the muted illumination of the foyer, the insignias danced with the brilliance of captured stars. The clerics placed their rifles upright in a gun rack just inside the door, the firearms joining several other weapons — including, Blackwood saw, a pair of wicked-looking crossbows.

Not once did the four youthful priests utter a sound, their faces practiced and neutral. With a nod to Dragoti, they turned and disappeared into the depths of the great house, called to other duties.

Blackwood switched his curious gaze to Big Hat, astonished their enigmatic companion wore no winter attire. He remained dressed the same as last night, and the night before, yet he looked none the worse for wear after marching through subzero conditions.

Catching Blackwood scrutinizing him, Big Hat winked.

A clock chimed in the distance, but otherwise the house remained muted; an endless warren of burnished wood-paneled halls and tassel carpets swallowed all sound. At Dragoti's behest, they started down a long corridor lit by more gas lamps. Scents of gingerbread, sage and lemon-oil polish grew more pronounced.

Big Hat turned and gazed over his shoulder at Blackwood, then smiled as if reading the reporter's thoughts.

"Yes, they're rather proud of this place. I myself find it quite comfortable, especially if you grew up in a hut in the desert like me. Little place called Bethany."

Blackwood barely registered the comment, distracted by a row of portraits showing a succession of local archbishops. One or two he'd interviewed for stories.

Sabrina, however, heard Big Hat very well. A puzzled expression flitted across her features as she struggled to recall something.

Before she could ask anything, McGowan spoke to their host.

"What is The Vicarage, Father? It seems to be more than just a house," McGowan asked Dragoti.

"Very perceptive, Mr. McGowan. It is in fact a kind of seminary for—how shall I put it?—a very special order," Dragoti said while maintaining the brisk pace. Blackwood guessed the priest to be in his 70s, yet he didn't seem winded at all. "Unique in the annals of the church, but I doubt you've ever heard of us: The Righteously Divine Order of the Hand."

"The Hand?" Blackwood echoed.

Dragoti's shoulders rose and fell as he nodded.

"We answer directly to the Pontifex Maximus," he responded, half-bald pate bobbing.

"The what?" McGowan whispered to Blackwood.

"The pope," Dragoti said, still pressing ahead. No problem with his hearing, either. "We answer directly to the Holy Father."

Footfalls muffled by the carpet, the company moved though ornate rooms richly appointed with overstuffed chairs, plush couches, shining candelabras and oil paintings, most depicting biblical themes. At one point they passed a classroom paneled in dark walnut with a high ceiling. Several young priests sat hunched over wooden desks, the surfaces piled high with books. Strange symbols Blackwood didn't recognize covered an old-fashioned blackboard, though Sabrina paused and stared for a moment. Her face scrunched up, mouth moving soundlessly as she examined the chalked images. The young clerics remained oblivious to their passage, scribbling furiously with old-fashioned fountain pens on sheets of curling parchment.

The companions entered a library next, passing without a word through floor-to-ceiling shelves crammed with endless rows of books, many of them leather-bound and gilt edged. To access the top shelves, one had to use ladders on tracks.

Most of the works appeared incredibly old, with the spines of several worn and cracked from age.

Intrigued, Blackwood split off from the group and approached a shelf, gently tracing a finger along a row of tomes at eye-level. He pulled out a few to peruse the titles. Most volumes in this section appeared to deal with Solomon, whom he dimly remembered as the fabled Old Testament king of the Israelites, said to be the wisest man who ever lived. (The image of two women arguing over a baby in a throne room came to mind). Peering closer, he examined the titles: Les Clavicules De Solomon. The Key of Solomon. The Testament of Solomon. La Livre de Salomon (curiously, this tome was shut with a lock, and the key nowhere in sight). Lemegeton, or The Lesser Key of Solomon.

Other titles danced before him as he strolled among the stacks, keeping an eye on the receding backs of his companions. The Grand Grimoire. The Red Dragon. True Black Magic. The Grimorium Verum. Grimoire of Honorius the Great. The Arbatel of Magic. Agrippa's Occult Philosophy. The Heptameron, or Magical Elements.

Sabrina materialized next to him, her gaze roving over the books.

"Not what I'd expect to find in a seminary," she said, appearing both puzzled and openly impressed. "Grimoires. Many of these are rare textbooks on magic or lost lore."

The volumes appeared to go on forever, and Blackwood could have spent hours scrutinizing the mysteries within, but he realized they had to keep moving. Dragoti wasn't slowing down.

Catching up with the others, they passed out of the library and turned a corner, entering a great hall under a vaulted roof. Religious-themed tapestries hanging between stained-glass windows lined the chamber. At the far end, bright light spilled from an open door.

When they reached the threshold, Dragoti turned and stretched out his arms.

"Welcome to my sanctum sanctorum," he announced. Dragoti strode through the door, signaling they should follow.

They entered a long, wide study. A fire blazed in the grate, the heat a comforting presence. Unaffected by the overcast day, tall windows admitted more than enough illumination. Wooden bookshelves, paintings of bluebonnets and pictures of the Mission Trail filled the open spaces. An old-fashioned mariner's clock atop the fireplace mantel dutifully ticked away. A huge desk cluttered with files and papers dominated the far end of the room, faced by two stuffed Queen Anne chairs. A rose-colored humidor loaded with unclipped cigars squatted at one corner of the desk.

Once everyone filed inside, Dragoti gently closed the door and addressed his guests with a determined air.

"Before we begin, let me explain about the Hand," he said. "My order predates the church of Rome itself, tracing its origins nearly three thousand years ago to the wise men in King Solomon's court. We are the spiritual descendants of those warrior-priests who protected the ancient Israelites against the forces of darkness. This house is a kind of academy to keep those holy arts alive. Consider me the headmaster. And the pleasant man in the floppy hat standing there, well, he is a kind of spiritual adviser."

The priest did not name the "pleasant fellow," Blackwood noticed, which he found odd. Big Hat, for his part, merely nodded at them wearing the wisp of a smile.

A light danced in Sabrina's eyes. She tapped a slender finger against her chin.

"That explains the Latin phrase on your car—'It went into oblivion.' And the grimoires in your library. You're exorcists?"

He nodded at her with a respectful air.

"Indeed, you are your parents' daughter. You're close to the mark, Dr. Hagen—Sabrina."

Dragoti thought for a moment before he spoke again.

"Let's just say we 'chase' troublesome things away."

Gazing at the others, he added, "Not everyone in the church agrees with our methods, nor, in fact, with our very presence. Hence the anonymity. We are something of an embarrassment to Rome. Nevertheless, from time to time, the Holy See requests The Hand's services. This happens to be one of those times, and I only hope we are not too late."

Dragoti pointed to several straight-backed chairs situated around a polished mahogany table.

"Please, sit," he requested.

The three guests took their seats wordlessly. Big Hat eased himself into a chair on the left. Dragoti remained standing at the head of the table, hands behind his back, balancing on the balls of his feet.

Their driver — Father MacKenzie, Blackwood recalled — entered from a side door, pushing a small trolley with a teapot, cutlery, dishes and a silver tray laden with pastries and fruit. He placed cup and saucer before each guest and their hosts, poured the tea and left sugar, sweetener and milk. He exited just as quietly as he'd entered.

"Please, refresh yourselves," Dragoti invited.

Soon, with the chill clinging to their bones banished by the food and fire, everyone appeared a little more at ease.

"Do you, Mr. Blackwood, believe in ghosts?" Dragoti asked, buttering a scone.

The question took Blackwood by surprise.

"Two days ago I would have said no," he ventured hesitantly.

The question reminded Blackwood of a Sunday school lesson that fascinated him years ago.

"But ... the Bible mentions the witch of Endor summoning a shade. If you accept Scripture as literal truth, that passage indicates spirits do exist," he said.

Dragoti dipped his head in acknowledgment, then sat down.

"I sense something of the scholar in you, Mr. Blackwood."

Blackwood didn't respond, only propped his elbows on the table. Outside the snow hissed, driven by the wind against the windows.

"But we're not here to chat about ghosts, are we, Mr. Blackwood? Reveal to me what you've seen."

CHAPTER TWENTY-TWO

Twenty minutes passed as Blackwood unburdened his soul, the words flowing like a torrent into Dragoti's receptive ears. The reporter omitted nothing.

Sabrina frequently chimed in, her sentences hesitant at first, but growing in clarity and conviction as the priest nodded mutely in agreement or understanding, his dark, gentle eyes holding hers. She began by describing what she still insisted were fatigue-induced hallucinations — hearing the disembodied voice and witnessing the arcane symbols dancing in the *Pactum est Maledictus.*

Dragoti raised his chin, acknowledging his familiarity with the phrase.

By the time both finished speaking, Blackwood felt as if a weight had been removed from his shoulders.

"You must think us utterly bonkers," Blackwood offered, his jaw set in a determined line.

Wearing a somber face, Dragoti rose quietly from his chair. Shadows thrown by the firelight made him seem stooped with ancient troubles.

"Not at all," he said, but the worried expression stamped into his features refused to go away. He paced across a timeworn area rug, lost in thought, then fixed the visitors' eyes with his own.

"'Twas a dark day indeed when the mad monk Pierre DeGulliot breached the hidden abbey of the Knights Templar and claimed for himself those cursed parchments locted from some dark hole in old Nazareth," Dragoti said.

His voice died away as he leaned over the conference table and fixed a cup of tea. Sabrina handed him milk in a small jug made of fine china. With a grateful nod, the priest stirred his tea and then strolled to the fireplace to regard the dancing flames.

He turned to the company with narrowed eyes.

"You speak of the Daughters, the lilin, Mr. Blackwood, but there is more to this picture than just these formidable agents of evil. They are merely a hammer, not the hand that wields the hammer," he said.

"Is that why Big Hat keeps popping up?" Blackwood said, pointing to the cloaked figure across the table.

"Are you tracking them?" he asked Big Hat.

The other man's bushy eyebrows shot up, a pair of mirthful question marks, but he gave no reply.

Dragoti cast a quizzical expression. "Big Hat?"

Sabrina answered for Blackwood.

"That's what John calls our bohemian-looking friend—Big Hat," she said.

"I see," Dragoti said, exchanging a mildly amused glance with the aforementioned Big Hat. They looked like a couple of chummy old pals sharing a private joke.

The reporter's face blotched with shades of embarrassment.

"Terribly sorry," he stammered. "It wasn't meant –."

The "bohemian" waved a hand.

"Big Hat will do nicely," he acknowledged with a grin. "Mind you, I've been called far worse."

Dragoti brought his hands together, allowing his gaze once more to circle the table. His somber mood returned and he spoke with words hard as flint.

"In our world, there are many who claim to have knowledge of the occult. Most are charlatans or simply misguided. But there also exist the authentic practitioners of forbidden lore, those malevolent few solely dedicated to eradicating all that is good. It is these sons of perdition who direct and control the Daughters; who have targeted you, Mr. Blackwood, because of your inquiries."

Dragoti waited patiently for his words to sink in.

"So who are these 'sons of perdition'? Is that what Grant wanted to discuss?" Blackwood asked.

After a ruminative pause, the Italian favored him with a bitter smile.

"Suffice to say that during Grant's research into the artifact, willingly or not he became a pawn of The Synod of the Noose."

For just a moment, the silence hung thick in the room.

"The Synod of the Noose?" Sabrina finally breathed, speaking to herself before staring up at the others. "Is that a cult?"

The edge in Dragoti's voice became sharp as steel.

"Oh, quite the contrary, my dear Dr. Hagen. It's far more than a cult. The Synod of the Noose constitutes one of the darkest, most dangerous organizations ever to exist."

The priest's expression changed, the wrinkles smoothing out around his eyes. His thick, working man's fingers drummed a refrain on the mantel.

"The Synod of the Noose is known by its sign — a circle embossed with the Roman numeral thirty, symbolizing the thirty pieces of silver paid to Judas Iscariot to betray Jesus Christ," Dragoti said.

A hand reflexively clasped the cross above his breastbone.

Blackwood's mind went "click" as another puzzle piece locked into place. The Daughter of Lilith had actually been telling the truth, then.

Yes, right before she tried to kill me, he reminded himself.

Blackwood pushed back his chair, stood and stretched his legs.

"So, the Synod of the Noose, eh? What's their story?" he asked.

Dragoti vented a pensive breath and didn't speak for seconds. Instead, he walked to his desk and selected a cigar from the humidor.

A match flared. After a moment, the priest returned to the subject at hand, puffing like a chimney.

"They are the fanatical servants of the renegade angel we've mentioned, Sarvael. They will go to any lengths to prepare a kingdom for him here on Earth. These dark disciples, who call themselves Adherents, practice forbidden arts in hopes of freeing Sarvael and his ilk from their impenetrable prison of ice, locked away in the void — a sphere outside of time and space. Hence the oft-repeated phrase, 'Break the circle.'"

He shared a worried glance with Big Hat.

"Exactly how they plan to accomplish this, we don't know," Dragoti continued. "We believe Mr. Grant discovered the answer to this mystery, but was killed before he could share the knowledge with you, Mr. Blackwood."

A plume of cigar smoke trailed upwards to the rafters. Dragoti watched the vaporous ribbon snake into the shadows before resuming his explanation.

"The Synod has recruited powerful allies. A cadre of turncoat Daughters, a brood of demonesses who spurned Hell, have thrown in their lot with the Adherents. They killed Grant as punishment for his betrayal, they induced the madness that claimed the life of Dr. Malory, they slaughtered the innocents at the Birkenstadt Haus and they harried you, Mr. Blackwood. The Synod is using them to cover its tracks ... which you 'inconveniently' keep uncovering."

Big Hat murmured an assent, tipping his forehead in acknowledgement of Blackwood's efforts.

"You're very dogged," he said. Blackwood brushed aside the compliment.

"Just what is it about that house? Is it haunted?" he asked.

Dragoti placed his hands behind his back, his cassock swishing as he passed in front of the fire, head slightly bowed.

"Not haunted. Accursed. You doubtless know the tale of the brewer who engaged in the dark arts after his son and wife met tragic ends?"

Blackwood nodded. "A few times, yes."

"Some say — and I believe this to be true — he explored the endless caverns plunging deep beneath the Birkenstadt Haus. Those tunnels lead to dark, forbidden chambers. I suspect in these eternally black grottos the Synod practices unholy rites. That ill-fated mansion is somehow the gateway to the caves, and the Synod protects its secrets with murderous fervor."

As Dragoti spoke of his suspicions, Blackwood's temper flared. Ghastly visions flooded his mind: three mummified corpses and Malory's pleading eyes just before he killed himself. Blameless victims, simply wiped out because they were in the wrong place at a really wrong time. Nothing could bring them back now, but if justice truly existed in the universe, those responsible for their senseless deaths would be exposed and made to pay for their crimes.

Blackwood silently vowed to see the wrongdoers punished, no matter what the effort cost him.

"So who belongs to this secret group?" he said, scribbling furiously in his notebook. So far no one seemed to mind.

Dragoti's visage grew as stern as the chiseled bust of a Roman emperor.

"The Adherents have always hidden in plain sight, Mr. Blackwood."

"Meaning what?" Sabrina interjected. Dragoti considered the question, his brows constricting.

"For starters, if my suspicions are correct, all roads lead to Mr. Grant's employer, Akel-dama. The name is a blatant giveaway," the priest said.

Blackwood edged a little closer to the fire. Outside, the moaning wind scratched at the windows, an orphan begging to be let in.

"Not to me, Father," the reporter admitted. "Please explain."

Dragoti took a spot next to Blackwood and extended his hands toward the grate, palms outward, to soak up the comforting heat.

"Judas Iscariot, the apostle who betrayed our lord and savior for thirty silver coins, felt remorse for his deed and hanged himself in a field which became known to all of Jerusalem as Akel-dama.'"

Dragoti pronounced the phrase as "ah-kell-day-maw," all one word, but that made little difference to Blackwood. What mattered was that another piece of the puzzle had slipped neatly into place, creating a pattern he could at least begin to understand.

"So that's the connection with the Synod of the Noose. You suspect someone in the Akel-Dama Corporation is a member?" Blackwood asked.

The priest's next statement didn't exactly shed more light on the matter.

"If only it was that simple," Dragoti said. He grasped a log from the wood rack and tossed the seasoned oak into the fireplace, producing a shower of sparks that twisted like lost fireflies. "Akel-Dama is just one company. The Synod is a sinister cabal exerting influence everywhere, from the highest levels of government to the boardrooms of the world's most powerful companies. The Adherents have had centuries to insinuate themselves into every walk of life ... subtly, like a slow poison that takes years before the deadly effects are felt."

He dropped into a heavy silence, chewing thoughtfully on the cigar. His cup of tea on the table remained untouched, going cold.

Blackwood pondered the coals in the hearth, but despite their glow the room seemed to grow darker.

"The Synod's membership — the Adherents — consider Judas Iscariot to be the true hero among Christ's disciples," Dragoti continued. "They venerate Iscariot. To them, he is not a sinner but a saint. They believe he merely followed a path chosen for him, and if he hadn't turned the savior over to the Sanhedrin, there would have been no crucifixion under the Roman Empire and thus no resurrection and the promise of life eternal."

The ash on the end of Dragoti's cigar lengthened, brightening into fiery orange circles before puffing out and turning gray.

"The Synod's loathing for the church cannot be measured," he added, scowling. "They blame the Holy See for turning their hero into history's greatest villain, and forcing Iscariot's descendants into centuries of hiding and persecution."

Big Hat pursed his lips. "The betrayer could have repented and found his reward in heaven, Louis. Instead, his act of self-murder cut himself off forever from God's grace."

A particular vehemence, something almost personal, colored the bearded man's statement.

Another long silence followed, and Blackwood frowned.

If only Grant had revealed even half of this when he called, Blackwood thought, there might have been a chance to save him.

But, would he have believed even half of Grant's story if he hadn't experienced some of these horrors for himself? Even more important, would the Daughters still have been able to find Grant if he'd been hidden away?

Maybe he could have delivered Grant to a church for a few nights. Hallowed ground, right? Sanctified against spiritual evil.

Blackwood knew that's what prevented the Daughters from following him when he drove last night onto the grounds of the Alamo, a former church mission. He'd sorted that out by now.

Dragoti studied the reporter's face and seemed to follow his train of thought, then shook his head sadly.

"The Adherents wouldn't allow Grant to live with what he knew, and so his hours were numbered. You couldn't have done anything to change that."

Dragoti rocked back and forth on his black dress loafers, and after a pause, said, "You're aware he called on me, right?"

Blackwood looked up at him, nodding.

"I assumed as much. Your name was on that card. When?"

The cleric consulted a calendar on his desk.

"Two days ago, he came to The Vicarage, demanding an audience with me because of my familiarity with the relic. He wanted to warn the church the Azad'dhul was no longer secure."

The priest gazed briefly into a silver-backed mirror mounted on the wall, giving himself what Blackwood could only consider a reproachful stare. The old mirror didn't lie. Sadness and disappointment marred his features as deeply as a boulder scoured by the wind.

"The night he turned up on my doorstep, Mr. Grant's fear bordered on hysteria. He told me about the negotiations with the museum, saying he hadn't realized at first the relic he was instructed to secure was the fabled Azad'dhul. But Grant was a bright man, and after some time he put two and two together."

Warmed enough for now, Dragoti stepped back from the hearth.

"My order and our friend here —" he nodded at Big Hat, who touched two fingers to the brim of his hat — "believe that book plays a key role in the Synod's plans for revenge."

Blackwood swallowed hard.

"So the *Pactum est Maledictus*, The Covenant of the Cursed and the—Azad'dhul—are all the same book? The Daughters mentioned the Azad'dhul by name," he said.

"Yes, yes," Dragoti said, impatient to get on with his story. "They are indeed one and the same. Of course the lilin would taunt you by mentioning it."

Goose bumps prickled on Blackwood's neck and arms, and a shiver shot through him.

"Do we know the ultimate origin of the artifact? Other than somewhere in medieval Europe?" he asked, licking dry lips.

Sabrina answered ahead of Dragoti.

"Not really. Research has shown the codex was copied in the early 1300s by Pierre DeGuillot from several much more ancient fragments of unknown origin looted in the Holy Land during the Crusades. DeGuillot belonged to an obscure monastic order in Grenoble, France. As I've mentioned, he was called the 'mad monk.'"

McGowan raised his hand like a schoolboy. Fingers sticky from a sweet bun left round, moist buttons on the table.

"Why the nickname?"

Sabrina favored him with a grim expression.

"It's rumored his work on the relic drove him completely insane. He's the one who dubbed it 'The Covenant of the Cursed.' That was just a guess on his part, because—like everyone else—he could never translate the symbols."

Blackwood flipped a page in his notebook.

"What happened to him?"

Dragoti, shrugging, supplied the rest of the story.

"He died in a mysterious fire. In fact, the entire monastery burned down, killing everyone. Only the book survived, and my order took possession."

At this juncture in the conversation, his heretofore avuncular tone shifted, turning judgmental.

"Now, may we return to the subject at hand?"

When no one objected, he continued: "I was appalled by what Grant told me, but even worse, I felt betrayed. Mimi Anderson swore an oath years ago to keep the Azad'dhul locked away and out of reach. Imagine my surprise when Mr. Grant revealed the cursed tome was about to become the centerpiece of a very public exhibit."

Dragoti stared at Sabrina with a look that could punch holes in steel. She seemed to want to melt into her chair.

"Only later did I learn Mimi had nothing to do with such a foolhardy venture. She was dead." Dragoti snapped off the last word like a brittle bone in a dog's jaws.

He continued glaring at Sabrina, his eyes shooting daggers like unspoken accusations.

The import of his words wasn't lost on her. She clenched her hands, the fingernails digging into the flesh until the cuticles bled white.

"No wonder my grandmother kept the relic hidden in the vault," she said in a voice trembling with misgiving. "I just thought she was being, well, eccentric."

Blackwood still had his pen and notebook out, jotting notes in that unique shorthand of his. Another question occurred to him.

"Father?"

"Yes?" Dragoti said, turning to him.

"Why didn't the Synod just send the Daughters to nick this Azad'dhul once they knew its location?"

Dragoti swiveled his gaze to Sabrina.

"Do you know why?" he asked, though his tone hinted he already knew the answer.

A glum expression darkened her face.

"When I found the relic, it was surrounded by crosses and a circle of salt. I'm pretty sure I mentioned that before. But there were other designs, too. In chalk. I didn't recognize all of them."

She looked up at Dragoti, her fists still closed. "Those are ... wards, right?"

"Wards?" McGowan said, putting down a table knife after lathering a scone in butter.

"Protective symbols to keep evil spirits away, representing venerated saints, the apostles and such," Big Hat explained.

Dragoti seemed to think for a moment before answering. He opened the door of his study and contemplated the vast library in the adjacent chamber.

"Drawn from the 'Lesser Key of Solomon' and blessed by a cardinal, no less," the priest said, nodding toward the rows of rare volumes. He closed the door. "We sprinkled holy water on the walls. The names of the three angels from whom Lilith fled are among the wards, too."

"Those were the names on the wall," Sabrina said, her statement answering her own question. The priest merely nodded.

Blackwood thought for a moment, nagged by an inquiry of his own, and then spoke.

"Could you spell the angels' names?" he asked. Not an unusual request for a reporter.

Nevertheless, Dragoti's iron-gray eyebrows rose.

"My, you're very thorough, Mr. Blackwood," the priest said. "But, they're not so much names as symbols. Here, let me show you."

He pointed at Blackwood's notepad, which the crime writer handed over. Dragoti gently pulled the pen from his fingers, his own smaller, thicker hand moving like lightning across the pages. When the cleric handed the pad back, Blackwood glanced down and saw three Hebrew letters scrawled on the page, each one on a single line apiece.

"Sanvi. Sansavi. Semangelaf," Dragoti said, pointing at the symbols. "Lilith's banes."

"Thank you," Blackwood acknowledged, studying the characters. "However, I must ask: How do you know so much about this vault?"

Dragoti's answer sounded almost smug.

"Because I designed the chamber — at the request of Mimi Anderson."

He cast a stern eye at Sabrina.

"The vault was never meant to be breached, young lady. That was a sanctified chamber. Those wards and blessings masked the Azad'dhul's presence. But the second you crossed the threshold, you set off a psychic alarm that alerted every foul presence on this plane of existence to the book's whereabouts."

Dragoti sank into a troubled silence, his breathing the low rumble of an idle steam engine. Though he didn't speak, the priest continued to deliver a disapproving gaze that spoke volumes. There was no mistaking his displeasure over Sabrina's decision grew by the minute.

Blackwood decided to steer the conversation away from any more finger-pointing. He needed more answers, not accusations.

"What's done is done," he said, walking over and gently loosening Sabrina's tightened fists. "Can't turn back the clock now. We've got to move forward."

He pinned Dragoti with a stare.

"You've said so yourself, Father," he said.

Dragoti heard him and thankfully took the hint. The priest's stern look softened, but only by a fraction. Perhaps he realized harboring resentments was a luxury he couldn't afford if they were all going to work together.

Cooperation is what Dragoti wanted, Blackwood sensed.

The priest blinked several times, forced himself to take calming breaths and then moved on.

"You're right, of course," he said at length.

Blackwood released a low sigh of relief.

McGowan, elbows on the table and chin resting in cupped hands, listened in fascination. Then he asked a very practical question.

"If this book is so dangerous, why didn't the church just destroy it?"

Dragoti barked a bitter laugh.

"The book cannot be eradicated, except by the power of the heavenly host. All efforts by man have failed over the centuries. Casting it into the ocean, throwing it into a volcano, hacking it to pieces—fruitless. Any overt, deliberate act of destruction always results in the book returning whole and unharmed, by some unknown means. Which is why the Church quietly left it centuries ago on the edge of a wild frontier by sealing it in a cave and erasing all records of its existence, or so we thought."

His mouth turned down in a severe frown.

"It was bound to be found again, no matter how hard your lot tried to hide the thing," Blackwood pointed out.

The priest blinked, not missing the implication.

"You may be right. Under great secrecy, in 1736, my order, accompanied by imperial Spanish soldiers from a garrison in Mexico, made the perilous journey to Mission San Jose y San Miguel de Aguayo here in San Antonio and delivered the relic to the safekeeping of a young and naive Franciscan, later a bishop, named Virgil Elizondo," he said. "We thought here, of all places, it would remain undisturbed."

Dragoti hesitated for just a second.

"In spite of taking a sacred vow never to disclose what he witnessed the night The Hand and the conquistadors arrived at

Mission San Jose, or his part in the drama, that addled cleric wrote an account in his private journal. We can only assume he meant his remembrances to remain private, but he later disappeared after being sent west."

An astonished breath escaped Sabrina. Dragoti cast a knowing glance in her direction, but he continued his narrative.

"We know a partial version of the journal secretly copied by Elizondo's personal secretary ended up under lock and key in the Archivum Apostolicum Vaticanum, only to go missing later. Then, just a few years ago, an Akel-Dama team stumbled across Elizondo's crypt at an abandoned church in New Mexico, and located the full, unabridged diary. From those crumbling pages, someone in the corporation was able to deduce the general whereabouts of the Azad'dhul in San Antonio. With a little more digging, this person or persons learned of its retrieval and traced it to the Anderson Museum."

"The Synod, apparently, has many eyes, many ears, and someone was paying attention to the museum's recent activities," Big Hat added, his voice dropping an octave.

He glanced at Dragoti.

"With the announcement of a public unveiling, Grant was then dispatched to negotiate a release," the priest said at length. "The Synod resolved the time was right to make its move."

Sabrina raised a downcast face. "That partial copy of the journal led my father to the discovery of the relic."

Big Hat spoke again.

"Your enterprising parents unearthed the artifact, Dr. Hagen, sealed in a limestone cavern protected by innumerable wards, on unhallowed ground just outside the mission and thus beyond the reach of the Archdiocese. The conquistadors rigged the cave with booby traps so it would collapse if violated. Those safeguards claimed the lives of your parents and their team, and the Azad'dhul was loosed upon the world."

Blackwood peered at Sabrina. Her shoulders shook as moisture brimmed in her blue eyes. Noticing her reaction, the utter dismay on Big Hat's face gave way to a sympathetic frown. Some of the tension dropped from his voice.

"If nothing else, at least your parents stayed a few steps ahead of the Synod, which also sought the relic," Big Hat said, searching her expression and offering a kindly smile. "Who knows? In the end, your mother and father may have bought us all some time by preventing the relic from immediately falling into the Adherents' hands. The Anderson Museum prior to the dig purchased the land, which meant the archaeological recovery reverted to its control. Meanwhile, your family's oil fortune and some very generous contributions to the political party in power at the time kept the government from asking too many questions."

Sabrina opened, then closed, her mouth. Bright pearls of red colored cheeks washed by a trickle of tears. Blackwood warred with himself whether to console her. Surprisingly, Dragoti got there first, handing her a crisp handkerchief pulled from a pocket in his cassock. She gratefully took the fluttering square and dabbed at her eyes.

"Because of the deep emotional loss she felt over the deaths of your parents, Mimi Anderson would not relinquish ownership of the discovery to the church, in spite of all our entreaties," Dragoti said, taking a step back, his face etched with regret. "Yet your grandmother understood the danger. She kept the secret well all these years, as she and I had agreed, but your decision after her death to make the Azad'dhul part of a public exhibit unfortunately accelerated the Synod's plans."

The priest's glittering eyes tracked across the cavernous study. He paused at Sabrina, appearing relieved her composure was returning. Dragoti rubbed his hands and pushed ahead.

"Mr. Grant said the Synod planned to embark on something truly monstrous, and begged me to join forces with him so the Adherents could be stopped. He didn't have all the details, not yet, but he promised to learn as much as he could while continuing to masquerade as their negotiator."

Dragoti paused. Blackwood wondered if the priest kept replaying in his mind the scene with Grant from that night. Dragoti's next statement answered his question.

"I must confess, I wasn't sure how much of Mr. Grant's story to believe. For all I knew, he was merely a lackey of the Synod attempting to lure me into a trap. I told him I would need more proof before initiating any drastic action on behalf of the church. The whole thing sounded so outlandish … at first."

He glanced at the reporter.

"I am sure in your business, Mr. Blackwood, you encounter your share of crackpots. So do we."

Blackwood couldn't fault Dragoti there; he'd thought the very same thing when Grant first phoned.

Dismay flooded Dragoti's voice with his next utterance.

"Grant argued there was no time for 'bureaucracy' or to seek pontifical dispensation. Yet my hands were tied by centuries of apostolic protocol. On such matters, the wheel does not turn very fast. Grant left … very frustrated. He vowed to find another way."

The cleric did not look at them now. His shoulders slumped dejectedly. Blackwood wondered whether Dragoti blamed himself as much as he seemed to blame Sabrina for this turn of events.

"As it is, when Grant departed this house, I believe his next intention was to go to the press, to 'blow the lid off' the conspiracy, so to speak. The pen is mightier than the prelate, or so he seemed to think."

So that's why he called me, the reporter thought.

Sabrina glanced at the others, nervously rubbing the backs of her hands. Her red-rimmed eyes had dried, but her pained expression showed just how heavily the emerging details weighed upon her.

"Poor James," she said in a voice as dry as a corn husk. "I wish he would've confided in me. I would have listened. I thought we were friends."

Dragoti waved his hand in the air with an imploring look.

"He may have been more of a friend than you know, near the end," he assured her. "Don't be too hard on yourself, young lady. I believe he developed an attachment to you, whether reciprocated or not. He genuinely feared for your safety. I think you are the reason he risked so much and came looking for help. He cared deeply for you."

Sabrina placed her palms flat on the table and said nothing. She seemed absorbed in willing her fingers to remain steady. There were still half-moon imprints in her hand from where she'd clenched her fists.

Her head shook doubtfully.

"There was just so much I didn't know ..." she whispered, then trailed off.

Dragoti glided back to her chair, reached over and took Sabrina's hands in his own, giving them a comforting squeeze. A heavy hush settled over the room. His earlier disappointment with her seemed forgotten, at least for the moment. He had, after all, helped save her life as a newborn, Blackwood recalled. That had to count for something.

The cleric's chest rose and fell heavily, and then his shoulders shook as though shrugging off some unwanted burden.

"We've all made mistakes lately, my dear. Now, let's just get past them and solve the dilemma facing us."

Blackwood pivoted, put his back to the fire and welcomed the heat crawling up his spine. Satisfied that a divide had been bridged, he asked: "Why are the Adherents allied with Sarvael?"

"Perhaps they feel a kinship with the Forgotten One, for he too was denied by heaven, the same as Judas Iscariot — at least in their eyes," Dragoti answered. "Doubtless Sarvael has made the Synod some promises about their exalted place in the new order."

"But why does an angel need a human cult?" McGowan said. "Aren't angels incredibly powerful?"

Big Hat spoke up.

"Because Sarvael is not physically manifest on this plane of existence, he needs someone to open the doorway on our side."

McGowan reached for a bear claw, and in-between mouthfuls inquired, "Now how do you know that?"

Big Hat crossed his arms and settled back in his chair.

"It's all laid out in the Azad'dhul, the book you call The Covenant of the Cursed," he said.

Sabrina's jaw dropped in astonishment.

"But no one has ever translated The Covenant of the Cursed," she protested.

It seemed Big Hat tried to keep his voice as polite and respectful as possible when he responded.

"No one has translated *Pactum est Maledictus*—that you know of, doctor," he said smoothly. "But the—ahem—organization I represent, the 'spiritual advisers' to the church, has access to records no one else has ever seen, including a kind of Rosetta Stone for Akhelabeith. Your grandmother, bless her soul, had no such resources, which is why she couldn't translate the book."

"Akhelabeith?" Sabrina murmured. "Never heard of it. Sounds Semitic, though."

Big Hat chuckled. "Oh, it predates any Semitic language. Or any other terrestrial tongue, to be precise."

"What is it?" Blackwood said.

The enigmatic figure stared down the length of the table, thoughtfully stroking the wisps of his beard.

"The language of the angels. Or at least of Sarvael and his cohort," Big Hat supplied. "The Azad'dhul is written in a variant called Twisted or Dark Akhelabeith. That is why no human has ever been able to translate it. The language was never conceived by a human mind, nor can it ever truly be encompassed by a human tongue. It is ageless. In fact, it predates the creation of the universe."

He regarded each of them in turn.

"It is so far beyond mortal comprehension that it would be easier for a salmon to read 'War and Peace' than it would be for a man to grasp Akhelabeith, much less Twisted Akhelabeith, a dark tongue that, when uttered precisely and correctly, perverts the very fabric of reality."

The temperature in the study seemed to drop by several degrees. Dragoti cleared his throat and took up the narrative.

"The Azad'dhul is the key, but there's more," he said. "During our brief encounter, Grant warned me about certain portents that would signal the beginning of the end. We are seeing those manifest now."

The priest began ticking off the "portents" on his fingers.

"As you know, the snows started very early, preceded by this uncharacteristic freeze. The kind of cold this region hasn't seen for ten thousand years. Soon, a blizzard of unprecedented magnitude will grip the city. Next, the ice sheets will spread exponentially, until the entire planet becomes a frozen wasteland. As nature slows to a crawl, Sarvael intends to hold what's left of mankind hostage until God capitulates and allows him back into heaven."

Blackwood couldn't hide his incredulity.

"How can he possibly hold the human race hostage?"

His gaze drifted to a large picture window. Blackwood thought he'd seen something moving in the bare trees across the drive, but now it was gone. The wind. Maybe.

Big Hat answered for the priest, his tone low but each word as clear as notes sounded on a bell.

"The Azad'dhul contains an incantation to keep everyone from dying," he said. "It's a way to indefinitely suspend death, in a manner of speaking. No souls for heaven, no souls for hell. Sarvael will use mankind as a bargaining chip to return to paradise and reclaim his seat among his angelic brethren."

Blackwood contemplated the fire, his silence merely the outward manifestation of a struggle to absorb such dreadful tidings. With thoughts hurtling at breakneck speed to weave together all the threads he now held, Blackwood realized one strand was missing.

"Did Grant mention when all of this would come to pass, Father?" Blackwood asked.

Dragoti locked hands at his waist, then strode quietly across the room, headed to the floor-to-ceiling windows behind the desk. He stopped, nose almost touching the glass, and felt his skin constrict at the frosty chill coming off the polished surface.

"Yes. Grant gave me a date," the cleric finally said. "Or rather, an event."

Blackwood's heart skipped a beat.

Dragoti smoothed the creases of his cassock.

"It is the solstice," he solemnly announced.

With a puzzled expression, McGowan ventured a question.

"The solstice?" he said. "What's that?"

But it wasn't Dragoti who responded.

"The winter solstice marks the shortest period of daylight during the year in the Northern Hemisphere," Sabrina explained, her expression revealing relief at contributing something to the conversation that didn't revolve around the decision to unlock the vault. "That's when the sun is at its most southern position, directly overhead at the Tropic of Capricorn. The reverse takes place in the Southern Hemisphere—it's their longest day and the beginning of summer. In many northern cultures, the winter solstice is a day of reckoning, when the doorways open between the realms of the living and the dead."

Realization dawned in Blackwood's eyes.

"The winter solstice," he said, snapping his fingers, "is not only the shortest day of the year, it's the longest night, too."

The room fell into a silence shattered by Dragoti a moment later.

"The winter solstice arrives shortly after midnight, Dec. 22," he said in a heavy voice.

Sabrina gasped. "Oh my God."

Blackwood stared at her in alarm.

"What's wrong?"

When she answered, Sabrina could barely keep her voice steady.

"The party at the museum, remember? We're unveiling the relic tonight — the same night as the solstice!"

CHAPTER TWENTY-THREE

Outside, in the deep gloom of the trees across the drive, just beyond the protective ring — how it burns so — of sanctified ground, something with glowing eyes brooded and watched the windows of Dragoti's study from the tattered boughs of an old oak. The Daughter of Lilith's hearing was very, very good. The ancient Hebrews had said the lilin could hear a fly snore from a league away. Perhaps there was some truth to this, for she could discern snatches of the conversation with little trouble, enough to know her master's plans had been discovered.

Right now the talk consisted of nothing more than childish prattle. Narrowing slitted eyes, she watched as the light spilling from the windows occasionally dimmed whenever one of the hairless primates walked back and forth, nattering away.

With black wings wrapped around her tensed body like a burial shroud, the abomination leaned forward to hear more. She easily detected the weariness in the Daughter of Eve's voice; close to the breaking point, the meddlesome woman struggled to hide her fears and regrets from the sons of Adam. The others with her — the foolhardy bard, the idiot shaman, the Lamb's tool and the feckless warrior — contributed little at this stage.

Suddenly the tips of the night hag's curved ears quivered. Something new here! Yes. The bard began discussing the unholy relic after uttering its true and venerated name — the *Azad'dhul*. The Celt spoke casually, with neither reverence nor regard for the deep mysteries the talisman harbored, powers his little simian brain couldn't even begin to comprehend.

Rage boiled within her. Low, venomous hisses sent snow flurries scurrying. Inside that cozy little room of theirs, the mortals' lips should be nailed shut for such effrontery. Had she been able to skirt the prayer wall and the protective wards, she would have swooped into their pitiful refuge and ripped out their throats.

Mawrgoth, for that was her name, especially wanted to see the light die in their gaping eyes as she drained their essence.

Instead, she merely bided her time and faded deeper into the skeletal lattice of tree limbs, the falling snowflakes popping whenever they alighted upon her scales.

Her masters' orders had been explicit: She was only to watch and wait.

For now.

•   •   •

A stunned silence seized the room after Sabrina's pronouncement about the impending solstice and the timing of the preview party. Coincidence? If so, it was a bad one. The worst. The relic would be left out in the open. Exposed. Ripe for the picking, and Blackwood knew who would come calling.

But now that we know about the solstice, is it really wise to go ahead with the unveiling? he wondered.

The Daughters are still out there. They haven't given up, not by a long shot.

McGowan beat him to the punch and voiced his concern.

"Wouldn't it be smarter to put the book back in that protected storeroom and call everything off?" the photographer asked.

Sabrina and Dragoti shook their heads simultaneously, but offered divergent rationales.

Sabrina spoke first, rising so fast from her seat the table shook.

"You can't be serious!" she exclaimed, giving the rest of them a flustered look. "Do you know how much time, money and work went into this exhibit? My parents died to retrieve the relic for scientific study and public discourse. I'm not going to let their sacrifice be in vain."

She stopped long enough to take a breath, but her agitation only grew.

"Plus, this is a major fundraiser for the Anderson. We need the revenue to stay in the black. Half of what I've heard today is only conjecture anyway, not enough to convince me to call off one of the city's most significant cultural events in decades."

Sabrina's lips compressed into a line so severe her mouth disappeared. Determination and indignation rolled off her in waves.

"We'll have plenty of security there. No one is stealing the relic, if that's what you're thinking," she added with an air of finality.

Her earlier regrets and misgivings seemed forgotten in the rush to protect the museum. In a way, Blackwood reflected, it was the only real family she still had left.

Dragoti cast a sour glance in her direction, then offered his own argument.

"I can't say I agree with Dr. Hagen's logic, but I do concur there is no point in locking away the relic. Now that the Synod knows where it is, they have plenty of human allies who won't be thwarted by chalk and candles in a basement storeroom."

Dragoti put his chin in his hands.

"Since we know the Synod faces a deadline, we have something of an advantage. They'll be coming for the relic, no doubt, probably sending the Daughters, but we'll be ready for them. We control the venue, we control the egress and the ingress, and we can put a stop to this madness once and for all."

Although both Sabrina and Dragoti seemed assured their ideas to safeguard the exhibit would prove adequate, Blackwood harbored his doubts. None of the others had seen the Daughters in action, faced their sheer cunning and ferocity. Not to mention all the people they'd slaughtered in the last 48 hours, including a child. Blackwood wondered whether they could mount any kind of defense against virtually indestructible beings.

He stole a glance at Dragoti, noting the priest's hardened jaw and squared shoulders. The cleric seemed assured of his plan, whatever it was.

But the priest wasn't ready to divulge any details. Dragoti asked them to remain patient a little longer, promising to explain everything soon. He urged them to regroup at the museum two hours before the preview party, which meant six o'clock. They would get their answers then, he assured them. Blackwood didn't like the idea, of course, but before he could protest too much he and the others found themselves politely ushered out of the study and back to the foyer by a phalanx of humorless priests, handed their coats and bundled back into the limousine for a return trip to the restaurant parking lot and their own cars.

•   •   •

Three hours later, as agreed, their little company sans Sabrina stood reassembled just outside the Anderson Museum. The weather hadn't gotten much better, but it hadn't turned any worse, either, so everyone made the trip without mishap. McGowan even showed up in a dinner jacket, as stipulated earlier by their host; perhaps the worsted wool vest stretched a little too tight around his midsection, and instead of a bow tie and black leather dress shoes, he sported a string tie with a Marine Corps EGA for the slide and wore his favorite pair of stitched Tony Lama alligator-hide boots. Though not attired in a dinner jacket, Dragoti also honored the ceremonial nature of the occasion and appeared in starched vestments and a cape Blackwood later learned was called a ferraiolo, traditionally worn by Roman Catholic clergy to formal, but non-liturgical, events. Big Hat, not surprisingly, eschewed the sartorial mandates and arrived in what Blackwood wanted to call "traveling wizard's garb"—the wide-brimmed hat, long cloak, homespun tunic and woolen leggings. A pair of sturdy hiking boots appeared to be his only concession to modern fashion, and the smile peering from the braids of his long beard telegraphed he remained unapologetic and unconcerned about what others might think of his fashion sense.

After parking their respective vehicles, the trio entered the museum and approached the ticket desk, where a dark-haired young woman in a sweater embroidered with flying reindeer noted their attire and simply waved them through.

"You want the Great Hall, down that way and to your right," she smiled through a slight drawl, pointing to a soaring chamber filled with dinosaur fossils.

Walking past a reconstructed long-necked Alamosaurus that appeared to smile through bony teeth, the four men mounted broad steps to a soaring entryway, the words Great Hall stenciled in bronze above the stairs. They moved inside. A blast of hot air from a ceiling-mounted heater washed over them as they emerged from a long hallway. The shining lights ahead welcomed them further into a massive chamber, the colonial wing.

A huge purple-and-gold banner emblazoned with "Myths & Magicks of Spanish Tejas" greeted them. The men's steps led them along a crimson carpet trimmed with gold tassels. Several eye-catching history displays, maps and dioramas showcasing the Spanish Empire's northward expansion in the New World crowded the room, but the real attraction — the legendary object drawing them here in the first place — squatted in a large glass-and-chrome box at the very center of the chamber, roped off and flanked by signs warning visitors to refrain from leaning over the barrier or touching anything, or risk sounding an alarm.

There it is, Blackwood thought, moving closer for a better look. *Pactum est Maledictus.* The Covenant of the Cursed. Or the Azad'dhul, if you prefer.

Frankly, no matter how frightful the legend, the relic did not leave much of a first impression, resembling little more than a collection of moldy, thick papers sandwiched between two weather-beaten leather boards. An iron band encircled the tome. A few of the pages spilled out, covered in some indecipherable writing just as Sabrina described.

Blackwood stared as hard as he could, but none of the symbols moved.

A platform with a podium rose behind the display case.

"That vile codex is an abomination to all mankind. It should never have seen the light of day."

A voice as cold as a chunk of ice rumbled next to him.

Blackwood swiveled to the right. Dragoti had crept up on him, standing two feet away. The priest remained riveted on the book the way a mouse watches a cobra.

"I'm still wondering if we're going to be able to protect this thing," Blackwood said, apprehension knotted in his voice. "We haven't even heard your plan yet."

The cleric kept his glittering eyes focused on the book.

"We'll discuss the plan when we find Dr. Hagen," Dragoti said. Only the muscles of his mouth moved, his eyes stayed fixed on the display. Blackwood stared at him, somewhat lost.

"No worries. She's found you," a voice announced. Both men rotated to spy Sabrina standing behind them.

Alluring in a sheer black dress and a coiffed French bob, her presence lit up the Great Hall. She regarded Blackwood steadily, those sapphire blue eyes connecting with his sad grays, her orbs electric, inquisitive. There was no question she was in her element; this was her exhibit, her museum, her turf.

With a radiant smile and a shake of her blonde tresses, she told them, "I'm glad you could make it. All of you."

"I'm glad you invited me — us." Blackwood quickly corrected himself.

McGowan and Big Hat drifted over from a re-creation of a horno, an outdoor adobe oven used for cooking by the converted indigenous natives at the missions, and joined them. Sabrina nodded in greeting, her eyes briefly lingering on Big Hat's less-than-elegant garb, and then pivoted, signaling to a caterer in a far corner setting up a bar.

"Champagne, please," she requested. Blackwood half expected Sabrina to clap her hands, a lady to the manor born. A young man in tails and a pink bowtie approached, adroitly balancing a tray of flutes. Sabrina grasped the slender tubes one by one, handing them to her guests. A cool glass slid into Blackwood's open palm before he knew what was happening.

She raised a glass of her own.

"Cheers," she said. "To the 'Myths & Magicks of Spanish Tejas' and the sacrifices that brought us here."

"*Diolch am y noson*," Blackwood responded solemnly, tipping his own glass.

She wrinkled her nose. "Oh my," she said, a hand fluttering to her throat, "that always burns a little when it goes down. I can feel the little bubbles bursting."

Blackwood sipped his drink while he studied her.

"What was that you said?" she asked him. "Your toast?"

Blackwood emptied his glass before replying.

"Welsh," he said. "Literally translated, it means, 'Thanks for the evening.'"

"You might regret that later," Dragoti muttered.

Sabrina eyed Blackwood with new appreciation. "You speak Welsh?"

He shrugged. "Not much. Mum's side, anyway. They're all fluent."

She seemed charmed by this.

Blackwood waved a hand at the room. "You've pulled out all the stops, it seems. Well done."

Dragoti grunted.

"Oh yes," she said, ignoring the priest. "This is a very important occasion for the Anderson — it's a significant development in our understanding of colonial Spain and the empire's relationship with the frontier church."

The blue eyes scanned Blackwood coolly from top to toe.

"You don't look half bad in a tux. A little underfed, maybe," she said.

"'Underfed'? — Bloody cheek, that," he said, his mouth twitching into a grin.

She, of course, looked gorgeous.

"I see you doffed the leather jacket," he said, searching for a spot to deposit his empty glass.

Sabrina winked at him. "Just for tonight," she said, taking the glass away and again signaling the busboy.

Dragoti sighed, obviously deciding they'd all heard enough polite banter.

"I think it's high time we discussed our plans to prevent any disruptions," he told the others, giving each of them a hard stare. "Agreed?"

Blackwood noticed he hadn't touched his glass.

•   •   •

Dragoti insisted they meet someplace away from the workmen still hammering and sawing, putting the last-minute touches on displays, their activity only slightly louder than the bustling crew of museum staffers setting up tables, hauling chairs and hanging signs.

Sabrina led the company to a service elevator that deposited them on the third floor. They traversed a long hallway with exposed pipes running the length of the ceiling. The featureless concrete floor soon changed to beaded board after they entered a door carved with vines and flowers that Sabrina unlocked with an old-fashioned brass key. Turning down a new corridor lined with cypress wainscoting, Sabrina came to another door, a much heftier specimen that looked hewn from the Round Table itself. With a single push, the door swung open. Sabrina entered an elegant, old-fashioned wood-paneled chamber, turned and stood waiting for the others. A thick red carpet swallowed their footsteps as they filed in. The smell of polishing oil greeted them, and the heat of a welcoming fire radiated from a marble-lined hearth. Glass cases filled with old maps and weathered documents made the chamber feel weighted down by dust and history. A massive table with leather-backed chairs anchored the heart of the room.

"As requested, Father Dragoti — a quiet place where we can speak frankly," Sabrina said, her wave encompassing the space. "Welcome to the boardroom."

Sabrina plopped down on a long leather couch, a sigh escaping her lips.

McGowan took a seat at the table, knit his hands together and placed them behind his head. Leaning back, he allowed his gaze to sweep the room.

"This place seems different from what else I've seen of the museum," he said.

Sabrina nodded. "Good eyes. You must be a photographer."

McGowan gave her a crisp salute.

"The Anderson is actually a gigantic building built around a smaller building. We're in the original structure now," Sabrina explained.

The others cast appraising glances around the room.

"How so?" Blackwood asked.

Sabrina pointed to the walls.

"This part of the structure is actually called The Armory, built by the U.S. Army in 1859 as an arsenal and supply depot. The Confederates seized it during the Civil War and also used it to house their munitions. The Johnny Rebs transported weapons on small barges from the San Antonio River, which flows right behind the museum, to a secret entrance at the basement level. Supposedly the Union Army dynamited the dock, destroying it. The hole they left in the wall was bricked up. They did a good job. No one alive today is even sure of the location. Anyway, after the end of hostilities, the U.S. Army moved back in, only to abandon the structure around the time of World War 1 and relocate to Fort Sam Houston."

"Makes sense. The post is only a few blocks away," said McGowan, the veteran. Sabrina didn't disagree and continued.

"Mimi loved to spin a tale that bootleggers moved into the building during Prohibition and smuggled moonshine into a speakeasy, also down in the basement and away from prying eyes. I've been told it was a pretty popular jazz club."

The revelation the venerable museum possessed something of a sordid past brought an ironic smile to Blackwood's lips. Sabrina caught his grin and returned it.

"When my great-grandfather bought the place in the late 1930s with his oil money, he closed what had turned into a reputable bar and started setting up the museum we all know and love today."

"Classing up the joint a little bit?" McGowan chided.

Sabrina offered a slight nod at the good-natured jibe.

"Actually, he didn't start building the museum until after the Second World War, using The Armory as the 'bones' of the new complex. Over the decades, the museum took shape around the older structure. Great-granddad eventually put Mimi in charge. I guess it gave my grandmother something to do besides tea parties and Fiesta coronations."

She arched her neck and rubbed a spot at the base of her skull.

"And so here we are," she finished.

Sabrina drew her knees up to her chest and wrapped her arms around them. She looked very tired. A second later, she put her face down sideways on her knees. The history lesson was over.

She shared a look with the others. "Father Dragoti, your plan? The hour grows late. The VIPs, guests and the donors will be arriving shortly."

She tapped her watch for emphasis, and Blackwood noticed her previously unadorned nails — hands for shifting and digging among ancient ruins—now sported a lustrous coat of red polish.

Dragoti cracked weathered knuckles and began to speak.

"It's simple, really. The priests of my order are placing wards at all the exits, entrances and windows. We will be discreet, of course, and your patrons — those who even bother to notice — will merely think they are art elements that belong to the exhibit. To the Daughters, however, they will serve as an impenetrable barrier."

He searched Sabrina's face for confirmation. After a moment, she yielded a reluctant nod.

"You have your own security here," Dragoti continued. "They may be adequate, but with your permission, I, too, will station some of my priests across the museum. They have some additional knowledge of the foe that will enhance existing safeguards. Again, we'll be the soul of discretion. Your guests will simply think they are delegates from the Chancery. Fitting, no, for an exhibit showcasing a relic of the Catholic Church?"

At least he didn't say "stolen" relic, Blackwood silently noted.

Sabrina tipped her head once again in agreement.

"And, finally, our little fellowship will be present, of course, including the inestimable Mr. Blackwood—who has actually bested the Daughters in a confrontation," Dragoti added.

The reporter's eyebrows rose quizzically.

"Um, point of fact, I ran away," he said.

Across the room, Big Hat shot him a grin. "No, you lived ... to fight another day. Look at it that way, John."

Blackwood wiped his palms on his trousers, not appearing convinced.

Dragoti settled into a meditative silence, slightly bowing his head and drawing his palms together. He waited to hear what the others thought of his strategy.

Sabrina clapped her hands and rose from the couch. A change had come over her, Blackwood realized. She was no longer the bewildered, grief-stricken woman he'd spoken to in her kitchen two days ago. That person was gone, transformed. Sabrina shone now, a proud woman of the Anderson lineage, part of the unyielding firmament of San Antonio society, possessed of an unswerving duty to her family legacy, her museum and her employees.

"No disrespect, but that sounds absolutely crazy and, in fact, I expected something better," she said, putting fists on slender hips. "But I'm going to have to trust your expertise in this, Father. I can't deny the strange and horrible things I've seen lately, and the clues my grandmother left me. Why she couldn't have just written a note explaining all of this, I don't know, but she was always eccentric."

"To protect you, to shield you," Dragoti softly said.

Sabrina sighed. She'd heard him.

"Maybe so. Either way, this night has to go flawlessly. The museum's future is riding on it. So, do what you must, set up your sentries, coordinate with my security ... Just keep a low profile, okay?"

She gestured at the door.

"Now, if you don't mind, I need to go mingle, shake a few hands and save my museum from financial ruin."

With that, she patted Blackwood on the shoulder, turned and walked out of the room, headed downstairs and to the grand unveiling.

The door shut behind her.

"Merry Christmas?" McGowan offered.

Blackwood didn't respond. The shadows smudged the corners of the room, and into their gloom he cast his gaze, wondering if anything would ever be merry again if they failed tonight.

CHAPTER TWENTY-FOUR

The Great Hall, normally the quietest of rooms this time of night, reverberated with the deafening hubbub of clinking glasses, conversation and footfalls echoing across the black marble floor. Waiters deftly weaving through the throng balanced platters loaded with drinks and canapés, the latter molded into cowboy boots and sombreros. Guests clustered around open bars. Track-mounted lights showcasing the trappings of a faded empire also reflected the sparkle of the one that rose in its place — diamond necklaces, strings of pearl, cufflinks polished to heady brilliance and glittering designer gowns.

Having returned to the ground floor with the others, Blackwood loitered in the colonial wing, automatically conducting a head count. He estimated eight hundred or more guests. Apparently the premiere of "Myths & Magicks of Spanish Tejas" was a big draw for San Antonio's elite, judging from the movers and shakers he recognized.

Gazing past a large diorama depicting the five Spanish missions erected on the banks of the San Antonio River, he did a double-take. Just behind the display, the attractive Latina TV reporter from yesterday's crime scene chatted with McGowan. A second later, they exchanged slips of paper, giving each other bashful nods before walking away.

Hmmm, Blackwood thought.

Above him, the melodic strains of a chamber orchestra on a balcony softened the din of the crowd. The musicians played in front of a gargantuan oval window three times a man's height and twice as wide, criss-crossed by a lattice of metal support bars. Recalling the museum stood on the banks of the San Antonio River, Blackwood assumed the window offered a picturesque view of the waterway below.

The Aspen pine towering over the balcony caught his eye next. A glittering star at the pinnacle brushed the vaulted ceiling. The green boughs of the Christmas tree twinkled with a thousand colored lights, and the heady aroma of a faraway forest filled the room. A small children's choir, the singers attired in red-and-green elfin costumes complete with pointed shoes and pointed hats, began arranging themselves on risers just below the spreading branches. They whispered and studied their sheet music.

Dragoti and Big Hat appeared at his elbow.

"Time to check on my priests," Dragoti said. The reporter spotted a few white collars floating among the crowd. He also noticed some off-duty police officers hired to beef up the museum's security force. Many he recognized; several waved or inclined their heads.

Dragoti and Big Hat strode into the crowd, parting the masses the way an ice breaker cuts through floes.

On the balcony, a man with a scruffy beard wearing a purple tuxedo emerged from a side door, clasping an accordion. The new arrival spoke briefly with the chamber orchestra. The other musicians grinned and nodded. Purple Tux began pumping the squeezebox. The chamber musicians enthusiastically joined in, switching from Mozart to the same tune, something with a little more local flavor.

The crowd roared with approval as the first strains of the Texas Tornadoes' "Hey Baby, Que Paso" reached their ears. Guests in black-tie, evening wear, boots and cowboy hats — only in the Lone

Star State do the styles mingle without reproach — formed a dance line. Blackwood edged away to avoid being swept into the gleeful fray. Taking refuge near a display detailing the conversion of the Payaya Indians, he once again regarded the guests.

The most prominent attendee held court a few paces from the podium: Mayor Raul Solis, dressed in a suit so sleek it looked sprayed on. In his early 40s, Solis—a lawyer by trade — radiated youthful exuberance except for a few deep lines chiseled by some unnamed sorrow around his eyes. A gaggle of dutiful City Hall functionaries flanked him the way groupies fawn over a rock star, laughing at whatever pearls of wisdom he cast. Occasionally someone new walked up, prompting Solis to throw out a big *abrazo*, enthusiastically embracing the arrival.

Weary of watching rich people dancing badly, Blackwood retreated from the Great Hall, searching for Sabrina. His footsteps led him to an arched doorway opening onto a long but smaller exhibition area. A sign over the door informed Blackwood he was entering the Folk Art of Latin America wing. As he took his first step over the threshold, very small, wetly gleaming markings across the lintel attracted his notice—shapes freshly painted in red. He froze in his tracks. Balancing on tiptoes, Blackwood squinted for a closer look. The marks resolved themselves into characters from the Hebrew alphabet. That's when he recalled Dragoti's promise to place wards at all of the entrances and exits.

If he remembered correctly, the symbols represented the angels Lilith promised to obey if only they would leave her and her dark offspring in peace ... Sanvi, Sansavi, Semangelaf.

He walked into the chamber. Sculptures and paintings lined the room, the depictions ranging from raspa vendors to the chili queens of the 1930s thronging Alamo Plaza.

A few people milled about, none of them Sabrina. Picking up the pace, his dress shoes pounded a tattoo against a Spanish-tile floor inlaid with colorful figures from Aztec mythology.

He ambled through another gallery, this one showcasing the Old West. The entrance displayed the same red symbols he'd encountered in the folk-art wing.

In fact, now that he knew what to look for, the wards seemed to be everywhere.

Dragoti and his lads have been quite busy, Blackwood mused.

Eventually he retraced his steps to the Great Hall. The guests no longer kicked up their heels, the music having returned to something more sedate. Enjoying the lull, he paused next to an exhibit featuring a 1700s mendicant friar ministering at a baptismal font. He downed a glass of champagne he'd grabbed along the way.

"Better watch the bubbly," a voice cooed. "You're on duty."

He turned and regarded Sabrina. She'd caught him by surprise again.

"Hullo," Blackwood greeted her. He waved at the room, visibly impressed. "You've managed to lure all the toffs here."

"Part of the job is knowing who has the deepest pockets," Sabrina said with a wisp of a smile, studying his reaction as she drew closer.

"Making new friends?" she asked, pointing to the penitent mannequin next to Blackwood. Clad in a homespun tunic and cowl, the friar loomed over the font with arms upraised, presumably performing a baptism.

"It looks quite authentic," Blackwood said.

Her chin rose. "Very much so. The font is on loan from the Alamo chapel."

"The Alamo?" Blackwood repeated.

Sabrina gave him a look that said he shouldn't be so incredulous.

"Don't be fooled by that silly John Wayne movie. Remember, the Alamo started as a Catholic church, long before the battle of March 1836."

Blackwood peered into the font, noting his and Sabrina's shimmering reflections looking back from a silver basin.

"And the water?" he asked.

She smiled. "Authentic, too. At Mimi's request, the archbishop himself blessed the font a few years ago."

She lowered her voice to play the part of a confidante. "I'm not Catholic, but I don't think holy water, once sanctified, ever expires."

She glanced at her wristwatch and sighed.

"Is it time already? The mayor is giving a speech, and I have to introduce him."

Absently twirling the ice in her glass, her eyes burned into his.

"Say, when all of this is over—whatever 'all of this' is—want to hang out for awhile? Just talk?"

Her question surprised him. He ran a hand through his straw-colored hair.

"I'd be delighted," he answered, embarrassed by how quickly he responded.

She gazed into his face, an unreadable expression on her own, and gently squeezed his hand. She seemed ready to say something else, but didn't, and was gone in an instant, swallowed by the crowd.

From under the boughs of the Christmas tree, the children's choir launched into a rendition of "O Little Town of Bethlehem."

•   •   •

"— your attention, please. Could I have your attention?"

The voice belonged to Sabrina, who now stood on the raised dais. Mayor Raul Solis, no longer surrounded by his entourage, waited by her side with a patient expression.

The children's choir went silent.

McGowan materialized next to Blackwood.

"Must be the big moment," he whispered.

Blackwood playfully punched his cousin in the arm.

"Who was that bird I saw you chatting up?" he asked the photographer. "Wasn't she at the crime scene yesterday? She's a reporter with one of the TV stations, right? KLIK?"

McGowan actually blushed, a rarity.

"Just a friend, that's all," he said, perhaps a tad defensively.

He didn't seem inclined to say anything further, so Blackwood took the hint and dropped the subject. He shifted his focus back to the dais.

Taking a cue from Sabrina's nod, a museum staffer dimmed the lights, leaving only the archaeologist and the mayor in a circle of illumination. Her eyes shone bright and quick, while a toothy smile swallowed Solis' features. The guests moved nearer to the platform. Several curious, expectant faces rose to regard the pair. Sabrina held up a hand, quieting the crowd's murmurs.

"Honored guests, welcome," she began in a voice as smooth as a margarita. "I'm Dr. Sabrina Hagen, interim director of the Anderson Museum."

She scanned the attentive faces of the audience before continuing.

"Tonight begins a new chapter in the study of southwest American colonial history with the unveiling of 'Myths & Magicks of Spanish Tejas,' an exhibit showcasing a little-known chapter in the settlement of Texas and the expansion of the Spanish Empire's mission system."

A ripple of polite applause circled the room.

"This occasion marks the debut of a truly unique addition to our city's rich history," she said, indicating the book and its case with a sweeping gesture.

Her voice dropped to a stage whisper. "Given the title 'The Covenant of the Cursed' in the Middle Ages by a French monk trying to unlock its mysteries, no one — in peer-reviewed academic circles, anyway — has ever deciphered the codex. Written in an unknown language, it has stymied all scholarly efforts to reveal its ancient secrets."

A hush settled over the chamber; the audience held its collective breath. Sabrina leaned forward, pinning the listeners with a penetrating stare.

"And yet ancient records hint the Roman Catholic Church considered the book very dangerous, enough so that the pope and the king of Spain decreed the relic should be conveyed to the New World and forever sealed in a hidden cave. Escorted from Mexico City by a special order of priests, and guarded by brave conquistadors, the book made its way north until reaching its final destination at Mission San Jose. There, it was sealed in the cave and forgotten. Church and state assumed the trackless wilderness would prevent anyone from ever finding the codex."

She paused to breathe.

"The book remained undisturbed for two centuries until it was discovered by my parents during their ill-fated excavation. As some of you may know, they and their colleagues paid the ultimate price for science."

A knowing undertone passed through the crowd. Most of the older attendees still remembered the deadly explosion and cave-in.

Sabrina's blue eyes narrowed and her lips pressed together. Not a peep emerged from the onlookers.

"And so today the Anderson proudly introduces this unique artifact as a permanent exhibit, 'Myths & Magicks of Spanish Tejas,' in the hope it will spark scholarly debate, encourage more research and continue a dialogue on the Spanish mission period."

The spellbound crowd listened, eager for more.

The public loves a good mystery, thought Blackwood, a man who knew a thing or two about catering to an audience fascinated by a whodunit.

Sabrina turned to the man in the well-tailored suit next to her.

"I've spoken long enough. Now, it's time to hear a few words from someone else, a person who probably needs no introduction."

Her words died away as the crowd waited with breathless anticipation.

"But I'll introduce him anyway.—Mayor Raul Solis," she announced, with all the gusto of someone presenting a beloved celebrity.

Stepping back, Sabrina joined the reverberation of clapping hands washing over Solis as he advanced to the microphone, exuding confidence. The mayor contemplated the crowd, his smile dazzling the appreciative listeners.

"*Felicididas esta noche*," Solis said warmly. More applause sounded, this time louder than before.

"Greetings, friends—*buenas noches, amigos*," Solis boomed.

The word "popular" didn't even begin to describe the reverence in which a majority of San Antonians held this native son. Most of the crowd gazed up at Solis with respect, a few with awe, and some—the women, old and young—with undisguised adoration. His West Side constituency — among the poorest inhabitants of the city, living in the *barrios* — affectionately referred to Solis as the "Mariachi Mayor" because of his folksy manner and high regard for tradition, especially *la familia*.

"My friends," Solis began, "today we rejoice, for we have arrived at a momentous crossroads where past, present and future converge."

The Havard University-educated mayor's dark, shining eyes seemed to share a personal greeting with every upturned face in the room.

"This new exhibit is a vital link to two hundred years of thriving Latino culture," Solis said.

Stroking the audience's ears with the aural equivalent of silk, his smooth politician's voice grew more solemn.

"Tonight, we have an opportunity to further explore this shared heritage."

He cast an introspective glance at the enshrined volume.

"I join Dr. Hagen in her call to the scientific community to research this artifact, to shine the light of knowledge into the darkness of the past. It will be a journey of discovery, just like the voyages the explorers from the Old World embarked on centuries ago when they came to our beautiful land."

As he spoke, waiters moved seamlessly through the crowd, handing out shot glasses topped with a golden liquid. Blackwood sniffed at his. Tequila. Not one of his favorites.

"So I say to you," the mayor intoned, raising his own glass, "that we welcome this opportunity to look both behind and forward, and toast our good fortune in true San Antonio fashion."

He brought the glass to his lips. "*Salud,*" he shouted. "*Viva San Antonio!*"

"*Viva San Antonio!*" the audience roared back. As one they downed the contents of their glasses, Blackwood included — though he winced at the pungent taste. Vigorous applause shook the rafters as a grinning Solis stepped back from the podium and spread arms wide. A mariachi band that replaced the chamber orchestra broke into a traditional ballad.

The crowd dispersed around the Great Hall, small knots of people swirling and forming little buzzing cliques in a kind of social Brownian movement. Sabrina took the proffered hand of the mayor and stepped down from the podium. The pair began conversing with waiting dignitaries.

Blackwood strolled over to the relic for another perusal.

Time-ravaged and motley, the thick volume sat on its small pedestal like a decaying log, gray and old. The cracked and pitted cover looked as if it could fall apart at any moment.

It was the furthest thing from a tome of ancient power that he could think of. But looks can be deceiving, he knew.

As before, Dragoti appeared by his side, as though materializing from thin air. The reporter wondered if the dour priest had assigned himself the task of monitoring the relic from some discreet vantage point.

"Enjoying yourself?" Dragoti inquired.

"Pins and needles," Blackwood said, though with an affable air. He straightened up from his examination of the codex. "By the way, are those symbols over the doors what I think they are?"

A strangely satisfied look creased Dragoti's tonsured brow.

"Saw those, did you? Yes, those are the wards I mentioned," Dragoti said. "As long as those symbols are in place, this hall is protected."

Blackwood opened his mouth to ask something else, but never got the chance. Dragoti's head rose and his palm came up in a peremptory shushing motion. The leader of The Hand scrunched his forehead as he peered across the room, spotting a boyish-looking priest with curly black hair trying to attract his attention.

Dragoti patted Blackwood on the arm. "Will you excuse me? It seems one of my lambs needs a little shepherding."

"Certainly," Blackwood said. The priest's expression revealed he sensed the reporter had more questions.

"We can talk later, after this regrettable ceremony is concluded," Dragoti said. "*Per favore sii paziente.*"

A trace of a smile graced Blackwood's lips.

"I don't speak Italian, but I think you said, 'Please be patient,' eh?"

Dragoti nodded, then answered him, "For one thing, we're going to have to decide on the dispensation of the relic. That will require some delicacy. In spite of Dr. Hagen's commercial designs, remaining on public display in the museum is not an option. I have my orders from Rome."

Blackwood's eyebrows lifted as quick as balloons in a storm, but he refrained from commenting.

Good luck with that, he silently replied.

Dragoti turned to go, thought of something else, pivoted and reached into a pocket, his blunt fingers fishing around. Extracting a small object, he then grasped the reporter's hand. Something cool and metallic slid into Blackwood's open palm. He glanced down to see a gleaming silver cross on a chain.

"A sacred gift. It will protect you. But remember, you must have faith or it's just a piece of metal," Dragoti admonished.

"That won't be a problem," Blackwood answered. "I'm a believer. Every time I turn in a story, I say, 'Please God, let it be right.'"

Dragoti searched the reporter's face for any hint of mockery, but found none. Blackwood actually told the truth — there are no atheists in a newsroom at deadline. Apparently satisfied, Dragoti closed Blackwood's hand over the cross.

With a firm nod, the crime reporter slipped the thin chain over his head. A thin smile briefly flickered on Dragoti's lined face, and then the cleric gently squeezed his elbow before turning to go. Blackwood watched him leave, with broad shoulders slightly stooped, as though the weight of the world rested there.

Barely five seconds passed before Blackwood felt a tap on his shoulder. Twisting around, he faced a beaming Sabrina. Obviously, she hadn't heard the priest mention spiriting away her relic or the smile would have vanished from her lips.

"Whew—finished making the rounds. Now, how about buying a girl a drink?" she said, brushing back her hair.

"Of course," Blackwood answered.

Sabrina's earlier edginess had dissipated, replaced by the glow one enjoys from doing a job well.

"What's the verdict?" she asked, an outstretched hand sweeping the chamber.

"Splendid," he said, and meant it.

Chuckling softly at his response, she leaned over and whispered in his ear. Her perfume conjured the image of an endless field of lavender bathed by dappled sunshine.

"Well, I think it was — how do you Brits put it? — smashing. Simply smashing. But I'd like to go sit down. These heels are killing me."

She drew back, gazing deeply into his eyes.

"Your office? A coffee?" he suggested.

"That," she said, hugging his arm, "is a great idea."

CHAPTER TWENTY-FIVE

Pascual Gonzales stood beneath the archway to the folk-art hall and sighed heavily. On his way to take a break after a night of hurried preparations for the unveiling, he'd glanced up and spotted red paint smeared across the lintel. The sight turned his smile upside-down. Now why would some *pendejo* tag the hallway, especially after his crew worked so hard to prepare for this important night?

He released another frustrated breath. The break would have to wait. Pascual's devotion to the museum wouldn't allow him to let the graffiti linger one second longer.

Turning, he glimpsed Dr. Hagen and a lanky man walking down the hallway. He waved, hoping she couldn't see the splotches. Smiling but looking preoccupied, she absently returned his greeting with one of her own, then disappeared around the corner, none the wiser.

Relieved, Pascual trudged off to fetch a ladder, a sponge and a bucket with soapy water.

• • •

Two floors below and a world away, the museum's basement stood eerily silent. Banks of overhead lights couldn't dispel the clinging gloom, only intensified the shadows between the paltry islands of illumination. As the lonely echo of footfalls reverberated off the walls, the arc of a powerful flashlight sliced through the blackness. Just outside its reach, a match flared into life, the flame licking the end of a cigarette. The flashlight beam jumped up, framing a man's desultory face just as he took a long drag.

Pablo Elizondo, the security guard holding the flashlight, scowled at the other guard, the one with the cigarette. The latter looked up, then down again. His face registered annoyance at being disturbed.

"Hey, Pat. No smoking inside the museum," Elizondo reminded his partner.

Pat Kinder shrugged. With his free hand, he swung a key on a chain attached to his belt. The key turned the locks in mechanical boxes placed around the museum, recording the time the security detail passed by. A duplicate key hung from Elizondo's utility belt, as well as a walkie-talkie. For legal reasons Elizondo never understood, the museum prohibited guards from carrying firearms — not that anybody would ever need one at the Anderson anyway.

"So write me up," Kinder answered with a surly growl.

"I just don't want to get fired," Elizondo shot back, parsing his words to avoid a quarrel.

The flashlight clicked off, as if doing so would hide the fact one of them violated the rules. Yet the end of the cigarette continued burning like a baleful eye.

Kinder, who looked like he combed his hair with a firecracker, tapped smoldering ashes into his palm. He didn't even wince. The older man's blue uniform, so wrinkled it could have just been snagged from a pile of laundry, stood in stark contrast to Elizondo's, with creases sharp as razor blades and a properly knotted tie (not a clip-on like Kinder's).

The men looked as unalike as apples and sausages. Elizondo could only assume he was down here to babysit the old goat; someone had to, he supposed.

Kinder scrunched his eyebrow, a single, thin band of scraggly fur crawling across his forehead like a mangy caterpillar.

"Kid, you ain't gonna get fired," he informed Elizondo with the air of someone who has seen it all. "Hell, they'd better be grateful we're working this here party in the first place, especially for what they're payin'."

Jabbing the air with the cigarette for emphasis, he waited to see if Elizondo offered a retort. When none came, Kinder snorted derisively.

"So don't be lecturin' me none," he said. Beady eyes that seemed eternally vexed glared from behind plastic-rimmed spectacles.

An uneasy silence settled between them. Elizondo knew enough to pick his battles and this wasn't one of them, so he just turned around, clicking the flashlight back on. The pair stood back-to-back, like mismatched bookends. The beam played across a cavernous expanse packed with crates, mothballed displays, vaquero mannequins, Aztec feathered headdresses and more of the museum's miscellany discarded or forgotten over the decades.

To be honest, Elizondo rarely ever visited the basement; no one came down here. Easy to understand why. Friggin' spooky.

Tonight, only he and Kinder patrolled the frigid chambers. Despite his misgivings about the creepy surroundings, he actually counted his blessings. With Christmas only days away, he could use the extra money, especially to put a few more presents under the tree for little Maria.

"Want one?" Kinder asked, hoisting a crushed pack of unfiltered Camels in Elizondo's face. Even in the dim light, Elizondo saw fingers stained yellow from a constant love affair with nicotine, ending in ragged nails.

He shook his head, his cap tilting.

"No thanks. I don't smoke."

"Humphh," Kinder acknowledged gruffly. "Probably smarter that way."

Elizondo swallowed a reply, instead letting the quiet roll over him. His thoughts switched from Kinder's flouting of the rules to his wife and daughter, at home safe and warm. He didn't feel like talking anyway, and visions of his family held more appeal than chatting with his irascible partner. After awhile, he realized the basement wasn't really all that silent; he detected a virtual symphony of background noise, barely audible until you actually paused long enough to listen. Groaning pipes, gurgling radiators, wind squeezing under the half-moon casements, water trailing down the walls, and the weary grumbling of stone as the aged building settled deeper on its foundations.

Elizondo knew the stories, of course, about how the basement served as an armory during the Civil War. He also heard how the Confederates stored gunpowder, cannon balls and Springfield Model 1861s down here. True or not, he'd even been told that punts disguised as logs plied the river and smuggled the weapons past Union checkpoints, delivering the munitions through a secret door to what was then a root cellar. The Union soldiers eventually discovered the ruse, and dynamited or bricked up the armory's entrance, but yes, it remained a part of the structure, hidden somewhere among the maze of storerooms.

The air reeked of damp stonework, too. Although the basement came with an air-filtration system designed to control humidity and keep everything in storage dry, the museum's proximity next to the river often made that a tall order.

Kinder spat into his hand, rubbed the spent cigarette in the wet swath and then dragged his palm down his sleeve. He cleared his throat a couple of times for good measure. Elizondo politely pretended not to notice.

Deciding it was time to resume his rounds, Elizondo started walking away when a sudden clatter froze him in place. The beam of his flashlight shot into the next room. The circle of light revealed dusty glass cases and cracked floors, but nothing else.

"Who's there?" Elizondo shouted.

Kinder placed a restraining hand on his partner's sleeve, the same hand cupping spit a moment ago. Elizondo didn't notice. He kept swinging the light around, the beam zigzagging in a nervous dance.

"Easy, kid," Kinder said, his whisper so faint it was barely audible. The older guard absently deposited the remains of his cigarette in a shirt pocket.

After listening a few moments, Kinder raised his shaggy gray head.

"It's probably just Santa Anna's gold-plated jockstrap that done fell off a shelf," he rasped. "Places like this old museum has bones; they move and shift in the night, just like my arthritis."

He managed to stretch the word into four syllables — "arth-ar-right-us."

Before Elizondo could answer, the old man steeled scrawny shoulders.

"I'll go check," he announced, filling his voice with a boldness that didn't fool anyone. Kinder's eyes bulged behind the Coke-bottle lenses of his glasses, reminding the other man of a startled bug. "It was gettin' kinda borin' anyway."

Kinder attempted to put on a brave face, but Elizondo knew his partner better than that. The older guard appeared distinctly uncomfortable.

Kinder's flashlight flickered into existence and he headed off. As the darkness swallowed him, Elizondo could still hear him muttering. Finally even that faded. The air hung still and cold.

Time passed. As he waited, Elizondo could feel the hairs rising on his neck. He shook his shoulders to rid himself of the sensation.

True silence — a deep, unnatural cessation of all sound — replaced the low-key symphony of grunts, whistles and gurgles from the pipes and casements to which Elizondo had grown accustomed. Eventually, the young man decided he'd had enough.

"Kinder?" Elizondo stammered. "You okay? Kinder!"

His mouth slammed shut with an audible gasp as something stirred in the shadows before him.

Elizondo understood why the hairs prickling on his skin refused to lie down.

Something's happening ... Something in the dark...

On the wall just across from him, he could see a bluish, ice-cold light shining not around but through the bricks, tracing the shape of a door. A big door, large enough for three men to walk abreast. A door made for cargo, he thought, then realized with a jolt, no, a door made for smuggling. The ribbon of light shone brighter, stronger, the outline taking on more definition. Elizondo wasn't sure he could trust his senses. The illumination seemed to emanate from the other side of the wall, pushing through the bricks like a searchlight broadcasting from behind a fence, creating a silhouette of each square.

What the hell, he wondered, taking a tentative step back.

At that moment Kinder reappeared, walking into the chamber where he was bathed in the chilly blue glow of the strange light. He held up a broken vase; another cigarette dangled from his lip at a gravity-defying angle. He paused mid-step in front of the shimmering wall and bellowed at the sight.

A groaning sound erupted from the bricks. Elizondo shouted a warning to Kinder, but he was drowned out as the masonry came crashing down. The ground shook. Thick dust clouds washed over Elizondo and left him gasping.

Kinder disappeared in the roiling cloud. Elizondo lost sight of him.

Elizondo's flashlight beam pierced a mass of dancing motes to reveal a long, arched tunnel lined with fitted limestone blocks, presumably stretching to the river outside. A faint patina of frost began glowing on the blocks. The carpet of ice crawled in his direction, spreading down the walls and coating the floor.

Shock rooted Elizondo to the spot.

After that, everything sped up, happening faster than his bewildered senses could follow. A pulsating, amorphous shape darker than any shadow shot out of the semicircular tunnel, only to be swallowed by the cloud of dust billowing across the storeroom.

Violently buffeted by a blast of air that felt uncannily solid, Elizondo's flashlight dropped from numbed fingers. The cylinder landed with a thud on a weathered oak barrel, only to roll off and hit the concrete with a clatter. Snowflakes blowing from the tunnel twirled in the beam. The metal casing slammed against the base of a display topped by a model of an ancient Mesoamerican temple. The lens cracked and the bulb shattered, plunging Elizondo into sudden darkness.

A pair of half-moon eyes glowing with the intensity of lava pools fastened on his panic-stricken expression. Nothing else was visible.

Something hard and leathery lashed out, striking him across the left cheek. The blow stung like fire. The impact knocked Elizondo back several yards, where he crumpled to his knees with a scream. As he clutched at the burning wound, ragged strips of flesh came off in trembling fingers. He moaned in agony and fear.

Fighting the excruciating pain, fueled by desperation, Elizondo groped blindly for the edge of a crate, somehow managing to pull himself up. Not knowing what happened to Kinder and with the flashlight broken, he realized the only course of action was to call for help, not seek a confrontation.

With hands shaking like rubber bands, he yanked the walkie-talkie from his belt. The overhead lights, which had gone off for some reason, flicked back on, but they did little to dispel the gloom.

He fumbled a few seconds, his fingers fighting to press the key grip. Blood flowed like a river from the gash stitched along his face, and his skin faded to the color of paste.

"This is Elizondo in the basement! Unknown assailant! I need backup! Request backup!"

The reedy, high-pitched utterance from his throat sounded strange in his ears, the voice of someone he barely recognized.

The box squawked with static, a ripple of wavering noise that mocked him. He repeated his frantic call.

"Backup requested! This is Elizondo in the basement ... Kinder missing! Do you copy? Unknown assailant!"

Just in front of him, an oval face pale and wild coalesced from the undulating wisps of gathering fog—a phosphorescent question mark smoldering with malice.

Elizondo could only stare in open-mouthed revulsion, another shriek forming on his lips. A cold rush of fear gripped him. The walkie-talkie slipped from his paralyzed hands, forgotten.

Twice he tried moving forward and nearly toppled, fingers convulsively digging into the crate for support. In some distant part of his mind, he wondered if his ankle had shattered. It kept wobbling. Every movement felt as if the bone and socket rotated on ground glass.

Fighting his mounting terror, Elizondo could not tear his eyes away from the indistinct shape in the swirling mist. But now he confronted a fresh horror. Something resembling two leathery appendages thrust upwards from the intruder's back, tapering to sharp points. The sight robbed him of breath, nor could he trust his eyes. But his vision didn't lie. He spied wings; unmistakably wings, like a bat's. A huge bat. The thing's head dipped down, a cascade of shimmering black hair falling over the moon-glow face.

The vaguely female figure started floating towards him. Not walking, but floating, a lascivious grin painted on features as white as the belly of a dead fish.

Every molecule of blood froze in his veins.

A tiny whimper pushed past clenched teeth. He shuffled back a few steps, his injured ankle screaming in agony, and his boot thudded against something on the floor.

He couldn't help but glance down. In the next instant, he bit back a scream, realizing he'd found Kinder. But what sprawled at his feet no longer resembled a man who'd drawn breath only minutes earlier.

A long time ago, Elizondo spent a summer working at a cattle ranch in Del Rio. His duties included collecting empty feed bags and stacking them in a burn pile.

Now, as his horrified gaze lingered on Kinder, or what was left of his partner, Elizondo couldn't help but think of those discarded burlap sacks. The old man looked as spent and as dry — as flat — as those empty bags in the burn pit. Even worse, a pair of black raisins in sightless sockets stared imploringly at Elizondo, as though he could do something.

The younger man swallowed a sob, but there was no time to mourn, to question how or why. He knew he was next.

Elizondo forced himself to turn from Kinder and focus on the woman — no, the thing — slowly approaching him. Out of the corner of his eye, he spotted two more of her kind emerging from the ice-coated tunnel. Drifting and bobbing like snowflakes on an arctic breeze, their bare feet never touched the floor.

The deafening chatter of his teeth competed with his thundering heart.

He tried like hell not to put any weight on his torn ankle, and the rip in his cheek burned as hot as a brand, compounding his misery.

The trio of ethereal women drew a bead on him, moving methodically, purposefully. Black wings beat sonorously against the dead air of the basement, sending foul breezes that burned his nostrils and throat. Elizondo's growing panic didn't stop him from noticing their near-state of undress, which was somehow arousing: bare breasts softened by tufts of fur and loins barely covered by some kind of pelt, held in place by rawhide belts studded with lustrous black stones.

The frost flowing from the smugglers' tunnel continued to creep like a stealthy beast over the floor, roof and walls. The shelves, shipping containers and artifacts transformed into glittering sculptures. Whenever the advancing ice sheet reached an overheard light, the tube flashed weakly and then shattered. Elizondo ducked several times to avoid flying glass.

He cast desperate glances left and right, fruitlessly seeking a way out. There was nowhere to turn, just endless pipes, valves and ductwork resembling a nest of snakes.

The unfairness of it all made Elizondo want to shriek until his lungs collapsed. Even if he could somehow sprint away with his hobbled ankle, some primal part of his brain warned him these creatures would be upon him in a heartbeat. The leader continued to close on him, while the other two split up to cut off any other route to safety. Elizondo's soul shriveled.

And as the dark drama of his final seconds played out, while the Daughters claimed another life, unbeknownst to all and forgotten, Kinder's still-smoldering cigarette — dropped from lifeless fingers when the last breaths fled his body—lay discarded under the papier mâché mask of a Mexican wrestler from some long-ago Fiesta parade.

The embers licked at the dry strips of paper and took hold, a ribbon burning small but bright in the dark repository of history's castoffs.

CHAPTER TWENTY-SIX

Blackwood leaned across Sabrina's desk, carefully pouring a second cup of coffee from a silver pot while avoiding the teetering papers covering every available surface.

"I swear they multiply when I turn my back," she said, thrusting an accusatory finger at the stacks.

For twenty minutes, their pleasant conversation touched on topics of mutual interest — history and politics, mainly — while thoughts of death cults, vengeful angels and demonic vampires faded into the background.

Blackwood opened his mouth to offer a pithy reply when frantic pounding on the door broke the spell.

The two exchanged worried glances. Sabrina straightened in her chair and said in a carefully modulated voice, "Come in."

Dragoti burst into the room. He seemed to have aged ten years since Blackwood last saw him. An unwelcome chill crawled down the reporter's backside.

Dragoti didn't waste time. "Both of you need to come with me. There's a problem."

Sabrina rose from her desk in one fluid motion, somehow managing not to tumble the scattered files.

"What's wrong?" she said.

Dragoti gave an agitated jab of his head.

"A guard in the basement radioed something about an unknown attacker and requested backup. Then, nothing."

"The Daughters?" Blackwood said, his good mood evaporating in an instant.

Dragoti waved his hand.

"I can't say. I sent my priests down there. I also told security to start asking guests to leave. I instructed them to say the weather was getting worse and the roads would be impassable if they didn't go now."

Sabrina looked ashen.

"I had two people in the basement. Are they okay?"

Dragoti's silence spoke volumes. He merely wheeled around and raced from the room. Without another word, they followed him down the hallway.

Blackwood, close on the priest's heels, cried out as Dragoti abruptly stopped. An "oof" pushed up from the reporter's ribcage as Sabrina slammed into his back.

The priest never registered their chain collision. Dragoti had gone stiff as a board, staring at something above the gargantuan wooden doors leading into the colonial wing. His eyes bulged to the size of hubcaps.

"Where are the wards?" he asked in a strained voice.

An icy hand closed around Blackwood's heart as he followed Dragoti's aghast stare.

"They were there—what, thirty minutes ago? I mentioned them to you!" he said.

Sabrina knit her brows, turning something over in her mind, and then snapped her fingers. A light bulb went off in her sapphire eyes.

"Pascual ... I saw him standing here when we went into my office. He was looking up and I couldn't figure out why."

Blackwood leveled a dumbfounded stare at her.

"He's head of maintenance," she hurriedly explained. Then a tremor shook her voice. "He didn't know about the wards."

Sabrina appeared to deflate.

"I'll bet he cleaned off the symbols," she added with a trill of alarm. "He probably thought it was vandalism. We've had some problems with kids in the area tagging the museum."

Blackwood noticed a ladder and a bucket tucked into an alcove next to a vending machine and the restrooms. Without a word, he pointed to the objects. Dragoti gasped.

"No!" he thundered. "If the wards are gone, then it may be too late already!"

Sabrina stared at both men, fear casting a shadow across her features.

"If Pascual wiped down this door, he would've cleaned all the others, too. He's very methodical."

Without another word, she grasped the ornate handle of one of the great doors, swung it open and waved the others in.

•　•　•

Blackwood wasn't sure what to expect. Pandemonium? Screaming crowds stampeding through the exhibits, knocking over priceless displays, shattering glass cases? But what they encountered instead as they came through the doors was simply a long line of guests calmly lined up, ushered by security guards who'd quickly erected a red velvet rope to create a path to the archway.

Sabrina heaved a sigh of relief. She also hadn't known what to expect, but was grateful to see this orderly procession.

Blackwood paused a moment and stabbed a finger at the employee exit at the other end of the chamber.

"There's only two exits from this place?" he asked. "Can't we split the guests up and move them through both?"

Sabrina started to reply. Dragoti cut her off.

"Absolutely not. The fewer ways into here, the better. In fact, the door to the employee hallway should be locked immediately."

Pursing her lips, Sabrina trotted to the faraway exit, moving fast even wearing the detested heels, and with a unladylike snort secured the locking bar.

That must be 20 fire-code violations right there, Blackwood mused. Sabrina returned just as one of the guards dashed past her.

She cried out, arms gesticulating.

"Charlie! — Charlie!"

The guard stopped mid-stride, swiveled and peered at her. He was a middle-aged, stoop-shouldered man, with strokes of ochre on old canvas for sideburns.

"Doctor Hagen?" Awareness dawned on his face.

"Hello Charlie," she said, inclining her head.

"Ma'am," he returned.

"Good work keeping the guests calm and moving. Let's make sure it stays that way," she said.

Charlie nodded again, looking puzzled.

"Yes ma'am. We got the choir kids out first, and then the mayor and his party."

He scowled. "Pardon my French, but what the hell is going on? Someone said there's been a break-in down in the basement."

Sabrina sucked down a series of deep breaths, marshaling her calm. Dragoti's stern expression told her not to reveal too much.

The guard stared at all three of them, waiting.

"Yes, Charlie, there might be … uninvited visitors," Sabrina said, carefully choosing her words. "So it's just best we continue getting the guests out of here smoothly and safely."

The tightly pulled corners of Dragoti's mouth loosened, showing he approved of Sabrina's terse explanation.

In the meantime, a slight edge crept into her voice. "Was anybody hurt in the basement?"

Charlie ducked his head. The guard couldn't hide the unease in his reply.

"We can't account for Kinder and Elizondo."

Sabrina swayed slightly on her feet. A shudder shook her frame and she opened her mouth to speak, but nothing emerged. Looking just as worried, Charlie glanced over her shoulder, eyeing Dragoti's starched white collar. He swallowed and found his voice.

"By the way, I'm looking for a preacher named Dragoti. Is that you, sir?"

Dragoti nodded curtly. His penetrating stare kept darting to the relic, as though assuring himself the artifact remained in the case.

"That's me," he said.

Charlie unclipped the radio from his belt and handed it to the Italian.

"Your guys down in the basement are looking for you," he said. "Just press and hold this button, then start speaking. Let go when you're done."

Dragoti did as instructed. His head jerked sideways when static squawked from the radio.

"Hello? This is Father Dragoti. Hello?"

A voice answered immediately, speaking with an Irish accent.

"This is Malloy, Father, down in the basement. We've had a breach. A wall came down. There's a tunnel behind it that leads to the river. Whoever it was came through that."

Dragoti's entire body tensed up. A tongue ran over dry lips.

"The smuggler's tunnel," Sabrina muttered under her breath, but her astonished voice was loud enough for Blackwood and Dragoti to hear.

"There must have been at least four feet of solid masonry. You'd need a wrecking ball to knock that down," she added, the perplexed look on her face mirroring her tone.

"A wrecking ball is insignificant compared to the power of the accursed," Dragoti whispered. "These abominations carry winter with them. Ice renders even mountains into dust."

Dragoti cleared his throat and spoke into the walkie-talkie.

"Is it the foe, Father Malloy?" he asked, his voice choked with trepidation.

"Aye, 'twould appear such, father," came the matter-of-fact reply. "There's frost everywhere. 'Tis a poxy business, innit? 'Taint natural. But no sign o' them beasties. Not yet, anyway."

Dragoti unconsciously backed up a step. Sabrina clutched his arm.

"Ask him about my guards," she said. Dragoti did.

"Aye, we're looking fer 'em now," Malloy said, his voice tense. "This place is a maze down here. Somebody wi' a few too many pints in 'im musta laid out this beauty. And, father, one other t'ing: There's quite a bit of smoke. Gettin' 'ard to see."

"Smoke?" Sabrina cried.

Dragoti ignored her.

"Proceed with caution," he instructed Malloy. "Get any civilians out of there, including museum security. Find the source of the smoke and neutralize it, if you can. And keep your assets handy."

Dragoti turned to look at the cross hanging around Blackwood's neck. Blackwood understood Dragoti's meaning and nodded. To him, Dragoti sounded more like a general barking orders to his troops than a priest and university lecturer.

The radio coughed up Malloy's brogue.

"Will do, father," he said. "*Infernales tenebras contendunt contra nos.*"

Dragoti drew himself up to his full height. Without hesitation, he responded in a voice ringed with steel, "*Infernales tenebras contendunt contra nos.*"

The radio went silent.

Blackwood turned to ask Sabrina the meaning of the phrase.

"Against the infernal darkness we strive," she supplied.

Later, he told himself, he would ask her how she knew Latin so well. If there was a later …

"What's next?" Blackwood asked the priest.

Dragoti shot a glance toward the arched doorway. The well-behaved line of guests snaking through the aperture moved briskly, but his expression said it still wasn't fast enough.

"I need to find some paint and see about restoring the wards," he said. "We must stop the Daughters before they get anywhere near the relic."

Dragoti looked at Charlie next.

"Bring all available security to this room, please," he said.

Charlie swiveled to Sabrina, who nodded.

"It's okay, Charlie. Do as he says—please," she said, only her request sounded less like an order and more like a plea.

The radio crackled. Malloy's voice rumbled out of the speaker.

"Father Dragoti! Do you copy?"

Dragoti pressed the key bar. "I'm here," he said.

There was quiet, and then a hiss of jumbled words before a voice emerged. Something was going on down there.

"We've found the guards, Father ... what's left o' the lads. 'Tisn't a pretty sight."

Sabrina's hand flew to her mouth and she let out a small, wounded cry. Instinctively, Blackwood reached out and squeezed her shoulder. Tears brimmed in the wide bowls of her eyes. Next to her, Charlie made a strangled sound.

"My god," he said, his voice hoarse.

Dragoti nodded sympathetically, but his grim expression said now wasn't the time to mourn.

"Assessment, Father Malloy?"

"Aye, 'tis the Daughters, that's fer sure. Their handiwork. Drained dry, th' pair o' them. No sign of the lasses, though."

The apprehension in his tone rang clear as a bell, and only became more pronounced with his next statement.

"We've another problem, too. There's a fire down here. No' sure how it started, but one o' the dead had a pack of cigarettes on 'im."

Sabrina and Charlie exchanged troubled glances.

"Kinder," Charlie sighed. "I don't know how many times I wrote him up for that."

Malloy's voice emerged from the walkie-talkie tinged with anxiety.

"We found some extinguishers, but they won't be enough. And the fire-suppression system hasn't activated … It may have frozen over. There's ice everywhere."

He drew a deep breath audible even over the radio.

"Tain't natural," he said once more.

"I need to call the Fire Department," Charlie gasped from behind Dragoti. He cast a glance at Sabrina for confirmation. "Dr. Hagen?"

She nodded vigorously, wiping with the back of a hand at a few tears stubbornly clinging to her lashes.

"Do that now," she said, her voice small and distant.

"I'll get all my security personnel in here, too," Charlie said. He inclined his head, tried to offer her a comforting smile, failed, and rushed off to locate a telephone.

Dragoti focused on his conversation with Malloy.

"Can you get out?" he asked.

An ominous silence followed, then the radio crackled with Malloy's answer.

"I think so," came the reply. "Th' tunnel tha' opened up, we can reach that and escape to th' river. Then we'll circle back and meet you lot upstairs."

The museum lights flickered. Blackwood tensed. Sabrina and Dragoti cast apprehensive glances upwards. The low babble from the packed line of exiting guests now became peppered with a few murmurs of alarm. Blackwood saw Sabrina's fists clench by her sides.

"The Daughters are trying to cut the power," Dragoti said, the worry in his tone plain.

Sabrina found her vocal cords. "Even if they do, there's a backup generator that will kick in. It's outside, but surrounded by a reinforced metal fence topped by barbed wire. We won't lose the lights."

She sounded like she was trying to convince herself more than anyone else. Blackwood's head rose.

"I don't mean to rain on your parade, Sabrina, but they'll find a way to disrupt any backup power," he said.

She responded in a taut voice.

"Even if they are ... not of this world ... there's still only three of them, right, John?" she said. "Surely they're not all powerful."

"They're not," Dragoti cut in, his tone firm to allay her apprehension. "But they are extremely cunning. And very, very old."

The lights winked out again, then snapped back on. The low ebb of chatter from the diminishing queue at the door spiked with a few dismayed cries, and the guards doubled their efforts to keep the visitors safely moving. Hundreds remained in line.

More museum security came through the door, as well as some of the off-duty SAPD officers Blackwood recognized earlier.

Blackwood pivoted in a tight circle, examining every inch of the massive hall. As his ears strained to identify even the slightest sound out of the ordinary, he spotted something that made his pulse race. There, very low to the floor, tendrils of smoke curled through the vents, probing the air of the Great Hall with questing tendrils.

"Bloody hell! Seems we have another problem," he said. "The fire is spreading."

The priest cast a dismissive glance at the vent, his concerns about the relic's safety trumping any other worries. He approached the display case at a brisk clip, the crepe soles of his heavy black shoes squeaking. He stopped just inches away. Squinting, he peered anxiously through the glass.

"We must secure the relic now. Help me get it out of here. The authorities can handle the fire," he said.

"As long as the hydrants aren't frozen," Blackwood added. The forlorn expressions on the others' faces told him they didn't even want to consider that possibility.

Sabrina marched to Dragoti's side, her jaw dropping. More smoke began rolling across the floor, pouring from other vents spaced along the wall at the opposite end of the hall. The acrid scent fouled the air.

She gazed at them in desperation.

"Gentlemen, this is a priceless artifact. The Anderson cannot afford to lose this antiquity. Nor, in fact, can we afford to lose the Anderson. The Fire Department will be here in minutes, and I have no idea what kind of damage they'll do in their efforts to 'save' the museum. In addition, and most vital, I need to get these people out of here."

Her voice took on an edge and she crossed her arms.

"Given the circumstances, I will consider a temporary—and I mean temporary—relocation of the relic to a location of your choosing, Father Dragoti. But I will remind you again — do not forget it is the sole property of the Anderson."

She glanced over their shoulders at the gradually thinning line at the door, but so many remained. The crowd had shrunk to about two hundred. So far no one noticed the smoke clinging low to the floor at the far end of the wing, slouching its way toward them like some dark beast.

Dragoti was silent for a moment, but his expression crumpled with relief. Perhaps he'd been expecting Sabrina to dig in her heels while her museum crumbled around her.

"Excellent choice, my child," he said, then faced Blackwood. "Young man, will you kindly help an old parish priest?"

"Certainly, Father," he said.

By now the smoke's billowing waves stretched to the mission dioramas, covering a quarter of the floor like a gray carpet.

That's when things went from bad to worse.

Someone in the crowd yelled, "Shit! Is that smoke?"

Not just smoke. Tongues of flame began shooting through the grates, lashing at the air. The alarms kicked in next, shrieking like banshees. The museum's overhead lights flickered, bathing the room in uneven shades of illumination and shadow before the fluorescents snapped back on.

"It's a fire," the voice yelped. "A fire!"

Blackwood learned a long time ago that yelling about a fire in a crowded space with only one exit never ended well.

Sabrina faced Dragoti, her jaw tightening.

"Do what you must," she said. "But the relic returns here when all of this is over."

Without another word, Sabrina walked towards the group, holding up her hands imploringly.

"Everyone, please stay calm!" she shouted. "Please!"

The crowd grew silent, attentive, for one lingering moment, collectively holding its breath. The spell broke in the next second when the vents behind Sabrina belched another burst of flame and choking smoke. A wave of heat washed across her back, and the guests felt it, too.

"The damn place is burning down!" a well-coiffed woman screamed, her twang like a buzz saw.

With a loud whoosh, a low-hanging banner burst into blazing stripes of orange and red. Sparks crackled, showering the group packed around the doors.

Bleating in panic, the crowd surged forward, a writhing, panicked mass charging the doors. As the guards struggled to maintain a calm and orderly flow, the press of humanity shoved the security detail against the angled portals. The combined weight pressed both huge oak panels closed, and the crowd flowed against the panels like a tide that had been dammed. Now all pretense of order evaporated in an instant as the hapless guards struggled to keep the mob from stampeding while trying to reopen the ponderous doors. The stanchions holding the velvet rope toppled, followed by a large woman in pearls and jewel-studded boots who tripped on the rucked-up carpet and landed on her face with a grunt. Others stumbled and fell behind her.

"There's no need to panic!" Sabrina cried. She approached the doors at a rapid trot, upraised hands thrusting at the crowd, palms out like a traffic cop. The only thing missing was a whistle.

Someone in the crowd noticed the staff-member exit at the opposite end of the hall — now locked, of course—and began running for it, heedless of the thickening smoke and growing flames in-between. Others followed, breaking off from the crowd at the doors. Sabrina stood in their midst, hands still up, yelling something when a man in a torn dinner jacket slammed into her. She stumbled backwards, falling against a display case that came down with a crash, taking Sabrina with it. Blackwood watched in horror as she vanished under a roiling collection of churning legs, shoes and heels, with some of the guests sent sprawling as their feet caught on her prostrate form.

"Sabrina!" he cried, trying to make his way toward her even as the crowd surged past and around him, the space filling with bodies, the air with shouts and screams. He spun around, barely able to keep his balance, and saw a wildly gesticulating Dragoti carried away by the frightened mob.

Tables laden with drinks and hors d'oeuvres went flying, street tacos and brie ground into mush under heels and boots, broken glass mixed with spilled alcohol.

A banging noise rang out, and Blackwood spotted a crazed-looking man using a fire extinguisher to force open the locking bar on the employee door. The metal bar crumpled and the crowd rushed pellmell through the aperture. Blackwood thought he saw a white collar and Dragoti's alarmed face bobbing among the flood of people before disappearing in a sea of arms, legs and torsos.

A loud shriek brought up Blackwood's head. The man who'd knocked Sabrina down — he recognized him as a prominent personal-injury attorney famous for lavish parties and bombastic television ads—beat frantically at flames crawling up his trouser leg. With lips pulled back in a shriek, the man reeled off into the thick smoke and disappeared from view, howling loud enough to be heard over the fire alarm.

Dodging other guests as they scrambled to and fro like a frenzied herd, Blackwood arrived at Sabrina's side and knelt down, doing his best to avoid being cut by shattered glass. A quick inspection revealed an ugly gash across her forehead and a ribbon of blood trailing from her mouth, but at least she breathed. Thankfully, the shattered case hadn't punctured any major arteries. He gently shook her slim shoulders. Her eyelids fluttered open.

"John?" she began hesitantly. Fingers probed the cut on her forehead, making her wince.

"There now, take it easy," he said. "Can you stand?"

Her eyes looked cloudy. He wondered whether she suffered a concussion.

"I think so," Sabrina said, though she sounded far from certain.

Looping his arm under her shoulder, Blackwood lifted Sabrina to her feet. She wasn't heavy. Even with the extra support, she still wobbled.

She scanned the room with a groggy stare, taking in the fire, the smoke, the overturned display cases and the hordes careening into each other like bumper cars. That brought her around better than any smelling salts. Her eyes snapped open in horror.

"Oh my god," she said, tears in every syllable. "It's all ruined. All of it!"

"Not everything," Blackwood said, the bleakness of his tone like a dash of ice water. She followed his gaze and spotted the relic resting snugly in the case, completely untouched.

She sagged a little in his grip. Worry flared in his features.

"Here, we've got to get you away from all of this," he said.

She fixed him with a weak gaze.

"Don't worry about me," she said, grimacing to hold back the pain. "Retrieve the relic. Do what Father Dragoti said."

Struggling to keep Sabrina upright, and worried she might lose consciousness at any moment, Blackwood started moving with her toward the case when the lights dimmed once more. This time the chamber remained dark for several seconds, and in the blackness the growing flames sputtered and spat like dragon's breath. More cries went up from the guests, running blindly in the clutching smoke.

The lights snapped back on and Blackwood let out an involuntary sigh. Sabrina searched his face, her expression crestfallen.

"This is terrible," she said. "I don't know –."

She didn't get to finish. Another voice, incredulous and even louder than the blaring fire alarm, rose above the din.

"What the fuck happened?"

Both of them looked up to encounter a stunned McGowan, who stood before them holding …

"Yeah, it's a margarita," he confirmed.

Blackwood's head and shoulders shook, partly from amazement and partly from relief.

"You're a daft bugger," he told his cousin. "Where the hell have you been?"

McGowan jabbed a thumb over his shoulder.

"Been in the can for a bit, limey, if you must know," he said, trying to sound miffed. He directed his next statement at Sabrina. "No offense, ma'am, but I don't think the ceviche aged too well, if you know what I mean. "

Carefully balancing the margarita in one hand, he rubbed his stomach with the other for emphasis.

Though Blackwood wanted to chuckle, instead his face darkened as he brought McGowan up to speed.

"Dammit. I go to pinch off a—to take a bathroom break and all hell breaks loose," McGowan said, frowning, after Blackwood finished. The photographer shot Sabrina an apologetic glance for his near slip of the tongue.

She let it go and instead gently disengaged Blackwood's arm.

"I'm okay now, but thank you," she said. Impulsively, she leaned into the hollow of Blackwood's cheek and gave him a quick peck.

Sabrina's lips lingered a moment longer, and then she seemed to transform into someone else. Her tone became firm, brooking no challenge. Once again, the blood of generations of ranchers and oil barons coursing through her veins gave her a burst of fortitude. Steely determination blazed in her blue eyes; she planted balled fists on her hips.

Blackwood stared at her in amazement: *And I worried she had a concussion?*

"Now, as I was saying before Robert made his triumphant return, the relic must –."

Before she could utter another word, an ear-shattering shriek of splitting wood thundered across the chamber. Blackwood's head whipped around so fast his neck bones popped. Heartbeat racing, he caught a blur of motion as both of the chamber's main doors erupted from their hinges and flew across the Great Hall, landing with a crash and splintering into a million fragments just yards from the relic, which remained unscathed. The same couldn't be said for those who'd been bunched up at the Great Hall's entrance. Mowed down by the hurtling doors, the crushed bodies of guards and guests alike lay sprawled and motionless as a cold, glinting fog ebbed through the entrance. An unnatural fog.

Blackwood felt every nerve go on high alert. The continued hammering of his heart, the blood turning to ice in his veins, told him all he needed to know even before he spied the trio of dim shapes moving through the murk.

Blackwood gripped Sabrina and McGowan by their elbows and started backing up, pulling them with him. Their mouths agape, they followed blindly. Blackwood only stopped when their backs bumped into the display case holding The Covenant of the Cursed.

The three Daughters emerged from the icy cloud. The temperature in the Great Hall began plunging almost immediately.

Held aloft by great, beating black wings, the nightmarish trio glided like death incarnate into the chamber. Forked tails flicked and swatted at the smoky air like serpents. They swept the hall with hungry, feral glances, their cadaver-white breasts heaving, mats of coarse hair bristling along their scabrous skin. Below their smoldering, slitted eyes, saw-blade mouths wore hungry, malevolent grins.

Sabrina screamed, high, shrill and surprisingly girlish, all semblance of a proud Texas heiress dropping as the scales might from a blind man's eyes. McGowan's drink slipped from a suddenly limp hand, the dumbfounded oval of his mouth parting his beard.

Blackwood stood resolute, muscles tensing, whispering a line from Shakespeare: "Something wicked this way comes."

"Noooo," Sabrina trilled in a single hot breath, clutching his arm hard enough to bruise flesh. "What are they? John, what are those things?"

Blackwood's mouth tightened in a thin, resigned line. The familiar trio spotted him, or rather the prized relic behind him, and changed course to head directly his way. Those deathly grins broadened as recognition flared in the dark holes they called eyes, and saliva drooled like wet ropes from distended maws. Matching sets of bared fangs gleamed like knives.

"The worst guests in the world," he answered.

CHAPTER TWENTY-SEVEN

Blackwood wasted no time. Clamping hands on Sabrina's bare shoulders, he gave her an apologetic look and shoved her into McGowan. Her slender frame collided with the photographer's whiskey-barrel chest. A surprised McGowan instinctively encircled her with beefy arms to prevent both of them from stumbling.

"Hey!" they shouted together.

Behind them, screams reached a fevered pitch as fleeing patrons caught sight of the Daughters. The horrors showed no interest in any of the guests, however. They kept heading straight for the relic, drawn like sharks to blood.

"Get out of here!" Blackwood yelled at McGowan. "Both of you need to go!"

McGowan released Sabrina and they stared at him, aghast. Sabrina's voice rose.

"What about you?"

"You needn't worry about me," Blackwood said, attempting to force some bravery into his voice. With a drawn face, he pointed to the employee exit, which now stood clear. The backs of the last guests could be seen disappearing down the hallway.

"You must leave," he pleaded with her. "Please."

Sabrina's jaw dropped.

"You're going to stay? You can't be serious. You'll be killed," she protested, fear collapsing her features.

McGowan barely paid any attention to their conversation. With growing unease, his gaze stayed glued on the Daughters as they drew nearer.

He suddenly remembered Blackwood's warning about the "glam" and broke contact with their empty, burning sockets. Instead, his eyes swept the room and alighted upon the twisted shape of a fallen police officer, the life crushed from him when the doors exploded from their hinges. With surprising speed, McGowan rushed over to the body, dropped to his knees and tugged at the man's leather belt. He rose a second later, clutching the policeman's Glock. It wasn't much use to the officer anymore.

It wasn't going to be much use, period, and Blackwood stopped quarreling with Sabrina long enough to say so.

"Robert, that won't work! Just take Sabrina and go."

The combat veteran ignored him. Planting his boots firmly on the parquet floor, McGowan took careful aim with the pistol and fired. Every shot hit its mark in the nearest Daughter, who only glared at McGowan, spitting and hissing. She never stopped moving, headed inexorably for the display to keep up with her dark siblings.

"What the fuck?" McGowan groaned. He looked at the pistol as though it must have malfunctioned.

Blackwood made an exasperated sound in the back of his throat.

"Guns won't work against the Daughters!" he shouted. "I've already tried that."

Witnessing McGowan's failed gambit, Sabrina clutched Blackwood's hand, her grip tighter than a vise. She started to tug on him.

"Please, John, we've got to get out of here! Grab the relic and let's go! All of us!"

Blackwood merely shook his head. He didn't have time to explain that no matter where they went, the Daughters would always follow. This was the last stand, here and now.

A visibly shaken McGowan, the useless pistol tucked into the waistband of his disheveled tuxedo, rejoined them.

"Uhh, guys...?" he said, looking over his shoulder at the approaching Daughters. "Can you argue later?"

Sabrina released her grasp on Blackwood, who wouldn't budge, balled her fists and shook her hands.

"If you're staying, then I'm staying!" She remained resolute, not dropping her gaze from Blackwood's flustered features.

Blackwood flipped his eyes up and down. Standing here dickering only wasted time. He searched her face in desperation.

"Please, leave!" he said again. "I'm only going to stick around long enough to distract the Daughters until The Hand arrives. They'll know what to do."

Sabrina opened her mouth, chin rising defiantly, the hollow of her throat flushed. With a flash of irritation, Blackwood recognized that even with certain death approaching, she was going to quarrel with him to the bitter end.

McGowan spared them further pointless debate. Without a word, he grasped Sabrina around the waist and lifted her with a grunt. She flopped over his shoulder, to him no heavier than a sack of feed at his dad's ranch. This wasn't a proper fireman's carry, but close enough. His Marine training didn't fail him. He started backing away, giving his cousin a mournful look.

"Don't die on me, limey," he said.

Stunned into speechlessness, Sabrina only growled in frustration. Bouncing and dangling the way a little doll might, the rear-facing woman glared daggers at Blackwood. Then, as the pair cleared the doorway, her expression softened and he heard her yell, "Oh fine! Be careful!"

"I'll do my best," he muttered, turning to confront the Daughters. Their leers widened as they closed the distance.

"Did you miss us, sweetmeat?" the one in front asked. He recognized her from before as the leader. "Oh, pardon my manners. I never properly introduced myself. I'm Mawrgoth."

Without waiting for an answer, she leapt for the wall and began crawling sideways in a blur of arms and legs. Stopping across from him, she flung herself from the perch, wings beating fast enough to part Blackwood's hair as she flew overhead. With surprising grace, she alighted atop a case holding the armor of a long-dead conquistador.

He could count the heaving vertebrae in her back as her head swiveled downwards, insect-like, blank eyes fastening on him.

"Salutations—Master John Gwydion Blackwood."

Her sisters merely floated forward, malignant glares painted on their dead-white faces. In seconds they circled him, but drew no closer than six feet. The black spaces where eyes should have been fixated on his chest. It took him a second to figure out why, and then his fingers grasped the cross around his neck. He raised the holy symbol; the creatures spat and drew back as though burned.

"Aye, protected ye might be, but ye leave unguarded that which we seek," one of the others said. Her rough voice recalled bones crunching.

The beast inclined her head slightly in a courtly fashion.

"Vhurtika," she introduced herself, executing an aerial bow. In answer, Blackwood raised the cross an inch higher; she emitted a little shriek and scooted back another foot. He felt the knobs of his spine brush against the case sheltering the relic.

Vhurtika's hairy chin rose a notch and she said, with as much venom as possible, "You are outnumbered, scribe. You cannot protect both yourself and the Azad'dhul."

"Only until the solstice passes," Blackwood said.

The sisters exchanged worries glances.

"That's right," Blackwood said. "We've sussed your plans, so sod off."

Their faces boiled with naked fury. Snarling, Mawrgoth launched herself from the conquistador display, joining her airborne brethren. In dizzying fashion, they rose and wove a circle above him the way vultures waiting for something to die will do, but didn't come any closer. Blackwood's grip on the cross tightened until the blood drained from his fingers.

Meanwhile, the flames continued their inexorable march across the chamber, setting alight anything that could burn. Untouched and aloft above the conflagration, the Daughters radiated icy cold, but below them the growing fires burned hot and bright. It was a different story for Blackwood. Little stabs of heat began to prick his exposed skin. The smoke, too, made breathing a challenge. Rising next to the balcony, the Christmas tree caught fire, the baubles dropping and shattering like discarded dreams.

Keeping the trio at bay was only a stalling tactic, nothing more, but fire or not, Blackwood didn't have a choice. The relic couldn't fall into the Daughter's hands. The solstice was less than an hour away.

An eternity. The blaze would reach him long before then.

Which is why Dragoti and the reinforcements need to arrive soon, he told himself.

The third Daughter spoke, cocking her head ironically.

"Ambergleiss at your service, son of Adam," she said, executing a bow in mid-air. "You may indeed ken our plans, but if you await succor from that fool of a shaman and his whelps, 'tis a misspent effort indeed. The sweet flames will claim you long before they arrive."

Blackwood swallowed with difficulty, as though a rock lodged in his throat.

Ambergleiss thundered with laughter. "Master Scribe, thee aren't too sore on the eyes. Let me take you into my soothing embrace. Never again shall ye worry about such things as fire."

Her little jest prompted titters from all of them.

Mawrgoth alighted upon a cornice, roosting there like some vile gargoyle. Intermittently flapping her black wings, the lava-like runnels of her face scrunched inward as she considered the next course of action.

"We'll just wait until you burn to a crisp, shall we, John?" she said, her expression hard as stone. "Then, we'll take the Azad'dhul as we please, sup upon the simmering marrow of your charred bones and return to the ones who command us."

She narrowed those hellish orbs, her forked tongue darting at the ashes swirling in the churning air. Her courtly manner of speech did nothing to hide the sheer malice rolling off her scaly hide in waves.

He made no reply. Instead, Blackwood's lips parted in a slow smile, a reaction clearly puzzling the hags. Expressions of uncertainty clouded their features, replacing the murderous scowls. They watched, mystified, as Blackwood's free hand reached into a pocket to extract a handkerchief. His other hand released the cross, the taut chain going limp. The holy symbol returned to its resting spot above his heart. Moving fast, he wound the handkerchief around his left fist.

The horrors watched intently, unable to come any closer.

Blackwood pulled tight on the white cotton, making sure the fabric covered his knuckles.

Breathing deeply, Blackwood wheeled around and slammed the fist protected by the handkerchief into the display case.

The shatter-resistant surface wobbled. Blackwood hit the glass again with all his might. A web of cracks began radiating from the point of impact. Redoubling his efforts, he struck again, and once more, grunting with each exertion. Finally, with a crash, the glass fragmented into dozens of jagged slivers that crashed to the floor, leaving the relic exposed.

In one fluid motion, Blackwood lifted the cross over his head, leaned into the case and wrapped the shining silver chain as many times as possible around the ragged tome. The holy symbol came to rest squarely in the center of the cover.

The Daughters screeched in rage.

"What have ye done, witless fool?" Mawrgoth shouted, her visage flaring with wrath.

Blackwood mentally reviewed his strategy. Legends said nothing could destroy the book. Thus, the relic would survive the fire even if he didn't, and the cross would keep the hags at bay until well after the solstice. They couldn't touch the tome while it was in contact with the cross, no matter how much they desired to do so. Meanwhile, with any luck, he would be able to lure them away, giving The Hand time to arrive, retrieve and secure the book. And even if the sisters stayed to figure out how to remove the cross, Dragoti and his priests would get here soon enough, dealing swiftly and effectively with the trio.

Either way, the Daughters would never take possession of the *Pactum est Maledictus*. Of course, Blackwood probably would die in the process. Not the best plan, he reflected, but better than none.

"Remove the lamb's seal now!" Mawrgoth bellowed, fury mixed with frustration.

Ripping off the handkerchief, Blackwood raised his hand and gave the Daughters the middle finger.

The howls erupting from the nightmarish brood shook the chamber's foundations and threatened to collapse the vaulted ceiling. Black wings beat the smoke with tornadic fury and claws rent the empty air with homicidal intent.

"Son of Adam, you will cast off that trinket now!" Blood and spittle flew from Mawrgoth's gaping maw.

Blackwood didn't stick around to offer a rebuttal.

Dodging under her swooping talons, he beat a hasty retreat from the chamber, skirting jets of flame while avoiding the bent and broken bodies scattered across the floor. Running as fast as possible, Blackwood's feet delivered him down the long corridor, now covered in thick sheets of ice that crackled and slithered like something alive. He emerged in Dinosaur Row.

The fire hadn't reached this wing yet.

Breathing heavily, he vowed to quit smoking while simultaneously admitting he was just lying to himself. He turned down a side corridor and slowed to a jog, then entered a gallery filled with Texas-themed paintings, including dozens of works featuring bluebonnets, the state flower.

He stood for a moment in silence, trying to catch his breath again. The respite didn't last long. He heard the creatures long before he saw them.

Good. They took the bait—him.

Ducking around a corner, he peeked across the gallery into a long mirror running the length of the room. The reflection from the far end showed a scene that defied belief — chairs spinning in the air, vases levitating and shattering against the wall, paintings ripped from their frames as if caught in a cyclone, even a very ornate 17th century writing cabinet — called a vargueno, according to a helpful placard he'd seen in a glance when rushing past — crushed as though an invisible boulder landed on top.

Just as in the parking lot when he gazed into the pickup's rearview mirror, the hags cast no reflection. Yet when he risked a furtive glance around the corner, not in the mirror, he spied all three Daughters coming his way, crescent eyes blazing with volcanic fire.

"It's better if you're alive to do our bidding, John," Mawrgoth screamed with homicidal fervor after spotting his fearful face. "But just an arm with a hand attached will do nicely in a pinch! The finger you just showed us should work!"

They came at him from various angles, with Ambergleiss in the lead. Her legs bunched and she jumped straight up, arms spread wide; Blackwood gasped as she clung to the ceiling fourteen feet above the carpeted floor.

She crawled upside-down toward him in the fashion of a spider closing on a hapless fly. She tucked and folded her wings to move even faster, and a corner of Blackwood's mind struggled to fathom how she so easily defied gravity.

As he gawked, a blur materialized in front of him. Vhurtika, he realized too late. Ambergleiss had created a distraction, and now Vhurtika plowed into his mid-section with so much force his teeth nearly popped out of his jaw. He sailed through the air and slammed into a sculpted column. A brass bowl brimming with potpourri atop the plinth flipped and showered him with its fragrant contents. He fought to draw breath, tasting dust and patchouli.

"Oh my, didst I cause thee an insult?" Vhurtika chuckled.

Choking back a cry, Blackwood struggled to get on his feet. She wasn't about to let him scamper off so easily. Before he could draw his next fractured breath, talons shot out and clamped around his ankle, her grip sinking deep into the flesh and threatening to crush bone. Blackwood kicked at her, struggling desperately to free his limb from that bear-trap grip, but she proved astonishingly strong. Within seconds she drew herself to full height, wings unfurling to blot out the overhead lights. A gasp of pain boiled up from within Blackwood as she lifted him by the heel and tossed him down the hall, expending no more effort than a petulant child throwing a toy. He flew several feet before his left side struck an antique chair, which splintered under the impact.

A horrendous yelp ripped from Blackwood's throat. Behind him cold, utterly soulless laughter rent the air. Twisting and turning his head to clear the fog, he dimly registered Vhurtika stalking towards him, her hands opening and closing in bloodthirsty anticipation.

With every nerve exploding in protest, Blackwood managed to crawl away, his frenzied fingers and feet digging into the fibers of the old carpet with as much tenacity as a baby turtle trying to reach the safety of the surf. He may as well have just stayed in place for all his trouble. Vhurtika loomed above him, screeching like some befouled bird of prey, her face contorting with animalistic rage.

She casually flipped him over and plopped down on his chest, effectively bolting him to the floor. The breath lurched out of his windpipe. The thing was far heavier than she looked. His head rang from the impact, his jaw burned from scraping against a rucked-up carpet. The moment became an eternity. He gazed up, transfixed by pain and horror, at a mouthful of gleaming teeth as she lowered herself to his exposed throat. He had no trouble seeing his own death staring back at him from the eternal darkness of her eyes.

"Yummy," the thing giggled. Red, foamy spittle dripped from her mouth, blistering his skin. He could sense in her coiled muscles the naked strength to gut him like a fish.

Blood roared in Blackwood's temples, throat, wrists and groin; he could feel her somehow calling to the precious fluid in the miles of veins that snaked under his skin, could sense her eternal hunger. The serum responded, as tides respond to the cold moon.

He tried twisting away, but she held him fast. The groping fingers of his right hand closed on something cylindrical and hard, which he dimly recognized by feel as a broken chair leg. She drew back, readying for the final strike, and then plunged towards him.

Acting on pure instinct, Blackwood blindly thrust upwards with the chair leg. The creature's eyes bulged in terror; too late, she realized her mistake. Momentum carried her irrevocably forward in her blind lust for his blood. The jagged stake of wood plunged straight into the very center of the beast's chest. The splintered tip slipped through the skin, a hot knife parting butter, slicing past supernal muscle and bone to pierce whatever shriveled thing passed for a heart underneath.

There was a sudden hush, a profound stillness; every atom in the room seemed to stop spinning in its orbit. And then the silence broke, displaced by the shrillest, most horrified scream Blackwood ever heard. The walls shook, the windows rattled. Lights flickered, switched off, flashed back on. The weight immediately lifted from his chest; he could breathe again, sucking in deep gulps of air. He rolled over on his aching hip, only to see Vhurtika lying spread-eagle on the floor just inches away, dark ichor pumping from her chest — more like gelatinous sludge than blood. The chair leg stood solidly embedded in her torso. Her hands groped weakly at the shaft, her face eaten by agony; legs kicked and squirmed with all the animation of a frog wired to an electric current. Underneath, her wings flopped uselessly like torn sheets stirred by the wind.

Blackwood watched in both revulsion and fascination as she continued writhing and screaming, her cries weakening, turning to whimpers. As she struggled, a startling transformation took place.

Like some sped-up film image, the hag's features rapidly altered, the skin aging, becoming as coarse and shriveled as old bark, turning yellow, then brown and finally black. Very quickly, the outlines of her ribs and collarbone pressed against her sagging flesh, which ripped like dry muslin as her body collapsed on itself, exposing her skeleton. Within seconds, she was nothing but a pile of quivering bones. And then even those dissipated, turning into calcified dust, until at last all that remained was a dim outline and a broken chair leg that wobbled upright for a second or two, then fell over with a thud.

An eerie wind sprang up and whistled down the hallway. He hazarded a quick look, unable to locate an open window or vent that would explain the wind. The creature's ashes began blowing away, like so much detritus in a fireplace. In seconds not even the outline remained. The breeze died down as swiftly as it arose. He shook away his astonishment and tried to slow his frenzied breathing, even while realizing his troubles remained far from over.

Down the hallway, the other two horrors — who had stayed back to let their sister have her sport — pinned Blackwood with truly poisonous stares. He felt sure his heart would burst and the eyes melt from his face if he returned their scrutiny for long.

Now it was personal, those malignant glares screamed.

Somehow ... some way ... he'd managed to kill one of them.

Blackwood scrambled to his feet and bolted from the room, wondering how long it would take before they caught up to him.

The answer came two seconds later. With loud crashes and keening wails, they pursued him full-bore, flying through the hallway at breakneck speed. He risked a glance over his shoulder and wished he hadn't.

Mawrgoth dragged her talons along the walls, shredding the yellow-rose wallpaper with all the tenderness of a flame through gossamer.

Blackwood put on a burst of speed, but in his heart he realized no real possibility of getting away existed. These things could track him anywhere. They were faster. They were stronger. He'd been lucky so far, but his luck was bound to run out sooner or later. The fire burning its way through the museum started making its presence known in this wing. Smoke thickened the air.

A large archway swam into view. As he raced for the opening, Blackwood gradually registered another sound besides the raspy breath echoing in his ears and the guttural howls of his rapidly gaining pursuers — a voice raised in song. Understanding dawned just seconds later when the arch opened onto a mezzanine fronted by a wide balcony. A grand staircase connected the balcony to a large foyer below, where another massive Christmas tree identical to the one in the Great Hall rose majestically from the parquet floor.

In the next second, he located the source of the singing. His heart sank even more.

A pretty little girl wearing a red elf hat and a green smock stood on a riser at the base of the Douglas fir performing a solo, her innocent voice uplifted in song. She seemed to be singing to keep herself calm. The slightest quaver underscored her airy tone. A small boy dressed the same way stood next to her, looking lost and nervous. His small right hand clutched a polished oak staff topped by a gleaming silver cross.

"Rump-a-tum-tum" the girl crooned. Even with the blood pounding in his temples, Blackwood recognized "The Little Drummer Boy."

He took the pair for carolers in the Christmas production. There must've been two groups, he reasoned, because the choir in the Great Hall had already cleared out, according to Charlie.

My god, Blackwood thought, somehow these children got misplaced in all the confusion. Or worse, forgotten ...

The singing and the good cheer evaporated the moment Blackwood skittered across the landing. The small girl's pigtails whirled around as she glanced up and caught sight of him on the balcony, her voice sputtering and a halting hand rising in his direction. It occurred to him as she started to scream that he must look a fright: bloodied, disheveled, eyes blazing. The boy yelled next.

Then it dawned on Blackwood perhaps he wasn't the star attraction. The skin crawling along his spine said as much.

Blackwood whirled around to confront the remaining sisters. The pair had taken up positions several feet behind him, their mouths staining the air with ragged grins. Those ghastly smiles made him think of Cheshire cats gorged on acid, all teeth, bloated gums and no face. Hs balls shriveled to the size of dried peas. Any hope he harbored of escaping evaporated on the spot. One blocked the doorway to the hall, preventing him from retracing his steps, and the second levitated at the top of the landing, her empty, raging sockets daring him to take a step toward the stairs.

Blackwood chanced a glance over the rail. He guessed the drop at 20 feet, straight down to the marble floor. A fall might not kill him, but likely would leave him a cripple. Whether he liked it or not, down seemed to be the only way out. That didn't have to mean straight down, though. Making a quick mental calculation, and trusting more to instinct than anything else, he spun smartly around, cursed, legged himself over the balustrade and leapt to the Christmas tree. There was nothing graceful about the maneuver; his arms flapped madly and legs pedaled as though riding an invisible bicycle. He felt a moment of sheer, heart-stopping terror before crashing into the uppermost boughs, stomach catapulting into his throat.

His good fortune held and so did the violently swaying branches, though he heard one or two small limbs crack. On the balcony, his tormentors' faces contorted in fury and surprise as they watched him once again outwit them. Blackwood sucked down great mouthfuls of air as he clung to the tree, arms locked around a sturdy bough. When the rocking motions finally steadied, he wasted no time shimmying down the trunk, surprised at his own agility even as the branches whipped his face.

The euphoria was short-lived. The tree began to bend. What started as an ominous creaking translated seconds later into a limb snapping under Blackwood's left foot, sending him plummeting the last several feet through clutching limbs. Decorations and strands of tinsel fell with him. He landed with a thud. Across from him, the children cowered against an antique roll-top desk.

Head spinning madly, the crime reporter brought his blurred vision into focus. Lying at two pairs of diminutive feet clad in green velour booties with upturned toes, Blackwood stared up and saw panicked expressions eclipsing the kids' fresh-scrubbed faces. The little boy, whom he guessed to be the youngest at seven or eight, sported a respectable gap between his front teeth, the kind that makes an orthodontist see dollar signs. The girl didn't look much older. The shapes of their noses and the freckles splashed across their cheeks suggested siblings.

In front of his face, the fuzzy lines of a discarded banner aligned into characters that read: "St. Paul's Episcopal Youth Choir Presents 'Ode to Christmas Joy.'"

Blackwood flipped on his back and groaned.

"Terribly—sorry—about ruining your performance," he gasped. His face stung from a hundred scrapes where the branches slapped his skin.

As his breathing slowed, he waited for the children to break the silence, to yell or start calling for their mum. Instead, the boy's head only rose a notch, his jaw going slack. The staff with the cross slipped absently from his fingers, the polished wood and lustrous silver hitting the floor with a clatter. A thin, wet line started to blot the boy's pants from his crotch to below the knee. The girl's head also jerked up. Their gazes became fixed on something past Blackwood. The bells on the peaks of their caps jingled as the kids screamed in unison and clutched each other in a protective embrace.

Grasping a corner of the desk, Blackwood hauled himself up on shaking legs and dusted himself off with a perfunctory air. He didn't need to turn around to see what lurked behind.

"Hullo, bitches," he said through gritted teeth.

Mawrgoth's sibilant voice, as sharp and sweet as a razor dipped in honey, confirmed what he already knew.

They had him cornered.

"Oh goody, John! We'll have a snack, shall we, before the main course? Two sweetlings!"

Ambergleiss chimed in. "Perhaps we'll fashion a necklace from their tiny little teeth!"

The sisters hovered a dozen feet from where he stood, their black tresses flowing behind them on an unseen wave, their mouths agape with distended teeth. They resembled a pair of ghastly mermaids suspended in a loathsome sea, a woodcut from the Brothers Pretty Damn Grimm. He didn't move an inch, except to cast his eyes around the foyer, seeking an escape route. Long, empty corridors extended in either direction; he calculated his chances at reaching either threshold before the women got their hooks into him and realized he didn't have a prayer. They would cut him off the second he tried to run. And then shred him — slowly.

Just an arm with a hand attached... That's all they needed.

Besides, he couldn't just leave these kids, and he knew they would never be able to outrun the Daughters.

"Move aside, scribe," Mawrgoth breathed, lips opening and shutting like mating slugs. "We'll make quick work of these morsels and save the best for last."

She drifted away a few feet and cackled, toying with him and the innocent children, who couldn't begin to understand what they faced.

Deep inside Blackwood, an ember of subdued anger flared into life.

"Let the children go," he demanded, the rage growing, burning. "They're not part of this."

Mawrgoth made a rude noise.

"But John, we steal children. We always have—especially males! Didn't your babbling friend tell you? He of the four days? The lamb's puppet?"

She studied Blackwood's blank, uncomprehending expression, then inexplicably erupted in mocking guffaws. She swiveled to face Ambergleiss, who also broke out in loud laughter.

"Oh, how sweet! The scribe knows not!" Mawrgoth screeched. "And here I was, thinking Celts so clever."

"Bah, we waste time talking of things long past," Ambergleiss hissed. "Vengeance for Vhurtika! For our sister."

Her sightless eyes became magma channels carved through blackest basalt, spitting sparks. She drew back a couple of feet, hair bobbing like a nest of eels.

"Heavy is the price you will pay, son of Adam," she added.

She spat the last words, naked contempt in her scratchy voice. Ambergleiss' chalky features glowed with dark glee, and her talons opened and closed spasmodically.

Blackwood steeled himself, wondering which Daughter would strike first.

The little girl behind him at last broke her silence, forcing words between great, hacking ruptures of frightened breath.

"Don't—let the—bad ladies hurt us, mister," she said. "Me and my brother Danny—want to go home for Christmas ... Please."

Her voice, so small and so filled with dread, tugged at his soul and breathed new life into his aching limbs.

"I'm won't allow the bad ladies to hurt you or your brother," he said.

He had no idea how to keep that promise, but he meant every word.

A weapon ... dear Lord, he needed a weapon.

Think, think, think, he admonished himself. And then it came to him. Hadn't he seen the little boy drop something on the floor? A long staff, topped by a piece of shining metal ... A cross.

Blackwood wanted to slap himself for not thinking of it sooner. *Yes! That should do nicely.*

He knew what had to be done, but that meant being very careful. And very fast. With a light, probing touch from the tip of his shoe, he located the fallen staff. He couldn't look down for fear the Daughters would discern his intention. Instead, he met their burning gazes head on, defiantly staring into those deep, endless holes of midnight. Having bested one of their brood, he sensed their "glam" no longer held any power over him.

Evidently reaching the limit of her patience, Ambergleiss' scabrous arms lifted into the air, gleaming claws distended to rend him to pieces.

Now or never. Blackwood made his move.

He ducked down. With the frenzy of a drowning man grasping a spar, his groping hand closed around the staff and held it fast.

He shot up as rapidly as a blast fired from a cannon, swinging the cross in wide arcs. It might have been a trick of the light, a reflection from the overheads, but in that moment the silver metal seemed to come alive and crackle with a pure white glow.

The reaction from his pursuers was no illusion, however. Both screamed in sheer terror and pulled back.

Blackwood's lips curled in a tight smile.

"I thought as much," he murmured. Relief surged through him. Now, they had a fighting chance.

The women spat and growled, strangled by impotent rage, and came not an inch closer. It seemed some invisible, impenetrable shield kept them at bay. Blackwood realized his vision was not playing tricks upon him—the cross actually did dance with a feathery nimbus of light. The glow became brighter with each second. He watched, fascinated, as the brilliance spilled over the edges of the metal, flowing down and across the wooden shaft, growing warm under his hands and flooding his muscles. A sensation of comfort and courage suffused every nerve.

With difficulty, he tore his eyes away from what seconds before had been nothing more than a silver icon, a juncture of two pieces of metal, a symbol of torture and capital punishment practiced by an empire dead for centuries, and stared down his attackers. This time, they refused to even look in his direction, drifting and bobbing like leaking balloons, keeping a wary distance. Their gazes shifted to the children, who cowered behind Blackwood. But they approached no closer. The few times they did hazard a glance at the cross, their expressions clouded with an emotion Blackwood had only seen once before, back in the Great Hall—abject terror.

He feinted at the pair with the staff. They threw up their claws and drew back with sharp slashes of breath, uttering little shrieks that would have been comical under any other circumstance.

He inched forward, never taking his eyes off the creatures. The sisters did their best to hold their ground, reluctantly backing away and venting more of those piteous little wails whenever they brushed too close to the religious symbol. Blackwood almost — almost — felt sorry for them, until he remembered all the dead left in their murderous wake.

The sisters' empty eyes wheeled with fire, glaring hungrily at the children. Save for the drama playing out among their number, the large foyer remained empty — still no sign of Dragoti and his priests. The hollow air echoed with the squeaking of Blackwood's soles. Somewhere, far down a hall, maybe toward the lobby, he thought he could detect raised voices, sounds of alarm. Off in the distance, the siren of a fire truck wailed. Help on the way? Too little and too late, he decided.

But at least the children no longer wept. Risking a glimpse over his shoulder, he observed both had gone mute, their mouths pressed tight enough to turn coal into diamonds. Their gazes stayed locked on the hovering monsters, their eyes puffy from tears. Though deathly afraid, the children made a good show of being brave. That let him breathe a little easier.

"Stay behind me," he said with a whisper, "and keep your backs to the wall. We're going to try for the nearest hallway.—The one to the right, I should think."

What was he forgetting? Oh, yes.

"And whatever you do, don't look in their eyes!" he said.

Blackwood motioned his new charges to start towards the hallway. As instructed, they clung to the wall, moving only a couple of feet at a time as the two Daughters tracked them step for step, never coming closer but never retreating. Blackwood kept the cross pointed forward, swinging it back and forth like a pendulum while trying to keep an eye on the children.

"Watch your step, Wendy!" the boy warned.

"I am, Danny," the girl shot back. "Don't tell me what to do. I'm eight—a year older than you."

A good-natured grin flitted across Blackwood's lips hearing her prim tone. He counted it a miracle the frightened pair found the sheer willpower to even put one foot before the other, much less speak. Had he been their age, he wondered how well he would have handled this little cat-and-mouse episode.

Now that he knew their names, manners dictated a proper introduction.

"Hullo Danny, Wendy. My name is John Blackwood. I'm a reporter," he said.

I'll wager that sounded impressive enough, Blackwood thought.

"Nice to meet you, Mr. Blackwood," the girl said, the very model of manners despite their predicament. "What TV station do you work for?"

His short-lived smile flipped into a frown. TV station indeed. What cheek!

Twisting around to offer a pithy retort, his arms moved with him and the headpiece of the staff dipped dangerously low to the floor.

"From the mouths of children ..." he muttered.

He almost learned too late the price of hubris.

Taking advantage of his carelessness as the cross practically scraped the floor, Ambergleiss attempted a flanking move calculated to bring her to the children from the opposite side. Mawrgoth tensed, ready to rush headlong for the kill the second Blackwood exposed his back.

As Ambergleiss lunged forward, she gave vent to an earsplitting shriek of triumph.

But cunning or not, the maneuver proved her undoing. Reacting from pure instinct, Blackwood at the last second did not turn around, instead raising the cross like a lance in a knight's joust. Before he even realized what he was doing, he blindly lunged forward and rammed the venerated symbol straight into the creature's exposed belly.

What happened next seemed so improbable, so far beyond even the realm of the fantastic, that Blackwood—in spite of everything else he'd witnessed—had trouble believing what his eyes revealed. The cross met just the merest resistance pressing against the thing's leathery flesh. The glow around the metal flared into a searing, golden corona.

Cleansing light, Blackwood would think later.

With all the force of a rock dropped into a pond, the top of the cross kept going, passing effortlessly into the Daughter. Her mouth ripped open in a howl of utter despair. The flesh of her abdomen puckered and became a huge burning welt. The light from the cross intensified, then enveloped the creature in pure white flames.

Blackwood flung a hand across his face. He felt but didn't see the explosion that knocked him to his knees. He could hear the children shriek as the same thing happened to them. When he next opened his eyes, the creature pinned on the end of the staff had vanished — vaporized or just summarily winked out of existence.

He gulped down great draughts of air to steady his nerves. It tasted, well, cleansed, on his tongue. Like a spring morning.

Ambergleiss was—what? Dead? He paused. Could these things actually die? Maybe "destroyed" worked better. Or banished. Never mind. The terminology didn't matter. She was gone for good, never to return. He felt the truth of that statement resonate in every fiber of his being.

No sign of Mawrgoth, but Blackwood sensed she lurked nearby, unseen, licking her wounds. Not giving up, though. Not by any means.

He glanced down at his hands, still tightly wrapped around the staff. The burnished wood remained untouched and otherwise unremarkable. The nimbus of light emanating from the top piece slowly faded, leaving only a brief after-image registering on his retinas. Even that vanished. The cross once again became a venerated prop for a kids' holiday recital.

He rose to his feet, wiping a patina of ash from his face.

"Everyone all right?" he asked the children.

Clinging to each other, the brother and sister stood up, shaking their heads.

"I think so," Wendy said in a tremulous voice. Her little brother just dusted himself off, too shocked to say much of anything.

The lad definitely will require therapy, Blackwood observed.

Satisfied the siblings remained unharmed, Blackwood turned his head left and right, resuming his search for Mawrgoth.

She was nowhere in sight. Blackwood wondered if the blast had claimed her after all.

Splendid news if true, his inner voice sighed. But he also knew that would be too easy.

Either way, the danger was averted — at least for now. Finally, he'd caught a break.

His watch no longer worked, but he guessed the solstice was only minutes away. Either The Hand would come to his aid before then or Mawrgoth would get the better of him, but no matter what, he would prevent her from claiming the relic.

He placed hands on the siblings' shoulders and gave a reassuring squeeze.

"I can't stay," he said, peering into their questioning faces. "I have to keep the bad lady from stealing something very important. But you're safe now. There will be firemen coming. Go to the main entrance and run outside; I think it's that way. And, take this cross with you. Your belief, your faith, will keep you safe. It's me the bad woman wants, and she's running out of time. Can you do that?"

Wendy's brows tightened in concentration and she nodded. At that moment, she looked much older than her eight years.

"Yes," she hesitantly answered. "Yes, Mr. Blackwood." More firmly that time.

Blackwood beamed at her. "Super."

With an air of gravity, he handed the staff to Danny.

"I believe this is yours," he said.

The boy grasped the wood with newfound appreciation.

Blackwood started down the opposite hallway, careful not to trip over his own tired feet.

As he rounded a corner, a surprising thing happened. He heard the children faintly wishing him a "Merry Christmas, Mr. Blackwood!"

CHAPTER TWENTY-EIGHT

The warmth hit Blackwood like a blast of tropical air as he rushed through the gift-shop doors. Overhead lights chased away the clinging shadows, sparing him any nasty surprises. Tower of the Americas replicas, plastic dinosaurs, Davy Crockett coonskin caps and mugs that matched the one in Sabrina's kitchen stuffed the shelves.

Exiting the store, Blackwood rode an escalator down to the wildlife section, his thoughts traveling at light speed.

He considered doubling back, but just as quickly rejected the idea. The object was to keep luring Mawrgoth away from the relic. The prickling on the nape of his neck told him she was never very far away, even if he couldn't see her.

At the end of the lift, positioned under a sign emblazoned with a neon feral hog and the words TEXAS FAUNA, Blackwood stiffened, his pulse racing as a familiar shiver trilled along his backbone.

She's here, he told himself.

He swung his head in a frantic arc, attempting to spot Mawrgoth before she ambushed him.

He didn't have to look far, only up. What he beheld froze his eyeballs. The Daughter dangled by a solitary arm from the railing just above his upturned face, a scaly vixen conjured from thin air.

"I'm quite cross with you," the creature spat. "You, a pittance of a mortal, have dispatched two of my sisters. Most assuredly you will pay. I will feed you your own guts."

Her mineshaft eyes narrowed to slits. The next words shot from her with the heat of a volcanic upheaval.

"In olden days, minstrels would sing of your deeds, but tonight your howls will shame the lamentations of the damned."

"I prefer New Wave —," was all Blackwood managed.

Throwing her head back to emit a bloodcurdling scream, she launched herself at him. The impact knocked every ounce of breath from his lungs. Tumbling in a tangled mass of arms and legs, the pair rolled down the escalator and through the entrance of the wildlife hall, past life-size displays showcasing stuffed armadillos, roadrunners and rattlesnakes. She landed on top; cloying scents of mold, blood and decay wafted from her hide, triggering Blackwood's gag reflex.

The Daughter gave a guttural exultation and lowered her jaws to within inches of his neck. With a cry, Blackwood threw up an arm. The Daughter's razor-lined mouth loomed over his exposed throat, his forearm straining against the creature to hold her at bay. A taloned hand entwined his straw-blond hair. With a savage yank, she jerked his head back to expose the jugular, but then just as quickly released him.

She wanted to show how completely helpless he was.

"I will dine on you slowly," the Daughter promised with soul-freezing malevolence. "And then, just before the last spark of life fades from your dull-witted eyes, provided I leave them in your skull, I will drag you to the Azad'dhul, where you will remove the sign of the lamb as your last act."

Her awful laugh boomed across the hall, nearly shattering his eardrums. Blackwood started kicking her as hard as he could, but the effort proved futile.

The pallid hag casually reached down, palmed his cranium and slammed his head against the floor.

"Stay still," she scolded. "I don't like my meals too lively."

Blackwood gasped in pain, stars swimming before his eyes. He turned his head, panting like a wounded dog, and caught sight of something glinting just a few yards beyond the floor-to-ceiling windows.

This level of the museum fronted the San Antonio River. The snow continued falling outside, more than he ever remembered seeing, even in Snowdonia National Park during the height of winter. The dark waters winding past the walls absorbed the flakes. The channel didn't amount to much more than a sizable creek, and it wouldn't be long before the sluggish current froze over.

Exhibiting a detached sense of curiosity, the monster followed his gaze.

"You fancy the river, John? Perhaps a swim?" she said, grinning wickedly. "What a wonderful idea!"

Her smile melted as quickly as a snowball in hell.

She lifted herself from him, beating her wings. Arms opened wide as the leathery appendages spread further, a churning pair of shadows come to life.

The night creature picked him up as effortlessly as a hawk snatching a hare. Blackwood's leg burned where her claws dug into his flesh; she hauled him upwards. Mawrgoth sailed from the hall, blasting out of the escalator and up to the next floor, where she soared like some hell-spawned carrion bird with her prey.

Mawrgoth circled the ceiling, deftly dodging cables, light fixtures and fluttering "Myths & Magicks of Spanish Tejas" banners, slaloming around as though he weighed nothing.

Within seconds she returned to Great Hall, where flames leapt and danced with abandon. Thick smoke wormed down Blackwood's throat, forcing a fit of coughing. The Daughter lifted him higher, gripping his calf as casually as a diner might swing a drumstick at a barbecue. The blood rushing to his head from dangling upside-down almost made him black out. Twirling in her grip, he spotted the relic.

The book remained undamaged in its case, a safe island amid a raging inferno. So, the legends didn't lie. The cross gleamed in the fire's light, still secured around the cover.

At that point the Daughter came to a sudden, gut-wrenching halt, great wings beating vigorously to stay aloft just under the vaulted ceiling. Hunter and hunted hovered the equivalent of four stories above the burning room.

"Mayhap I should just drop you now?" she mused aloud. Blackwood moaned, trying not to retch.

Somewhere along the way, he'd bitten his lip; crimson drops twisted as they dripped to tiles that seemed miles below.

"My apologies, John. I got a bit carried away," Mawrgoth chortled. "Naturally, one must first learn to fly before learning to fall."

A breathless hush fell over the cathedral-like chamber; even the crackling flames sounded tiny and distant. Mawrgoth gave herself a little push and soared towards the majestic oval window overlooking the river. Scattered across the balcony that fronted the window, Blackwood could see where the musicians had dropped their instruments, even the accordion.

Without warning, the abomination drew back an arm corded like a steel cable and let fly, hurling Blackwood into space. Shrieking, the reporter had just enough time to cover his face before smashing through the window's massive panels. Shards of glass, indistinguishable from the glittering snowflakes choking the sky outside, nicked his face as he spiraled through the frosted air.

He landed on his stomach across a steel support girder protruding from the moon-shaped window, a long piece of metal that looked like the start of an unfinished observation deck. The impact shoved a scream from his lungs. Convulsively wrapping arms and legs around the beam, he hung suspended above the black ribbon of the nearly frozen San Antonio River.

The girder vibrated under Blackwood as he shifted his weight. The chattering of his teeth sounded worse than a child shaking a piggy bank. Then, as things went from worse to totally screwed, he started sliding down the beam, which was coated in thick ice. Gibbering with animal panic, his freezing hands frantically clawed for purchase.

A raised metal knob fastened like a large rivet at the end of the beam gave Blackwood something to grab as he slipped over the edge. Clutching desperately at the mushroom-shaped object, his numbing fingers lost and then regained their grip in one heart-stopping second. He swung in the cutting wind like a broken marionette. Blackwood risked one look below his dangling shoes and felt his breath seize up—it was a long fall to the dull, surly waters.

Swallowing hard, Blackwood waited for the beam to stop shaking. Too weak to pull himself up, he just hung there, limp as a scarecrow. Far below, the river became more sluggish as ice built up in the current.

Right. What now? he wondered. He kicked weakly at the frigid air, but his legs felt as heavy as sacks filled with rocks. It wouldn't be long, he knew, before his hands lost their hold.

"Hanging around? That's unlike you, a man of action."

At the sound of the unearthly, mocking voice, Blackwood reluctantly craned his aching neck to gaze upwards. The Daughter floated in the air just above his head, the steady flapping of her wings creating a breeze that ruffled his hair and tickled the cuts crisscrossing his face.

"I don't know what's more offensive," he said, swallowing painfully. His breath came out as little white puffs. "Your jokes or your stench."

A wicked grin split her tortured visage.

"You think yourself clever, Celt? So prideful, the mighty slayer of night hags?"

Murderous rage fired the empty holes of her eyes, like molten rock glowing in deep craters.

She alighted on the girder. A yelp escaped him as the metal bar bent several inches under her bulk. Showing delight at his fright,

Mawrgoth jumped up and down experimentally, the way a kid might test a trampoline. When his hands slipped, she giggled uproariously. He experienced a moment of brain-freezing vertigo, then managed to clutch the rivet once more. All sensation had fled his fingers, which felt as dull as wood.

She scowled, revealing her disappointment that he hadn't yet plunged to his death.

"Ready to enjoy a cool dip, John?" she asked, arching eyebrows like charcoal rubbings. "Let me help."

She daintily walked-hopped toward him down the steel beam with steps as prim as a ballerina's. He wanted to move away, but he had nowhere to go. With a mischievous leer, she reached down and began prying his fingers off the girder one by one.

Blackwood's eyes doubled in alarm.

She glared at him. Every time she pulled a finger away, he managed to put it back just as she started to dislodge the next.

"Oh, you're no fun," she said. "Let's try a different approach, shall we?"

Straightening her back, the Daughter raised a cloven hoof — *when did her feet transform?*, he wondered — and stared darkly into Blackwood's blanched face.

"Bollocks," he croaked, realizing her intent.

"This is so going to hurt you more than me," the Daughter said. Then she stomped hard on his right hand.

A pain-filled yelp barreled up from deep under Blackwood's ribcage as his fingers lost their tenuous grip. Clinging desperately to the girder with his other hand, he scrambled to once again wrap his throbbing right fingers around the rivet. The world spun like a pinwheel in a tornado.

But she wasn't finished with him. Blackwood didn't see the other hoof come down, only felt the jackhammer crunch of phalanges rendered into broken shards. Blackwood groaned and lost his grasp.

With rushing wind filling his ears, he plummeted to the glacial current below.

But mere inches from slamming into the torpid flow, that familiar but detestable grip as strong as iron encircled his wrists and lifted him bodily into the night. With her twisted expression upraised, the Daughter climbed with powerful thrusts from her wings to the coal-sack skies above, the black caul of her shadow crawling along the frosted brickwork of the museum. Pushing into the wind, unfazed by Blackwood's limp weight, the massive wings propelled her over air vents, antennas and satellite dishes dotting the Anderson's roof until she made a long, sweeping loop and headed for the shattered oval of the big window. Out of the corner of his eye, Blackwood saw the flashing lights of several fire trucks and police cars lined along the curb, and knots of shivering guests clustered under the barren trees. Several glanced up and began gesticulating.

Mawrgoth paid them no mind.

"They'll be dead or in chains soon. Or food," she announced with a dismissive glance that tore at his soul. She swept back inside the Great Hall, came to a complete stop in the center and hovered above the Lucite-encased display holding the accursed book. Lowering herself about ten feet, her great wings fanning the flames, she twisted to the right and dropped Blackwood. He crashed into a display packed with Spanish imperial coins. The metal frame buckled inward with a crumpling noise.

He rolled off the twisted metal and glass, moaning and swearing in the same breath, and tumbled like a sack of potatoes to the floor. His every nerve felt blistered, he couldn't move the fingers of his left hand, and he heard small, twig-like noises popping inside his ribcage. Something warm and tasting of salt flowed from his lip.

"Bloody hell, did you have to drop me?" grunted Blackwood, who lay very still on his back on the uncomfortably warm marble floor, limbs splayed.

The Daughter landed with a whump, folded her bat-like wings and strode over to him, features radiating contempt. She waved a taloned hand and Blackwood felt a sudden chill sweep across the immediate area. In an instant, the nearest flames winked out of existence, replaced by a glistening carpet of frost that somehow kept the fire at bay.

"I have known your kind before, scribe, always meddling, always standing in our way. A foolhardy breed, you heroes," she said, delivering the last word with a bone-cracking kick to his right side.

Blackwood shrieked and arched his back as though someone rammed a hot poker into his chest. She kicked him again for good measure and a second scream burst from torn lips. If he'd doubted before, now he knew for certain something was broken — most likely a few ribs. With a mocking smile, the Daughter rolled him over with one hand and casually raked her claws along his cheek. She licked her chops at the sight of the blood streaming from the freshly opened stripes.

Mawrgoth flipped him back over and kissed his gritty, sweat-streaked forehead. The imprint of her mouth left a stinging welt. He made a feeble effort to shoo her away.

"Be thankful I didn't kiss your lips," she chuckled. "They say the experience adds years to your life. But, my master wants you to suffer for your affronts."

"You—you're wasting time. The solstice is almost here," he said when he finally found his voice.

"There's time enow," she tittered.

She grabbed Blackwood under his leg and side, then hefted him over her head like some trophy. His cheek brushed a wing as she thrust him into the air. The tip, which felt about as soft as petrified wood, left a stinging cut below his left eye. The membranes of her wing rippled as she twisted around and bashed him against another exhibit. The shatter-resistant glass fractured, forming a jagged outline of his body. Through a red haze, he saw his blood drip through the cracks to spatter several aged parchment maps of the Texas frontier.

A cry tried to explode from his sternum, but the Daughter cut it short when her taloned hand encircled his throat. She jerked his body off the case with no more difficulty than lifting a limp noodle, then held him aloft so they were face-to-face. His feet kicked feebly as he tried to punch her with his unbroken hand.

The effort brought an approving leer to her lips, which bulged with veins the size of worms.

"I admire your spirit, John," she acknowledged with grudging respect. "Perhaps the blood of great warriors flows in your veins."

She stared at him for a long moment, her features taking on a puzzled aspect.

Lowering nostrils shaped like a squashed bell pepper, she sniffed at Blackwood, then peered into his eyes as though searching for something buried deep within. A second later, her mouth curled in a cruel, satisfied smile. Her eyes continued to probe him.

He dropped his gaze, not wanting to tempt those churning maelstroms of soul-sucking emptiness when he was so weakened.

"There is something ... very familiar ... about you," she whispered. "Yes, I can smell it. I can taste it! How delicious!"

She smacked swollen gums like a sommelier over a particularly pleasing vintage, then giggled.

"Hmmff," she said. "You've no idea, do you, Celt?"

He gave no response, but then again, the claws wrapped around his throat made that difficult.

Wings snapped open like taut sheets. She sighed.

"No matter. The past is the past, and I have my appointed task for here and now. Mustn't tarry. Still ... the irony. Not just a scribe after all, hmmm? Much, much more. Yet I shall end your reign before it ever starts, your majesty."

More cackles punctuated her speech, the sound of unwary bugs crackling in a fire pit. Questions about what she found so ironic about him hardly seemed important, though. His grip on life felt as thin as a strand of gossamer.

As he watched through blood-rimmed eyes, the Daughter sized him up with a newfound appreciation.

"You have vanquished not one but two Daughters of Lilith. Indeed, you have led me — the mightiest of all, second only to our unholy mother — on a merry chase. No easy feat," she said, every word sheathed in ice. "But you have also angered my master. You go places you shouldn't, ask questions that best remain unasked, and challenge a great power of which you remain woefully ignorant. My master has foreseen that you could put our designs in jeopardy."

Blackwood's good hand fluttered once more to her claws, vainly trying to pry them from his windpipe. He may as well have attempted to peel the color off the sky.

She didn't seem to notice. Or care. But she kept talking.

"We are too close to the dawn of our dark reign, to unlocking the power of the Azad'dhul, to have our plans thwarted. The age of man is over. The affronts to my mother will be avenged."

The grip on his throat tightened as her sentence trailed off, but the reference to Lilith sparked a memory.

They say just before you die, your life flashes before your eyes. In Blackwood's case, however, only one thing came to mind, a single memory echoing repeatedly in his brain. Over the pounding of blood in his ears, he could hear the kind, authoritative voice of a certain "old parish priest" regaling Blackwood and his companions with an incredible tale from antiquity during their first encounter. The story was important, even crucial.

The lingering recollection gave Blackwood one last idea. A very insane idea.

"One ... final ... request?" he sputtered, the words pushing through his narrowed windpipe. The surface of her arms and hands had grown as hard and sharp as the scales of an iron fish, nicking his tender skin. The curling horns sprouting from her ridged head ended in wickedly sharp points. He struggled to stay focused, but with his airflow siphoned off, all his broken body wanted to do was shut down. Eyes bulged. Hot coals burned where his lungs used to be. His mouth opened and shut.

She pulled him so close he could smell every grain of grave dirt packed in her fetid breath.

"Ah yes, that little ritual," she whispered, and he recognized the acidic drip of mockery in her voice. "You wish to plead for your life? To beg Mawrgoth for mercy? Your end will be soon. That is my mercy. You don't want to be here for what is coming. It will be more terrible,"—her voice rose in adulation, "— more magnificent, than anything your pitiful little ape mind can comprehend."

Ice water flowed through his veins as the words spewed from her obscene mouth. He tried hard to ignore the implication of her warning.

"Please," he said. "Please, just let me have ... the honor .. of showing my devotion. I will do anything you ask, but do this for me. I beg you."

The Daughter continued holding him at arm's length, the tips of his trailing shoes scuffing the charred floor, but now her grip around his throat relaxed just a tad. Yellow spots still traced circles in his eyes, just not as many as before.

"What trick is this?" she demanded, steam in her voice.

The Daughter pulled him so close their noses almost touched. The smell of her breath made him want to rip his own nose off.

"No trick, no trick," he said imploringly, raising his one good hand in a piteous, beseeching manner. Every cell in his body screamed for release from this broken existence. "I am defeated. I know a queen when I see one ..."

Her expression brimmed with contempt.

"I should have known. Even though the blood of a conqueror flows in your veins, you snap as easily as a twig. Paugh!"

The gob she spat landed thickly on the side of his neck, scorching him. Tears welled in his eyes.

"Very well, whelp. I will grant you this last request. I am not ... unfamiliar ... with the adoration of the males of your kind."

She released him and he crumpled to the floor, a heap of broken bones and bleeding wounds. Moaning, he turned away from her. Mawrgoth opened her arms wide, ready to receive his supplication.

"Pray to me, son of Adam. Acknowledge Mawrgoth as your mistress. Sing your orisons!"

The crag of a chin lowered to the leprous scales of her chest. "And as your final act of love, you will remove the Son's sign so that I may claim what is rightfully ours."

Blackwood drew a haggard breath, forcing down smoke-filled air that scraped his aching throat. His trembling hand dipped into a pocket, withdrawing his notebook.

Out of her view, covering the notebook with his quivering frame, he opened the cover and flipped the pages, dripping blood on each one, until he found that which he sought.

He quietly and carefully tore out the page. Using an elbow to hold the single white square steady, but still keeping the sheet hidden, he separated three strips with oddly precise movements. Then, with sobbing breaths, he twisted around and began crawling to where she balanced on cloven hooves the color of old bone.

The Daughter's thick eyebrows peaked in grudging acceptance.

"Pray to me, little man," she demanded. "Foreswear your God and accept my master as your lord eternal — Sarvael the Forgotten One."

Blackwood whimpered like a beaten animal seeking any token of mercy. Pain boiled in every pore and crashed like tumbling boulders in his skull.

His shaking hand caressed one of the hooves. Up close now, he noticed strange, arcane symbols carved into the pitted surface, marks that reached through his agony and chilled him to the depths of his soul. They matched the script scrawled on the vellum pages of the relic.

Shielding his movements with his body, he quickly arranged the three slips of paper in a circle around her misshapen feet.

Raising his eyes and meeting Mawrgoth's smoldering gaze head on, Blackwood opened his mouth.

"There is only one God," he said. "And it's not Sarvael."

She did not reply, but a cold fury smoldered in her eyes.

The world was tipping and Blackwood felt close to going over the edge, but he couldn't give up now. His mind raced, keeping time with the rapid beating of his pulse. He wondered which would give out first, his heart or his brain?

The Daughter, who stood so motionless she could have been a statue in a graveyard, uttered a furious growl. Brandishing talons dripping with reflected light from the red and orange flames, she started to bend down toward him, ready to tear Blackwood into clumps of meat.

Except she couldn't.

Coughing more roughly, crimson spattering his once immaculate tuxedo, Blackwood summoned a last erg of energy and rolled away from her. Mawrgoth grunted dully, like a boar in a trap, and tried to follow, but her hooves wouldn't obey. She stood in place, held fast as though sunk in concrete.

"Fie, what trickery is this, mortal?"

Blackwood smiled, a slow, cold smile, and instructed her, "Look down."

She followed his trembling finger, still struggling to make her legs move, her wings to beat, but going nowhere. At first, her uncomprehending eyes remained as blank as smooth stones, but gradually as awareness began to dawn within those deep recesses, Blackwood could see the fires burst into shooting stars. What she at last recognized on the slips of paper at her hooves elicited a howl so terrible the glass shattered in every case within a thirty-foot radius, the ones that hadn't already succumbed to the panic of the fleeing crowd or the flames and mounting heat.

Revealed on each ragged fragment of paper was a single word, each written in an ancient tongue and now perhaps the key to averting the downfall of man.

Words symbolizing faith. Words symbolizing mercy. The most powerful forces in the universe.

A day ago, he had asked Dragoti to write down these very words in the study of The Vicarage. A good reporter always asks how to spell an unfamiliar phrase. In this case, three of them.

Sanvi. Sansavi. Semangelaf.

The angels to whom Lilith, mother of all vampires, owed an eternal debt. An oath that could not be broken.

Mawrgoth's eyes blazed with a rage more searing than a supernova. Had the wards not been in place, Blackwood felt certain he would have burned to a crisp.

"You have bound me under the ancient edict!" she screamed, ceasing her struggles as she recognized the futility of the effort.

"The shaman taught you well," she sputtered.

Her eyes narrowed and a coy smile broke across her ghastly visage.

"You're more clever than I thought," the Daughter said in a low voice. "But when I free myself, and I will, rest assured the tortures of hell itself will pale in comparison to what I shall do to you, Master Blackwood. The fire approaches, and these scraps of paper will burn. I won't."

In spite of her threatening demeanor, Blackwood's weak smile managed to get bigger. Forcing his good eye to stay open, he studied her chiropteran features as they hardened into a rigid mask promising a lingering death — his.

Undaunted, Blackwood painfully rose to his feet. The Daughter renewed her guttural roars of mounting frustration, but stayed frozen in place.

Blackwood regarded the ravenous being before him; this bloodthirsty, nightmarish shadow fiend. Time for her to go.

A paroxysm of violent coughing seized him. He gulped down a wheezing breath.

The Daughter stopped her cries and gave Blackwood a fiery appraisal, a slow, deceitful smile darkening her gash of a mouth. She spoke to him oh so sweetly, changing tack.

"I can give you whatever you want. Riches, fame, that tasty Daughter of Eve you've been sniffing after—anything! Merely release me. You can rule with my master, share his reign over your kind. You will be the most powerful mortal who ever lived."

Blackwood wiped his mouth with the back of the hand that still worked and began casting around the room. In seconds, he found what he was looking for and, miracle of miracles, the basin remained unscathed.

Mawrgoth began weeping. He hadn't thought so vile a being capable of such an expression, then decided it was only more trickery.

"Mercy, please! Show mercy, good king!" she cried. "I will tell you all your secrets, the secrets you don't know about your family, your past. Your timeless lineage. Everything ... I promise!"

He ignored her. The crocodile tears stopped. Mawrgoth began threatening to damage every inch of his body in the most vulgar and abhorrent terms. The imprecations barely registered in his ears as he shambled to the baptismal font. The silver bowl atop the ivory-colored onyx stand (a singed wall card informed onlookers) once occupied a hallowed corner in the Alamo chapel — just as Sabrina had explained. (He prayed she was safe, that all of his friends were safe).

Sabrina's words drifted back to him: "I don't think holy water, once sanctified, has an expiration date."

The memory, only an hour or two old, seemed like an echo from a lost age.

"Let's hope you're right," he said.

Once more, Blackwood peered over the side of the font's ornate bowl, barely recognizing the bruised and torn face peering back at him from the shimmering water.

Blessed by the archbishop himself, she also said.

Blackwood's vision wavered. His legs wobbled, knees close to buckling. A tidal wave of weariness threatened to swamp him. He had to work fast; remaining conscious might not be an option soon.

Summoning whatever reserves of strength remained, Blackwood lifted the bowl—surprisingly light—from the basin and cradled the cool silver in his arms. The sloshing water thinned the blood clumped on his dress shirt.

Careful, he warned himself. *Don't spill it!*

Gritting his teeth so hard he could hear the enamel grinding, he walked through patches of fire, broken glass and twisted metal to stand in front of a spitting, growling, cursing abomination borne of a woman's scorn before history began.

When the black holes in Mawrgoth's twisted features beheld what he carried, she only doubled her exhortations, but now her screams and threats turned to renewed pleas for mercy. This time, they sounded real.

Blackwood paid her no heed.

"Bottoms up," he said, pouring the holy water on her.

What emerged from her mouth next was not so much a scream as an ululation of pure misery that rivaled the explosion of the Big Bang itself. Faster than the eye could blink, Mawrgoth began to rip apart and melt in the same instant, the way chunks of wax slide off a candle. Soon enough, her cries turned to muddy gurgles, until at last she was nothing more than a smoking, bubbling puddle. Even that presently disappeared, leaving only a mound of green-tinted ash piled between the three slips of paper.

Wearing no expression, Blackwood dumped the last of the holy water on the ash, stepped back and waited. As before, a wind with no discernible origin sprang up, captured the particles and carried them out through the shattered oval window, disappearing into the night.

And so ended Mawrgoth, chief daughter of Lilith the spurned, herald of Sarvael, servant of the Synod of the Noose. Of her nothing remained. Nothing except the nightmare in men's minds that she once existed.

A trail of victims had been avenged, not just those of the last two days but nameless others over countless centuries past.

Never again would she or the other night hags trouble humankind.

"The circle remains unbroken," he gasped to the empty hall.

One problem resolved, but now Blackwood faced another threat. Around him, the flames tightened like a net, tongues of heat biting deep. His reddening skin protested, telling him he needed to move, but his rubbery legs wouldn't listen. Thickening smoke shoved a bitter fist down his sandpaper throat. The sounds that rang in his ears he dimly registered as his own phlegmatic coughing. Above, sections of the roof began caving in, and beyond their jagged edges, Blackwood could see stars. Not billowing clouds pregnant with snow, but stars. Shining bright. In a clear sky.

The solstice must have passed ... and the planet remained whole. That was the good news. As far as his situation went, though, nothing short of another miracle would save Blackwood, and he'd run out of those.

He dropped to his knees and toppled over. The swollen eye stayed shut, but the other traced a path straight to the display case containing the relic. The ragged old book sat on its pedestal untouched, the cross he'd tightly wound around the cover shining in the firelight.

Satisfied by this outcome, which had never been certain, he shut his remaining good eye. With slowing heartbeats, he waited for the pain—the raw, burning agony screaming from every muscle—to finally stop. He was ready for whatever came next, because it had to be better than this.

So imagine his surprise when a familiar voice whispered in his ear, "Rise and shine, lad. You get to live today."

Grudgingly, Blackwood forced his eye open. The good one, even though that hurt like blazes. A blob swam into view, but after a few seconds the fuzzy lines resolved themselves into an oval with gentle eyes, a long beard and a silly, floppy hat. Big Hat knelt over him, concern etched so deeply on his features that his brow looked as rumpled as an unmade bed. One hand grasped a little bottle hanging on a chain, the contents pulsing like a beacon. The impossibly long fingers moved nimbly and removed a stopper made of cork. The man tenderly lifted the mortally wounded reporter's head to the bottle.

"Here, drink this. You'll feel better," Big Hat said, the urgency in his voice unmistakable. "But just a drop, mind you. No more."

In the next second, a hand gently tipped the phial forward. A clear drop gathered at the lip of the glass and then plunged downward. Just a single, insubstantial drip, nothing more, but it pulsed like a burst of starlight just before disappearing into Blackwood's yawning mouth. He swallowed, tasting honey, sunlight and hope. At first nothing happened. Then, a strange, inexplicable energy surged through every nerve, muscle and shattered bone, only to fade away seconds later. Fatigue stole over him. He'd never felt so alive and yet so tired in his life.

Try as he might to remain awake, Blackwood found himself floating off, yet he felt no fear, no frustration, no resignation. Only contentment. He couldn't say why, but he didn't care at this point.

The world became a watercolor someone left out in a storm, all colors and shapes running together, as he began his descent into a well-deserved slumber. But something still nagged him, something very important ...

He tried to speak, even as he felt himself lifted bodily from the floor and carried away. The flames for some reason had no power over them. In fact, did they part as Big Hat moved through them?

Again, it didn't matter. He didn't care. Only one thing was important.

"What ... what's your name?" he mumbled, tongue heavy as lead. "The real one."

"Hush now," he heard his benefactor firmly say. "Hush and rest. The world owes you a great debt, but this is just the beginning. You have some very trying times ahead of you, John."

Yet the question burned in his mind.

"What's your ... name?" he stammered.

His rescuer gave a resigned sigh, an admission he realized Blackwood simply wouldn't close his eyes without an answer. As they passed through the great doors on their way to the lobby and the world outside, Big Hat bent over and breathed into Blackwood's ear, murmuring the way one might mention a long-forgotten friend. Even through the thickening fog of sleep, Blackwood heard. The crime reporter's eyes flickered opened.

Unless he was mistaken, he could have sworn Big Hat said, "Lazy horse." Lazy horse? Blackwood frowned. That couldn't be right. What kind of name was Lazy Horse?

And then it hit him. Not Lazy Horse.

Lazarus...

But by then, sleep finally took him into her sweet embrace, and he could remember no more.

THE END

John Blackwood will return.

ABOUT THE AUTHOR

Photo by Jason Hennington

Thomas Edwards was one of the longest-serving police-beat reporters at the San Antonio Express-News in Texas, covering homicides, gang wars, arsons, kidnappings, occult crimes, Death Row and a militia uprising. He also co-hosted a radio drive-time crime show, and served as executive editor of several newspaper chains including one where he chronicled a horrific cross-country murder spree. Today he is the executive editor of Granite Media Partners, Inc. He and his wife live near Austin on a rural property they share with two horses, six cats and a naughty Corgi.

NOTE FROM THOMAS EDWARDS

Word-of-mouth is crucial for any author to succeed. If you enjoyed *Daughters Drear*, please leave a review online—anywhere you are able. Even if it's just a sentence or two. It would make all the difference and would be very much appreciated.

Thanks!
Thomas Edwards

We hope you enjoyed reading this title from:

www.blackrosewriting.com

Subscribe to our mailing list – *The Rosevine* – and receive **FREE** books, daily deals, and stay current with news about upcoming releases and our hottest authors.
Scan the QR code below to sign up.

Already a subscriber? Please accept a sincere thank you for being a fan of Black Rose Writing authors.

View other Black Rose Writing titles at www.blackrosewriting.com/books and use promo code **PRINT** to receive a **20% discount** when purchasing.

www.ingramcontent.com/pod-product-compliance
Lightning Source LLC
Chambersburg PA
CBHW020551120726
47903CB00001B/224